THE
SPIRIT MAGE

Book II of
The Blackwood Saga

Layton Green

To the Dreamers

THE SPIRIT MAGE, Book II of the Blackwood Saga, copyright © 2017, Layton Green
All rights reserved.

Published by Cloaked Traveler Press
Cover design by Sammy Yuen
Interior by QA Productions

Books by Layton Green

THE DOMINIC GREY SERIES
The Summoner
The Egyptian
The Diabolist
The Shadow Cartel
The Resurrector
The Reaper's Game (Novella)

THE BLACKWOOD SAGA
Book One: The Brothers Three
Book Two: The Spirit Mage
Book Three: The Last Cleric (Forthcoming)

OTHER WORKS
The Letterbox
The Metaxy Project
Hemingway's Ghost (Novella)

ZEDOCK'S CITADEL, URFE
-1-

A rising tide of fear threatened to swallow Will Blackwood whole as he placed his palms on the glass wall and stared down at the swamp surrounding the obelisk of Zedock the necromancer. Ghostly tendrils of Spanish moss hung from the trees, brackish water and clumps of cypress roots stretched to the horizon. Less than an hour ago, he and Caleb and Yasmina had returned through the portal to Urfe and managed to kill Zedock. While savoring the fact that they were still alive, the portal had been destroyed and they had no idea how to get home.

"Guys," Yasmina said, her lilting Brazilian accent sounding less dazed and more shrill than the last time she had asked the question, "where are we?"

"Hell," Caleb said. He was sprawled in Zedock's high-backed chair near the center of the room, feet resting on a telescope, wavy dark hair framing his face.

Will took long deep breaths through his nose, corralling his emotions. He was bolstered by the knowledge that his brother and Yasmina needed him.

Yasmina: PhD student in zoology, brilliant and beautiful, Caleb's ex-girlfriend and the only woman back home he had dated for more than five minutes.

A relationship which had brought her nothing but grief, Will thought, culminating with Zedock kidnapping her for leverage and dragging her through the portal. Will tried not to look at the shattered ring of azantite on the other side of the room, a constant reminder that they were trapped in this world of dreams and nightmares.

"Tell her," he said to his brother. "Tell her everything."

Caleb shrugged, and then he did.

Told her how Zedock the necromancer had come to New Orleans to steal the sword their father had bequeathed to Will, how Salomon had given them a key that transported them to a world called Urfe, how the three brothers had traveled with the adventuress Mala and her team of mercenaries across the wilds of the Southern Protectorate to find a trio of magical items hidden in a geomancer's keep.

The last part she already knew: they had returned to Earth through the now-broken portal to wage an epic battle against Zedock, defeating him with the help of the necromancer's own arrogance, a dose of luck, and a sword—Will's sword—that could somehow cut through magic.

Yasmina's hazel eyes had opened as wide as an owl's. Her long limbs collapsed like a folding chair as she sank to the floor, her back against a bronze chest. Will watched her carefully. He knew all too well that the fine line between panic and control was the difference between life and death in this world.

"Are we dreaming?" she asked quietly, squeezing her eyes shut and then pinching herself. "Tell me I'm dreaming."

Caleb slowly shook his head.

"What do we do?" she whispered, her voice quivery but laced with an undercurrent of strength. "How do we get back?"

She's taking it better than we did, Will thought.

"We don't know," Caleb said, "which is why I vote we stay put. We have shelter, there must be some food around here, and I have no interest in traipsing through the Swamp of Death."

"And when the supplies run out?" Will said.

"We'll deal with that when it happens. Maybe Salomon will come and get us."

"Salomon stood and watched while Zedock tried to kill us. We're specimens under glass to him."

"So what's your grand plan, little brother?"

Will rested his hand on the hilt of his sheathed sword. The movement was becoming instinctive. "I vote we go to New Victoria. We're not getting home by staying here."

"New Victoria?" Yasmina echoed.

"It's New Orleans," Caleb said, "only it's not. Trust me, it has to be seen to be believed." He turned back to Will. "And if we make it through the swamp alive, then what? Walk into the Wizard District and ask someone for help? They'll throw us straight in the Fens."

"It's a huge city," Will said. "There's got to be someone there who can help us. Someone who knows *something*."

Caleb gave a bitter laugh. "I sort of gathered that the whole portal-between-worlds thing is extremely rare. I don't think we'll find one at the corner magic store."

"Zedock had one. There has to be others."

Yasmina was looking back and forth between the two of them as if they had just sprouted horns and tails.

"Don't forget," Caleb said, giving the vertical shaft in the center of the room a nervous glance, "that we just killed a wizard. What if the Congregation finds out?"

"How would they?"

"I don't know, the same way they travel across worlds and fly through the air and raise the undead?"

"They're not all-powerful. Like you said," Will said grimly, "we just killed one."

"Whatever." Caleb kicked his feet up and put his head in his hands, pausing for a long beat before he looked up. "What about Val and Lance?" he said quietly. "We just left them."

Yasmina walked over to squeeze his hand. "You didn't leave them. You came for me."

Will shuddered away the memory of their oldest brother and Lance in the cemetery, surrounded by hordes of the undead. He could only pray that when Zedock had gone through the portal, it had severed the connection to his creations. "Even more reason to get back," he said.

Caleb, looking like a dashing pirate captain in his leather breeches and a frilly white shirt, sleeves rolled up to expose the black leather bracers their father had left him, took a slender iron filing out of his pocket, and rose to inspect the bronze chest next to Yasmina. He ran his fingers over the surface, then probed the iron clasp and padlock. Will knew he was still processing the loss of Marguerite, his lover who had suffered a grave—perhaps fatal—injury in Leonidus's dungeon.

"Caleb?" Yasmina asked, surprised.

"A few skills I picked up over here," he said.

Dressed in a brown leather vest and breeches, Will tossed his chin-length blond hair out of his face and watched his brother work. The long hair and stubble were products of the month-long journey to the geomancer's keep.

"Seems okay," Caleb muttered to himself, then removed the padlock and lifted the lid. A dazzling array of gemstones and coins glittered back at them. Yasmina's eyes widened again.

Will scooped up a handful of rough-cut diamonds. "These won't hurt our bargaining power."

With a dexterous movement, Caleb pocketed a handful of coins. "I wouldn't mind spending this loot in the French Quarter, but it won't help us survive the swamp. And I haven't agreed to go anywhere yet."

Will threw his hands up. "Someone's going to come here and check on Zedock eventually. What if it's another wizard? Or a majitsu?"

Caleb paled at the mention of the frightening warrior monks, themselves possessed of low level magical ability, who served as bodyguards for the wizards. He started to respond, but Yasmina cut him off with a finger. "Did you hear that?"

Will stilled to listen. From somewhere down below, increasing in volume as it echoed up through the wizard chute, came the clink of metal armor and the slap of booted heels.

Someone was climbing the stairs.

NEW YORK CITY

-2-

Valjean Blackwood checked his watch once again. A twitch of the wrist that had become an obsession over the last few days, ever since his younger brothers had traveled through a one-way portal to the citadel of a feared necromancer named Zedock.

Will and Caleb were trapped in a dark fantasy version of Earth—and Val had no idea how to help them.

According to Salomon, an old man with silver eyes who might be a crackpot and who might be a two-thousand year old wizard of immense power, time passed at a different rate in Zedock's world. Presently, a ratio of sixty days in the other world for every one on Earth.

Which meant, if the time differential held, that his brothers had been trapped on Urfe for months. At best, they had found a way to escape but were stranded.

And at worst . . .

Val, too, had visited the other world. When he and his brothers had found Zedock's fortress at the end of their journey, they were forced to pole through a swamp full of undead creatures reaching mindlessly out of the water, horrific creations of the necromancer.

So Val didn't want to think about *the worst*.

Reeling from lack of sleep, shaking with rage and impotence, he stared at the sprawl of Manhattan outside the fiftieth-floor window of his law office and thought about how impossible it seemed that there was another dimension, or world, or universe out there from which Val had narrowly escaped. A world of manticores and cave fiends, magic swords and potions, spirit mages and necromancers. Wizard-monks who could shatter walls with their fists, a city of colored spires so beautiful it took his breath away.

His eyes slipped to the staff hidden behind his desk. Five feet of fortified oak topped by a crescent moon of azantite, a milky-white stone so thin and strong a professional jeweler said it shouldn't exist.

A staff Val's father had left for him before he died.

A wizard's staff.

Someone knocked on the door. Val blinked away his exhaustion. "Come in."

With hooded eyes, Val watched Mari Winslow step through the door in red-rimmed glasses and a grey pantsuit that clung to her svelte figure. A half-American, half-Swedish brunette, Mari was only five years older than Val's thirty-one but already head of the powerful Compensation Committee.

She was also Val's mentor, and was probably checking in to see why he hadn't left his office for two days straight. *Just what I need*, he thought.

Masking the turmoil raging within, Val arched his eyebrows and extended an upturned palm towards the sofa. Mari smoothed her pants as she sat. She looked a decade younger than her age, and the suitors who had crashed against the rocky shores of Mari Winslow were outnumbered only by the legions of defeated opposing counsel.

Spit it out, Val wanted to say, *and let me get back to work.*

"What is it, Mari?" he said wearily.

"How's the Myrddinus research coming?"

Val stilled. The Myrddinus was a secret society dedicated to the exploration of magical phenomena, and his only hope of reaching his brothers. Val's godfather, Charlie Zalinski—the man who had told Val and his brothers about Urfe, before he was turned into a zombie by Zedock—had claimed to be a member of the Myrddinus, along with Val's father.

Despite his best efforts, neither Val nor his junior associate had turned up anything about the Myrddinus other than what Val already knew, which was that *Myrddin* might refer to a Welsh historical figure who may or may not have inspired the Arthurian legend of Merlin.

"Fine," Val said, wondering how Mari knew what he was researching.

Her mouth curled into a smirk. "Myrddinus. A strange name for a research project."

"It's a project for a financial firm in Wales." He waved a hand. "They think a competitor might have set up a shadow company and absconded with certain assets."

"And? Have they?"

"I'm still researching," he said evenly.

"Perhaps you're not taking the right angle."

"It's possible. I just need a little more time."

"Or," she said, leaning forward to place a business card on his desk, "perhaps you need a little assistance from the inside."

Val's breath caught in his throat as he reached for the card. On the front was a colorful depiction of an Ouroboros, a serpent eating its own tail. Inside the motif was a collection of runes and astrological symbols. He flipped the card over, already knowing what name would be printed on the back.

Myrddinus.

She rose. "Tomorrow night, midnight, my office. Don't be late."

"Tonight," Val croaked, as Mari rose for the door. His voice sounded hoarse and desperate to his own ears. "It has to be tonight."

"I have plans—"

He grasped for leverage. "You're aware of what happened in New Orleans on Halloween?"

Mari stopped with a hand on the door. "A terrorist blew up a cemetery. The whole country's aware."

"A terrorist?" Val said. "You really believe that?"

She paused a beat. "And?"

"Did you know Charlie Zalinski was my godfather?"

Her face betrayed no surprise. "Was? Do you know where he is? We haven't heard from him since—" her eyes widened—"Halloween."

"Tonight," Val said, leaning forward and pressing his palms into the desk. "We meet tonight."

"What happened in New Orleans, Val?"

He refused to respond, and Mari's eyes flashed before she swept out of his office.

Ten minutes until midnight. A cold November wind buffeted Val's camelhair coat and expensive jeans as he strode through the subdued streets of Lower Manhattan. Not knowing what to expect, he ignored the stares of passersby and gripped his father's six-foot azantite staff. He was also carrying the Amulet of Shielding and the Ring of Shadows he and his brothers had found in the castle of the geomancer Leonidus.

After a few more hours of fruitless research at his Lower East Side loft, Val had spent the evening riding waves of feverish hope and tempered expectations. Even if Mari *was* part of the Myrddinus, the organization might have no clue how to bridge the two worlds.

Memories crowded his head. Charlie breaking the news that his father had fallen to his death while searching for Durendal, the lost sword of Charlemagne, during an archeological expedition. Val's mother wandering the mental institution in her dressing gown, adrift in her own mind since losing her husband.

The deaths of Alexander and Hashi and Fochik. Mala lost, Lance crucified by Zedock. Caleb racing for the portal after the necromancer escaped carrying Yasmina. Will diving after Caleb and plunging through the portal with him.

Val willed his thoughts away when he reached his building. He took the elevator to the fifty-fifth floor and strode down the deserted hallway to Mari's office. She was sitting behind a pile of documents stacked neatly on her desk, looking fresh and alert. When Val walked in, her eyes latched on to his staff like a cobra mesmerized by a snake charmer.

"Nice walking stick," she said. "Bad knees?"

Val sat across from her, deciding not to mince words. He rarely did. "If you knew who I was, why'd you wait so long to approach me?"

"Your father's instructions. He asked us to hold off until you exhibited an interest in finding us."

Val balled his fists to control his anger, reminding himself she wasn't aware of his brothers' plight.

Or was she?

"Obviously, your father didn't tell you very much. You don't know anything about us, do you?"

"How many of you are there?"

She shrugged. "In North America? A few handfuls." She rose to throw a red leather jacket over slacks and a form-fitting black sweater. "Let's take a walk."

"Where?"

"To the home of the Myrddinus in New York City, of course. I think you'd be an asset to the organization, and we have something you might be interested in."

Val folded his arms. "Stop being coy, Mari. What is it?"

"Your father left something for you."

-3-

Will, Caleb, and Yasmina crept to the edge of the wizard's shaft in the center of the floor. They risked a glance down and saw a knight in full plate mail climbing the staircase that spiraled upward through the center of the shaft. The slits in the knight's visor glowed with an eerie green light, and his gloved right hand was gripping a broadsword.

"You still want to stick around?" Will whispered to Caleb.

Caleb was crouched on the balls of his feet, like a wild animal that wanted to bolt but had nowhere to go. Yasmina backed away from the shaft. "What do we do?"

"We run," Will said.

Yasmina flicked her eyes at Will's sword. "Can't you fight it? I saw what you did in the cemetery."

"Those were skeletons and zombies magically animated by Zedock. My sword cut right through them. I have no idea what that thing coming up the stairs can do."

"*Quiet*," Caleb said in a fierce whisper. "It's almost here. We've got to do something."

Will eyed the walkway leading to the staircase. The only access to the bottom of the obelisk.

His gaze spun around the room. Three chests, a telescope, the high-backed chair, and the writing desk. On top of the desk was an obsidian helm that looked decorative, as well as a set of transparent pens filled with a substance that looked suspiciously like blood. An orb lamp suspended from the ceiling lit the room with a soft golden glow.

"Caleb," Will said, "take Yasmina and hide behind the desk. As soon as we start fighting, hit the stairs and go for the pirogue. I'll be right behind you."

"That's the plan? Aren't you a chess whiz? A master of strategy?"

"You have a better one? We've got about five seconds to decide."

The metallic rustle of the knight's armor sounded as if it were right beneath them. Will saw Caleb's eyes flick around the room and then settle on Yasmina. Her face was pale, and her designer jeans and fitted white T-shirt looked pitifully out of place.

Caleb grabbed Will by the arm. "Stay alive."

"That's the idea."

Right after Caleb and Yasmina crouched behind the desk, the knight's helmed head appeared in the stairwell, the unnatural green light burning like a laser. Was the knight one of Zedock's magical creations, subject to the power of Will's sword? Or was it a true undead?

Will positioned himself near the edge of the shaft. As soon as the knight saw him, it raised its sword and advanced. The movements didn't look human, but neither did they appear mechanical. They were somewhere in between;

they were *wrong*. Will backed away, centering his bodyweight and gripping his sword as Mala had taught. The knight followed and backed him towards the wall. Once they passed underneath the orb light, Caleb and Yasmina sprinted across the walkway and bounded down the stairs.

The knight turned at the sound, and Will took the opening. His first goal was simply to strike it and see if there was any magic to be severed. He tried to stab the knight in the chest but it turned and parried Will's thrust at the last second. Then it advanced with two quick strikes, the last of which Will blocked by falling to his knees and barely raising his sword above his head in time. He had to scramble backward to regain his feet.

The brief exchange was enough for him to grasp the situation: this being far outclassed him, and whatever its magical nature might be, the metal in its sword was all too real. True undead or not, the knight would run him through before he got a chance to utilize the powers of his sword.

Will circled and tried to reach the platform. The knight cut off his approach, backing him closer to the wall. Forced to exchange another series of blows, Will escaped by rolling away and diving behind the desk.

The knight kicked the desk aside. Will threw the obsidian helm at its face. It caught the helm in midair and set it down, with an oddly careful movement. Will tried to attack one more time, feinting twice and then trying for a side thrust, but the knight parried, knocked him senseless with a gauntleted backhand, and almost ran him through before Will could dive away again.

He had seen enough. He couldn't win this fight. After desperately scanning the room for an escape, he ran straight for the side of the vertical shaft, dropped his sword into the hole, and jumped into midair. He crashed atop the metal railing of the staircase on the next level down, losing his wind and almost plummeting into the shaft.

The knight bounded down the stairs after him. Will clung to the railing with both arms, flailing to regain his footing. His toes found the staircase just as the knight stabbed downward, and Will dove head first down the spiral stairs, careening halfway to the next level before righting himself. He gained his feet before the next blow came and then sprinted down the stairs, the knight right behind him.

Out of the corner of his eye, Will caught a glance of Zedock's laboratory, morgue, and army of inanimate skeleton creatures. By the time he reached the creepy parlor at the bottom of the stairs and recovered his sword, Will had gained three strides on the knight and could see the exit. He started to sprint away but tripped over something on the floor, sprawling on his face in a pool of sticky red liquid.

Frantic, he splattered through the blood to avoid the knight's next swing, scrambling over the decomposing body of the majitsu he had killed before diving through the portal for the first time. Just a day ago to him, but two months on Urfe.

Zedock's headless body was lying next to the corpse. Will ended up on his back, sword raised to block the deathblow he knew was coming. As the knight's sword descended, a knife clanged off its visor, causing it to falter at the last second.

"Hurry!" Caleb screamed.

Will rolled to the side, just avoiding the sword thrust. He scrabbled backwards, sprang to his feet, and sprinted after Caleb. The knight followed, but couldn't catch them as they ran on to the floating platform outside the obelisk, down the long rope bridge, and then jumped into the pirogue still tied to the dock.

Yasmina was waiting on the flat-bottomed boat, pulling in rope as fast as she could. Caleb helped her, and as Will used the long pole to push off from the dock, the knight stood at the edge of the platform and watched them leave, unnerving in his stillness, the strange green light swirling like swamp gas inside the helm.

Hours later, with dusk creeping through the vines and Spanish moss, they had put Zedock's obelisk far in the distance. Or at least they thought they had. They were horribly lost, so they didn't really know.

Will's arms ached from the strain of poling through the water, though he liked that Yasmina had twice complimented his forearms. Caleb's three turns had lasted about ten minutes each, and he had shown zero shame about his lackluster performances.

"I think we should find some shelter," Will said, "even if it's in the trees. We could be going around in circles on the water."

Caleb was sprawled on his back, hands behind his head. "I like the safety of the boat."

"You would, since you're not the one poling."

"I'm proud of you, little brother. You were gifted with strong hands and a Puritan work ethic."

Will snorted. Tall and fine-boned, with a face so pretty women blinked twice when they saw him, Caleb had skated through life on charm and good looks. If he wasn't such a happy-go-lucky guy, Will would have resented him.

He had learned on their journey, however, that when pushed to the edge, even Caleb had a dark side to his personality.

That everyone did.

It was warm and humid. Yasmina's caramel-colored hair hung limply down the back of her sweat-soaked T-shirt. She said, "But surely we can't stay in the boat all night?"

"Why not?" Caleb asked. "We can tie up to a tree, and we only have to deal with mosquitoes. Out there," Caleb jerked his thumb at the shore of the sluggish swamp channel they were traversing, "we have to deal with snakes, gators, leeches, ticks, and a million other nasty things. And that's just from *our* world."

Her mouth compressed as she surveyed the ominous green and black wilderness surrounding them, moss-laden branches dipping into the water, the ridged backs of gators rippling through the scum. "Why do you want to go to land?" she asked Will.

"In the morning, we can navigate by the sun and cut a straighter course. I was watching when we flew in the first time. We've got to be in the Jean Lafitte Swamp. New Victoria—New Orleans—is almost due north. Even if we miss it, we'll hit the Mississippi."

"What about all the," she waved her arms, "dangers?"

"Caleb's right, the swamp's deadly. But we don't have a choice. We need water."

"Which plodding through the swamp will only make worse," Caleb said.

"On land, we can build a fire and boil water."

"With what?"

"We'll find something." Will stopped poling to let the burning in his arms dissipate. "Look, we could be close to the city already. If we stick to the boat, what's your plan for tomorrow night, when we're even more lost and dying of thirst?"

Caleb had no answer.

Dusk congealed into a moonless night. Everyone agreed it was too dark and wet to do anything other than tie the boat to a tree and wait for dawn. In the morning they would make a decision.

The night was misery heaped upon misery. Minutes after securing the boat, the mosquitoes attacked *en masse*, and the three of them were forced to cover themselves in mud, a trick Will had heard about but never tried. The mud alleviated some of the torture, but left them damp and sticky. The temperature cooled until they were huddled together in the middle of the pirogue, shivering and mud-covered, wondering if they would make it to the morning.

The diurnal chatter of the swamp turned into an ear-splitting cacophony after dark, as if battalions of insects and amphibians were waging an all-out interspecies war. Will heard larger things as well, slitherings and ploppings and scratchings that left the three of them clutching the sides of the boat. More than once they heard the throaty cries of a jungle cat, and they also feared the appearance of a crocosaur, a monstrous reptile that could capsize the pirogue and devour all three of them.

"We should have made a canopy in the trees," Will said.

"We should have never left New Orleans," Caleb muttered.

"Shut up. You know we didn't have a choice."

Caleb didn't respond, and Will said, "Yasmina? You still with us?"

"Yes," she whispered. "Still here."

Will knew that if he had been alone with the terrors of the swamp, without Yasmina and Caleb to look out for, he might not have coped. Caring for others brought out the best in him. Val called it a hero complex; Will saw it as displacement of his weakness.

Though after what Will had been through over the last few months—and especially the last few days—not even the terror and discomfort of the swamp could keep his body from shutting down, his eyelids gumming closed and his fingers wrapped around the hilt of his sword.

                    *   *   *

They woke with the dawn. By a two to one vote, and with Yasmina vowing never to spend another night in a pirogue, Will's argument won out. Wet and cold and starving, they poled until they found a section of semi-dry land, then left the boat and headed perpendicular to the sun, tramping wordlessly into the marsh. The muck and swamp grass tugged at their feet, and Will used the pole to test for gators and sinkholes.

"We can't go much farther without water," Caleb croaked.

"It's South Louisiana," Will said. "It has to rain soon."

An hour later, his throat a piece of sandpaper, Will almost danced a jig when the sky darkened and a morning shower washed away the grime. Yasmina, raised in a city in Brazil right on the bank of the Amazon, taught them the trick of drinking rainwater running down a vine, as well as how to hollow out a piece of deadwood and fill it with spare water. Her knowledge of animals helped them steer clear of predators by studying tracks and listening to their cries.

As the sun started to descend, the soggy marsh turned firmer, hardwood hammocks replacing the endless clumps of cypress. The insect swarms eased from catastrophic to merely inhumane.

Caleb slumped against the base of an oak as Will doled out a ration of water. "Let's find a place to set camp," Will said. "Some of these sticks are dry enough for a fire, and I'll search for food."

"If we have to," Yasmina said, "we can survive on insects."

Caleb made a choking sound. "Will's going to search *real* hard."

Thirty minutes later, they collapsed in a glade of shortleaf pine. After collecting wood and pine needles, they managed to start a fire using a piece of flint Caleb found in the set of thief's tools Marguerite had lent him.

Will set off to find something to cook, leaving Caleb and Yasmina by the fire. Half a mile from camp, Will got lucky and found a pond stocked with frogs the size of dinner plates. He managed to impale three of them with his sword, and even began to whistle a tune as he trudged back to camp. If they could avoid predators and survive the night, he felt sure that another day of walking would bring them within striking distance of New Victoria. He would *will* his way out of this mess, he decided, giving an exhausted chortle at the pun.

The smoke from their campfire guided him on the return journey through the forest. He tried not to jump at the shadows dappling the woods. After passing a glade full of wildflowers, he heard the strange, pig-like grunts at the same time he saw a wart-covered face and a pair of curved tusks, fierce and terrifying in the failing light. Holding a barbed spear pointed right at Will, the squat, five and a half foot tall humanoid advanced with a shifty, waddling gait. Clumps of bristly hair covered its slate grey arms and legs, and strands of oily hair hung from its scalp like lichen. It wore a soiled red tunic, a leather breastplate, and black thong sandals tied to the bottoms of its lumpy feet.

Five more of the goblin-like creatures emerged from the brush, also training spears on Will, leaving him no choice but to surrender. Still grunting, the first one approached and took Will's sword, then picked him up and tucked him against his side like a football as he marched to Will's campsite. Three more of the creatures were gathered around the smoldering remains of the fire. The two groups of goblins exchanged a series of nuanced grunts, including finger pointing and spear jabbing at Will.

Oddly enough, he thought he could understand their language, but that fact was buried by the skull-pounding terror he felt at his predicament, and by the sight of Caleb and Yasmina hanging upside down from a tree branch, swinging slowly back and forth as another of the horrid creatures poked them with the pirogue pole.

-4-

Val followed Mari on a ten-minute walk from the firm to an unmarked door in a crumbling brick alley. The hidden byway felt more like Old World Europe than the middle of Manhattan.

He remained silent as she unlocked the door and entered the rear of a narrow, high-ceilinged chapel with a thick layer of dust on the pews and effigies. Stepping confidently through the abandoned church, Mari descended a spiral staircase in an alcove near the altar. The staircase spilled into a cellar with a

locked wooden door. Using another set of keys, she opened the door to reveal
a stone-walled passage tunneling into darkness.

She flicked on a pocket flashlight and seemed to enjoy Val's unease. Cob-
webs clung to the rounded ceiling, and he had an uncomfortable flashback to
the dungeon beneath Leonidus's castle.

The muted roar of the subway echoed in the hallway just before it dead-ended at a modern steel door. Mari stood in front of the keypad with crossed arms.
"What happened in New Orleans?"

She was going to make him pay to play. It was smart, Val thought—except
she had no clue as to the magnitude of the game.

He rubbed his thumb against his staff. "What do you know about my father?"

"I know he was an archaeologist and Charlemagne scholar."

"What did he leave for me? Why didn't any of you give it to me when he
died?"

"I don't know what it is. His instructions were to bring you to his locker if
you sought us out."

Val studied her face and found no signs of deception.

"Tell me what you know," she said, "and we'll walk through this door together."

After seeing this place, he had no doubt of Mari's involvement in the Myrddinus. But how far was she willing to go?

"Do you believe in magic, Mari? Real magic?"

"I'm Myrddinus. Of course I do."

He chuckled to himself. "Let me rephrase. Have you ever *seen* real magic?"

Her response was slow to come, a prolonged, "No, not personally." But Val
read the underlying tone, the intense eyes and thrusting jaw, loud and clear. *I've
never seen real magic, but I'd do just about anything for the opportunity.*

Val's guess was the Myrddinus wanted magic to be real, they sought it out
and catalogued mysterious phenomena and played their shadow games, but
they didn't have a clue about Urfe.

Or at least not most of them. Why had his father played along? And who
was the original Myrddin?

He saw no reason to lie, so he told her about Salomon's key and the door between worlds, about the terrible beauty and magic of that *other* place, and how he had to return, at all costs, to help his brothers.

He left out plenty, including the fact that he was a fledgling wizard. He didn't expect her to believe him, but when he finished, the best way he could describe Mari's expression was one of hunger. Not an *I'm ready for a steak dinner* kind of hungry, but a *starving, lone wolf in the frozen tundra, chew off its own leg for a meal* kind of hungry.

Mari swallowed and keyed in the access code. The metal door swooshed outward to reveal a cavernous rotunda with marble pillars, a stone floor covered in thick Persian rugs, and six closed doors spaced at regular intervals. As they entered, Mari slid her arm through Val's, her soft hair spilling across his shoulder and tickling his neck.

The contents of the room were even more incredible than its existence. Twenty-foot tall bookshelves lined the perimeter, shelving thousands of brittle tomes and grimoires. Glass display cases contained every magical accoutrement Val could imagine: staves and wands and star-shaped brooches, potions and alchemical displays, scrolls inscribed with complex mathematical formulas.

Val walked up to one of the books on display, an illustrated codex depicting a variety of fantastical creatures. He swallowed—one of them was the titan crab that had almost killed him in Leonidus's dungeon. He read the plaque beneath the case. "The Voynich Manuscript? I thought the only copy was at Yale?"

"This is the prototype. Without the missing pages."

"Where did it come from?"

"No one knows."

Val whistled.

She opened one of the doors, revealing a room full of file cabinets, desks with reading lamps, and a bank of computers. "We're extremely serious about our research."

"I can see that."

He had so many questions. What was the connection between the two worlds? Were there any other real wizards involved?

"I'd like to see what my father left me."

"There's one more thing, if you'll indulge me," she said. She moved to a corner of the file room that contained a few dozen safes set into the wall, each secured with a keypad. She selected a safe near the center, entered a code, and the door popped open with a release of pressurized air. She extracted a folder containing a stack of photos and documents.

The first photo depicted a man with wispy gray hair and silver eyes sitting at Caleb's bar, cradling a cup of coffee while he watched Will from across the room. It was the same man Val had seen in the cemetery the night they fought Zedock, watching events unfold as if he were eating popcorn at the local cinema.

Salomon.

Val looked up, his voice sharp. "Who took this? Charlie?"

She waved a hand at the documents. "Keep going."

Val ran through a few more photos of the same man in various places: Walking into the British Museum in London, standing next to the Astronomical Clock in Prague, peering up at the Taj Mahal. In one black and white photo, Salomon—looking the exact same age—was seated in the corner of a café with Albert Einstein. Val started. "Is this real?"

"The next photo is with Nikola Tesla. The one after that, a daguerreotype with Faraday. We also have an eyewitness account describing an old man fitting this description talking to the Italian scientist Ettore Majorana the day before he disappeared off the face of the earth. Oppenheimer, Schrödinger, Heisenberg—our people have spotted this man chatting with virtually every important theoretical physicist since photography was invented."

"You think he's learning from them?"

"That or he's *teaching* them." She leaned into him. "Who is this man, Val? Why doesn't he age? He's a wizard, isn't he?"

Val shuffled through the remaining documents, photographs, and write-ups of the various encounters. "I wish I knew," he said slowly.

Mari's gaze lingered on him before she replaced the contents of the safe, locked it, and took him by the arm. "This way," she said. Her normally modulated voice was thick and sticky, as if coated in molasses.

She led him back into the main room, through one of the other doors, and into a sprawling stone-walled chamber that reminded Val of a medieval country club. Tapestries and rugs and buttery leather furniture filled the room.

There was even a fireplace, though Val had no idea how the ventilation functioned this far underground.

Against the far wall, he saw a series of oak-paneled lockers, each with a bronze nameplate. Near the middle was a plaque engraved with the name Dane Maurice Blackwood.

Dad.

Val could feel Mari's eyes on his back as he stood in front of his father's locker. He had dealt with those emotions long ago, but this hidden piece of his father's puzzle sent a shiver of both grief and anticipation coursing through him.

"We've never understood the lock on your father's door," she said.

At first her words confused him. Then he looked down and understood. Unlike the other lockers, secured by padlock or keypad, the only apparent ingress to Dane Blackwood's locker was a curved sliver of space in the center of the door. Val stared at it for a long moment, uncomprehending, before holding his staff lengthwise and inserting the inverted crescent moon of azantite into the slot.

The two ends of the staff clicked into place. Val turned it left and then right. On the second try, there was another click and the door swung open. As Val extracted the staff and peered inside the locker, Mari gripped his arm and hovered over his shoulder.

Resting on top of a footstool was an ornamental wooden box. Inside he found a gilt-edged letter, a sack of gold coins bearing the stamp of the Realm, and a crescent moon sliver of azantite similar to the one on Val's staff.

Val stood for a long moment, fighting his emotions. While Mari looked at the coins in awe and let them slide through her fingers, Val took the azantite token and the letter and walked to the center of the room.

Dearest Valjean,

If you have read my journal and opened my locker, then I fear the worst has come to pass. I've been pursued across the ether. You should know that except for Charlie, no one in the society knows the truth. Take care what you reveal. The two worlds are not ready to collide, and perhaps they never shall be.

The crescent moon is a portal formed of spirit. Connecting it to my staff will transport you to Urfe, my home world. If you need to protect the family, use the portal as a last resort, and be sure to consult my journal at every step. The situation on Urfe is complicated. I detailed the names of those who can help you survive and how to find them. I also left basic supplies in my lodging in New Victoria.

A note of warning: the azantite portal, as they say on Earth, is a one-way ticket. There are other ways to reach Urfe, but they are exceedingly difficult and, at this point, far beyond your reach. I can only hope that you will follow in my footsteps, unlock your power, and one day manage to return on your own.

And finally, in the unimaginable event that this letter must serve as our goodbye, you should know that while I have traversed the cosmos, I have never come as close to understanding the reason for existence as the day I gazed upon my firstborn son.

Dad

"Mari," Val asked, his voice thick with emotion, "could I get a glass of water?"

"Sure," she murmured, squeezing his arm as she passed. "Are you okay?"

"Yeah."

Mari walked to a corner of the room and opened a wooden cabinet. As soon as her back was to him, Val strode to his father's locker, picked up the sack of gold coins, and touched the crescent moon token to the top of his staff.

When the two pieces of azantite connected, Val felt a mild electric shock. There was a prolonged flash of blue-silver light as his body seemed both to vibrate and dissolve. During that moment, Mari turned and dropped the pitcher, ran across the room, and flung herself at Val.

Just as they collided, he had the familiar sensation of the molecules in his body disconnecting and then being jerked forward by an impossibly strong force, and then

the world

went

black

-5-

A flash of red, then a starburst of color.

Colors so deep and profound they made all the colors Mala had known before, the splendid colors of the normal world, seem muted, monochrome.

She blinked and realized these otherworldly hues were not flashes of light but were all around her, preserved in solid state. Bridges and loops and pathways of color. Honeycombed archipelagos of color, floating grottoes of color, spiral tunnels of color, polyhedra of color. Shapes and pigments for which she had no name. There was no sky or ground, no up or down, no left or right—just dimensions of color, stitched into the fabric of this place.

But there was something else, too. Flat, one-dimensional circles of darkness loomed in the distance like suns during an eclipse, dozens of them, pockmarking the palette of color. Some primal instinct told her that there she must not go.

She realized she was drifting slowly through this dreamscape, and had a moment of panic. *Where was she? How had she arrived?*

Then she remembered.

Fighting the majitsu outside Zedock's obelisk.

Quaffing the Potion of Movement to try to even the odds, give herself a fighting chance.

Still unable to hurt the warrior-mage.

Forced to use an Amulet of the Spheres she had recovered from an ice fortress in Lapland, right under the nose of a powerful Snow Mage, she had wrapped her arms around the majitsu in a desperate attempt to take him with her, fulfilling her debt to Will by giving him and his companions a chance to escape.

Majitsu.

She spun and saw him drifting twenty feet behind her. Shaved head, black robe cinched at the waist with a silver belt. Part of an elite order of martial artists who supplemented their craft with low-level magic and served as personal attendants to the Realm's wizards.

After blinking his eyes in wonder at the Place Between Worlds, the majitsu's eyes found Mala and narrowed. Tightened even further when he saw the circular blue amulet looped around her neck, pulsating with jagged streaks of silver. She clutched it tighter. The amulet had never throbbed before.

The majitsu snarled and came for her. One hand grasping the amulet, the other reaching for her sash, Mala tried to swim backwards to get away, flailing her arms and legs.

She went nowhere.

Panicking, with the majitsu rapidly closing the gap, Mala took a good look at him and realized he didn't even seem to be trying. Arms extended, he drew towards her as if gliding.

She tried the same thing, and realized she could fly.

She couldn't describe the odd sensation any other way. It wasn't exactly flying, but neither was it anything else. When she extended her arms and willed herself to go in one direction, there she went, drifting through the vortex of color like a gnat flitting across a rainbow.

Terrified of getting lost, she turned her head and saw, a short ways behind the majitsu, something that resembled a cave mouth lurking underneath a vivid pink and fuchsia overhang. The filmy opening was a black semi-circle streaked with mahogany and blue and green, and it was less substantial than its surroundings, as if she could slip right into it.

This, she sensed, was the doorway back to her world. Whether she could access it without the amulet, she had no idea.

Mala tried to circle back, but the majitsu cut her off, forcing her deeper into the honeycomb. She noticed more of the gauzy black cave mouths as she flew, dozens more. Hundreds. The kaleidoscopic landscape extended as far as she could see, and her mind cringed at the implications.

She had to think of something fast. Whether because he was heavier or because her potion of movement was wearing off, the majitsu was gaining ground. If he caught her, she knew he would kill her, strip the amulet, and return through the doorway to their world.

Of course, were she in his position, she would do the same thing.

A shadow appeared and disappeared to her left, something long and fluttery and ominous. She started. *Is there something in here with us?* She had heard stories of wraiths floating through the Place Between Worlds, devouring the souls of travelers.

She grimaced and willed herself forward. She had plenty of tricks left, but nothing that would stop a majitsu. He was ten feet behind her, palms open at his sides, mouth cruel and relaxed.

They drifted through a curving corridor of splattered hues, exiting into a gold and violet canyon with walls so high she couldn't see the top. Dozens more of the insubstantial cave mouths were scattered about the canyon, at varying heights.

A keening erupted out of the silence, a high-pitched rush of air that sounded like a tea kettle starting to boil.

Mala paled. The fabled astral wind, buffeter of souls.

If it caught her, so the legend went, it would fling her through the Place Between Worlds like a sheaf of paper in a hurricane. Even if she managed to survive the wraiths and the majitsu, she would lose her world forever. It was said that spirit mages prepared for years to navigate the Place Between Worlds, and here she was, floating through it like a babe set adrift in the ocean.

As the howling wind drew closer, stray gusts buffeting them forward, the majitsu drew within seven feet, then five, then three.

If Mala had to, she would take her chances and throw the amulet into the void, then try to double back to her world when the majitsu went for it. But she was wary. Would her body whisk into the nearest world if she removed the amulet, like a jinn sucked into a bottle? Would her soul separate and float forever in this place, a lost and formless thing? Would one of the wraiths come for her? Would she simply cease to be?

She decided she didn't want to take the chance with either the astral wind or losing the amulet.

Which left only one option.

Just before the majitsu reached her, Mala darted a few feet to her left, diving with fingertips extended into a cave mouth the color of morning fog, set into the side of the canyon.

Another flash of red light, and then she was falling.

-6-

Mari crashed into Val, her momentum sending them both sprawling across the room.

Only it wasn't the same room anymore, Val thought. Or the same city.

Or even the same world.

They stumbled into a knee-high table that splintered on impact. Dishes shattered, shouts filled the air. Val's face ended up pressed against a stained wooden floor that reeked of stale beer and vomit.

He pushed to his knees, whipped around, and saw a room full of people with tattered clothing and grime-streaked faces. Soiled bed sheets spread over reed mats took up half the room. A cane rat peered down from a hole in the ceiling.

Dripping bits of gruel and foul-smelling ale, Val pulled Mari off the floor. Her eyes looked twice as big as normal and she was unsteady on her feet.

The shouting ceased when the people in the room stopped moving and got a good look at Val and Mari. He thought they would be in a fight for their lives, but then he noticed the downcast eyes, stooped shoulders, and furtive glances at his staff. The piece of blue-white azantite he had connected to the top of the staff had disappeared, leaving the original upturned crescent moon.

Two people in strange clothing teleporting out of nowhere. An azantite-tipped staff.

These people thought they were wizards.

Which, he thought with a grimace, he supposed he was. Just not a very good one.

"I'm sorry," he muttered to the crowd of indigents as his eyes found the door on the opposite side of the hovel. "I'm really sorry."

He took Mari by the hand, staff held high, and backed towards the exit. No one moved or uttered a sound, afraid to be singled out. Two children scuttled away from the door like lizards, then returned to scratching the bright red sores covering their bodies.

Val left the room and strode down the darkened hallway without a backwards glance, his heart slapping against his chest. Mari was clutching his arm, fingernails digging into his flesh.

"Jesus Christ," she said. "Jesus *Christ.*"

Not until they reached a staircase, descended two flights to ground level, and stepped outside into the tepid night air did Val exhale. Then he saw where they were, and sucked in his breath again.

"I guess Dad's neighborhood has seen better days."

Mari didn't seem to care about the crumbling tenements lining both sides of the empty street, or the preternatural calm that exists in neighborhoods where people are afraid to go out after dark, or the two hunched figures that eyed them and slunk into a recessed doorway. The intense light had returned to her eyes, brighter than ever, glowing at a fever pitch.

"We're here," she said in a daze, head swiveling to take it all in. "It's real."

Val grabbed her by the arm and led her down the street. If she hadn't jumped through the portal, he could have at least slipped on the Ring of Shadows until he made it out of this slum. If he used it now, she would appear alone to any observers, and they would be in even more danger. "Keep it together, Mari. You have no idea what a stupid thing you've done."

Val stepped as quietly as he could through the mud and potholes pockmarking the cobblestone street. Assuming this was New Victoria, he had no idea in which section of the city Dad had once lived. He just knew they had to get out of it.

Once again, the loss of his father's journal was a blow that left him reeling.

"Tell me all about it," she gushed. "I want to see the magic, Val. The *magic.*"

"Mari," he said, his voice tight but soft, "surely you can grasp what a dangerous place this is."

She lowered her voice as some of the initial shock and hunger drained from her eyes. "Of course. But I saw the way those people looked at your staff. You're some kind of wizard here, aren't you?"

Val ran a hand through the cowlicks in his normally trimmed brown hair, which had grown to his eyes over the last few months. "I don't know what I am," he said, "except that I'm as lost and helpless as you are."

She looped an arm through his as they walked. "Somehow I doubt that."

Val crouched behind an abandoned cart at the next intersection, peering around the corner as a rat clambered through a pile of garbage. "You're not getting it," he said. "Wizards, *real* wizards, rule this place, and if they find you, they'll squash you like a roach or throw you in the Fens, a place which makes this slum look like Disneyland."

"Is that who we're trying to avoid?" she said, a secret excitement creeping back into her voice. "The wizards?"

"Right now we're trying to avoid the thieves and murderers who no doubt prowl this area and would love to have their way with you."

Mari blanched, then regained her composure as quickly as if a jury were watching. "I need knowledge to survive, right? So educate me."

They hurried to the next intersection. Again the scenery looked uniform: moonless streets, decaying architecture, weeds and vines arcing out of cracks between the potholes.

"My guess is we've landed in the slums of New Victoria. This world's version of New Orleans."

"Which explains the humidity," she said, unzipping her jacket. "What time period are we talking?"

"It's not an exact correlation, and it's like nothing you've ever seen. But for starters, think Victorian era mixed with Medieval. There are parts of the city that are surprisingly sophisticated—these buildings are blocking the view of the Wizard District."

"So no guns?"

"No guns. As far as I've seen, magic has replaced most technology. But don't let that fool you. I'd rather face a team of Navy Seals than a wizard."

Not to mention the majitsu, and the sentient monsters, and the terrifying things roaming the countryside. Val sucked in a deep breath and balled his fists, unable to believe he was back. "You're taking this far better than I did when I arrived," he said. "Than I still am."

"That's because I *believe*, darling. And I've had the benefit of the Society archives. It's all there in history, if you know where to look. The myths and legends that are far too aligned and widespread. The ancient obsession with magic and the occult. Humanity used to be much more attuned to it, until technology replaced superstition."

Val frowned. "Are you implying our world used to be like this?"

"No, just that we've always believed that there's a *source*." She looked around, her tone reverential. "And here it is."

A few blocks down, the scenery took a turn for the worse. The streets narrowed into alleys, a thick layer of mud and sewage overlaying the cobblestones. Val swore. He hated to backtrack, but neither did he want to delve into that wasteland.

"So how does it work?" she asked.

"Sorry?" he said, trying to decide which direction to go.

She was staring at his staff. "You know what I mean."

Val barked a low laugh. "I wish I knew. I think magic's an innate mental skill for some that can be developed, like an athletic ability for the mind, but beyond that—"

Val lurched backwards as someone slid out of the darkness in front of them. He was tall and wiry, dressed in worn but colorful patchwork clothing that looked stitched together. A black sash was tied loosely around his waist, similar in length to the one Mala wore.

"Lost, me friend?" A green top hat, combined with poor posture, made the man's angular frame looked unbalanced, as if he were about to pitch over.

Val risked a quick glance over his shoulder, and went cold at what he saw. Men and women in similar clothing and black sashes slipping out of alleys, approaching the intersection from every direction. At least fifteen of them.

"Just passing through," Val said evenly.

"That right, is it? Ye don't look like yer just passin' through. What ye look like is someone wearin' fine togs who's lost where he shouldn't be lost."

Val opened his palms. "Take our clothes, then. I have a few coins as well."

The man grinned, revealing a mouth full of rotting teeth. "Oh, I'll be takin' yer coins and clothes," he said, leering at Mari. "And whatever else I want, too."

Mari flicked her eyes at Val and took a step forward, her tone imperious. "Can't you see that he's a wizard?"

The leader advanced towards Mari, head cocked, his laugh a shovel scraping against ice. "If 'e was a wizard, I'd be dead, and we wouldn't be 'aving this conversation. If 'e was a wizard, 'e'd be far too proud to muddy his boots in the Gypsy Quarter." He stepped forward until he was a foot away from Mari. "If 'e was a *wizard*," he said, thrusting his face into hers and roughly cupping her breasts in his hands, " 'e wouldn't stand and watch while I 'ave my way with 'is woman."

Mari tried to push away, but he caught her wrists in cloth-wrapped hands. She kneed him in the groin, which caused him to stumble and suck in his breath—and then stab her in the gut.

Val hadn't even seen him draw the knife. Mari's scream rattled in his ears as the leader of the gang shoved the blade deeper into her stomach, then ripped it to the side as he pulled it out. Without thinking, Val whipped his staff downward, the razor-sharp azantite slicing clean through the assailant's wrist.

The man bellowed and stumbled backwards, blood spewing, while Mari moaned and fell in a heap. Clutching his bloody stump to his chest, the gang leader pointed a shaking finger at Val. "Kill 'im!" he screamed to the others. "*Kill 'im!*"

-7-

Snuffing and snorting, two of the ugly creatures tied Will by his hands and feet to a six-foot pole. They hoisted the pole on their shoulders, then lowered Caleb and Yasmina from the tree and did the same.

Hanging upside down like a sloth, bouncing to the heavy tread of goblin feet, Will was forced to stare at the scars and calluses on his hands. He'd acquired quite a few badges of honor on the jobsites of his building contractor gigs. Ah, the jobsite: that theater of war where he had been fearless and respected—and where no real danger existed.

Will had always wanted the chance to make a difference, save the damsel in distress. Prove to everyone he wasn't just an average kid with good test scores, poor life skills, and no future. Prove he could overcome his severe panic disorder, which had disqualified him from even working in the local fire department.

Prove he was more than just a fantasy geek.

The only thing he had longed for more than being a hero was that fantasy could be real, that something rich and wonderful existed beyond the mundane reality of his life on planet Earth. Something to make him forget about the overdue rent, the foreman with the squirrel-size brain who resented Will's snappy comebacks, the girls in the bars who liked his forearms and tool belt but wouldn't look past his lack of a college degree.

Will laughed out loud, resulting in a kick to the ribs from one of the goblins. Oh, how he had gotten his wish.

He forced his mind elsewhere, face to face with the terrible things that had happened on the last visit to this world, the only way he could control the panic swelling inside him like a rising geyser.

The arrow spurting through Akocha's chest . . . Hashi dissolving into the acid . . . Charlie's animated corpse lurching towards Will . . . human spiders slicing open the cocoon next to him and feeding on that poor woman . . . .

Will shuddered and gritted his teeth, the panic seeping back down.

No, he was no longer the same Will.

He craned his neck to observe his surroundings, but saw only a line of goblins marching north through the forest, Caleb and Yasmina bouncing along behind him.

The goblins carrying Will began speaking in their harsh language of grunts, snorts, and garbled voices. Able to concentrate a bit better, he was now sure of what he had suspected the last time: he could understand them. The words popped into his mind in pigeon English, with what he assumed was goblin syntax.

"Grilgor pleased he be," the creature behind Will's head said.

"Three strays they are," the other agreed with a snort. "No marks. All limbs and bones they have."

"Flesh on bones too much for Fens. Come from swamp they did."

"Where go they now?"

The first goblin gave a puzzled grunt. "No matter."

"Grilgor send men to mines. Eat the skinny girl, we do?"

"Grilgor decide."

The other one made a wet, slobbering sound that raised the hair on Will's arms. "Eat her now, we do. Too long with no flesh. No ask Grilgor."

"Too close to camp we are."

They quieted, and minutes later they arrived at a clearing in the forest alight with a huge bonfire. At least twenty more goblins lounged about the camp, gnawing on hunks of meat stuck on the ends of sticks, drinking from clay mugs, and bantering in their coarse language. On the far side of the camp was a group of the ugliest equines Will had ever seen, mottled brutes the height of small ponies but with legs as thick as oak stumps. Their faces looked like smashed gourds, and a ridge of spiky red hair ran from the backs of their heads to the tips of their stunted tails.

Steeds as ugly as their masters.

To the left of the horses, obscured by the trees, a group of people sat in a circle around a mature hickory. Will's eyes moved downward, to the thick iron chain that encircled each of the humans at the waist and connected them together.

An enormous goblin rose from his seat around the fire, licking his hands after stuffing a hunk of meat in his mouth. A foot taller than the others, this goblin wore a necklace of desiccated human ears, a black ring on each tusk, and his greasy hair was tied back in a matted ponytail. A rawhide headpiece with jagged ridges sat on his forehead, a parody of a crown.

Grilgor, Will presumed.

The huge creature walked up to Will and began sniffing. Will tried not to gag; the creature smelled like a compost heap. After grunting a few times, Grilgor moved on to Caleb and Yasmina, then flung a hand in the direction of the people chained around the tree. The goblins carrying Will looked like they wanted to say something, but swallowed their protest and dropped Will on his back, untying him and prodding him with their spears towards the circle.

A goblin unlocked a padlock between two of the men, and the captives shuffled to widen the circle. Another goblin brought out four lengths of chain, fitted a circular iron belt around the waists of the three newcomers, then closed the circle again by reconnecting the chain to include Will, Yasmina, and Caleb.

Six feet of chain separated each of them, and at least they had put Yasmina between Will and Caleb. To Will's right was a ferret of a man whose golden brown skin and soft beige eyes reminded Will of a puppy. To Caleb's left was a slope-shouldered, shirtless brute with lash marks on his chest and back.

"Hang in there, guys," Will whispered, thinking it best not to discuss what he had heard earlier, especially the part about eating Yasmina.

Caleb's head was bowed. Yasmina looked terrified but defiant. Some of the people in the circle engaged in low conversation, but most sat cross-legged with downcast eyes and an unhealthy pallor to their skin.

An hour later, a goblin approached the circle carrying a burlap sack and a bucket. With wart-covered paws, it reached into the sack and tossed chunks of food at the captives.

Will picked up the piece of meat at his feet. It looked like boiled chicken, and he didn't think he wanted to know what it really was. He forced it down, though it tasted on the verge of being rancid. When the jug came around the circle, he followed the lead of the others and took a long swig. Lukewarm water slid down his throat.

"You going to eat?" someone said to his left.

When Will looked over, he noticed that neither Caleb nor Yasmina had touched their food. The brute beside Caleb, the one who had spoken, was eying the untouched meat. Caleb looked away, saying nothing.

"He's gonna eat it," Will said.

The larger man had olive skin, a beard, and a unibrow that hung like an unruly hedge over dime-size eyes. He glanced at Will, then reached down and snatched Caleb's meat.

Caleb's eyes rose and then fell.

"Give it back," Yasmina said.

The man bit into the chunk of meat. Will lunged over Yasmina and Caleb and snatched it out of the brute's hand, just able to reach him before the chain tightened.

The larger man bellowed and stood, then reached for Will with both hands, crowding past Caleb and Yasmina and dragging two men along behind him. Will stood and head-butted him in the face, then kneed him in the groin before he could recover. The man dropped to his knees, and Will barreled into him, ended up straddling him, and started punching him in the face. On the fourth punch, someone jerked Will into the air from behind, and he smelled the fetid odor of goblin.

Grilgor was stomping forward from the bonfire, waving his stumpy arms. "To the pole," he roared in English. "Take both!"

*   *   *

The cat o' nine tails lashed across his back for the eleventh time, and Will's eyes rolled with pain. The man beside him, the one Will had fought for Caleb's food, screamed in agony.

Will did not.

Another searing lash. Another scream from the man.

The muscles on Will's back and hamstrings spasmed. The pain from the cramping was almost as bad as the whip.

Don't give in, he told himself. *Don't give them the satisfaction.*

Will's hands were tied above his head, to a wooden pole stained with blood. He knew he could pull it down, but worried that if he did, they would flay him alive and eat him. Instead he took his punishment as best he could, knowing he would do the same thing again if given the chance. He hated bullies, and he sensed he had to let everyone know where he stood, right from the start. Especially with Yasmina and Caleb to protect.

Another lash. Blood from the man's back beside him splattered Will's face and chest.

He gritted his teeth and took short deep breaths through his nose. The pain from the poison dart in Leonidus's keep had been worse than this. "What else you got, pig face?" he muttered.

Another lash, harder.

This time Will screamed.

Yasmina stroked his hair while Will lay curled in a ball at her feet. A goblin had lathered some foul-smelling paste on his back that stung worse than the lashing, which he assumed was to prevent infection to their human chattel.

"How bad is it?" he asked.

"It's fine," she murmured. "You'll just have a few beauty marks, no?"

"Liar."

Caleb was squatting next to her, looking at Will as if he was on his death-bed. The goblins had moved the brute who had stolen Caleb's food to the other side of the circle.

"Really, I'll live," Will said to Caleb. "I've been wanting a tattoo for a while. This will do."

"You don't have to fight my battles, little brother."

"Yeah," Will said, "I do. I see red when someone touches my family."

Caleb was staring into the darkness. Yasmina reached over to stroke his cheek, and Will said to Caleb, "You're a pacifist. I respect that. Mankind is a violent, terrible race. It takes a big man to turn the other cheek."

"Or a coward," he murmured.

"You're a gentle soul," Yasmina said, and then to Will, "I've never seen that side of you. Where did you learn how to fight like that?"

Will felt a flush of pride. "I had a good teacher. Listen," he said in a low voice, "I think I can understand their language."

Caleb sat up. "Come again?"

"I've no idea why, and it's a bit like hearing evil toddlers converse. The only thing I can think of"—he winced as he lifted his arm an inch off the ground, drawing their attention to the inch-wide circle of iron wrapped around his biceps—"is this thing I found near the ogre-mage. I think he might have been wearing it as a bracelet."

"Ogre-mage?" Yasmina asked.

Caleb looked down at the armband, engraved with the image of a fat tongue sticking out of an oval mouth. "There's an easy solution to this. Take it off and see what happens."

"Yeah . . . that's the problem. It won't come off."

"Why on earth would you put on something the ogre-mage had?"

The side of Will's mouth curled in a sheepish grin. "It looked cool."

"It does suit you," Yasmina said.

Caleb shook his head, his dark hair flicking across his face. "Wow, little bro. I thought I was the vain one."

They all shared a nervous chuckle, and Will looked down at the lewd engraving, hoping it wasn't cursed.

Or maybe understanding languages *was* the curse.

"So where are our skin-care challenged captors taking us?" Caleb asked. "Maybe I'll end up as a courtesan to some duchess."

Yasmina rolled her eyes. When Will didn't respond, Caleb said, "Will?"

The healing salve had finally numbed the pain in his back. Will shifted an elbow to support his head. "I don't know," he mumbled.

Caleb and Yasmina fell quiet, both knowing he was lying, neither sure they wanted to know the truth. The moment of false levity they had shared melted away like snow on warm pavement.

"*Psst.* You awake?"

Will wasn't sure whether he had fallen asleep, was going insane, or someone was whispering to him.

"I'm no *krakey*, I promise. Let's talk."

It was a voice, he was sure of it now. Coming from his right.

It hurt, but Will managed to flip onto his side to regard the slight, beige-eyed person chained up beside him. With only a hint of stubble shadowing his smooth brown face, the prisoner looked a few years younger than Will, and he couldn't have weighed one hundred-forty soaking wet.

"*Rucka*, but you took a beating. Think you'll live?"

"I hope so," Will said, keeping his voice as low as possible. He had no idea how well goblin ears could hear.

"Stupid question, sorry. You only screamed once, though. I noticed. Marek wailed like a woman. Not that I wouldn't have. *Aike.*"

Will had no idea what some of the words the guy was using meant, and his arm bracelet wasn't helping. Maybe it was gibberish.

"What's your name?"

"Will."

"Normal name, weird clothes and accent. Where you from, Will? The North? Viking Land?" His eyes brightened. "Further?"

"Further. You?"

His mouth parted slightly, as if about to tell an important secret. "Macedonia. Family of wizards."

"Doesn't that mean you're . . . ." Will trailed off, his eyes widening.

He clicked his tongue. "Wizard born. Keep it quiet, of course. They'd kill me or turn me over to the Congregation if they knew."

"The Congregation is worse than this?"

"A non-citizen, unregistered wizard in Congregation territory? They'd see it as an act of high espionage. Death by fire, without a doubt."

"Ah." Somehow Will doubted the Congregation would consider his fellow prisoner an agent of high espionage. Maybe just plain espionage. "But why can't you—" Will nudged his head towards the chain—"just escape?"

"I'm still learning." His eyes roved downward, to his leg clamp. "And snapping iron isn't a simple task."

Still learning, Will thought, *or not very strong?*

"Dalen the Illusionist," he said, answering Will's next two questions. "Never met an illusionist, have you?" He kept speaking without giving Will a chance to respond. "Not many of us, 'tis true. I know we're not the most respected wizards. At least, not most of us. The Kalaktos conjurers are a different story. Break your mind, they will."

He looked around as if he had spoken a forbidden name, and Will took the chance to talk. "Where're we going?" Will said. "What are these things? I mean, I assume they're goblins—"

"*Rucka*, where are you from? Goblins have the ears, tuskers the snouts. Tuskers can smell for miles. That's probably how they found you."

Nope, they pretty much spotted our campfire from a mile away.

"It'd take two goblins to equal a tusker. Maybe three. And a brute like Grilgor?" He shuddered and inched closer. "Strong as a gorofant. We ran across a pack of leggers in the Eighth, and I saw him rip one apart with his bare hands."

"Thanks for that. Listen . . . I've heard rumors we're headed to a mine?" Will didn't want to give away his odd ability to understand tusker speech.

"My guess is Fellengard Mountain. Plenty of other mines in the Ninth, but everyone knows The Protectorate—" he snorted "—the *Congregation*—is hoarding tilectium like a barrow fiend." He cocked his eyebrow. "Suspicious, I know. Something's brewing, and everyone knows it. *Aike*."

"I don't get it," Will said.

"Get what?"

"The connection between the tuskers, the mines, and the Congregation."

Dalen's mouth opened in soundless mirth. "You think the Congregation would let tuskers operate east of the Ninth? Who do you think pays them? For the last year the slavers—tuskers, goblins, trolls—have been picking up strays and outcasts from the First on down, and carrying them to the mines."

"Where they disappear," Will said.

"Where they disappear," Dalen said grimly. "That's why I wanted to talk."

"To tell me I'm about to disappear? I've got that covered."

"To tell you we have to escape. I was impressed with the way you handled Marek."

Will looked around the silent camp before he spoke. "You have a plan?"

"*Aike*. Not yet. But if Fellengard is the destination, we have to think of something before we get there. Because no one escapes that mountain."

-8-

As the black sash thugs closed in, Val froze like an exposed rabbit. With trembling hands, he backed away and slipped the Ring of Shadows on his finger. His assailants whirled in confusion when he disappeared into the gloom.

"Where'd 'e go?"

"'E *is* a wizard."

Val scrambled to the side of a building, knowing if they shone a light on him the effects of the ring would be negated. He turned to see what looked like buckets of blood spilling over Mari's fingers. At least ten men and women had gathered around her like crows, pawing through her clothing and removing her jewelry. The rest of the gang milled about in a wide circle, peering into the darkness.

"'E's not a wizard, fools," the leader said. He snarled and wrapped his bloody stump with his sash. "Do ye think a wizard would let us live after that? 'E's got a potion or a ring. Get the light stick!"

One of the women whipped a short, battered stick out of a cloth bundle, shook it until it glowed, then handed the rod to the leader. Val shrunk against the building as the stick emitted a cone of light in a ten-foot radius. The gang leader whisked the light back and forth as he advanced, his movements jerky. "Where are ye, knave? Ye'll pay for me hand in spades, ye will."

Mari's face had lost all color. She lay crumpled on her side, unmoving. Val burned with an anger so intense it threatened to overwhelm him, blurring his vision and dumping adrenaline into his system like water from a burst dam. He reached deep for the magic, willing it to consume his enemies in a burst of fire, not having a name for the spell but knowing he had to help Mari.

Focus and *release*, he remembered, trying to concentrate through the chaos. *Focus and release*. Dig deep and find the magic and *focus and release and focus and release and*

Nothing happened.

Not the barest of sparks, not the whisper of a breeze. After trying again with the same result, he had to dive away from the approaching cone of light. As the thugs advanced in his direction, Val was forced to back away, deeper into the alley.

The hard truth was that he couldn't access his limited magic at will, especially not in the press of battle. His only weapon was his staff, and Val was no warrior. As soon as he attacked someone they would swing the light around. Even if he reached Mari, he only had the one ring.

But he couldn't just leave her. He slipped off the ring and let the men see him disappearing down the street, then doubled back at the next intersection and raced around the block, back to Mari. The street gang had moved on by the time he arrived, leaving her alone on the street, sprawled on her back like a discarded toy.

Her breaths were short and quick and far too shallow. He took her hand and pocketed the Ring of Shadows, so she could see him. "I'm here, Mari. Stay with me."

She moaned, and he eased her head into his lap and stroked her hair. "I just wanted to see the magic," she managed to whisper, and then her breathing stopped and her body seemed to deflate.

Val tried to revive her, pumping on her chest and blowing oxygen through her lips, over and over.

She was gone.

"There he is! I told ye he'd go back!"

Val jerked his head up and saw the street gang rushing towards him, still led by the scarecrow in the green top hat. The adrenaline rushed back in, and Val rose, ready to cleave the leader in two with his staff and accept the consequences.

With a shudder, he stepped away from Mari and slipped the ring back on. His colleague was dead, he couldn't win this fight, and there was a chance his brothers were still alive and needed him.

The leader of the gang was seconds away, sweeping the cone of light from side to side. " 'E went this way," he said, a dozen of his men right behind him. "I can smell 'is strange perfume."

Val ran.

Frightened and exhausted and filthy, his stomach lurching whenever he thought about Mari, Val stumbled through the slum for hours, unable to believe how large it was. His Ring of Shadows in place, he slunk through the nightmarish ghetto like a feral cat, jumping at every sound and movement.

The Ring of Shadows was not a true ring of invisibility, and as the first hues of dawn appeared, Val looked down in horror as his form adumbrated in the soft morning light.

He turned a corner and looked up, seeing a sight that made him shiver with relief. At the edge of his field of vision, a line of glow orbs emitted a pale halo of light. Glow orbs meant safer environs. As the sunlight strengthened and his form continued to solidify, he sprinted to escape the slum, waving his staff like a banshee at the few beggars who raised up as he passed.

A wide cobblestone boulevard separated the blighted neighborhood from the nicer one defined by three story brick townhomes and oak-lined streets lit by the gentle radiance of the glow orbs. Not until Val was safely across the boulevard did he stop to catch his breath. After making sure no one was watching, he removed the ring.

He decided to walk down the wide avenue rather than delve into the residential neighborhood. A few tradesmen, bakers and blacksmiths and general store owners, paid Val no mind as they swept the walkways in front of their shops. Trying to block the last image of Mari from his mind, nervous about his staff and exotic clothing, Val hugged the side of the road and prayed he didn't run into the authorities or, God forbid, a real wizard.

Five minutes later, a horse-drawn carriage clacked down the road with *For Hire* painted on the side. Forcing himself not to wave gold pieces like a madman, Val flagged it down and climbed on board.

He still didn't know where he was, but at least he knew where he was going.

Salomon's Crib.

That was what Caleb had dubbed it, the house on Magazine Street where the old man with silver eyes had first sent them. When Val and his brothers had arrived, whisked through the interdimensional ether, three bedrooms were already prepared, as well as trunks of clothing, weapons, and gold.

This time, Val guessed his father's portal had deposited him and Mari somewhere west of the French Quarter, because after he gave instructions to the driver, they angled south through a series of residential neighborhoods similar to the one he had just left, crossed over St. Charles Avenue, then turned right on Magazine.

It all came back in a rush: the timber-framed buildings and muddy cobblestone streets, the disorienting lack of cars and electrical wires. The clarity of the air, unspoiled by pollution. The little details eerily endemic to both worlds: wrought iron balconies, courtyards shielded by banana trees, the sickly sweet smell of decaying vegetation.

And in the distance, like a billboard screaming *you're not in Kansas anymore*, was the awe-inspiring sweep of the Wizard District: hundreds of multicolored spires piercing the sky high above the city, rising like celestial needles out of domes and manors and phantasmagorical creations of dripping stone.

When they neared the modest stone-and-timber façade of Salomon's Crib, Val paid the driver and hurried inside. As before, the lock clicked into place behind him, despite the fact he had opened it without a key.

He walked past the windowless great room, made of rough stone blocks and lit by standing iron candelabra, then carried on down the bedroom-lined hallway to the kitchen at the far end of the residence.

Just like the last time, three loaves of bread awaited, next to a dish filled with creamy yellow butter. Val consumed an entire loaf, washing it down with a bottle of ale from the cellar. When he was done, he held the bottle in his hands, then rose and smashed it against the wall.

"Salomon! I know you're out there! What have you done to us?"

Exhausted to the point of delirium, Val took a bath and laid down for a short rest, relieved that another huge chunk of time would not pass for his brothers every time he slept.

Mari stumbled through his dreams, clutching her intestines as they spilled out of the jagged hole in her stomach, looking at Val with confused eyes.

When he woke again it was morning.

*   *   *

As Val debated what to do, he buttered some bread and prepared a coffee—the pantry was stocked—in the sock-like contraption on the counter.

Mari was gone, and there was nothing he could do about it. He clenched his fists in anger, whispered a final goodbye in the silence of the room, and made a promise to extract what revenge he could. Then he shoved the rest of the universe aside in order to focus on the only thing that mattered.

Find his brothers.

He wanted to think they had escaped or possibly even killed Zedock, but he feared the necromancer was far too powerful in his own stronghold. Either way, Val had to be sure.

He needed information.

Salomon had left him with plenty of gold, but he didn't know where to spend it. He wasn't a citizen, and he knew if he started advertising his wealth, he would be robbed or thrown in the Fens or worse.

Mala was gone, and he had no idea how to locate Allira or Marguerite. He supposed he could ask around at the Thieves Guild, but that did not sound like a healthy proposition. He could think of only one person in the city who could point him in the right direction, and who he might be able to trust.

The morning sun blasted down as Val set a brisk pace down Magazine, the humidity already moistening the inside of the high-collared dress shirt he had found in one of Salomon's trunks. He had also donned a pair of dark woolen pants, brown leather riding boots, and cuff links. He left his father's staff hidden in the cellar so as not to attract attention.

He saw the date, the third of January, displayed on carved wooden blocks in the window of a bakery. According to the sixty-day time differential, that was four months earlier than it should have been.

He paled. *Or eight months later.*

When he reached the corner of Trafalgar and St. Charles, he peered both ways beneath the canopy of gnarled limbs festooned with Spanish moss, looking for a sign of the New Victoria City Tour operator he had once hired. Though it was still early, an hour after dawn, he supposed the driver might have left for the day, or was waiting at a different stop.

Val took in the twenty-foot high glow orbs in elegant bronze cages lining both sides of St. Charles, the stone mansions separated by wrought iron fences, the marble steps and stained glass windows and gardens of bougainvillea, all of it wrapped in a gauze of lingering morning mist.

"Step right up, good man, step right up and catch the Realm's first and only city tour."

Val whirled and saw a bearded man in a black top hat sitting atop a horse-drawn carriage, approaching from the north side of Trafalgar. It was the same driver as before, still chewing on a pipe and holding the same placard advertising the tour.

"Six groats apiece for the tour," he boomed, "only six groats. We just need three more to get started, should be soon enough."

Val stepped up as the carriage pulled to the curb. "If I recall," he said, "it was six groats apiece or a silver drake for everyone."

The driver took his pipe out of his mouth, his eyes shrewd. "You've 'ad one of me tours before, 'ave ye?"

Val flipped a silver drake up to the driver. "I'd like to hire you for the day."

The driver caught the coin and whisked it into his jacket, then peered closer. "Ye do look familiar."

Val climbed aboard the open-top carriage. "I was with my brothers and a friend last time. You were good to us."

The driver wagged his finger. " 'At's right, 'at's right, I remember. The out o' towners, was it?" He slapped his knee and laughed. "Ye gave me a good tip and plenty o' laughs."

"That's right," Val murmured. "Just last October, right?"

"That's it, that's it," the driver said, and Val breathed a sigh of relief. Only two months and a few days had passed here. "Say, where are yer brothers? They return, where was it, back north?"

"They're busy today."

Another stagecoach passed right beside them. Val caught a glimpse of a woman in a silken dress inside the carriage, chin held high, carrying a ruby-tipped wand and staring haughtily out the window.

A wizardess.

Though the woman had no reason to accost him, Val shrank from view.

The driver clicked his tongue, and the horses started down the wide, smooth-stoned road. "If ye like," the driver called back, "since ye've been here before, I'll toss in something extra. How about we swing by Bayou Village? If ye haven't been, 'tis quite the sight."

"Actually," Val said, "I didn't hire you for the City Tour. I need a driver for something else today, and you're the only one I know."

The burly driver stopped the horses and turned to face Val.

"I need information," Val said, holding up another silver drake. "As you know, we're new around here, and I'm not sure where to turn."

The driver eyed the coin. "What kind of information?"

Val rubbed his tongue against his teeth. *How to say this?* "I've lost something I need to get back. Something important. The problem is, I have no idea where it is."

Val remembered, when discussing magic with Alexander, that the geomancer had told him about a group of psychics called augurs who could receive impressions of the future. "Perhaps an augur could help?"

The driver clamped down on his pipe and blew a few smoke rings. "Plenty of those around. Too many, if ye ask me. Problem is, more likely than not ye'll get a charlatan. And even if ye find a good one, she'll spout some mumbo jumbo about the future that probably will just confuse ye."

Val pressed his lips together. "I see."

"This thing ye've lost, is it valuable?"

"Extremely."

"Do ye 'ave a few gold pieces to spare?"

"I do," he said evenly.

"And are ye brave?"

"I'm desperate."

"Then what ye need," the driver said, grinning through crooked, tobacco-stained teeth, "is a gazer."

-9-

Will's days passed in a blur of pain and hunger, his nights a gauntlet of cold and despair. Every morning, the tuskers separated the circle of prisoners by unlocking the padlocks, then secured a pair of captives to one of the squat, ugly steeds. Will rode with Dalen, Caleb and Yasmina right behind them. Tusker guards hovered on either side.

They rode from dusk to dawn, stopping only for five-minute breaks, making Will think the tusker mounts had steel for bones and iron for joints. Were they a native species, he wondered, or created by one of the legendary menagerists?

Caleb and Yasmina spent the journey slumped in the saddle with drawn faces and listless eyes. Even Will, who was used to never-ending slogs on the jobsite, had trouble managing the lack of food, the back pain, and the never-ending jostle of the ride.

On the fifth morning in, a lukewarm rain started to fall. They had left the marshlands behind and were traveling through copses of shortleaf pine and hardwoods. Despite the terrible nature of the journey, Will couldn't help but admire the beauty of the old growth forests of this world. Everything was bigger and brighter, more pristine, more mysterious.

He raised his manacled hands to wipe rainwater off his face, then leaned forward to sneak in a chat with Dalen. "If the mines are out west," Will whispered, "why are we headed north?"

"Too many natives due west. Not to mention Mayan war parties ranging up from the south. I don't know about you, but I'll take my chances with tuskers before I'll have my beating heart ripped out of my chest by a battle mage and thrown into a volcano. *Aike.*"

Dalen, Will had learned, was not averse to a little melodrama.

"How far away is Fellengard Mountain?" Will asked. "I'm not sure how long Caleb and Yasmina can keep this up."

"You think this is easier than pounding rock out of a mountain until you die from exhaustion?"

"Good point," Will muttered.

"Never been to the Ninth, have you? The Protectorate built a few byways, but most of it's wild. A whole new world. Treasure, Will. Mountains and valleys and caves full of treasure. And the Barrier Coast, *rucka*. I've heard all kinds of tales about that. Gypsies are out there, of course, but that's fine by me. Gypsies leave you be unless they're trying to pick your pocket. Except the Black Sash gypsies, now they'll slit your throat from ear to ear."

"Have you ever been to the Ninth Protectorate?"

"My *da* and I crossed the Great River once, on a Queen's Day ferry. Just a quick out and back, but I've heard the stories. Believe me."

One of the tuskers shook his flail at them, and Will quieted. He wished Val were here. He would figure something out. Or Mala—she would just reach into her pouch, find something to help them escape their chains, then lead a slaughter of their captors.

But they're not here, buddy. Caleb's a pacifist, and Yasmina's still wearing a T-shirt.

This one's on you.

Around midday a cloud of black smoke blotted the sky in the distance. The goblins stopped to confer, then sent one of their scouts ahead to investigate. After the scout returned to confer with Grilgor, the party resumed its pace, heading straight towards the ashen horizon.

An hour later the forest broke, revealing the smoking remains of a village nestled by a stream. The tuskers led the captives to the center of town, then halted the march to rummage through the charred remains. Will could tell the village had once been attractive, a collection of brick and thatch-roofed homes surrounding a leafy central square.

"Notice what's missing?" Will said to Dalen, blinking through the tears caused by the lingering smoke.

"Bodies."

"Exactly. And the tuskers are bringing sacks of coins out of the houses. Why wasn't this place looted by whoever burned the village?"

"Good question, Will From The North," Dalen murmured.

After the tuskers finished looting the ruined settlement, they spurred the steeds into action. A few minutes outside the village, on the banks of the stream, Will found some insight into the mystery—and wished he hadn't.

Swarming with carrion birds, piled in neat rows next to the stream like stacks of human firewood, were the corpses of the missing villagers. The wind shifted, causing him to recoil as the smell of decomposing flesh drifted to his nostrils.

Yasmina vomited behind him. He glanced back and saw Caleb staring at the pile of bodies, rubbing his bound hands together as if kneading a pile of dough.

"By the Queen," Dalen muttered.

Later that night, Will lay on his side, eye to eye with Caleb. Yasmina was facing away from them, already asleep. Almost a week had passed since their capture, and the tuskers had picked up four more prisoners.

"So, genius," Caleb said, in a voice too low for anyone else to hear, "you thought of a way out of this yet?"

"Some genius," Will said. "My main intellectual achievement was memorizing the entire contents of the AD&D Monster Manual when I was twelve."

"It's better than bar menus."

"Glad to see you still have your sense of humor," Will said.

"I'm not as frail as you think, little brother. I've been around longer than you, remember. Got a few more gray hairs."

"Three whole years? And the day you find a gray hair is the day you have a nervous breakdown and check yourself into the Mayo Clinic."

"Beware, brother mine, of jealousy. 'Tis the green-eyed monster which doth mock the meat it feeds on.' "

"Who said that? Stephen King?"

"Yeah . . . that would be Shakespeare," Caleb said.

"Since when do you read Shakespeare?"

"I had to say something when my ex stole my iPhone. She was a literature major. I looked the quote up."

"Didn't she catch you cheating?"

"So break up with me. Don't steal my iPhone."

Will rolled his eyes. "This world isn't ready for you."

"They won't have to put up with me much longer."

Will's voice turned serious. "What's that supposed to mean?"

"I heard you talking to Dalen about the tuskers taking us to some slave mines."

Will couldn't deny the truth of that, so he decided not to talk about it. "How's Yasmina?"

"I'm not sure, to be honest. I've been filling her in on what we know about this world. Mainly she listens and stares straight ahead. I think she's taking it in, but . . . I don't know, Will. She's a tough girl, from Brazil and all, but she's middle class like us. Her parents were teachers." His eyes slipped downward. "I was the one who suggested that campfire."

"I took the key from Salomon, Caleb. This is on me."

"You did what you thought was best at the time. Dad brought this on us, if you want to blame someone."

"Don't," Will said.

"Why not? Why is it such a sacred memory? All he did was lie to us our entire lives and leave us at the mercy of Zedock."

"He left us the weapons and his diary. We don't know all the details. He did what he could."

"Did he?" Caleb said. "I don't doubt that he loved us, but he came to our world for a reason, and I don't think it was Netflix and thin crust pizza. When you play with fire, Will . . . you know the deal. It's one reason I'm a pacifist. Violence is a never-ending cycle. And it usually carries on to the next generation."

"Really? You're blaming Dad instead of Zedock?"

"Dad was a wizard. A member of the *Congregation*. I loved him, too, but do you think his hands were clean?"

Caleb turned to go to sleep, and Will lay on his back, staring at the stars. He didn't do well with shades of gray. He wanted the world to be black and white, good and evil.

Especially when it came to people he loved.

"Psst. Will."

He shifted to see Dalen on his side, peering at him. Except for a few sentries too far away to hear, no one else seemed to be awake.

"We need to figure something out. A plan."

"Yeah," Will said. "We do."

"I think I've got a way out of these chains."

Will almost shot up, but he forced himself to look asleep.

"But *lucka*, it has to be the right time," Dalen continued. "Have you seen the guard with the missing tusk, the one who unlocks the circle every morning?"

"Sure."

"Every few nights he drinks too much grog and falls asleep with the keys around his neck."

"Can't you just," Will flicked a wrist, "bring the keys over here? Once they're asleep?"

Dalen looked embarrassed. "I haven't quite mastered that spell."

Will wanted to say, *isn't that about the easiest spell in the book?* But he held his tongue. He didn't know anything about how magic worked. "So what're you going to do?"

"Tools of the trade," Dalen said mysteriously. "But I need you to take care of the tusker once I lure him over. Can you do that?"

I'll do it or die trying. "You better believe it."

"Good. I'll unlock the four of us, then leave the key for the next person while we slip away."

"What do we do after that?"

"*Lucka*, Will. We run."

Will woke stiffer than usual the next morning. Talking to Dalen had given him a glimmer of hope, though his stomach churned at the thought of having to take on a tusker by himself, weaponless, with his hands chained.

He spent the morning recalling the lessons in hand to hand combat Mala had given him. The thought of her brought a pang of memory.

She had sacrificed herself for them. For Will.

What he wouldn't give to see her alive once more. He would find a way to prove himself, to make her look at him despite the fact that she probably dated six-foot-five Viking warriors who looked good in tunics.

No, he thought. Mala was too smart for that. Too *cool*.

He put his hands to his temples. *What are you doing, Will? She's dead. They're all dead. Mala, Hashi, Fochik, Alexander. Maybe even Lance and Val. They're all dead and they're not coming back.*

The lowland forests had ended some time ago, and they were traveling through a region of dry grass, bare trees, and undulating terrain. After crossing a stream and rounding a bend, the path led into a shallow canyon. Not far in the distance, a line of tall hills appeared like brown gumdrops beneath a roiling sky.

Soon after they filed into the canyon, the tusker steeds started making a noise halfway between a grunt and a whinny. A few of the prisoners gasped and pointed to Will's left. He turned to look and then paled.

Standing atop a low bluff about fifty yards away, guarding the approach to hill country, was a group of enormous humanoids dressed in rough cut animal skins. They had to be at least eight feet tall, and each one carried a spiked club half as long as their body.

"*Lucka*," Dalen breathed in front of him. "Hill trolls."

-10-

Mala was wrapped in gray.

A leaden mist cloaked the narrow valley in which she stood, the sky thick and hoary as gravy, the forested hills choked with leaves that hung like ashes from the trees.

On the opposite end of the valley, she could just make out the outline of a few low structures. A farmstead, she guessed.

The air was cool but not cold, still but not dead. No sun in the sky. The valley smelled like mushrooms and wood smoke.

There was no grass, just a bluish-gray ground surface with the slick texture of clay. Perhaps it was clay.

The curiosities of this world were a distant item of interest compared to her survival. She grasped her amulet and slid her fingers into the grooves of silver, ready to re-enter the Place Between Worlds and retrace the passage to her own world, hoping the astral wind had passed.

Nothing happened.

Mala stared at the amulet in shock, then remembered the words of the fence she had consulted in Londyn.

With an amulet of power such as this, my dear gypsy explorer, it is impossible to predict how many charges it holds. And this type of item has limits. Perhaps its magic will function once, twice, three times. Perhaps it will work once an hour, once a day, once a year. Only the Magecrafter who fashioned it can know.

Did her amulet need to recharge, she wondered, or was its power spent? Might she be stuck in this place forever? Heart fluttering in her chest, her short sword and curved dagger appeared in her hands as if by magic, and she crouched to survey the barren landscape.

No sign of life. Not even a birdcall to break the silence.

Just as she decided to scout the homestead from the safety of the trees, a hole in the air opened and closed in the blink of an eye, and her majitsu oppressor tumbled onto the ground.

Mala whipped another dagger out of her boot and hurtled it at the warrior mage, almost as fast as the portal had opened. She was hoping to catch him off guard or, better yet, perhaps the laws of magic did not work the same on this world.

She had no luck on either account. The majitsu reacted in time to use his magic to harden his swarthy skin, and the dagger bounced off him as if striking a stone wall. His smile appeared like a paper cut beneath his shaved head and sturdy nose.

He leapt forward with the distinctive movement of the majitsu, a cross between hurdling and flying, each step covering five paces. Mala whirled her weighted sash into his face. That bounced off him too, and she tossed a few ineffective fire beads before turning and sprinting for the forest, knowing if he caught her he would shove his fist through her heart.

She could feel him behind her, grinning, confident in his superior ability. She *hated* him for it.

Ten feet separated them. She rolled to the side, coming up with both blades at the ready, poised to engage. The majitsu turned to face her, hands loose at his sides.

She feinted and backpedaled. As he lunged for her, something steel gray and slithery shot out of the air and attached itself to the majitsu's wrist, jerking him backwards and then coiling around his body at an impossible speed, rendering him immobile.

Mala spun to the right, just in time to see a huge hag-like creature point a crooked finger at her. Another gray tendril shot out of the hag's fingertips.

Mala tried to evade the missile, but it landed on her arm with the soft impact of a snake dropping from a tree, then coiled around her faster than she could react, tightening her arms against her sides and causing her to topple over, just like the majitsu. The coils felt slimy and thick against her skin. *What type of strange magic is this?*

One of the coils covered her mouth, muting her shouts but allowing her to breathe through her nose. She turned towards the hag and saw two similar but smaller creatures standing behind her.

They were hideous things, taller even than the majitsu but squat like toads, with arms and legs disproportionately short for their torsos. Each wore shapeless, loose fitting wool smocks with pouches sewn into the middle, and their exposed skin looked like chewed gray leather. They wore no shoes, and the six wrinkled protrusions at the end of their feet resembled knuckles more than toes. Each had six stubby fingers as well.

The larger hag had a nest of white hair that sprouted in all directions and hung past her shoulders, a squashed nose with three nostrils that covered half her face, and a choker made of bark and affixed with a series of ivory hooks holding live, two inch-long worms. As the invertebrates wriggled in place on her neck, the hag barked a command in a language Mala had never heard. It sounded like raspy gargling.

The two other hags, one bald and one with pale red hair, waddled over to Mala and the majitsu, then carried them back to their mistress as if they were sacks of grain.

The lead hag tore off one of the worms around her neck and popped it into her mouth, then hunched over Mala and probed at her face with a clawed finger. Mala recoiled from the slimy touch of the worms dangling against her skin. The hag's powerful odor washed over her, rot and disease and some pungent but unidentifiable herb. Mala choked back her vomit as the thing babbled in its guttural language.

After lifting off Mala's amulet and placing it around her own neck, the hag muttered something to the other two creatures, then took a spongy root out of one of her pouches and passed it under Mala's nose.

She swooned.

*　　*　　*

When her eyes opened, Mala found herself looking at the underside of a peaked thatch roof. Still clothed, unhurt as far as she could tell, she was hanging upside down in a room with rough stone walls.

Her feet were secured to a giant iron hook with the same disgusting ropy tendrils the hag had used to subdue her. The hook was attached to a ceiling beam. When Mala tried to wriggle, she realized her entire body was bound, wrapped like a mummy.

To her right, a small window showcased a gloomy view of the valley.

To her left was the majitsu.

He was hanging upside down from an identical iron hook. His brown eyes bored into hers. "Why didn't you escape with the amulet? You couldn't, could you?"

She would tell him nothing. He could simmer in the arrogance of his kind.

"Why would you do such a stupid thing, portaling into an unknown realm?"

Her lips curled. "Better that you kill me in the Place Between Worlds? I think not."

The majitsu flicked his eyes towards the wooden door. "There are fates worse than death."

"Perhaps. But I'll choose an uncertain fate over a certain demise."

The majitsu struggled to free himself, then stopped and squeezed his eyes shut, as if concentrating. When he opened them again, Mala asked, "Why can't you break these bonds?" She had not known many things a majitsu could not break.

"Because they're constructed of a stronger magic than mine, obviously. Yet it's strange," he muttered, as if speaking to himself, "that I don't recognize the basic structure. It's like nothing I've ever seen."

"I believe that's why they call it otherworldly."

"What do you know about other worlds, gypsy? I'm surprised you left your wagon."

Mala resisted the urge to spit in his face, and then explain in exacting detail just how far she had traveled, the wonders and terrors she had seen that surely dwarfed his limited experiences gleaned from a lifetime of servitude to the wizards.

No, this *gadje* majitsu didn't deserve an explanation.

"As if working for a necromancer is a higher calling," she mocked. "Did you graduate last in your class at the Academy to secure such an honorary position?"

"Watch your tongue, wench. Zedock is an adjunct member of the Congregation."

Mala didn't bother with a response. In her mind, the Congregation and the leadership of the Protectorate were so corrupt, so ludicrously unworthy of respect, that anyone who stated otherwise was a fool.

And everyone who propped up their incestuous regime, herself included—they were fools, too.

But again, better to be a fool than dead.

Shuffling footsteps approached from outside. As the door creaked open, Mala's eyes flicked to the ominous curve of the hook above her head, disliking the train of thought that resulted.

The door swung wide, and the hag mother shuffled through the entrance, the other two fiends crowding in behind her.

-11-

"A gazer?" Val asked, as the horses clacked down St. Charles.

"A gazer. Ye know, a phrenomancer."

The second term sounded familiar, but Val couldn't recall where he had heard it. "I don't think I'm ready to consult a wizard."

I'd love to consult a wizard, he thought, *if I had any faith they wouldn't kill me or toss me in the Fens.*

The carriage driver brayed and slapped his knee. "There's the laddie I remember, doesn't know an intelligent monster from a wood rat. Gazers aren't wizards—well, now, come to think o' it, I suppose some of 'em are in a fashion, or at least that's what they say. But they're certainly not part o' the Congregation. They can see things others can't, now that's without a doubt."

"See things how?"

"Well, now, 'tis a clever question. Ye've heard, o' course, about the philosophy of phrenology?"

"Of course," Val lied.

"Power o' the mind and all that. I don't buy into it much me'self—me own noggin tells me when I'm hungry and tired, and that's about it. But real gazers —not just philosophers but the ones who can go inside yer head, like the one I'm taking ye to—they can see all sorts o' crazy things. How?" He cackled at his own question. "You'd 'ave to ask one of 'em. Won't get a straight answer, though. A bit like the augurs when it comes to that." He spat, then swiveled to cock another toothy grin. "Ye'll see."

As they passed through Ambassador's Row and the rest of the Garden District, those enchanting colored spires looming in the background, Val relived the wonder and terror he and his brothers had experienced at seeing the sights of New Victoria for the first time.

The busy commercial district with its dizzying array of sights and races filling the cobblestone streets, lizard men and albino dwarves and cloaked, misshapen figures hinting at even stranger origins. The Bestiary, the silver gleam of the Spectacle Dome, the shops that had so excited Will: *Gareck's Alchemical Supplies*, the *Adventurer's Emporium*, the *New Victoria Magick Shop*.

The thought of his beloved youngest brother, of his innocent spirit and ability to be moved, caused a shudder of rage and grief to course through Val.

They can't be gone. They simply can't.

Forcing thoughts of his brothers away, he snapped his fingers as the carriage passed a bamboo walkway leading to an open door and a *Phrenomancer Available* sign hanging from the window. He remembered this part of the tour from last time, and knew he had seen that word before.

"We're not stopping?" Val asked.

"I'm taking ye to the French Quarter. A little place known as Bo'emian Isle."

"What's wrong with this phrenomancer?"

"That shop's for the tourists, lad."

Next came the Guild Quarter, followed by the imposing monoliths of the Government District. As before, one of the enormous stone sphinxes guarding the bronze and marble Fifth Protectorate Capital Building tilted its head to regard the carriage as it passed. Val locked eyes with the mythological beast, searching for answers in its timeless gaze.

They passed through a section of fancy shops and cafes, then turned right on Canal Street. The pearl of New Victoria's downtown, Canal brimmed with brocaded carriages and avant garde restaurants with velvet-draped entrances.

Instead of heading towards the silver bridge arcing above the river at the end of the street, the driver crossed Canal and headed into the chaos of the French Quarter. The change in environment was intense, even more pronounced than back home. This world's French Quarter was bigger, dirtier, louder, more grim. Three and four story wooden buildings leaned over the street, creating an aura of perpetual gloom, and Val tensed as the carriage crept through the labyrinth of filthy streets and alleys, slowed to a crawl by potholes and crowds of degenerates. Women in low bodices—and some with no bodice at all—beckoned to Val from crumbling balconies.

Whenever the crowd grew too dense or aggressive, Val's driver would stand and curse, and the throngs would shift to let them through. A few of the rougher types even gave friendly waves, and Val wondered what his driver did in his spare time.

Perhaps he was more useful than Val had realized.

They went ten blocks deep, turned left, and went ten blocks more before the street dead-ended at a canal full of brackish water. A footbridge crossed the canal, leading to an island of tightly packed lanes similar to the rest of the French Quarter, except the buildings were painted various shades of pastels that had long since begun to fade and peel.

"Bohemian Isle, I presume?" Val said.

The driver cackled. "Paradise on Urfe. See that street 'tween the green and purple buildings? Follow it right to the center. Take the alley across from the fountain, underneath the gargoyles, then ye'll see the phrenomancy sign on yer left. Look close or ye'll miss it."

"You'll wait here?"

"Aye."

Val climbed off the coach, trying not to inhale the canal's toxic odor of refuse, spilled ale, and human waste. Without his staff or a weapon of any sort, he felt as if he were walking into a courtroom without documents.

Except in this court, you got stabbed if you weren't prepared.

After a final glance at the chaos behind him, Val stepped across the footbridge, entering the slightly less manic atmosphere of Bohemian Isle. As he delved into the heart of the neighborhood, he saw the same taverns, opium dens, gaming houses, and brothels as in the rest of the French Quarter, but he also saw minstrels playing for groats on street corners, artists working on canvas sheets, jugglers and flame throwers practicing their art.

And then it got weird.

A snake charmer coaxing a three-headed cobra out of a basket. Two street artists collaborating on a wall mural, starbursts of color worked into an impressionistic desert landscape—only the artists didn't have any brushes, and appeared to be painting with their minds. A cross-legged swami levitating above the ground, his topknot floating three feet above him. Groups of lizard men tossing dice. A shop that sold various goods appearing to be hybrids of magic and technology: model pirate ships that circled the shop in the air, an ornate grandfather clock with a human face that spoke the time, a selection of globe orbs for the home.

A few streets in, Val passed a sign depicting a voluptuous naked woman with fangs and claw-tipped wings. Soft mocking laughter emanated from an open second story window.

Come in, a voice spoke in his head, the whisper of flesh on satin. Val felt a sensation of overwhelming desire course through him. *Come in and try me.*

He pushed air through his teeth and hurried forward, thinking it would be best if Caleb never stumbled across that particular establishment. Jittery by the time he reached the circular fountain that served as a drinking trough in the central square, wondering how they purified the water, Val paused to scan the crowd of artists, drifters, and street urchins. True to the driver's word, Val spotted an alley across the square, flanked by two gargoyles leering off of waterspouts.

As he surveyed the scene, a woman came striding out of a side street, dressed in a simple gray caftan and clutching a scroll. Three blue dots formed a triangle on her forehead and the backs of her hands. The crowd quieted, and the people who noticed her scurried to the side as if she carried the plague.

The woman walked straight towards the fountain, speaking with the self-assured tone of the converted. "Abandon your ways, sinners and nonbelievers. Turn to He who ruleth from above the mountains and below the seas, He who formeth the heavens, He who sprangeth from the Void. Embrace the power of Devla. Embrace Him or perish with the wicked, in the golden fire that shall consumeth the earth."

That's a comforting theology, Val thought.

The woman was almost to the fountain. The center of the square had emptied, and Val hurried around the perimeter to the entrance of Gargoyle Alley, joining the rest of the crowd as they watched the woman. The crowd seemed apprehensive but eager, as if they knew something titillating was about to happen.

The woman climbed onto the lip of the pool and raised a fist. "The Disciple of the One True God hath come to the Realm! He shall lay His enemies low, sayeth the Prophet, in a storm of spirit and lightning!"

Two helmed guards in gold and crimson uniforms burst into the square, heading straight for the woman with raised halberds. She kept speaking as they came, her expression unchanged, fist raised.

Just before the guards reached her, she dropped something into the fountain, and it erupted into molten blue fire, immolating herself along with the guards. The men screamed as they burned, but the woman stood calm and composed while the flames engulfed her.

As the smell of crackling flesh filled the square, some of the bystanders began shouting and pointing skyward. Val followed the line of fingers to what looked like a blazing arrow coming from the direction of the Wizard District. The shape coalesced as it drew closer, until Val could see a wizard in a red cloak, riding a ten-foot wave of fire with vaguely formed head and limbs.

The pyromancer hovered above the square on his fire mount, then passed a gauntleted hand in the direction of the burning guards and woman. The flames died. The pyromancer clenched his fist, showcasing a giant ruby in the center of his gauntlet, and the woman flew towards him as if shot from a cannon. The wizard's fire mount secured her with cords of flame—Val assumed they were heatless—then returned skyward, blazing out of sight like a comet in reverse.

As the guards writhed in pain, the bystanders muttered in subdued voices, as if the pyromancer might still be watching. Val backed away, shuddering, then turned and strode down the alley.

The problems of this world were its own. He had work to do.

Gargoyles marked every peaked roof on the claustrophobic lane, as if the building code had required each owner to hire a macabre artist to complete the structure. Unlike the rest of the colorful streets of Bohemian Isle, these buildings were grey and decrepit, creaking with age.

The street was deserted, but Val felt an uneasy sense of not being alone. He didn't feel as if someone or something were watching, but rather as if traces of old magic had collected in the grime of the windows and door stoops, humming with forgotten power.

The phrenomancy sign was halfway down the street, carved into a wooden doorway in a tight, archaic font. Val stepped close to read it. The residence looked abandoned, three angular stories of worn stone and boarded-up windows squeezed between its neighbors.

He knocked. No one answered.

After a few more moments, he turned the knob, eased the door open, and stepped into a windowless parlor with a low ceiling. A half-cracked interior door faced him, with an *Open* sign hanging from a hook. Val opened that door and traversed a stone hallway lit by guttered candles set in sconces overflowing with melted wax.

After passing four closed doors, he encountered a beaded entryway at the end of the hallway. He pushed through and saw a man lounging in the center of a small den strewn with tattered rugs and cushions. Candelabra provided illumination, the wax again overflowing and collecting in coagulated mounds on the floor.

The man's smile was as lazy as a summer day. A mass of dark, tangled hair spilled to his waist, stubble shadowed his face, and his threadbare clothing, navy pantaloons and a white dress shirt unbuttoned halfway down his chest, looked as if it had once been of fine quality. "Yes?"

Val's eyes swept the room and picked out a battered gourd on the floor next to the man. Though disheveled and at least forty, the man was still quite handsome, and his red-rimmed, mandarin colored eyes simmered with a penetrating intelligence.

"Are you the phrenomancer?" Val asked.

"I am *a* phrenomancer."

"I was told you're good."

"That depends."

"On what?" Val said.

The man's eyes were unfocused, as if half-dreaming. "On what you're look-ing for."

Val stepped closer and folded his arms. "I'm looking for my brothers."

"Oh? And where might they have gone?"

"They might be . . . ." Val took a deep breath, unable to say the words. "They fought with a wizard. I don't know the outcome."

"That does not sound promising."

Val didn't reply.

The phrenomancer shifted an arm that was splayed across a cushion. "You haven't yet inquired about the cost. That is everyone's first question."

"I don't care about the cost. I care about results."

"Is that so?" The man leaned over to sip from a copper straw protrud-ing from the gourd. Then he leaned on an elbow, his eyes suddenly focused. "Where are you from?"

"North. Beyond the snows."

The phrenomancer's smile faded to a neutral expression. Val could tell he didn't believe him.

"Have you seen a gazer before?"

"No," Val said.

"Do you understand what phrenomancy is? What we will do here? Why they call it gazing?"

Val hated to admit weakness. It was the cardinal sin of a negotiation. Un-fortunately, he needed knowledge more than he needed leverage. "I assume you'll look into a crystal ball, or read tarot cards."

The phrenomancer chuckled, a low and throaty sound. "No no no, my friend. Oh no. That is not *at all* what I will do."

"Then what?"

"I'm going to enter your mind. Gaze into your soul."

Val stared at him for a few seconds before responding, his expression un-changing. "How will that help me find my brothers?"

"Good," the phrenomancer said, with an approving nod. "Most flinch at that knowledge. Either you have no secrets, or you are desperate. My guess is the latter, since every man has secrets. My name is Alrick. And with whom do I have the pleasure of doing business?"

"Valjean. Val."

"And your brothers?"

"Will and Caleb. You never answered the question."

The lazy smile reappeared. "To try to locate your brothers I'm going to take a journey, Valjean. Inside your mind."

"I don't understand."

"Who does? We may not understand it, but we can still try to perfect it. The mind is the gateway to the universe. The mind, the soul, the realm of spirit, we are all one. And if you follow the pathways far and deep enough, and manage to survive the journey," he spread his hands, "who knows what you'll find?"

Val had to work to keep the disbelief from his voice. Trying to understand this world was like trying to complete a business deal in Chinese without an interpreter. "So you're going to go inside my head and search for my brothers?"

"Not just your mind, but theirs. Following the pathways. Looking for connections. I can't promise we'll find them," he took another sip from the gourd, "but I can promise you I'm the best there is in New Victoria." He ran a hand through his hair and gave a low chuckle. "At least that's the reputation. Who can really say? Perhaps there's some mad gazer rotting deep inside the Fens, locked in his own mind, talking to the Great Architect as those around him boil leather for supper."

"Will you be able to tell—" Val's jaw worked back and forth—"if they're alive?"

"Is the connection between you strong?"

"Define strong."

Alrick waved a hand. "You've seen them in the last year? More than once? Are you close in spirit?"

"Yes to all," Val said. Despite his strained relationship with Caleb, he loved both brothers equally, and more than anything else in the universe. "Very."

"Then I will know if they're alive."

Val felt a wave of both fear and relief at the knowledge. At the very least, he was going to know that.

"So how does it work?" Val said.

The phrenomancer pushed to his feet. "Come."

*   *   *

After locking the door at the other end of the hallway and switching the sign to *Closed*, Alrick led Val into a windowless room the size of a large closet. The walls and rear of the door were painted glossy black.

The only objects in the room were two chairs placed on either side of a square wooden table. Atop the table was a curious device: a brass stand that rose a foot off the table and then branched into two circular apertures spaced a foot apart, and sporting adjustment knobs and leather chin pads.

Alrick, still moving as if underwater—Val assumed he was intoxicated, which did not inspire confidence in the procedure—produced a stopper of amber-colored liquid.

"Secure yourself in the oculave," the gazer said, nodding towards the device on the table, "and I'll insert the drops."

Val hesitated, and Alrick said, "Forgive me, it's your first time. As they say, the quickest route to the soul is through the eyes, and it just so happens that it's true. After inserting the glow drops, I'll secure myself across from you, and our gaze will be locked. You can sever the connection at any time by removing yourself from the oculave or simply shutting your eyes for a prolonged period. But I counsel you to maintain the soul gaze until I sever. I'll know when we've gathered what we can."

Val sat and placed his chin on the padded square, so that his head was leaning slightly forward, like a visit to the optometrist. "Ready." *I think I am, at least.*

Alrick lit a candle and placed it on the table, then shut the door. After gently tilting Val's head back and inserting two drops from the stopper, he tightened Val's oculave by rotating the knob. Val couldn't move his head, which unnerved him, but after loosening and retightening the knob himself, he felt comfortable he could escape if needed.

The drops caused a brief sting and then settled. Alrick inserted his own head into the opposite oculave, then adjusted the height until his and Val's gazes were locked a foot apart. Just before Alrick blew out the candle, Val saw an alertness in the phrenomancer's eyes that had not been present before, an eagerness bordering on hunger that left Val feeling unsettled, as if Alrick was about to gain some illicit pleasure from the procedure.

Then there was darkness.

"Can you see my eyes?" Val asked.

"Perfectly. Count to ten as I lock in my gaze, think of the last time you saw your brothers, and then don't utter another word."

"Don't you need more information? What they look like?"

"Your memories will tell me everything I need to know," Alrick murmured. "Now count."

One, two, three

Val looked straight ahead and saw the red-rimmed, pale orange eyes of the phrenomancer staring back at him. As Val counted, he thought of the battle with Zedock in the cemetery, just before his brothers dove through the portal.

Four five, six

Or wait, should he think of the last time they had been in this world? Did it matter?

Seven, eight, nine

Was Alrick really going inside his head? Was any of this real, or just a complicated trick to relieve Val of his gold—

He heard a scraping sound, smelled sulfur, and then light flared into the room, the kind of instant glow a wizard would create. Alrick whipped himself out of the oculave, shook out his match, and slammed his palms on the table.

"Why didn't you tell me you were a wizard? You're not with the Congregation—who are you? And those memories—those mechanical things, those cities—*where are you from?*"

Val unfastened the apparatus and backed away from the table. "If you really saw inside my head, then you know I'm from someplace far away. Another world. I know it's strange—this is all strange—but it shouldn't affect this transaction."

The gazer kept staring at him, and Val compressed his lips. If Alrick was the real deal, then he couldn't lose this chance to find his brothers. "To answer your other questions," Val continued, "I'm certainly not with the Congregation, and you didn't *ask* me if I was a wizard. Why would it matter? I'm begging you, don't turn me away."

Alrick's laughter was brief and off-kilter. "Turn you away? No, my friend, that is not something I will be doing. Of course I know there are other worlds, though I've never gazed upon a place such as that. And as to your being a wizard, it matters a very great deal. It matters because I can take you with me."

-12-

Will expected the hill trolls to brandish their clubs and come charging down the bluff, but instead they stayed on higher ground, shadowing the tusker caravan through the canyon. He stared in fascination at the oversize heads and cartoonish muscles of the hideous humanoids, their misshapen faces, topknots of bright orange hair, and almost simian lope. The sight of them caused him to break out in a cold sweat.

Were they going to slaughter them at the other end of the canyon? Kill the tuskers and eat the humans?

The canyon wound through the dry hill country for miles before leveling out. Still the trolls loped along beside them. Will could smell them, a foul body odor even worse than the stench of the tuskers.

"These creatures . . . ." Yasmina murmured from behind him, in an awed voice. "They're remarkable. Did they descend from Neanderthals? A new species entirely?"

"I don't know, Yaz," Caleb muttered. "Does it matter when they eat us?"

The trail spilled into a settlement of fifteen-foot lean-tos made of tree branches, animal hide tarps, and stones securing the base. Dozens of male and female trolls milled about the homestead, the women cooking over bonfires or stirring enormous pots, the men curing animal skins and sharpening clubs. There were even troll children running about, their carrot tops framing lumpy bulldog faces as they kicked a ball around the rocky, uneven ground.

Will swiveled to address Caleb and Yasmina. "I've been trying to figure out where we are, based on the geography and rate of travel. My best guess is Arkansas."

"Can't say I've had the pleasure of visiting that great state," Caleb said, "but if you're right, I gotta say the scenery looks about how I imagined it."

Near the center of the village, a gargantuan troll stepped out of a cowhide yurt. Wearing a headdress of bone, accompanied by a cadre of warriors, the chief waited with crossed arms as Grilgor approached. The hill troll was easily twice the size of the tusker leader. Will was too far away to hear the discussion, but Grilgor tossed a small bag of coins to one of the bodyguards, and the troll chief waved them through.

On the other side of the village, Will got a closer look at the children, and realized he had been mistaken about the ball.

It was a human head they were kicking.

The trolls escorted them half a day past the canyon. The hills resumed and the tusker caravan spent the next two days in troll country, passing through five more villages, paying off the chief of each clan. Despite the civilities, the tuskers looked nervous during that stage of the journey, posting extra sentries at night.

After troll country, the caravan headed west, across a horizon of flat golden plains. They made good time, the tusker steeds pounding out a steady rhythm under the weakening sun of early winter. Will overheard the tuskers discussing a desire to reach the mines before the snows came.

Yasmina, model-thin even before the tolls of the journey, shivered so hard during the night that Will thought she was having seizures. Caleb didn't fare much better, and the ordeal had also taken a toll on Will's hardy constitution. He kept expecting their captors to toss out blankets at night, but they never did.

The first night on the plains, Will fell asleep huddled between Dalen and Caleb, trying to protect his exposed limbs from a bitter night wind. At times, the screams of slain animals interrupted Will's sleep, and every time he woke, he couldn't stop thinking about the trolls behind them, the mines in front of them, and Dalen's tales of monsters roaming the Ninth Protectorate in between.

"Yaz," Caleb whispered, turning over to spoon her willowy form. He pressed as close as the chains would allow, burying the side of his face in her long brown hair, doing his best to rub her arms and keep her warm. "Yaz."

Will's chest rose and fell with the rhythm of sleep, but Caleb was too cold to drop off. He had just heard Yasmina murmuring to herself, and wasn't sure if she was awake or having a nightmare.

"Mmm," she murmured, as if unconcerned whether the conversation continued or not.

"You still with me? Hang in there, okay? We're going to figure something out."

False emotion wasn't Caleb's strong suit, but apart from his family, there was no one he cared for like Yasmina. He felt the need to do something, anything, to lift her spirits.

So he decided to tell the truth about something.

"There's something I've never told you," he said.

She didn't respond, but he could feel her hips shift, the corner of an eyelash twitch.

"When you broke up with me because I wouldn't change my habits . . . well, it's true I didn't want to change. But it's not true I wouldn't have changed for you."

Her hands were crossed against her chest, and Caleb could feel her heart beating faster. "The thing is," he said, "it's not the drinking and the women I'm worried about. It's *me*. Who I am. Yaz, you're such a better person than me, that I . . . I know I'll never deserve you."

She turned and reached up to stroke his cheek. "That's not true," she whispered, and he realized she wasn't as frail as she looked. Just conserving her energy. "None of us are any better than anyone else. We're all so very flawed, no?" She drew him close, then cupped his face in her hands and gently kissed his eyelids. "It's okay, *meu amor*. I knew who you were from the beginning, and I still loved you."

She hesitated, as if she were going to add something else, a statement in the present tense. He moved to kiss her, and she moved aside at the last moment, pressing her cheek against his instead. "I'm terrified," she said. "And freezing."

"Me, too."

Caleb rubbed her chest and arms, her hands and legs, willing the heat from his body to flow into hers. He had asked a guard for a blanket, and received a backhand to the face. "We'll make it through this," he said. "I promise."

"You never promise anything," she said, just before she closed her eyes and fell silent in his arms. "It's one of your better qualities."

* * *

Still the plains stretched before them. There were moments of excitement: twin tornados that spun on the horizon like maddened tops, perhaps controlled by a rogue aeromancer; a creature Dalen called a night shamble that resembled a pile of corn husks with claws and a face, and which climbed out of a barrow one night and ate one of the tusker scouts; a caravan of Romani wagons that crossed an intersection in the distance one morning, each side eying the other with raised weapons. One of the captives shouted to the caravan for help, and a tusker whipped her into silence. Even if the gypsies had wanted to free them, there were only three wagons, and unless they had a wizard or some serious warriors—both of which Will doubted—then they would only have been slaughtered by the tuskers.

The tuskers picked up a few more humans on the plains, though Will had seen no evidence of settlements, and assumed they were stray travelers. "Doesn't anyone live in the Ninth?" he asked Dalen.

"Plenty," he said, "Settlers, traders, hunters, prospectors, tribes of natives—though you'll never see any of those unless they wish to be seen. Lots of non-citizens, too. Gypsies, religious clans, people who don't want to be told what to do."

"So it's take the oaths or risk the Fens," Will said, with a shake of his head. "And maybe get slaughtered in your village."

"Under Lord Alistair it is," Dalen said darkly. "It wasn't always that way."

Will decided to ask a blunt question. "Are you a citizen?"

"Why do you ask?" Dalen replied, after a long moment. "Are you?"

"No."

Dalen turned to face him, looking relieved. "Me neither. I was on my way to New Victoria to take the oaths when," he waved a hand, "this happened."

Earlier, Dalen had told Will he was from Hellas, a city in Macedonia, and offered no further details. Will hadn't pressed, not wanting Dalen to realize the extent of his ignorance.

The midday sun hovered overhead, though it failed to banish the chill. Will saw a herd of buffalo grazing in the distance, and vultures wheeled beneath an archipelago of clouds to the north. He lowered his voice. "We're running out of time."

Two nights before, the tusker with the keys had gotten drunk and fallen

asleep. Will had urged Dalen to try to escape, but the young illusionist said he
was still tweaking his plan. Will was beginning to doubt his nerve.

"We've a ways to go before Fellengard," Dalen said. "Once we reach the
mountains, according to the maps I've seen, we still have to travel many days
north and west."

"We're getting further and further away from New Victoria," Will said, annoyed. "And what's your plan, go back through troll country?"

"Head south and find a Byway. There has to be one eventually."

"I thought you were afraid of the tribes to the South?"

"*Aike.* I'm more afraid of trolls and winter."

Will didn't respond, because there was nothing to say. Even if they managed to escape, their choices were depressing.

"We'll have an easier time hiding out in the mountains," Dalen said. "The
tuskers can see us for miles on the plains."

"Yeah, but other things can hide in the mountains, too." Will glanced at his
brother's lowered head. "Listen, Dalen. If you want my help, it has to be the
next chance we get. No matter what."

Dalen didn't respond at first, then gave a slow nod. "All right," he said softly.

The next day the plains disappeared and they entered a land of dry scrub and
surreal rock formations, backed by a glowering line of peaks.

"New Mexico?" Caleb asked. "Colorado?"

"Dunno," Will said. "Never been to either one. But it's beautiful."

The trail wound through jagged towers of sandstone, the rock strata stag-
gering him with their variety of colors. When they crested a plateau and saw
the afternoon sun lowering into a mauve and crimson valley, an egg yolk sinking into a field of heather, the sight took his breath away.

They camped at the base of the first high peak, surrounded by the mythic
landscape. The higher elevation brought even colder air, and when Yasmina's
numbed fingers spilled her bowl of gruel, earning her a lash, he knew they had
to act.

The tuskers seemed to be in a good mood, and partied louder and longer
than usual with their leather flasks of grog. Throughout the evening, deep into
the night, Will's eyes never left the guardian of the keys. He was one of the last

tuskers to go to sleep, and when he finally stumbled onto his bedroll, thick fingers clutching a flask, the set of iron keys dangled enticingly from his belt.

The last two tuskers dropped off. After Will was sure no other guards were awake, he exchanged a grim nod with Caleb and Yasmina, then turned towards his new friend. Dalen was wide-awake and staring at the sleeping tusker.

"It's now or never," Will said. "You ready?"

Dalen swallowed and rubbed a thumb against the back of his fist. "*Aike*. I'm ready."

-13-

"Gathered wizards of the Conclave," Vice Thaumaturge Rainsword proclaimed, "I give you Lord Alistair, Chief Thaumaturge of the Congregation and First Wizard of the Realm at large."

Jalen Rainsword, a powerful electromancer and lead representative of the Sixth Protectorate, ceded the floor to Lord Alistair, who stepped onto the silver-blue dais of hardened spirit to face the semicircle of thirty-one wizards who formed the Conclave, the governing body of the Congregation.

Three wizards for each of the nine Protectorates, three representatives from Albion, and the Chief Thaumaturge.

"Fellow citizens and mages," Lord Alistair said, azantite scepter in hand, "I thank you for your attendance. Please accept my apologies for this irregular meeting, but there are urgent matters that need addressing."

He had their attention. Besides being an elder spirit mage and Chief Thaumaturge, Lord Alistair was a tall and imposing man, his silver widow's peak the punctuation mark on a regal face and square-shouldered frame that, while nearing two hundred years old, seemed to defy the ravages of time. Only eyes of different hues, one pale blue and one almost black, marred the symmetry of his features.

Lord Alistair held an upturned palm in the air. Though impeccably dressed in trousers of fine wool and a dress shirt with Bavarian cuffs, he was not one to adopt the latest fashions. "My leadership style has never been evasive," he said, "so let me be direct. The Revolution is spreading."

Though no one spoke, the rustle of clothing and almost imperceptible shifting of position was a clarion call to Lord Alistair. These were highly-trained Congregation wizards, most of them elder mages, and the slightest reaction meant they had heard him loud and clear.

As he knew they would.

"I'm afraid I don't understand," said a sylvamancer from the Fifth, his worn cloak and emerald-studded walking stick indicative of his preference for the outdoors. "I thought the situation was under control. Have the rebels become a *threat*?"

"It is not that the rebels themselves pose a problem," Lord Alistair said, his scornful smile relaxing the crowd. "It is the ideas they represent which are of concern. We long ago eradicated the scourge of religion, and who here wishes a return to that epoch of ignorance? None, I should hope. Let us never forget the tragic history of our kind. The millennia of persecution of the wizard born. The Culling and inquisitions. The pyres."

One of the trio of women representing the First, a blond aeromancer with the delicate features of a sparrow, asked, "How could events on the Barrier Coast possibly affect the Protectorate at large?"

Lord Alistair watched as heads turned to regard the three wizards from the Ninth Protectorate—the lands west of the Great Victoria River—grouped on the far left of the Conclave. No one blamed the representatives for the rebel activity. The Ninth was a vast territory, largely unexplored and still under de facto control of the various tribes, clans, and creatures who called it home.

And the Barrier Coast, unreachable except by great expense and journey, had long been home to gypsies and other undesirables who risked life and limb to get there.

"Because revolution is a plague," Lord Alistair said, "spreading like spirit fire across the land." He raised a palm, rings glittering above his embroidered cuff. "The blame falls on us, the governors of New Albion. We have been lax in our persecution of those who foment rebellion."

"But what do you propose?" said the aeromancer. Her name was Kalyn Tern, and she wore a dress of blue silk that spiraled down to her ankles. "Our prisons are full, the Fens overflow."

"Then we make room."

"Executions?" Kalyn responded, with a nod. "I've been in favor for some time. Only the worst elements, of course. Blights on society of whom we can make an example."

"Can we not build more Fens instead?" asked Garbind Elldorn, the sylvamancer from the Fifth. "We've plenty of space."

"That would set a bad precedent," Alistair countered. "The public would rather see cleaner cities and fewer undesirables than more prisons and fens. I would also propose strengthening restrictions on Byway travel, bolstering the Oath Guard, increasing city checkpoints, and sending more patrols to the villages."

"Aye aye," said a handsome, dark-haired cuerpomancer from the Third named Braden Shankstone. At forty-four Birth Years, he was the youngest member of the Conclave but already a close advisor to Lord Alistair. Most viewed him as a likely successor.

They took the proposals to a vote. Thirty of the wizards gave their assent in a matter of moments. After a long hesitation, Garbind slowly raised his hand.

Lord Alistair paced back and forth on the six-foot wide dais, his expression grave. "There remains one other thing to discuss. I am of the firm belief that a message needs to be delivered to the leaders of this rebellion. Strike a blow that will remind them with whom they are dealing—a blow that will ricochet to our northern and southern borders as well, preparing the way for future incursions."

"Be more specific," Kalyn said. She hailed from one of the oldest wizard families in the Realm and was unafraid to speak her mind. "What sort of blow? What are the logistics involved? If reports are to be believed, the rebels count a number of rogue wizards among their ranks. Nothing of concern, of course, except that we would have to send a few of our own to address the situation."

Lord Alistair exchanged a glance with the three wizards from the Ninth, who had sat quietly during the meeting, already aware of the events Lord Alistair had set in motion. "There is something I have in mind," the Chief Thaumaturge said, his smile as cold as a winter's evening.

*　　*　　*

After the dispersal of the Conclave, Lord Alistair exited the towering, midnight-blue pyramid called the Sanctum—the headquarters of the Congregation—by flying down the wizard chute from the Gathering Room to the columned entranceway flanked by two thirty-foot colossi guardians, then through the invisible force field surrounding the structure, an extremely complex multi-discipline ward passable only by those bearing the imprimatur of the Congregation.

Most of the wizards arced upwards in flight, towards the tops of their respective spires. Lord Alistair did the same, soaring high above the pathways of mosaic tile that wove through the manicured gardens separating the wizard compounds. The vista of colored spires needling high above the city never failed to move him. Each was a different length and hue, symbols of the beauty and progress of the Realm—and the might of the Congregation.

Alistair's two personal majitsu accompanied him. Most majitsu did not possess enough magic to sustain flight, but these were two of the strongest of their order. As they neared Lord Alistair's residence, half the size of a city block and the largest compound in the District, the majitsu peeled away, alighting at the base of the moat. Lord Alistair flew past the topiary and polychromatic fountains, all of which served defensive purposes, and continued towards the blue-white central tower, linked by Gothic bridges and archways to the surrounding beehive towers whose dun-colored stone flowed and smeared in surreal patterns.

He flew through his ward and into an opening halfway up the central tower, landing on the plush sheepskin rug of his private chambers. The period Oriental furniture and Luxorian tapestries had remained unchanged since the death of his wife, a cuerpomancer from a prominent Londyn lineage. As always, Lord Alistair's eyes lingered on the portrait of his wife and daughter, holding hands beside a loch of purest blue.

Amber orb lights kindled and then faded as Lord Alistair ascended the wizard chute, illuminating his workshop, library, artifact rooms, and finally the observatory atop the tower.

It was an observatory befitting an elder spirit mage: artistic renditions of the astral plane wrapping the support columns, celestial maps and astrological charts covering the walls, a tinted glass ceiling showcasing the glory and mystery of the heavens. In the corner of the room, a circle of darkness pulsed with streaks of silver light, twelve feet in diameter and framed by a thick layer of azantite.

A long ivory pew ran along one of the walls, above which hung a row of obsidian helms. Lord Alistair plucked one marked 'Inverlock Keep' and strode to a raised dais in the center of the room, which supported a silver throne that revolved and tilted to allow for observation of the heavens.

And a spirit mage, of course, did far more than just observe.

Lord Alistair sank into the throne and fitted the helm to his head. His vision blurred as a spirit signal whisked across the ether. When he could see again, he found himself looking at the workshop in his cloud fortress through the eyes of Fesoj Gelmene, a wizard banished from the Realm for the unlawful practice of menagery.

"My Lord," Fesoj said in Lord Alistair's mind, the spirit helm neutralizing Fesoj's sibilant lisp.

"Excellent," Lord Alistair said. "You're already in the workshop."

Through the helm, Lord Alistair could see the five azantite pods in the center of the room, each bearing a window of translucent spirit glass showcasing the transformation taking place within.

Each, that was, except for the empty pod whose door and inhabitant had both disappeared—an occurrence which Fesoj and Alistair did not yet understand.

"There is still no sign?" Lord Alistair said, his gaze resting on the barren interior of the pod.

"None, my lord. Rest assured I've performed every test possible on the others, and they exhibit no aberrations."

Lord Alistair clenched the sides of his throne, trying to control the surge of anger that sent cracklings of dark matter flaring across his fingertips. "How could this happen? Did the subject dissolve into spirit? Blood and stone! If it is alive and able to communicate—I think I need not explain what would happen. What the Conclave would do."

"No, milord," Fesoj murmured.

"One day they will understand, but not today. No empire lasts forever, and those that do not innovate and expand, respond to the challenges of the world, perish first. Rest assured our enemies have no qualms in developing new methods of warfare."

"Of course."

Alistair knew his genius menagerist could not care less about the machinations of world politics, as long as he was allowed to perform his experiments. A necessary evil, employing one such as he.

"How long before they're ready?" Alistair asked.

"I plan to open the pods in three days time, and judge the state of the subjects."

"If the tests are favorable, I think you know the nature of the first task."

"I do."

Fesoj started pacing the room, wisely diverting Alistair's attention from the empty pod. When his menagerist passed the wall of shadow glass, Alistair saw the dark glitter of the menagerist's reflection: a tall, angular wizard with the bald head and placid face of an archivist. Only the off-kilter line of his mouth, whose lips always seemed half-parted, belied the cruelty within.

"Have you consulted our phrenomancer again?" Alistair asked.

"Indeed."

"And the sword? It remains in our world?"

"It does. Of that he is certain."

How did it get here? Alistair wondered for the thousandth time.

He realized Zedock must have carried the sword through the portal without informing him, but why? The only explanation was that the necromancer had desired to usurp Alistair's power. Alistair was far more powerful than Zedock, but putting Spiritscourge in the hands of any elder mage would be a devastating combination.

Which, of course, was why Alistair wanted the sword for himself.

"What of the identities of those responsible for his death? Still nothing?"

"I did as you asked, and found a second phrenomancer willing to gaze with Zedock's ghost knight. The result was . . . unfortunate."

"The phrenomancer perished?" Lord Alistair asked.

"I'm afraid so. From what I understand, traveling the pathways of the dead is quite perilous, even for an experienced gazer. Madness and death commonly result."

The dark lightning returned to Lord Alistair's fingertips, now spreading up his forearms like a writhing, three-dimensional tattoo. "It had to be the sword, but wielded by whom? One of Zedock's majitsu? And where is it?" He allowed his energies to relax. "Did our gazer have anything else to add?"

Fesoj hesitated. "He said the negative probabilities have risen. Almost to the point of equality."

"Which probabilities, Fesoj? The last time we spoke, we discussed several prophecies revealed by the phrenomancer."

Fesoj stopped pacing, his side reflection in the shadow glass now reminding Lord Alistair of a crane standing beside a lake, head bent and poised to strike.

"That when the sword born of spirit returns to Urfe," Fesoj repeated slowly, reluctant to speak the words, "war is imminent, and one born of Roma blood will destroy you."

Lord Alistair didn't speak for long moments, waiting for his rage to subside. "The lost subject will have to wait," he said, his voice thick but under control. "As soon as the first Spirit Liege is ready, send it to Zedock's obelisk. Send it after the sword. "

"Yes, milord."

-14-

"How did you know I was a wizard?" Val asked.

Alrick looked at him askance. "Because of your psionic signature, of course."

Of course, Val muttered to himself. *My psionic signature.*

"Will you go?" The gazer said, his eyes boring into Val's. "Will you lock gazes with me?"

"Will it help me find my brothers?"

"You'll be able to affect the journey, so yes. It is dangerous, I won't lie. And you must *never* leave the path. Let me guide you, and if you see something connected to your brothers, I'll know. The pathways will appear."

Val took a deep breath. He didn't trust something he didn't understand, but there was no time to learn. "How do I stay with you?"

"You'll understand once we start. It will take a burst of will to separate from me. Remember, where we're going, place and time do not exist in the same way. You'll see impressions, memories, future possibilities. Sorting through them is the trick."

"Why can't we leave the path?"

Alrick relit the candle and extinguished the wizard light. The candle flickered in the darkened room. "Because of the beings that roam the Void. Some gazers, near the end of their lives or if they go insane, veer off the path and seek them out." He handed Val the glow drops. "They never come back."

Val placed a drop in each of Alrick's eyes, noticing no effect.

"At times, you might see something of interest and be tempted to cross the Void. Don't."

"What exactly are these . . . roaming beings? I prefer to be prepared for all contingencies."

The phrenomancer gave a low grunt. "No one knows. Entities beyond human comprehension. Other things lurk inside the Void, but those are the most dangerous, at least as far as we know." He smirked. "No one really knows what lies within the Void."

"What are the odds of encountering one?"

"A gazer can look inside his mind for days and not be in any danger, as long as he travels his own psionic veins. The further out one ventures, away from known pathways, the more dangerous the journey." He held a hand up. "I will keep us in good stead, unless you are someone who is predisposed to . . . lose control over one's mind?"

"That would be out of character," Val said, re-fastening his oculave. "So what do I need to know?"

"Just look into my eyes and open your awareness. Think of your brothers. I will link and guide us."

"Won't we be in your mind, too?"

"I will shield it."

"A final question," Val said.

"Yes?"

"All real gazers are wizards, aren't they?"

Alrick's voice already sounded far away. "Of course. They have to be."

The gazer blew out the light, and the darkness returned, broken only by the golden glow of two enlarged pupils staring at Val from a foot away. It was an unsettling sight, and Val started counting again.

One, two, three

Alrick's leonine eyes were mesmeric, reeling him in. Val felt consumed by them, as if they were enlarging at the same rate Val was shrinking.

Four, five, six

He felt a tickle in his brain. It was the best way he could describe it, a feeling that someone or something was gently probing the inside of his head.

Seven

The golden orbs merged and expanded to fill the room. Behind the glow, as if at the end of a tunnel, Val saw an approaching wall of blackness crisscrossed by silver filaments, like a giant spider web in outer space.

Eight

The tickle became a prod

Nine

He felt weightless in his chair, as if someone had lifted him

Ten

The golden orbs moved past him and disappeared, leaving him wrapped in silver lines and darkness as he rushed down one of the silver pathways, deeper and deeper and deeper. The world had somehow become more than three-dimensional, the silver filaments branching like floating capillaries, tens of thousands of branches stretching in all directions into the distance, with no discernible pattern. He realized he was seeing not with his eyes, but with his mind.

Though he couldn't see Alrick, Val had the sensation of being carried, and he gave in to the feeling, allowing the gazer to guide the way.

The images started as soon as the first silver line split into five pathways. Alrick chose the one to the left. Val and his mother enjoying a game of Scrabble when he was ten, then watching movies together on the couch with a bowl of homemade popcorn, then running hand-in-hand through a leaf-strewn park as his mother's brown hair tossed in the wind, her playful blue eyes sparking brighter than the sun. *Mom,* Val whispered to himself, *you're young again. And you're not insane here.*

The images began playing at high-speed, like one of those horror movies where everyone in the psych ward moves too fast. Val felt as if he could slow them down, but he didn't want to interrupt Alrick.

As the pathways branched, the images changed. Val teaching Will how to

play soccer at the levee. Val and his friends walking to the neighborhood pizza joint, combining their funds to order breadsticks and Cokes and play the
jukebox. Val telling his father about a fight at school, his father ruffling his hair
and making it all go away. Val watching Caleb kiss girl after girl on their front
porch. Their father packing his bags for the trip to France, uncharacteristically
serious, holding Val tight and telling him he loved him. The gutted feeling at
hearing the news of his death, their mother collapsing in the living room and
then leaving in an ambulance, Val forced to change his life and take care of the
family. Standing in a witness room at a police station in Manhattan, explaining
to two detectives why he had met with Mari at midnight the day before she
disappeared. Val with grey hair, arguing in court before a jury. Val in prison.
Val standing on the ramparts of a multi-tiered castle in the clouds, black electricity crackling from his fingertips, nightmare creatures made of ice climbing
the walls.

*These last things—they haven't happened yet. Am I seeing what could have
been? Or what might be?*

He felt a tug, as if someone had pulled on the reins of his mind. He remembered he was supposed to be thinking of the last time he had seen his brothers.

It wasn't that easy. As he tried to focus on Will to filter the images, the
silver pathways branched faster, until they became a random blur. He did his
best to slow the reel, focusing harder on Will as the pathways sped by, filtering
through images of his youngest brother's childhood. Will's constant pranks,
the first of his devastating panic attacks after their father died, Will's off-the-
charts test scores and inability to focus in class, the Navy and the New Orleans
police and even the fire department denying his applications, the refuge he
sought in the world of fantasy—

There.

Will and Caleb in the cemetery, fighting off skeletons and following Zedock and Yasmina through the portal . . . and then something Val hadn't seen
before. Approaching quickly was a four pronged branch, each a distinct hue
of silver.

He had no idea what to do, so he thought of Will again and *whooshed* down
the pathway on the far right, the lightest of the four.

More images of Will, often with Caleb and Yasmina. Fighting Zedock in
his obelisk. Racing through the forest. Shackled in an underground cavern,

hacking at a vein of minerals in the wall. Sleeping in a pirogue in the swamp. Kissing Mala on a windswept plain. Thrusting his sword at Val in anger. Fighting a winged demon that was holding Caleb in one of its claws. Falling into a chasm, arms flailing, calling Val's name as he plummeted to his—

Val shuddered and tried to close his eyes, then realized he couldn't. The images kept changing, at times leading to branches in the distance with even more nuanced shades of silver. Eventually the movie of Will's life grew weaker and more ephemeral, and the silver lines became harder and harder to see. Finally they disappeared altogether, ending at a wall of blackness.

Val was confused for a moment.

Then it became all too clear.

His brother was dead.

No he screamed in his mind, his anguish expanding outward like a phoenix bursting into flame. As he roared, he felt the magic inside him pop, and the entire fabric of the place, the silver filaments and the limitless black space in between, pulsed and warped as if a bubble of mercury had plopped onto a table. In that instant of time, he saw a field of new pathways, filaments of a thousand colors branching in every possible direction, the hues forming patterns of breathtaking multidimensional beauty.

The pulse ended, the landscape returned to normal, and Val was once again staring at a wall of blackness. He had no idea what had just happened. He didn't know where he was, he didn't understand any of this, and he didn't care. One of his brothers' pathways had terminated, and he didn't need a mystic to tell him what that meant.

But Val had power. He knew it, and he was going to dive into that infinite dark and snatch his baby brother's spirit from the maw of death.

He propelled his mind into the blackness, ignoring the tug from behind, rushing forward until the glow behind him ceased. Until there was nothing left at all.

At first there was an absence of light, of sound, of smell. A darkness so visceral and complete it made the darkest of caves seem well-lit. Val pressed forward, welcomed the black. In his mind, he extended his hands and flew, faster and faster and faster.

He wasn't sure how long it took for the presence to emerge behind him. *Alrick*, he whispered in his mind? *Is that you?*

No answer.

The sense of a presence increased exponentially, a feeling that made Val feel as if he were a child wandering alone in the darkness as a child, searching for a lost toy in the back yard while the mystery of the night sky pressed down from above, suffocating him.

The beings that roam the Void, Alrick had said. *Some gazers go to them. They never come back.*

In the distance, a light appeared, soft and silvery.

Val shuddered at the implication.

Will.

He could bring him back.

Faster, he willed his mind. Faster.

He felt the presence approaching behind him like an avalanche gathering steam. Whatever it was, Val sensed that it was both a wondrous and terrible thing.

Immense. Eternal.

The silver glow increased, coalescing into a line. A pathway! Was this what he had to do to bring his brother back, cross the void and link the pathways? He would find a way to do it with his magic, or break his mind trying.

A cold wind brushed his shoulders. The first physical sensation he had felt since entering the void. *How could that be?* Despite his anguish over Will, fear clawed at the edges of Val's mind.

The entity was almost on top of him. The silver thread in front of Val was still quite far, and he knew he wouldn't reach it in time.

Still he pushed.

He had to try.

Cold all around, roaring in his ears, the sound of a thousand thunderclaps, the smell of every food he had ever tasted, a feeling of pleasure and pain so intense it paralyzed his mind, too intense, he couldn't bear it, the beauty and the terror and the *power*—

"Val!"

Someone slapped him across the face. A light so bright he had to shield his eyes.

Another slap, and then a gush of cold water in his face.

Val's eyes opened. He caught Alrick's hand just before it slapped him again.

There was an empty bucket on the floor beside him. "I'm here, Alrick," he said in a husky voice, half-inside a dream.

Alrick had already unfastened the oculave. Val stumbled out of the chair, face dripping water, his body feeling unconnected to his mind. He moved for the door.

"Where are you going?" Alrick said.

"Does it matter? One of my brothers is dead. Probably both of them."

Alrick grabbed him by the shoulder and spun him around. "Oh no, my friend. That is not what just happened. Oh no no no. And your brothers are very much alive."

"What do you mean?" Val said, after Alrick led him back into the cushioned room. Val's roiling emotions made him feel as if the floor was unbalanced, like he was trying to stand on a waterbed. "I saw the wall of blackness. The end of the path."

"You saw the end of the trail of probabilities pertaining to your brother's life before he stepped through the portal," Alrick said. "Since we don't know where he is, we have no clue which trails after the portal were true and which were false. Even if we did know, time and space, past and present, real and unreal, can be muddled in the Void. One can never be certain about what one sees."

"Then how do you know he's alive? Especially if the Void contains future probabilities?"

The phrenomancer shook his head. "If he were dead in this world, his pattern would look different. It's something a gazer is trained to recognize. Of the four pathways after the portal, only Zedock's exhibited an atypical pattern. *Zedock* is dead."

When that sunk in, Val put a hand on the wall to steady himself. "They're alive," he whispered. He looked up. "How do you know who Zedock is?"

Alrick reached for his gourd. "I've gazed for him. His death is common knowledge in New Victoria, by the way. Someone found his headless body at the base of his obelisk." He turned and arched an eyebrow. "Your brothers?"

"I've no idea," Val murmured, as if in a trance.

Alrick sipped on the gourd, his eyes never leaving Val's. "The psionic veins we followed—the silver pathways—were your own memories. Later those of your brother. The interconnected minds of this world. Anyone with a touch of power can find them. What you just did with your magic, however . . . those colors, the pattern . . . the link between all lives, all worlds, all pathways . . . we call it the Grid. Most don't have enough power to see it, and those who do practice for years to learn. You did it in a moment. How?"

"I have no idea. Do you know where my brothers are?"

"You saw what I saw. After they entered the portal, the probabilities are too attenuated. There's no way to guess which path they followed."

"Going back inside wouldn't help?" Val asked. "Even to that other place?"

"You mean the Void? Where you almost died? No. Assuming we could reach it again, it's far too dangerous, even for me."

"Then how much do I owe you?"

Alrick released the gourd with a sigh of pleasure, and sank into the cushions. "Valjean Blackwood, you've rewarded me more than you could know. Come back to me. I can teach you. That is my price."

Val left a stack of coins on the floor and started for the beaded doorway. "Thank you for your help."

Alrick pushed to his elbows, his expression incredulous. "You don't wish to know more?"

"I just want to find my brothers."

As Val swam through the beads, Alrick said, "There is one other way."

Val turned. The phrenomancer's grin looked sinister in the dim light, and his long hair framed his pasty, malnourished face like a wig on a ghoul. "You must promise me you'll come back. Gaze with me again."

Val gave a slow nod. "If I find them, you have my word."

Alrick reached for his gourd. "Join the Congregation. Become a spirit mage."

"I'm sorry?"

"The final test for every spirit mage is to complete the Walk of Planes. If you manage that feat, then you will step through the final portal to become a full-fledged spirit mage. A member of the Congregation. *Don't go through the portal.* Behind it, you'll see a lake as black as the Void. This is the Pool of Souls, a portal created by one of the elders for times of war. Think of who you desire most to see, then dive into the pool and you will find them." Alrick's grin curled into a wicked smile. "And don't get caught."

Val's mind catalogued the information. "How do you know about this?"

The phrenomancer pushed up his left sleeve to reveal a tiny octopus tattooed—no, Val realized, *imprinted*—in vivid colors on the underside of his biceps, as if painted by a master artist just that morning. The symbol of the Congregation, he knew.

"Because I've been there," Alrick said.

-15-

The camp had fallen silent except for the snoring of the tuskers. A dome of stars crowned the inky night sky, sage and juniper infused the air.

Trying not to vomit from nerves, Will rubbed his hands together to ward off the cold while Dalen handed out a fistful of root tips that resembled brackish bulbs of garlic. "Rub in this stinkweed," Dalen said, his face contorting as he bit into one of the bulbs and then crushed it between his palms. "It will mask your smell."

Caleb held the potent herb out from his body. "Rub it in where?"

"Everywhere."

"Then what?" Will asked.

"Then be ready." Dalen put a finger up and lay on his side, his line of sight facing the single tusker guard holding the keys.

Will bit into the stinkweed and spread the brown pulp over his body as best he could, recoiling at the smell of morning breath soaked in urine. Yasmina wrinkled her nose and joined him, and Caleb did the same. As Will worked, he watched a ball of silver moonlight form in midair next to Dalen and grow to the size of a tennis ball. The will o' the wisp shot forward, until it was a foot away from the sleeping guard.

The ball danced in front of the tusker's face, shooting in and then retreating, dodging back and forth, brushing against his tunic. Just as Will thought the exercise was pointless, the tusker stirred and opened his eyes. Instead of sounding the alarm, he tracked the silver ball with his head, then rose to his feet in slow motion.

Dalen moved the ball backwards a few feet at a time. The tusker followed with the movements of an automaton. Dalen led the guard through the pile of sleeping tuskers, each near collision costing Will a year of his life.

After the guard passed through the center of camp, Dalen guided him towards the circle of prisoners. Will glanced at his brother. Caleb was squatting on the balls of his feet, hands ready. Yasmina hugged her knees beside him, shivery and wide-eyed, watching the scene unfold.

The silver ball danced in front of Will, then glided past him and hovered a foot from Yasmina. As the sleepwalking guard stepped towards her, Caleb leaned forward and, fluid as a snake, lifted the ring of keys off the guard's belt. Will balled his fists and held his breath, but the guard didn't stir.

Dalen held the ball in front of Yasmina, moving it in a slow figure eight to hypnotize the guard while Caleb fumbled through the keys. Yasmina swallowed but held her position. After the longest fifteen seconds of Will's life, Caleb found the key that fit the lock binding his length of chain to Yasmina's. He eased the bonds to the ground, then searched for the key that unlocked the circle of iron around his waist.

None fit.

Will made frantic gestures with his hands for Caleb to hurry, then watched as his brother retried every key on the ring.

Still nothing.

They had seen this same guard chain other people to the circle; *where was the key?*

Just as Will started to panic, Caleb held up a finger and blew out a silent breath. He turned so Will could see him reach around the back of his waist manacle, press down with his thumb, and insert one of the keys.

The click of the lock sounded like a clap of thunder to Will. He stood as still as stone as his heart thumped against his chest. The tusker gave a soft snort but didn't wake up.

Dalen kept the ball moving while Caleb unlocked all four of them, setting the manacles gently on the ground. He paused in front of the red-haired woman sleeping beside Yasmina; she had been kind. Will caught Caleb's eye and wagged a finger; they had already discussed this. *Not yet. Not until we're ready to flee.*

There was one more thing to do. While Dalen kept the guard in the trance, Caleb handed the keys to Will and slipped into the darkened camp, heading for the stash of provisions where the tuskers kept the prisoners' weapons.

Moments later, Caleb's shadowy form reappeared on the edge of camp. He was wearing his bracers and holding Will's sword. *Well done, Caleb.*

Will took Yasmina by the hand and curled a finger at Dalen, just as someone behind them coughed. Will recognized the sound; one of the older men had been having coughing fits the last few nights.

The coughing quieted, and Dalen maintained the spell. Then the coughing returned, louder this time, and the tusker in Dalen's thrall blinked.

Will clenched his fists.

The silver ball danced back and forth.

The tusker relaxed again, but the prisoner beside Yasmina stirred and gasped when he saw the tusker, before anyone had a chance to quiet him.

The tusker's eyes popped open.

Will tossed the keys at the prisoner beside Yasmina, then rushed to tackle the guard, driving his shoulder into the creature's chest and tripping him at the ankles as Mala had taught him. He landed on top of the tusker, pressing both hands over his mouth and nose to quiet him. Out of the corner of his eye, Will saw Dalen freeze beside Yasmina.

The tusker grunted and squealed beneath him. Will's palms muffled the sound. It took all of his strength to hold the creature down and quiet it, and he didn't know how to hurt it without losing his grip.

Caleb was racing towards them with the sword. The tusker bucked and reached for Will's eyes. He head-butted the creature, then realized what a bad idea that was. His forehead felt as if it had just struck a cement wall.

Dazed, he fought to keep his hold, but the tusker jerked upward, slicing Will's biceps with its lone tusk. Will lost his grip, and the tusker bellowed, causing shouts from the camp.

Fighting not to panic, his left arm spurting blood, Will grabbed his opponent's good tusk with his right hand, then jerked the appendage upwards as hard as he could, his strong forearms ripping apart the monster's face. The tusker emitted a wheezing scream, and Will pushed off him. Yasmina ran up and hit him on the head with one of the manacles.

Caleb ran up and handed Will the sword. The injured tusker stumbled away, clutching its ruined face. Will whipped around to find Dalen, frantic when he didn't see him, then heard a whistle and saw the illusionist waving at him from behind the nearest rock tower.

A few of the other captives had freed themselves. Tuskers bellowed from below as Will and Caleb and Yasmina sprinted towards Dalen. The clash of steel rang out behind them, and Will turned to see the freed prisoners using their chains as weapons against their captors.

Will and the others rounded a mound of sandstone with a curved lip. Dalen led them deeper into the forest of rock formations. Footsteps pounded behind them, and Will felt the black wings of terror beating at his back, snatching his breath and propelling him forward.

Will heard some of the tuskers shouting in their rough language. "*Four more there be.*"

"*Grilgor kill us all if no find them.*"

The sounds of pursuit drew closer. Will heard the harsh whinnying of the tusker steeds. "By the Queen," Dalen cursed. "They've got the steeds out."

"Please tell me you thought further ahead than this," Caleb said, as they dashed between two boulders.

"You doubted?" Dalen asked, his smile quick but grim. He swiveled his head as he ran, veering towards a cone-shaped formation with a sizeable over-hang, like the rain flap on a tent. Will and the others crowded in as Dalen herded everyone against the back wall. "Keep as still as you can," he said. "I can merge us with the darkness, unless they illuminate us directly."

Which is a distinct possibility, Will thought.

The hoof beats drew closer, until they passed right by the hiding place. One of the tusker steeds turned and snorted. Will thought that was the end, until he saw Yasmina facing the steed, her palms bobbing up and down in a pla-cating fashion. She looked deep in concentration, and her lips were moving without speaking.

The animal quieted, but one of the tuskers had a torch, and he swung it underneath the overhang. Will pressed his body as tightly as he could into the rock. The light swept towards them, illuminating the dusty ground inches from Yasmina's feet. Finally it retreated, and the tuskers moved on, grunting and wheezing and cursing.

Long minutes passed until Will dared to speak. "Didn't they smell the stinkweed?" he whispered.

"Of course they did, but there's stinkweed all over this hill. *Lucka*, where do you think I got it? It's amazing what one can find while relieving oneself."

Will squeezed his shoulder. "You did good, Dalen. We owe you."

"I can hide us in the shadows, but sunlight is something else, *aike*. We have to be gone by morning." Dalen drew up his shoulders like the real wizards Will had seen, stroking his chin and considering the situation as if he had been there a hundred times.

Despite the false bravado, Will had to give him props. Dalen may not have much power, but he had used it cleverly.

"How did you soothe that horse?" Will asked Yasmina.

She looked embarrassed. "I . . . was just trying to help."

"Yaz has always had a way with animals," Caleb said. "They love her."

"I'll say," Will said, wondering if something else wasn't going on.

"Listen," Dalen said. "These rocks are facing west. Let's use their cover and head south tonight, then east at first light. We'll walk all day if we have to, and find a place we can defend. They won't risk a delay for four prisoners."

" 'Tis a good plan," a new voice growled, followed by a group of short, albino, burly humanoids emerging from the darkness like liquid slipping out of cracks. "Except for us, that is. Ye might fool the piggies with yer little tricks, but ye won't fool me."

-16-

As the lead hag shuffled forward, the other two crowded in behind her. Mala grimaced and tried to push away her dread. Whatever was coming, it wasn't going to be pleasant.

"What do you want from us?" Mala asked.

"I serve Zedock the Necromancer," the majitsu added. "If you know anything of wizardry, you should know that you shall regret the day he comes to look for me."

Mala couldn't believe what she had just heard. Spouting threats while hanging upside down from a giant hook? The arrogance of the wizard born never ceased to amaze her.

The larger hag waddled over to Mala. The creature was almost eight feet tall, the top of her head level with the soles of Mala's feet. She watched in surprise as the hag began sniffing her toes.

Three nostrils flaring, the creature sniffed her way down Mala's body, kneeling as she worked her way to the ends of her dark hair hanging loose below her head. After finishing with her, the hag moved to the majitsu and repeated the procedure.

When she reached the majitsu's head, she stopped, took his face in her hands, and began sniffing harder around the top of his skull. Her mouth parted and her eyes rolled, an expression Mala took for one of pleasure or excitement, and the hag curled a finger at her minions. They waddled over and joined her in sniffing the majitsu's head. After that, they began babbling in their language.

"What are you doing?" the majitsu said, trying to bend at the waist. "Get away from me, you filthy beasts!"

The lead hag made a few hand gestures and a parting remark, then left the room. One of the younger hags released Mala by slicing through the gray tendril holding her in place with her claw. She threw Mala over her shoulder, the other hag did the same to the majitsu, and they carried them outside.

Still bound tight, lugged like a child, Mala swept her gaze around the compound, taking in as much information as she could. Just in front of them were two low-slung, rectangular structures: the farmhouses she had seen earlier. The low ceilings made Mala guess that the hags had not built the homestead. Her assumption was strengthened by the three conical huts at the base of the hill near the rear of the compound, in the direction the lead hag was waddling.

The smaller hags carried Mala and the majitsu behind the farmhouses, to a building made of ash-colored wood, low and long like a kennel.

There was no door. Just a dim entryway lined with straw. The stench from inside was dung-ridden and gamey, like a barnyard.

The hags hoisted them inside, ducking when they entered. A walkway of wooden planks led to the rear of the tight structure, lined on either side by latticework cages made of the same ropy gray tendrils.

Inside the first cage was a unicorn.

The beautiful equine watched them pass with sad eyes, unable to stand because the cage was too small, its horn poking out of the top of the cage even while splayed on its haunches.

A two-foot tall imp ran back and forth in the second cage, its tail swishing against the sides. The hag holding the majitsu bent to slice open the door, and the imp shrieked and backed as far away as it could. The hag set the majitsu down, grabbed the imp by its neck, and pulled it out. Zedock's majitsu cursed and fought, but the hag shoved him inside and shut the door, then re-secured it by producing more gray material from her fingertips.

The majitsu locked gazes with Mala after they stuffed him inside. He was breathing hard, not from exertion but from rage. His eyes slid away, and he cursed again and grasped the bars of the cage.

They passed three more enclosures on each side, all occupied by a creature. Mala saw a nymph, a mermaid with her tail stuck in a dirty basin of water, a golden fox that teleported to the back of the cage when Mala looked at it, and three lizard-like creatures, each with two heads and a blue humpback. As she passed the last one, she heard a voice inside her head that sounded as if both heads were talking at the same time.

You must help us, the voice said. *A terrible fate awaits.*

Mala didn't need a voice inside her head to tell her that.

The final two cages, one on either side, were empty. The hags shoved the imp in one and Mala in the other. Mala didn't bother pleading; she knew no quarter would be given. Instead she processed what she had seen and tried to devise a plan of escape, however unlikely the prospect might be.

But what she really wanted to do was scream.

-17-

Val retraced his steps through Bohemian Isle to find his driver parked alongside the swampy canal, reclining in his seat and smoking his pipe. One of the horses snorted as Val approached.

The driver took out his pipe and cackled. "From the look on yer face, ye got what ye needed. And maybe a bit more."

Val climbed into the carriage. "Yes I did. Thank you."

"My pleasure, laddie, my pleasure." He took the reins. "Where will it be, then?"

Val took a deep breath. *As they say, in for a penny, in for a pound.* "The school for wizards."

The driver paused with his pipe halfway to his lips. "The Abbey?"

"If that's the wizardry school, then yes."

"Laddie, if I may, why on earth would ye want to go there?"

"To sign up."

The driver slapped his knee, his braying laughter trailing away when Val's expression didn't change. "Are ye a wizard?"

"I'm about to find out. How does one apply? Is there some sort of entrance exam?"

The driver stared at Val as if he had just sprouted an extra head. "All I know is hearsay, but they say there's a testing period at the start of each semester, where hopeful wizards from across the Realm line up to see if they've got enough power to join the Abbey. If ye make it in, the new class starts every year on the tenth of January. One week's time."

"What does the test entail?"

"A display o' power, they say."

"What happens if you fail?"

"Some become majitsu. Some go rogue. And some . . . well, they just fade away, I s'pose."

Lovely, Val thought. *A display of power on demand is exactly what I'm not prepared for.*

"They say ye can try again after another year if ye fail," the driver said, picking up on Val's tightened jaw.

"No, I can't."

There was an uneasy silence, and the driver said, "Laddie, can I ask ye a personal question?"

Val lifted his eyes. "Sure."

"Are ye . . . a citizen of the Protectorate?"

After a long pause, Val slowly swung his head back and forth.

"Ye can't attend the Abbey if ye ain't a citizen, or at least a registered visitor." The driver's brow darkened. "And they'll throw ye in the Fens for tryin.' "

"How does one register?"

"Ye take the Oaths and apply."

Val crossed his arms and reclined into the seat. "Then I suppose our first stop is wherever it is that one takes the Oaths."

The driver puffed on his pipe, eyed the descending position of the sun as he blew a perfect smoke ring, and spurred the horses.

The driver took Val to a pillared building in the Government District that looked crafted out of black granite. A steady stream of people entered and exited the boxy edifice.

"The Tribunal," the driver said. "It'll be a line, but I'll wait for ye. Listen, laddie . . . my name's Gustave Mortimer Scurlock. Call me Gus. My wifey, she's got a cousin who married a lad from the north. *Way* north, like you. Tiny village name of Talinmar, just outside the Protectorate. Lad's surname is Kenefick." Gus put his hands up. "Maybe ye don't, but if ye be needin' a name to use for the Oaths . . . if it ever came up . . . we'll vouch for ye."

Val flipped a gold piece to the driver. "Thank you, my friend."

Gus's eyes widened as he took the coin. He tipped his hat. "Thank *ye*."

Val walked through the imposing pillars and into a grand foyer filled with civil servants, uniformed guards, and long lines of people that snaked into adjoining hallways. He found the line marked 'Registered Visitors,' and spent the next hour waiting to reach a desk where, under the alias of Val Kenefick, he responded to background questions from a bored official.

After paying a levy of one gold piece and two silver florins, Val received a vellum Certificate of Registered Visitation and was ushered into a long corridor, where he waited in line to take his Oaths. When his name was called, he entered a room with two rows of benches running along the longer walls. Opposite to him, sequestered behind iron bars, was a raised platform supporting five desks arranged in a semicircle.

"Approach the platform, please," said a white-haired man sitting in a green-backed chair behind the center desk. The other seats were occupied.

Val stepped forward.

"Your certificate?"

He placed the vellum certificate on the desk. The administrator leaned forward to peer at the document.

"Val Kenefick from Talinmar Village, do you understand and agree that by swearing the Oaths of the Protectorate of New Albion and receiving a Certificate of Visitation, you will be bound, on pain of incarceration or expulsion, not only by the laws of this land during your period of visitation, but by the letter, principles, and spirit of these Oaths?"

"I do."

The judge looked up at him. "Place your hand over your heart."

Val complied.

"Do you hereby swear that you possess no religious faith or belief, nor do you adhere to or practice any religious creed or doctrine?"

"I swear."

"Do you hereby swear that should anyone attempt to incite you to worship any god or goddess, or attach yourself to any religious creed or doctrine or body of worshippers, that you will immediately and forthwith report that individual or individuals to the nearest Tribunal?"

"I swear."

"Do you hereby renounce any allegiance to any gypsy clan, native tribe, or other group that operates under archaic belief systems that are in direct contravention to the laws of this land and the principles of these oaths?

Ah, there's the kicker for the gypsies, Val thought. "I swear."

The judge pressed his wooden stamp against Val's certificate with a *thump*, and waved him through.

After making arrangements to meet the next morning, Gus dropped Val at a pub named Falrick's Folly, two blocks down from Salomon's Crib. Val wasn't about to step foot in the Minotaur's Den, the mercenary pub where he and his brothers had once been assaulted.

The next morning, Gus picked him up and drove past the French Quarter to the edge of the Goblin Market. They traveled down Esplanade alongside a twenty-foot wall, then passed through the tall iron gate marking the border of the Wizard District.

As before, a pair of majitsu guarding the entrance waved Gus past the line of tourists. Val gave the guardhouse a sidelong glance, not wanting to attract the attention of the shaven-headed warrior monks milling about inside. Lithe and intense, dressed in black robes cinched at the waist with silver belts, the majitsu unnerved Val almost as much as the wizards.

Just as it had the first and only time he had visited, the Wizard District made his heart skip a beat. The hundreds of spires piercing the sky like a pageant of tropical minarets. The assortment of domes, obelisks, ziggurats, poly-sided towers and fantastical creations of stone that supported the spires, some the size of a small chateau and some five times that size.

From his last visit, Val knew the Wizard District wasn't all handsome topiary and otherworldly architecture. Lord Alistair's compound was a maze of wards and potent magical defenses cleverly disguised within the landscaping, and Val suspected the rest of the compounds followed suit.

The carriage rolled along the tree-lined pathways of mosaic tile separating the compounds. They passed the midnight blue Sanctum, the red-and-gold-marble Hall of Wizards, and then continued to the southeast side of the district, further than Val had ventured before, to a squat manor of pale blue limestone topped by a quartet of spires. Behind the manor, a beguiling collection of buildings lay nestled among serene groves of palms, bougainvillea, banana trees, and live oaks laden with Spanish moss.

"The Abbey," Gus announced.

People milled about the stone fountain fronting the manor, and a wizard in brown robes flew inside one of the obelisks rising out of the foliage on either side.

What if the wizards guess where I'm really from? Val thought as the carriage slowed to a halt.

What if I fail the test?

What if the test kills me?

Most people, his brothers included, thought Val had nerves of steel. On the contrary, his nerves were just like everyone else's, jittery and unsure.

It was stubbornness and willpower that carried him through.

"Ye know I've got no love for wizards," Gus said, "but I wish ye the best of luck. If ye get in, at least there'll be one I trust."

Val nodded in response, hopped down and took a deep breath, strolled to the ornate bronze door with his head held high, and stepped inside.

The first thing he saw was a grand foyer with walls and flooring of striated blue marble. He assumed the heraldic banners hanging from the ceiling represented the houses of esteemed wizard families.

A line of people waited to be seen by a wizened old man behind a counter at the far end of the room. The line moved quickly, and when Val reached the front, he presented his Certificate of Visitation and was given a wooden marker. The clerk pointed down a wide hallway and told him to have a seat.

As Val approached the waiting salon, a powerfully built older man flew past him with a dejected look on his face.

Val swallowed, watching the wizard wheel around the corner while hovering three feet off the ground. If someone with that much power had failed the test, what hope had he?

The waiting salon was an oval chamber filled with plush furniture. He slid onto a silk-covered divan and avoided contact with the other applicants. He didn't want to see the confidence in their eyes or the magic alive in their hands.

Instead, he looked within.

Searching for his magic.

Val had accessed it before, and knew he could do so again. Just not at the level he wanted. Unless his or his brothers' life was in immediate peril, he couldn't do much more than float a paperweight across the room.

Whatever the coming test entailed, he had a feeling it wouldn't involve toying with office paraphernalia.

Alexander's words of advice came floating back to him.

Focusing the will requires extreme concentration, but magic also requires release. The balance between the two is the key, and the hardest lesson to learn.

Focus and release, focus and release, focus and release.

Val had practiced it over and over, triggering that pressure point in the mind which he knew released the magic. It was almost like learning to ride a bike: wobbling back and forth until finding that sweet spot of balance that allowed one to stay upright, then practicing until it became an automatic response.

Except bike riding was simple, and magic was unimaginably complex. Reaching the source of his magic was just the beginning, and he didn't know how to use or expand his power.

Concentrating until beads of sweat formed on his forehead, he reached inside again and again while waiting to be called, diving in and touching that wellspring of power.

"Val Kenefick, Talinmar Village?"

He looked up at the man with the clipboard who had poked his head into the alcove. Somehow, two hours had passed. One other person remained in the room, and she looked as nervous as Val felt.

He stood. "Ready."

The clerk collected Val's marker and led him down the hallway to an open door. He had more butterflies in his stomach than during his first day in court. At the time, his performance before the watching partners had felt like the most important thing in the world. Looking back, it seemed a triviality.

After Val entered, a mahogany door swung shut behind him. To his right sat two men and a raven-haired older woman wearing a crimson robe and a platinum circlet in her hair. One of the men wore a purple robe, the other a robe the color of crushed garlic. All three wizards sported blue and white striped stoles.

Val eyed the strange array of objects on the marble floor in front of the wizards: a gold block the size of a stove; a large clay bowl full of white orbs that resembled ping pong balls; and a tub of molten lava that steamed, hissed, and flamed within a silver container Val assumed was magical.

He kept a blank face, but his stomach roiled at the implications. He had been hoping the test would consist of one of the wizards probing his mind for evidence of innate magical ability.

"Proceed to the testing square and remain inside," the dark-haired woman said without introduction. She had a hooked nose and a strong, almost masculine, chin. A ruby ring in the shape of a seven-pointed star adorned her right index finger.

Val looked down. A three-foot square of silver tile occupied the space in front of the lava basin. He stepped onto it. No heat emanated from the lava.

The woman said, in a rote voice, "Lift the gold block and hold it at head height."

Val had been afraid of that. There was no telling how many thousands of pounds that thing weighed.

He breathed through his nose and remembered Alexander's instructions. *Allow your mind to move inward . . . focus, forget, find, and control.*

Release, Alexander had said. *Not just focus, but release.*

Find the magic and control it.

Focus.

Release.

Balance the two.

Val let his mind go blank, focused and released, merged the two. *Again*, he thought. *Again and again and again.*

He found the elusive touchstone of magic inside his head, then put everything he had into moving the block of gold, straining so hard he felt as if he was causing an embolism in his brain.

The block tilted a fraction of an inch, and then settled. Normally Val would have fallen over in stupefied awe at his success, but judging by the glances of amusement exchanged by the three wizards, he knew his effort wasn't good enough.

Not nearly so.

"When I release the glow orbs," the woman said, scorn dripping from her voice, "hold as many as you can in the air, then replace them in the box one by one."

She flicked a finger, and the entire box of white spheres flew into the air above Val's head, dozens of them, scattering in a wide pattern. They stopped just below the ceiling, hovered for a moment, and then fell.

Even if he had ample time to focus, Val couldn't have done what she asked. The orbs plummeted towards the floor, and he only managed to hold two of them aloft. Just before the rest of them hit the floor and shattered, the woman opened her palm and the entire lot floated gently back into the bowl. Val tried to guide the two orbs he had stopped into their container, but he couldn't manage both at one time. One would drop while he held the other, and he ended up losing control of both.

He choked on his wounded pride as the woman had to replace the final two orbs in the bowl. Val hated to fail at anything, even if it was a test of wizardry of which he had no hope of passing in the first place.

The two men had smirks on their faces. Val wanted to wipe them off.

The woman was unsmiling. "That will be all," she said coldly. "There is no need for the lava test. Elgan?" she called out. The clerk appeared in the doorway. "Please add this man's name to the *Do Not Return* register."

"Yes, Dean," the clerk said.

Val stepped forward, to the edge of the silver tile. "Please. Let me try again. I have power but can't always summon it."

The woman looked down her hooked nose at him, as if she were a queen and Val were a peasant who had just asked for her hand in marriage. "I think not," she said.

Desperate for a solution, Val thought fast. The two times he had used magic of any consequence—not counting whatever had happened with Alrick—Val's or his brothers' lives had been in danger. He didn't know if there was a trigger beyond mortal peril, but he knew that if he didn't try something extreme, his quest was doomed before it began, and he had no hope of finding his brothers.

Attacking the wizards was suicide. They would snuff out his life in a heartbeat. He kept thinking, and a crazy thought popped into his head. The woman's eyes clouded. One of the men pointed at the door. Val bowed his head and turned as if to leave.

Instead of walking away, he plunged his left hand into the basin of lava.

The pain was like nothing he had ever felt, shutting down his brain, a wind tunnel of fire roaring through his nerve endings. He screamed and stumbled backwards, the flesh of his hand melting like wax on a candle. Somehow through the pain he remembered why he had done it, and he focused his agony and rage on the giant cube of gold.

It flew into the air and exploded upwards in a million shards, coating the ceiling with gold buckshot.

The woman jumped to her feet, her eyes intense and narrowed on Val. No trace of a smirk remained on the faces of the two men. Val moaned, sinking to the floor and cradling his burnt hand, fighting not to black out from the pain.

As he writhed in agony, the woman reformed the block of gold from the suspended fragments, then lowered it to the floor. "Elgan," she murmured, her gaze locked on Val, "take this man to the infirmary right away. Then have him added to the student registry."

-18-

Hammers and pick axes in hand, the albino dwarves fanned out to pin Will and his companions against the rock formation. The stumpy humanoids looked as dense as pit bulls, at ease with their weapons, and far more sinister than dwarves were supposed to look.

"Who are you?" Will asked, trying to sound tough but knowing he sounded weak and lost. They had been so close to escaping.

"I'll be asking the questions around here," the lead dwarf said. His knee-length red tunic showcased the bunched muscles in his arms and calves. A white goatee hung six inches below his chin, and his yellow eyes, possessed of two vertical slits like cat's eyes, glittered in the darkness.

The dwarves took their weapons and prodded them back to the tusker camp. Grilgor looked cowed when he approached the lead dwarf, whose name Will overheard as Farzal. As they talked business, four of the tuskers locked Will and the other escapees back into the chain of prisoners.

Will noticed a tusker dragging a dead human captive towards an iron cauldron in the middle of camp. It was the woman who had been chained next to Yasmina. Marek, the man whom Will had fought over Caleb's dinner, was giving Will an accusing stare across the circle. He couldn't blame him. "She's dead because of us," he said, feeling as if he might be sick.

"Not just dead," Dalen muttered. "Breakfast."

That almost tipped the scales, but Will choked back his vomit. It was a harsh world, and he knew that if he wanted to survive, he had to learn to cope.

The dwarves handed over five sacks of coins to the tuskers, then herded the line of prisoners towards the rock formations. Will was behind Dalen, and whispered as softly as he could, "Did you expect this transfer?"

"Not this soon, but it makes sense, *rucka*. The delvers don't want the tuskers in their mountains."

Delvers, Will thought.

Half an hour into the mind-blowing rock formations, the entourage stopped at the entrance to a cave. Fifteen more delvers joined them at the cave mouth. Thirty in total.

"Listen well," Farzal boomed, addressing the crowd from atop a boulder. "It's a two week journey through the Darklands before we reach the mountain. If ye know anything about the Darklands, then ye know that what ye just tried with the piggies," he looked right at Will, "would be exceedingly stupid down there. If ye want to live, shut yer mouths and do as yer told."

"Why should we?" shouted one of the female prisoners. "You're taking us to the mines. We'll never survive."

Will shrank, thinking Farzal would send one of the delvers to punish the speaker. Instead Farzal gave the woman a ruthless smile that chilled Will to his core.

"We'll provide food and shelter in the mines, which is better than most of ye were doing before the piggies found ye. And if ye work long and hard for us," he grinned again, "who knows, maybe ye'll see the light of day again."

"*Lucka*," Dalen muttered to Will. "Delvers never free anyone."

"And if ye still have doubts," Farzal said, "remember there are fates in the Darklands much worse than the mines."

They traversed a series of caves deep underground, the forks in the passages so convoluted that even Will quickly lost track. Delvers on either side of the captives carried torches so the humans wouldn't trip in the darkness.

A few hours into the journey, far beneath the surface, they reached a bronze door set into the cave wall. An alien scrawl of runes covered the face of the metal.

"King's Blood," Dalen said in an awed voice. "A real entrance to the Darklands."

Farzal touched a series of runes in unison, too fast for Will too follow, and the door swung open on silent hinges.

"Is he a mage?" Will whispered.

"Delvers aren't wizard born," Dalen whispered back, "though they can do things with stone and metal that seem magical. My Da said they use geomancers and warders to augment their work."

The door opened onto a wide tunnel with an arched ceiling. Will estimated it was seven feet high at the apex. Giant blocks of stone, fitted together smoothly and without mortar, comprised the walls of the tunnel.

"Thank God," Caleb murmured behind Will. "I was worried I wouldn't be able to stand."

Every fifty feet, lanterns lit the tunnel with a sickly green glow, barely enough light to see by. When they passed one of the lamps, Will looked inside and saw a cluster of phosphorescent minerals.

The delvers didn't talk much, but when they did, they spoke in raspy but fluent English. Will assumed they had their own language, but he had yet to hear it.

The tunnel continued for another few hours, until they reached an enormous natural cavern with five identical tunnels exiting in different directions. Stalactites and stalagmites filled the grotto, as well as a pool of murky water. A colony of bats hung from one corner of the ceiling, and a pair of mineral lanterns provided faint illumination.

The delvers had set a brutal pace. When they gave the order to stop marching and set camp in the grotto, the prisoners slumped to the ground.

"Break it down," Farzal ordered, and the delvers orchestrated a symphony of coordinated action. They arranged the prisoners in a circle near the basin of water, set up the mess area and began preparing dinner, posted sentries in the tunnels and at the entrances to the cavern. One of the delvers applied a salve to Will's bloodied arm, presumably to insure his value in the mines.

After a meal of cold stew and cave water, Will eyed his ragtag companions.

All of them were suffering from malnutrition, exhaustion, and the chill of the Darklands. He was on his last legs himself.

Yasmina had been shaking and vomiting since they entered the caves, making Will think something more sinister than cold and exhaustion was plaguing her. He had no idea whether it was day or night, but as they settled in to rest, one of the guards, a delver with a flat nose and a ponytail of dreadlocks, approached Yasmina and asked if she would like something to warm her up.

"Please," she said.

He unlocked her from the circle while three more delvers looked on and smirked. "Just follow me," he said, his eyes roaming her body with a hungry gaze.

Yasmina hesitated.

"I'll keep ye as warm as ye've ever been."

She stumbled back to Caleb, and the guard laughed and chained her up again. "If ye get too cold, lassie," he said, shoving her into Caleb's arms, "ye just remember Fargar's offer. I'll hold it open for ye."

Yasmina curled into a ball, and Caleb waved Will closer. A faint blue rash had formed on the exposed skin of her arms. They pointed it out to Dalen, who swore.

"What is it?" Caleb asked, hovering over Yasmina like a mother hen.

"Breakbone Rash. From chewing the stinkweed bulb. *Aike*. It's rare but I think she's got it."

"What?" Will said. "Why didn't you tell us about this?"

"Would it have changed your mind?" Dalen shot back. "We took a risk."

"What's it mean?" Caleb asked. "I mean . . . how bad is it?"

Dalen couldn't look at Yasmina. "Some people survive," he said weakly.

A while later, as the delvers drank and chatted amongst themselves, Will turned on his side to face Dalen. "You asleep yet?"

The illusionist's eyelids fluttered. "Yes."

"We need to talk."

"About what?" Dalen asked, in a defeated voice.

"About escaping."

"In the Darklands? *Lucka*, Will, forget it. We'll never find our way out of here."

"Isn't getting lost down here better than facing the mines? Surely we can figure something out, if we can get away."

"For starters, delvers are much cleverer than tuskers. And crueler. They'll kill one of us as an example if they catch us. But that's not it. Don't you understand where you are? No one knows the Darklands except the delvers and whatever else," his eyes flicked to the shadows, "lives down here."

"What *does* live down here?"

Dalen threw a hand up, then realized he had made a sudden movement. He and Will waited in tense silence until sure no one was looking. "*Aike.* Rock wyrms, titan crabs, cave fiends, darrowgars, darklings. And those are just the commons. From what they say, the delver tunnels are only the beginning. The Darklands go deep, deeper than you can ever imagine. Old things live down here. Even if we escaped the delvers, we'll be lost or eaten within days, if not hours. Not to mention the lack of food, water, and light."

"Sounds promising," Will muttered. For once, he didn't get the sense Dalen was exaggerating. His eyes found Caleb and Yasmina, huddled on the floor beside him.

"*Lucka*, Will, *wizards* don't come down here. At this point, I'm more worried about reaching the mines alive than trying to escape."

The next two 'days' were an endless series of tunnels and intersecting caverns. Judging by the position of the lanterns, most of the time they were traversing a gentle downward slope. Thinking of how far underground they had journeyed gave Will a queasy feeling.

On the fourth day, they descended a narrow staircase that led straight into a chasm. The dwarves lit the torches for the prisoners, but outside of the penumbra of light, Will saw nothing but darkness in every direction. It was terrifying.

After the chasm, which descended for at least a mile, the tunnel leveled out for the rest of the day. They encountered countless more intersections, some of which contained jagged holes that the delvers crept around as if something would spring out of them. Will peered inside one and couldn't see the bottom.

Did Urfe have a mantle and a molten core like back home, he wondered? If so, how close were they to it, and what lived down there?

At the end of the day, the passage spilled into a cavern with a vast underground river flowing through it, so wide Will couldn't see the other side. Sandy soil the color of blood filled the cavern, and giant phosphorescent mushrooms, most as tall as Caleb, sprouted from the weird topsoil.

"It's beautiful," Yasmina said, startling Will. She had barely spoken since their descent into the Darklands. The rash had grown more pronounced and she had developed a fever.

Caleb took her hand and squeezed it with a grave expression, as if realizing the need for a moment of happiness. "It is."

The delvers set up camp next to the river, which was the same crimson color as the topsoil. The surrounding mushrooms towered over the four-foot tall delvers.

Will noticed a somberness to their captors' demeanors. Less ale was quaffed during dinner, more sentries were posted, and the delvers' yellow pupils kept flicking into the darkness.

"What do you think is out there?" Caleb asked, hands hugging his knees.

"Dunno," Dalen said, "but I hope it *stays* out there."

The delvers had stashed Will's sword in one of the burlap sacks they carried, and he felt naked without it. If something decided to attack the camp, he would be as helpless as a babe.

The prisoners huddled together, as close as the chains would allow. After a long period of lying awake in silence, Will finally fell asleep, until his eyes opened at some point deep into the night. The camp was quiet, the river still, the cavern an eerie dreamland lit by the green and yellow glow of the mushrooms.

Before his eyes closed again, he glanced around, as if to reassure himself that nothing was out there.

And saw a creature creeping into the cavern from one of the side tunnels. The thing resembled a giant pink salamander, only with a long and narrow head like a crocodile's, its jaw lined with hundreds of dagger-sharp teeth.

The creature was creeping upside down along the ceiling, above the two sentries. Sticking out of its mouth was the limp torso of a delver.

Will opened his mouth to yell, but one of the sentries beat him to it.

"Darrowgars!" the delver roared. "DARROWGARS!"

-19-

The woman huddled in a damp corner of the cell, clutching her gray caftan as her lips formed a continuous string of prayers. She was not afraid, just cold and wet and miserable. When the time was right, Devla alone would decide to save or take her life, and that knowledge made her feel secure. Her god had formed the world, raised the mountains, filled the seas—he possessed more power in a single breath than all the wizards of the Congregation combined. If He wanted to free her, then He would.

The heavy door creaked open, allowing light to flood in. Two days had passed since the pyromancer had snatched her from the fountain on Bohemian Isle and deposited her in this stone prison. She was weak from hunger, thirsty beyond belief.

Her downcast eyes caught the legs of three people entering the room, and she heard the door close behind them. Legs clad in the finest of wool, feet shod in smooth calfskin boots. *Wizards.*

The woman's eyes lifted and then widened in surprise. The tall, stately wizard in the middle she knew on sight.

Lord Alistair, Chief Thaumaturge of the Congregation.

Accompanying him was a handsome dark-haired man, as well as a delicate blond woman with cruel eyes and a thin but expressive mouth.

Lord Alistair opened his palm towards the prisoner, forcing her to stand against her will. The woman tried to wriggle free, but she couldn't even twitch. *Filthy, evil wizards.*

"What is your name?" Lord Alistair asked.

She glared back at him, defiant. Knowing her name, Magdala of Clan Argentari, would give the wizards leverage over her family.

"Who sent you to the fountain?" Lord Alistair asked, when she didn't respond.

The woman spat. "You know who. The Prophet."

"And where is this illustrious teacher who commands the immolation of his followers?"

"Embrace the power of Devla, nonbelievers. Embrace Him or thou wilt burn."

"Braden?" Lord Alistair said. "If you will?"

The dark-haired mage stared at the captive. She felt a terrible pain in her fingers, looked down, and watched her fingernails peel away and fall to the floor. She gritted her teeth.

"It will be better if you talk," the blond woman said. "Trust me."

The captive spat. "Knowest there is nothing thou canst do which would cause me to betray my prophet or our God. *Nothing.*"

Braden flicked a wrist. One of the prisoner's arms shot straight out to her side. She tried to lower it, but it wouldn't budge. As she watched, horrified, her elbow began to invert at the wrong angle, bending further and further until it snapped.

As she screamed, Lord Alistair took a step closer, looming over her. "I care not about your fictional deity. But, young lady, you *will* guide me to the Prophet. Do you understand who I am? Who stands here with me? The sort of power we wield?"

The woman's arm was still outstretched, the urge to cradle her broken wing almost unbearable. She was hyperventilating from the pain, and had to gasp her words. "If thou thinkest thou can break me, thou dost not understand our beliefs. Compared to the agony of eternal damnation, the pain of this world is a drop of water in the ocean."

"We'll just have to see about that," Lord Alistair said, nodding to Braden.

The cuerpomancer's liquid eyes betrayed no emotion as they focused on the captive. As he raised a hand, her shirt flew off her body, and she shrieked in pain as her skin peeled back from her fingers and palms. The process continued all the way up her arms and across the top of her chest.

"We prefer not to continue," Lord Alistair said. "But we will."

When she still refused to speak, Braden gave a contemptuous flick of his wrist that sent the flayed husk of skin flying into the opposite corner, where it settled like a piece of soiled laundry. The prisoner's arms and upper chest were a red mass of exposed flesh.

The pain was almost as intense as her immolation had been. She lost control of her bowels, and forced herself to remain conscious long enough to deliver her final words. "Thou shalt burn for eternity in golden fire for thy wickedness," she screamed, her body convulsing in waves of uncontrollable spasms from the pain. "*Thou shalt burn.*"

-20-

It was Registration day for wizard school.

Jittery with anticipation, Val prepared a pot of coffee as the sun broached the horizon. Sleep had never been a priority for him.

After caffeinating, he replaced the bandages on his hand. A cuerpomancer in the infirmary had managed to repair most of the damage and somehow re-grow the skin, but Val had to keep his hand out of the sunlight while the scars formed. He didn't know what the cuerpomancer had done, but most of the pain had subsided—less than a week after plunging his hand into a basin of hot lava.

It wasn't impressive. It was miraculous.

Next he downed two eggs and a ration of bacon he prepared on the wood-burning stove, as well as a piece of fresh-baked bread with butter. He had found an excellent provisions store three blocks away. After a quick wash in the clawfoot tub, he donned tan breeches and a high-collared dress shirt, put a handful of gold coins in his pocket, and left his staff in the cellar again. He didn't want to draw attention to himself at the Abbey.

Gus was waiting by the curb. He and Val had settled on a monthly fee of ten gold coins for transportation to and from the school. Val knew it was a steep price, but he believed in paying his people.

The horses trotted down Magazine Street, sharing the road with a bustle of pedestrians and smaller carriages. Val was pensive on the way to the Wizard District. At his request, in a last-ditch attempt to seek information, Gus had asked around about their old traveling companions. The carriage driver had heard of Mala and was impressed Val knew her, but no one in the city had seen her for months. Allira was also a ghost, and Gus relayed a rumor in the Thieves

Guild about a woman fitting Marguerite's description who, after treatment by a cuerpomancer, had traveled west seeking adventure.

So Val was left with the Abbey. He had no idea what he was getting into, and worry for his brothers consumed him. He had spent most of the last week pacing Salomon's Crib, avoiding the danger of the streets and wishing school would start so he could concentrate all of his energies on reaching the Pool of Souls.

Despite himself, he was curious. It was *magic* school. Unlike Will, Val had never been interested in fantasy or the supernatural, but if wizardry was his birthright, then he wanted to know what it was all about. And there was, in fact, one thing about magic that interested Val very much.

Because Val was interested in power.

The streets of New Victoria passed by in a blur, and before he knew it, Gus was reining in the horses by the front entrance of the Abbey. Val was glad to see some of the other students—those who didn't fly in—arriving in carriages as well.

"How do the wizards afford these towers?" Val asked as he stepped off the carriage.

"Inheritance, I s'pose," Gus said. "And they oversee the taxes, reserving a nice bit for themselves."

"Taxes for what?"

"Defense of the Realm, public works, I dunno, just bein' wizards. How do rulers always get paid?"

"About like that," Val murmured.

When he entered the marble foyer of the Abbey, the faces of the budding wizards reminded Val of his former law school classmates, skittish with nervous energy yet at the same time imbued with a sense of destiny at the promise of their bright futures.

Nearly one hundred students filled the foyer. The genders appeared equally represented, and he was glad to see a range of ages. At thirty-three, he seemed to be in the older third of incoming students, though not by much.

He joined the line behind the sign marked 'Registration.' After reaching the booth, he presented a silver medallion he had been given in the infirmary. The medallion was engraved with his name and status: 'Val Kenefick—Acolyte.'

The aging counter clerk eyed the medallion, sifted through a box at his feet, and handed Val a vellum scroll. "Down the hallway to your left to select your first-year discipline," the man intoned. "The Lyceum for electives."

Val murmured his thanks, then retreated to a corner to open the scroll. It read like a typical class schedule.

Val Kenefick
10:00 Daily Basics of Wizardry I
14:00 Daily History and Governance
16:00 Daily Discipline I
09:00 Sat Elective

Val closed the scroll and followed the other students down a long hallway lit by mauve glow orbs. A series of closed doorways lined the corridor on both sides, and above each door hung a sign designating the core disciplines: Pyromancy, Aquamancy, Sylvomancy, Geomancy, Aeromancy, Cuerpomancy, Alchemancy, and at the very end of the hall, Spiritmancy.

A line of students snaked beside all of the doors except for cuerpomancy and spiritmancy. Did one need special permission to apply to be a spirit mage? Was his quest for the Planewalk doomed before it could start? He had no idea, but he followed the philosophy that it was better to ask forgiveness than permission.

He felt eyes on his back as he strode the length of the hall. When he reached the spiritmancy door, he gave it a solid rap, frazzled with nerves but not about to show weakness in front of the other students.

The door opened of its own accord, and Val stepped inside a marble-walled room, empty except for two leather armchairs facing each other in the center. A fiftyish man with burnt orange eyes and a fluffy red beard reclined in one of the armchairs. Lying next to him was a staff similar to Val's, except the azantite tip was a milky orb instead of a half-moon.

The varieties of human eye color on Urfe continued to amaze Val. He assumed that, like species of tropical birds, the spectrum of hues resulted from the presence of different evolutionary pigments within the iris.

The man smiled at Val, his eyes warm like the glow of a hearth. He had an avuncular face, broad and familiar, the kind of face you felt you knew as soon as you saw it. Val wondered if he was looking at his first spirit mage.

Besides his own father, that was.

"Come in, please, come in," the man said, in a rich brogue. "I was starting to wonder if Damon was our only incoming student." The man put a hand out and said, "If I could just ensure all is in order . . . ."

Val got the hint and presented his medallion. When the man touched it, the marker glowed with a pale blue light and a symbol appeared under Val's name, an eight-pointed ruby-red star enclosing the initials *DVS*.

"Ah, bonnie lad, there's Dean Varen's approval. You must have impressed her." He returned Val's marker and indicated with an upturned palm for him to sit. Val complied, feeling light with relief.

"I'm Professor Groft, Dean of spiritmancy. I like to extend a personal welcome to all of our Acolytes."

"A pleasure to meet you, Sir," Val said.

The professor clasped his hands in the folds of his brown cassock. "I always ask three questions of each new student. After you give your answers—rest assured this is a wholly subjective test—I will stamp your Acolyte token and you may proceed to the elective room. All I ask is that you tell the truth to the best of your knowledge."

Val waited for the first question while Professor Groft crossed his legs and folded his hands in his lap, eyes twinkling as if he and Val were sharing a private joke. "Who are you?"

Val stilled, wondering if the spirit mage somehow knew his true identity. Val didn't want to tip his hand, but he also sensed Professor Groft would know if he was lying.

He opted for semantics. "I'm not sure I understand the question. Who is anyone? I am who I am."

The professor's eyes never blinked. Val tensed, expecting to be asked to explain further, but Groft said, "Do you fancy yourself a man of evil or good intentions?"

What kind of a question was that?

Professor Groft's odd inquiries caught Val off guard. Nor did he believe for a second the test was wholly subjective, or that Groft did not have an agenda of some sort. Everyone had an agenda.

"Is there such a thing as a truly unselfish person?" Val replied, honestly. "I believe the polar extremes of *good* and *evil* are too simple to describe a human being."

The professor gave a slow nod, his expression unchanged. "Final question. Why do you want to be a spirit mage?"

Again Val hesitated. *Was he passing or failing?* He couldn't tell the real truth, of course—that he wanted to sneak into the Pool of Souls and find his brothers—so he told a pair of lesser truths. Maybe they would add up to a whole.

"Because spiritmancy is the most demanding discipline," Val said, "and I like to be challenged. It would be an honor and a privilege to be accepted."

"Good, good," the professor said, though Val didn't get the sense that he was passing judgment. "Your registration scroll, please."

Val unfurled his scroll. Professor Groft leaned over and touched the face of his ring against the vellum, leaving a glowing, blue-white imprimatur of a dragon eating its own tail, in the shape of a figure eight.

The same emblem used by the Myrddinus.

Val concealed his shock. Had the original Myrddin been a spirit mage?

The professor slapped his palms on his knees. "Well, then."

Val took his cue, rising and thanking him for his time, unnerved by the odd exchange. He felt uncomfortable when he couldn't read other people's motives, and he had no idea what Groft's game was.

"Good luck," the professor said gravely, just before Val turned to leave.

Surprised by the change in tone, Val risked a glance back and noticed the professor's eyes had turned sad and distant, as if the mysteries of the universe swirled within.

Val wasn't sure where to find the Lyceum, but he saw a number of students proceeding through a doorway at the end of the hallway. He followed suit and found himself in the rear of a modest size auditorium. Colorful booths separated by marble pillars lined the perimeter. Students milled about in small groups in the center or waited in line at the booths.

A room full of budding wizards. Val got a shiver at the thought.

And then remembered he was one of them.

Next to him was a booth marked *Potions*. A smiling older woman in a thin white robe stood behind a counter filled with inch-high liquid stoppers. Val read some of the labels: Wizard Skin, Vigor, Owlbear Sight, Astral Aura, Dragon's Tongue. On the left side of the counter, an unfurled registration scroll displayed a list of names and corresponding disciplines.

"Would you care for a sample?" she asked.

"No thank you," Val murmured, wary of imbibing something he wasn't ready for.

He backed away and squeezed through the auditorium, eying some of the names above the other booths. *Relics. Zoomancy and History of Menagerical Specimens. Combat Wizardry. Pedagogy. Basics of Oriental Magic. Shamanism. Applied Electromancy. Cyanomancy.*

In a corner of the room was a booth lined with black velvet and filled with a variety of animal skulls, jars of desiccated specimens, and vials of liquid that smelled like formaldehyde. Val turned away with a shudder when the stern-faced necromancer behind the stall leveled his gaze at him.

Val had to pick something. He decided on *Relics*. It had a number of people waiting in line behind a booth displaying unusual items in glass cases, and he preferred a larger class in which he could hide. It also sounded like one of the electives least likely to subject him to embarrassment. Maybe he would even learn something about Will's sword.

As he waited in line, he caught a glimpse of the two items on display—a unicorn's horn from the Withering Forest and something called the Girdle of Girardius.

When he reached the front, a wizard in gold robes with bushy white eyebrows stamped *Relics* on Val's registration scroll. With a nod, he left the Abbey and returned to his waiting carriage. Classes started the following morning.

On the ride home, reliving the events of the day in his mind as the horses trotted past the Goblin Market, Val felt as if he had truly, deeply, and utterly fallen down the rabbit hole.

And wondered if he would ever climb out.

-21-

The mushroom cavern exploded into action. Darrowgars swarmed inside from all four entrances, springing onto mushrooms, climbing the walls, scuttling across the ceiling.

Instead of panicking, the delvers gathered into formation in the middle of the cavern, responding to Farzal's roared commands. Shields and pickaxes and hammers came up, clashing with the darrowgars as they rushed across the floor and dropped down from above.

Caleb and Dalen jumped to their feet beside Will, joining the line of prisoners backed against the river. Yasmina pressed against Caleb's back, her hands on his waist, forehead slick with fever.

The darrowgars were quick as striking snakes, snapping with elongated jaws while their rubbery bodies contorted at impossible angles. Will watched as one of the creatures sprang to the side to avoid a blow, then bent its body in half as it reached back to snatch a delver's legs in its jaws. The warrior's screams echoed through the cavern.

But the sturdy delvers had experience and discipline on their side. They kept their formation, interlocking shields and impaling the darrowgars as they leapt down from the ceiling and sprang sideways off of mushrooms. Farzal was a particularly fierce warrior, fighting with a war hammer and a double-sided battle-axe, twirling his two weapons as fast as the darrowgars could strike.

Will watched the battle in morbid fascination, having to root for their captors since the darrowgars would surely eat the prisoners if they won. He thought the mushrooms would be an advantage, but whenever one of the delvers backed against a giant fungi, a darrowgar would bend its body around the thick trunks, or spring atop and attack from above.

Dalen shouted for help. Will whipped to his right and saw a darrowgar that must have leapt over the delvers. The creature was rushing towards the line of prisoners, and Dalen stood right in its path. The young illusionist formed three balls of green light and thrust them at the darrowgar's face, one after the other, but it didn't seem to notice. Frantic, Dalen waved his hands in the air, and then there were three of him: he had somehow created two replicas of himself, illusory doppelgangers who moved exactly as he moved.

The casting was imperfect, and Will could tell that two of the doppelgangers were more insubstantial than the real Dalen, but the spell confused the darrowgar. It changed direction and sprang at Will instead, lunging for his legs before twisting its torso at the last second for a throat strike. Will stumbled backwards, just managing to slip his hands around the creature's slimy throat.

The darrowgar pressed forward, its slender neck much stronger than Will had expected. It pushed Will onto his back and put two sticky salamander feet on his chest, thrusting its elongated jaws forward. Will's wrists and forearms were his greatest assets, naturally thick as well as strengthened by years of working as a contractor, but he could only slow the darrowgar down. The jaws inched closer and closer to his face.

Will tried to buck the thing off, and Caleb and Dalen beat on it with their fists. Still it pressed forward, until Will was staring at two jagged rows of teeth and inhaling the fetid odor of its breath.

The darrowgar's front feet slipped forward, and the brunt of its weight landed on Will's chest. He yelled and tried to thrust it off him, wondering why it hadn't bitten him, then saw a battle axe sticking out of the creature's back and realized it wasn't moving.

Farzal reached down and jerked his weapon out. "I don't appreciate darrowgar eating me prisoners," he said, giving Will a wink and a wicked smile before helping him to his feet. His grip felt like a steel clamp.

The delver leader walked off, leaving Will shaking from the near-death experience. Dalen was huddled off to the side, hoping none of the delvers had seen his magic display. Caleb stepped out from behind a mushroom with Yasmina, who was pale with fever.

The battle was finished. Three dead delvers—and the severed torso of another—had been laid out in a line near the center of the cavern. Two more moaned on the ground, blood pouring from the stumps of severed limbs and soaking into the topsoil. A delver in a green tunic attended to the injured, pouring a tawny liquid onto the wounds.

The rest of the delvers had whipped into a flurry of action, which made Will think there might be more darrowgars on the way. Some of the delvers broke down camp, while others dragged the bodies of the slain next to the river, leaving them heaped on the bank. Another delver poured a few drops from a stoppered bottle onto his fallen comrades, and their tunics burst into flame.

Farzal strode to the nearest cavern wall and stuck his ear against the stone. After a few moments, his head jerked up. "Move!" he roared.

One of the delvers stuck his hands in the river and came out holding a heavy chain. Another joined him, and they tugged the chain out of the water as fast as they could, until a long wooden skiff drifted into view.

As they pulled the skiff to shore, Farzal crowded everyone on board. The prow of the boat dipped almost to the water. Delvers picked up the six oars lying on board, pushed off the bank, and started rowing in time to Farzal's command. The boat flew across the water.

Halfway across the river, just as the opposite shore emerged from the darkness, the water near the bank they had just fled erupted, spraying so high it soaked the boat.

An enormous creature with grub-white skin burst out of the water. It had the head and forelimbs of a Tyrannosaurus Rex and the body of a great white shark. Three suckered appendages extended from either side of its torso, twenty feet long and grasping in all directions.

It used its tiny forelimbs to drag its body onto shore, and Will watched in horror as each of the suckered appendages grabbed a darrowgar corpse and shoved them, one by one, into its gaping maw. The crunch of giant teeth tearing into darrowgar flesh reached all the way across the river.

The monster finished its meal and slipped back into the water. The delvers rowed harder than ever, and when the boat reached the opposite bank, they tied it down and rushed ashore. Held until last, Will and the rest of the prisoners scampered along behind them, tripping over their neighbor to not be the last in line.

After the fight with the darrowgars, Farzal marched the party an hour past the underground river, until they reached another cavern with multiple exit tunnels. Yasmina collapsed when they stopped for the night, curled on her side with her hair spread in a halo, an angel slumped on the cold cavern floor.

Caleb had to shake her awake the next morning. As soon as she stumbled to her feet, the dry heaves began, lasting throughout the day's march. Will and Caleb pled for help. Their captors finally allowed her a few drops of a healing potion, which stopped the vomiting but didn't improve her pallor.

The next morning, Yasmina was awake before Will. When Caleb stirred, she leaned over him and smiled, her hair brushing his face.

"Good morning," she said. Her voice was spritely, and it chilled Will to his core.

Caleb put a hand to her forehead. "God, Yaz, you're burning up."

"Am I?" she said, in a puzzled voice. "It's such a nice day today."

Caleb stared at her.

She giggled and moved her hands in a circle, as if twirling through a meadow. "Can you smell the lavender? I love days like this."

Will swallowed, his mouth dry with worry.

Farzal called out for them to march.

"Sure thing," Caleb said, helping Yasmina to her feet. "Let's go to the park."

She started walking, her smile as warm and bright as the sun they might never see again.

Sick with worry over Yasmina's health, Will was nevertheless awed by his surroundings. The journey took a turn for the fantastic, leading them through territory filled with molten geysers, multi-hued underground streams and lakes, rock formations that boggled the mind, fields of mushrooms and lichen and strange plants clinging to the cracks and fissures, insects and aquatic life unlike anything Will had ever seen. If the Darklands was an undiscovered country, this section was its national park.

The bottomless chasms, navigable rivers, and gaping holes in the stone floor sparked Will's imagination, making him feel as if they had barely glimpsed the wonders of the Darklands. When they skirted a chasm with a set of rough-hewn stairs leading into the blackness, it made him think of the *old things* Dalen had mentioned, and fear laced his curiosity. He also sensed danger lurking in the shadows at every turn, unwilling to face the might of the delver expedition.

Dalen was right. Even if they escaped, they wouldn't have lasted five minutes on their own.

Two days later, during the evening march, Yasmina collapsed. She was unresponsive to Caleb's pleading, and Farzal stomped over to her. "If she can't continue," he said to Caleb, "she stays behind."

Caleb's face was ashen. "You can't do that."

Farzal smirked and waved for the delver with the keys. He ran over, and Caleb stepped in front of Yasmina. "No!"

The delver shoved him aside and unlocked Yasmina's chain. Caleb stepped towards him. "Unlock me, too. I'm staying with her."

Farzal rasped a laugh. "And lose an able body for the mines? I think not, laddie."

"Give her to me," Will said in desperation. "I'll carry her."

The delver with the keys shrugged and tossed Yasmina's limp form at Will, then returned with Farzal to the front of the march.

Yasmina's emaciated figure felt as light as a child. Will put her on his back and draped her arms over his shoulders.

"Thanks, little brother," Caleb whispered. "I'll take her when you get tired."

Though unresponsive, Yasmina was semi-conscious, able to relieve a bit of the burden by clinging to Will. Despite her reduced weight, Will was ready to collapse an hour into the journey. He gritted his teeth and kept going. Caleb wasn't a reasonable option; Will knew he wouldn't last five minutes.

Half an hour later, Will stumbled, falling to a knee. He struggled to his feet and lurched forward, unable to accept defeat, knowing Farzal would leave her to die without a shred of remorse.

Will stumbled again, his hamstrings cramping, and Yasmina slid off his back. Dalen and Caleb moved to help him, each of them struggling to pick her up.

"Leave her," a voice rang out.

Will looked behind him, to the prisoner who had spoken.

"I'll carry her."

The speaker was Marek, the muscle-bound cretin who he had clashed with the first night of their captivity. Will hesitated, though something in the man's eyes told Will he could trust him with Yasmina.

And there was no choice. Will guessed they had at least another hour on the day's march, and he couldn't carry her any further. Caleb gave a reluctant nod, and Will squeezed Yasmina's hand and left her on the ground.

As Marek passed her in line, he scooped her up as if she were an inflatable doll, then slung her over his shoulder.

After they set camp, shoveled cold stew into their mouths, and lay down to sleep, Will overheard Caleb whispering to Yasmina. Her eyes were open but she was catatonic and feverish. The delvers hadn't even bothered to chain her.

"Wake up, Yaz. Please wake up. Will and Marek can't carry you all day. Farzal will leave you if you don't come around." He buried his head in her chest, his voice cracking. "Please, Yaz."

Will turned the other way and tried not to listen.

The next day Marek and Will swapped out carrying Yasmina during the morning march. When they tired, arms cramping from the strain, Caleb and Dalen took ten-minute turns, managing to survive until the short lunch break.

After lunch, Will bent to pick her up, knowing he wouldn't last much longer. Even with Marek's help, they wouldn't make it through the day.

Someone whistled, and Will turned to see a muscular woman on the other side of Dalen, one of the newer arrivals, waving a hand. With a grave nod of thanks, Will passed her on.

During the rest of the day's march, every able-bodied prisoner took a turn carrying Yasmina, passing her along the line until each man or woman tired. She became a child in the care of the village, kept alive by a spark of human goodness in that darkest of hours.

Will had put a pebble in his pocket each morning to track their journey. On the afternoon of the thirteenth day, after a long slog through a mind-numbingly uniform series of tunnels, the party stopped inside a cavern with a high ceiling and five exit tunnels, similar to any number of caverns they had passed.

Farzal stepped to the center of a wall and placed his hands on the surface. The wall glowed with blue light, illuminating a set of spidery runes swarming the wall. The delver moved his hands over the runes in a rapid pattern. A concealed door swung inward, revealing a staircase ascending a vertical chasm.

Will was surprised to find two sentries waiting inside the door. They waved Farzal through, and he led the party up the stone staircase.

Hugging the edge of the rock wall, the stairway seemed to last forever. Every hundred yards or so they passed a wide platform lit by mineral lamps and manned by a pair of sentries fronting a tunnel.

Will was carrying Yasmina when they reached the top of the staircase. His arms felt like wheelbarrows full of wet cement. Two sentries stepped aside as Farzal opened another of the rune doors, and the party stepped through the portal, this time onto a large platform manned by another set of guards.

Wide marble stairs descended on both sides of the platform, and a five-carriage funicular on bronze rails was anchored to the ledge. Will inched forward and caught his breath. Far beneath them, in a cavern so enormous it boggled his mind, a vast underground city had been scooped out of the earth, built entirely of silver-hued stone glowing in the emerald light of a million hanging mineral lanterns.

Farzal turned to address the line of captives, showcasing the view with an upturned palm. "Welcome to Fellengard," he growled.

-22-

Night fell soon after the hags stuffed Mala and the majitsu inside the cages. Eerie sounds emanated from the forest: hoarse growls and ragged barks, a series of prolonged shrieks, and the alien chirping of whatever species of insects populated that world.

Once reasonably sure the hags wouldn't return for the night, Mala whispered, "Majitsu!" as loud as she dared, not caring if the creatures inside the kennel heard her. Surely they despised their captivity as much as she.

A pause, and then, "My name is Hazir."

At the front of the kennel, when the hags had led her in, Mala had noticed an open storage bin filled with discarded belongings. She hadn't seen her edged weapons, but her sash and pouches had been dumped on top of the pile.

It got her thinking.

"I assume you've tested our bonds?" she asked.

"Of course. The gray coils are impervious to magic. Or at least to mine."

"See if your magic works outside the cage. Try to move something, a piece of straw."

A longer period of silence, and then, "It does appear to work outside the cage, but you must know I'm not strong enough to hurt—"

"That isn't my objective. At least not yet. If you can reach my pouches, float the red one over to me."

Hazir gave a harsh laugh. "And aid your escape?"

Mala swallowed her retort. To have any chance of escaping this nightmare world, she had to cooperate with the arrogant majitsu and deal with the consequences later. "I've a potion that can render me small enough to escape this cage. I propose a truce while I search for a way to overcome the hags."

"Do you think I'm daft? Why would you return for me?"

"Because the amulet is our only way home, and the larger hag wears it around her neck. I'll need your help retrieving it. And I'm afraid you don't have a choice, unless you have another plan."

The majitsu didn't answer, and Mala added, "If you're thinking of using the potion for yourself, know that I've many potions, at least half of which are poison. Choose wrongly, and you doom us both."

Mala held her breath as she waited on the majitsu's decision. When her red pouch containing the Potion of Diminution floated into view, she prepared to reach for it, but it stopped moving just outside her cage.

"Your word that you won't leave me behind," the majitsu said.

"On the honor of my clan, I swear that if it is within my ability to leave this world, I shan't do so without you. We will use the amulet together."

The pouch drifted within reach. Mala squeezed a hand through the latticework opening, searched through the pouch, and extracted a green vial. Since nothing else would be of use and there was no place to hide the pouch, she had Hazir return it.

Before she quaffed the potion, she said, "I'll need your word as well, Hazir. That if we return to Urfe, we go our separate ways, the past forgotten."

"Of course," he said.

"Swear it," she said. "On your oath as a majitsu."

She could sense him gritting his teeth. "Should we reach our home world, then on the oath I swore to join the Order of Majitsu, I promise to honor our pact and grant your freedom."

Not believing a word he said, but wanting him to think she did, Mala stripped, put two drops of the potion on her tongue, pushed the vial and all of her clothes except her shoes–which wouldn't fit—through the cage, and began to shrink.

Two drops shrank her to the size of a grasshopper. She was just able to jump up and over the bottom latticework of gray tendrils. The other creatures watched with listless eyes as Mala huddled naked on the wooden planks, her new world a towering and frightening place, hugging her knees to her chest as she waited for the potion to wear off.

Half an hour later, after returning to normal size, she dressed and pocketed the vial. When she passed Hazir, they exchanged a grim nod.

An expert tracker, Mala slipped soundlessly into the night to learn the lay of the land. The clay-like ground felt moist and sticky beneath her bare feet.

There wasn't much to the compound. Besides the kennel and cluster of low farmhouses, she saw only the three conical huts she assumed the hags stayed in.

She searched the two farmhouse buildings first, both of which were piled haphazardly with cobweb-covered furniture, piles of clothes, and random junk. She found her weapons tossed just inside a door, and breathed a sigh of relief.

Next she explored the valley, roaming right to the edge of the forest, wary of stepping inside the woods. She felt a presence flitting through the darkened trees, something dangerous and unfamiliar, and decided not to venture into the forest unless forced.

Frustrated, shivery from cold and unwilling to risk waking the hags, she was forced to return her weapons and race back to the kennel as the muted dawn light broached the horizon. After relieving herself outside—there was not even a pot inside the filthy pens—Mala took two more drops and returned to her cage.

The smaller hags returned just after dawn, tossing each prisoner a pile of mush that looked like tripe. Mala forced down enough of the vile meal to keep from starving. The creatures stopped by again at dusk, slopping another round of food into the cages.

Following the next dawn visit, Mala waited long enough for the hags to wander away, then took another dosage. After checking to ensure the hags were nowhere in sight, guessing they had gone into the forest, she ran to the edge of the trees behind the three huts and hid in the foliage as she observed the windowless dwellings for the better part of an hour.

The huts were made of dried mud with thatched roofs. Like everything else in the settlement except for the farmhouses, everything seemed to be of organic origin.

Mala saw no movement inside the huts. It was time to take a risk.

Creeping down the hill on bare feet, nerves endings bursting with adrenaline, she took a deep breath and reached for the door of the first hut.

-23-

When Val arrived at the Abbey on the first day of wizard school, there were signs guiding the students to different coteries. According to his registration scroll, he was part of Coterie III.

He left the carriage and followed the signs behind the main hall on foot, down a brick walkway that led through a citrus grove, to a handsome granite bungalow in a clearing shielded by curtains of bougainvillea. A large koi pond covered the left half of the clearing, and climbing roses brightened the granite. Standing beside the pond, taking in Val's approach with folded arms, were two majitsu.

Val tensed as he approached. *Is this typical for students?* he thought. *Majitsu guards?*

He entered the house promptly at nine a.m. and found four people sitting in a tidy lounge decorated with tapestries and oil paintings. He took a seat on a velvet sofa, between a bookshelf and a glass cabinet stocked with bottles of amber spirits.

The other students were trying to observe each other without being noticed.

Typical behavior in a new group, exacerbated when that group was a collection of prospective wizards at the most exclusive school in the Realm.

To his left, an attractive, pale young woman with turquoise eyes and a waist-length braid of blond hair shared a couch with a tall, thin black man about Val's age with a bald head and a high forehead. The man was dressed in a one-piece outfit of stitched silk, a strange hybrid between a robe and a business suit.

In another chair sat a swarthy young man closer in age to the woman—mid-twenties—with curly dark hair, hairy forearms, and a strong build. With his chocolate pants of fine wool and white shirt buttoned to the neck, left thumb tapping his crossed legs with nervous energy, Val knew his type right away: the type A, over-eager associate. The brash negotiator.

"I'm Adaira," the pale young woman said, rising to grasp Val by the shoulders and kiss him lightly on the forehead. A linen pantsuit, flared at the shoulders and wrists, complemented her turquoise eyes. Silver riding boots hugged her calves, and a matching belt accentuated her narrow waist. She wore no jewelry other than a choker of black pearl. The *fashionista*, Val assumed.

"Val," he replied.

Before she sat, her eyes made a confident sweep of his face, as if cataloguing his features. "Charmed," she murmured.

"Chakandida," the bald man said, tripping over a foot-stool as he rose. He righted himself with a self-aware chuckle, then grasped Val's arm at the elbow. "Call me Dida."

"Sounds easier," Val said.

"Yes, yes," Dida laughed. His accent was heavy and his diction precise. Val liked him at once.

"Gowan," the curly-haired man said, with a curt nod. Val responded in kind.

The door opened, and two more people entered. Despite his vigor and swarthy good looks, the tall man holding the door with aplomb appeared at least a few years older than Val, his age betrayed by the lines around his eyes and streaks of silver in his V-shaped goatee.

The woman behind him was a fish woman.

Val could describe her in no other way. She entered the room with a strange rolling gait, like a sailor just off the boat. Her face was green and gilled at the cheeks, with a wide and pleasant mouth, nostrils so flat they were almost imperceptible, and lidless eyes the color of aged tobacco leaf. Sinuous blue-green scales covered her body.

Val had seen the representation of a similar humanoid before, on the zelo-mancy board in Leonidus's castle. *Kethropi*, Mala had called them. A race of fish-people.

The woman raised the back of her hand in a limp-wristed movement, curled the corners of her mouth, and announced herself as Riganthalaag Kothvi of Nelandia. "Perhaps you should call me Riga," she said, after everyone regarded her with a blank stare.

"Xavier at your service," the man behind Riga said, bowing after he closed the door, "and you may call me whatever you fancy. Hopeful sylvamancer, fa-ther of two, Southern Protectorate freeholder. My gads are Catalonian, nei-ther wizard born, and I'll be shocked if I pass the discipline exam. But I'll be damned if I don't give it a whirl." He spread his palms and grinned. "Just so you know."

Soon after the two new arrivals took their seats, a large-framed man with a comb-over—taller even than Xavier, but with the mushy build of an academ-ic—entered the room from a swinging door beside the bookcase. He sported a gold robe with one of the blue-and-white striped stoles.

He clapped once, then strode to the cabinet. "I see we've all arrived. I trust the first few decades of everyone's life have been relaxed and pleasant? Be-cause—" he poured himself a highball of the amber liquid –"the next three years, if you last that long, will not be."

His voice was arrogant and highly intelligent, reminding Val of his law school professors. "I'm Professor Gormloch," the man said. "You may call me Professor Gormloch."

Adaira and Xavier chuckled.

The professor plopped down on the sole remaining chair, crossed his legs, and swirled his highball. "Basics of Wizardry," he said. "The essential tools ap-plicable to all disciplines of magic. As well as mastering core skills, we shall delve into the shallow end of the major disciplines, both to familiarize our-selves with the traditional spectrum and to elucidate your own career path. Change of discipline is natural, and may be effected at the beginning of any semester—all that matters in the end, of course, is whether you pass the exam for your chosen discipline."

"Can we take the discipline exam at any time," Val asked, "or only after graduation?"

The question caused Gowan to snort and finger his collar, and Adaira to glance his way with interest.

"Young man," Professor Gormloch said, "you may take the exam at any time you wish, including this very moment! Shall I gather the deans?"

The class tittered, and Val leaned back and crossed his arms. *Rebuke accepted.* "That won't be necessary."

"It is highly, *highly* recommended that you complete your coursework before attempting your discipline exam. Individual classes may be repeated up to three times, but the discipline exam may be taken only once." He peered down his nose at Val. "And for an aspiring Spirit Mage, well, there have only been three students in the history of the Congregation who have successfully accelerated their spiritmancy studies, and all three were savant-level talents whose decisions were necessitated by time of war."

The mention of Val's chosen discipline garnered a reaction among all of his peers except Riga, whose cool-eyed stare never wavered. Adaira and Xavier raised their eyebrows, Dida gave Val a thoughtful look, and Gowan looked as if he had just swallowed a live toad.

The professor noticed the reactions. "Given the difficulty of wizardry studies, we prefer small coteries and a low teacher-student ratio, as well as a diverse range of disciplines. Always remember that you are here to *help* each other. Some of you will have talent in an area where others might fall short."

He rose with his drink. "Please consider the facilities of this house as yours to use at any time, including," he swept a hand towards the liquor cabinet, "the amenities." After pausing to regard each of them in turn, as if searching for a reaction to some hidden question, he said, "Come."

Val fell in line behind the others. The class followed the professor down a hallway to a windowless room of polished stone at the rear of the bungalow. The house was deceptively large.

The square classroom contained six chairs with lap desks, placed on circular daises raised a foot off the ground and arranged in a semicircle. The daises had no visible support. On top of each desk was a fountain pen and a cream-covered, unlined vellum notebook. Val chose a dais between Adaira and Dida.

The students faced a higher platform with a standing lectern. The professor floated up to his dais and set his drink in a cup holder, then placed his palms on the lectern. "I'll begin with an inquiry. What," he said, drawing out the pause, "is magic?"

Dida raised a hand. "The funneling of the unseen forces of the universe in order to achieve a wizard's purpose."

"Hand raising is unnecessary. Speak boldly and with command. And I did not ask for a definition of the result of the utilization of magic, I asked what *is* magic."

"Magic is spirit," Gowan said. "Power."

Gormloch smirked. "Obviously."

"Magic is here," Adaira said, touching her fingertips to her forehead. "The psionic signature. Studies have recently isolated the region of the brain kindled when magic is employed by the wizard born."

"A knowledgeable answer from our aspiring cuerpomancer," Gormloch said, which elicited almost as much interest as the pronouncement of Val's discipline. "And still incomplete. Please, let me know when you resolve this question, because we would all like to know. No one knows what magic is or why it only responds to the wizard born, why mages and magical creatures vary widely in strength, why some spells take far longer to master than others, or why some mages are better at creating wards, some are skilled at fire storms, and some have a facility for working with the dead. Magic," he looked down his nose again, "is magic.

"What we do know," the professor continued with a finger wag, "and what we are very, very good at, is how to harness and utilize this most powerful of forces."

He paused to take a drink. "In front of you is a notebook. As I am sure you know, though aids such as wizard stones have proven helpful to some, a mage does not need written words—or anything at all—to work magic. But most students find that note taking aids the learning process. Inscribe what worked for you and when. Ponder it when you return home at night. *Why* did a particular technique work? Did it feel natural? Can you replicate the feat?"

"Can we bring our notebooks into the discipline exam?" Val asked.

Gormloch leveled his gaze. "Will you consult your notebook when falling from an airship during the flight test? Battling a spirit elemental during a challenge exam? Or after graduation, when you are assigned to the border for your apprenticeship and a Battle Mage from the Kingdom of the Mayans attempts to rip your heart from your chest?"

A snicker rippled through the room. Val was unperturbed. In his mind the question had been valid, and the opinion of others had never mattered to him. "Duly noted."

"Are we allowed to bring our wizard stone to class?" Xavier asked.

"So sure of our discipline, are we?" the professor asked. "We do not allow physical aids until your second year. A wizard stone should not be a crutch."

The professor waited to see if there were any more questions, then spread his hands. "Please, raise your concerns at any time. I will rebuff them in kind. Now, shall we begin the lesson?"

The light from the four glow orbs dimmed and then extinguished, casting the room into darkness.

"Riga," the professor said, "create light, please."

After a prolonged period of silence, the room remained dark.

"I cannot," Riga said, embarrassed.

"Gowan?"

Again nothing. After a few more moments, the professor called on Xavier and Dida and then Adaira, all with the same result.

"Val?"

Val had already risen and felt his way to the door. When the professor called his name, Val opened the door and allowed light to flood through from the hallway.

Adaira laughed and then covered her mouth with her hand.

Gormloch re-illuminated the glow orbs, then shut the door with his mind. Val expected to be chastised, but was surprised when Gormloch murmured, "Well done," and flicked a wrist for Val to return to his seat.

The professor swept his gaze across the semicircle. "Two very important lessons. One is the first law of magic: one cannot create something out of nothing. You were all focused on reigniting the glow orbs, but not enough light remained in the room. A high level spirit mage can extract light from darkness, but that is far beyond the purview of this class."

"The second lesson," Gormloch continued, "is not to forget that you have a brain. Wizards weaken. Wizards face situations requiring wisdom and common sense. Wizards are mortal. *Never forget.*"

He paced back and forth on his floating platform, the size of a round dinner table. "We will spend the rest of the morning perfecting Light, the most basic of spells. Unlike your discipline deans, I've yet to judge your strengths. One by one, I'd like to see you use the illumination from the glow orbs to flare the room with light, bring it into near-darkness, then return the illumination to the proper level. Xavier, please begin."

The light in the room wavered and then slowly increased, until Val had to shield his eyes. It took Xavier five seconds to dim it, and the light source wobbled as he worked to bring it back to the original level.

Gormloch gave no indication of judgment. "Riga?"

The kethropi woman performed marginally better than Xavier.

"Gowan?"

The pyromancer waved a hand in a contemptuous gesture, and the light flared so bright Val had to shut his eyes. When he opened them, the room was almost completely dark, and a moment later it returned to the same brightness in which it had begun.

"Adaira?"

Without twitching, Adaira matched the speed and precision of Gowan's Light spell. Dida did the same.

"Val?"

Had Gormloch proceeded in order of perceived strength, Val wondered? If so, he was about to be sorely disappointed.

Since the first name had been called, Val had been concentrating on accessing his magic. A trickle of sweat already rolled down his forehead. Focusing on the wall behind the professor, Val blotted out the room and reached deep inside. When he found the wellspring of magic, that mental state he could now slip into like inserting a key into a door, he tried to seize the light from the glow orbs and increase it.

The light in the room flickered but remained at the same level. Val pushed harder, knowing force wasn't the right tool but not knowing what else to do. The trickle of sweat increased, stinging his eyes.

"Think of the tiny motes of light," Gormloch murmured. In the back of his mind, Val wondered how this world knew about motes.

His metaphorical key kept slipping inside the keyhole, as if the hole were too big. He tried to do as Gormloch said, imagining the light in the room as tiny particles of light and brightening them.

The light increased.

"More," the professor commanded.

Val lost concentration, and the light dimmed. Face flushed, he worked to recover, trying to compartmentalize the concentration needed to reach the magic while at the same time flaring the light.

It worked. The light increased.

"De-illuminate," Gormloch said. "Shrink the motes."

Val focused his will and tried to dim the glow orbs. Instead of a decrease in light, they extinguished.

Someone snickered. Val thought it was Gowan.

The professor reignited the glow orbs, and Val wiped his brow.

"Again," Gormloch said.

He said it many, many times.

Basics of Wizardry ended at one in the afternoon, after three hours of intense mental concentration far more taxing than any law school class. They had practiced the basic light spell for the entire period, working on refining the brightness, controlling the expansion of the light within different areas of the room, splitting the light source into separate factions, and creating spherical balls of light beyond Val's ability. He understood the concept, though—using his will to refine and shape the particles of light into usable objects—and he vowed to practice relentlessly. Not only did he hate failure, but increasing his skills would help him survive.

He also reminded himself that he didn't have to finish the semester—he just had to find a way to access the Pool of Souls and find his brothers.

It was all so confusing, exhilarating, and terrifying. What was the nature of this otherworldly thing inside him? Did the magic really stem from his psionic signature? And what did that *mean*?

It was real, at least—that he knew for sure.

Real and powerful.

*   *   *

Though the students were free to do as they wished before the two o'clock class, all six students in Val's coterie elected to have lunch on the rooftop patio of the cottage. Each coterie was assigned a personal chef, and the cottage also had wash facilities, a study room, bedrooms for overnight stays, and a private garden.

They sat on cushions around a low table as they waited for their food, cradled by tropical foliage, breathing in jasmine and gardenia, eyes raised to admire the vista of colored spires rising all around. A few hundred yards away, just over the top of the wall protecting the Wizard District, Val spotted the indolent curve of the river, winding alongside the Goblin Market.

Xavier slumped into the cushions, interlacing his hands behind his head. He looked as exhausted as Val felt. "If we're going to be classmates," Xavier said, "we might as well get to know each other." He turned to Dida. "I confess I've never met an African wizard—" he pronounced the last two words in the precise diction and supercilious tone used by Professor Gormloch, eliciting chuckles—"in person. You are African, I take it?"

"I am indeed, though Africa is a very large place. I hail from the Kingdom of Great Zimbabwe." He tipped his bald head and raised it back up, an easy grin in place. "It is an honor to study with my fellow students at the world-renowned Abbey of New Victoria."

"Your discipline?" Riga asked. Her voice was a spool of silk reeled from the back of her throat, somehow both rough and smooth.

"Though most of the wizards in my kingdom are geomancers who work with the stones and soils native to our land," Dida said, "I have chosen to study the art of bibliomancy."

He flashed a wide smile, as if expecting everyone to clap. Instead, they all regarded him with a blank stare.

"Ah, yes. I see the discipline is unfamiliar to you. Bibliomancy is the art of inscribing magic into words and runes."

"A warder," Gowan said. "That's what we call it."

"Warding is important to my art, but bibliomancy involves others skills, such as rune translation and inscription, divination through characters, and scroll working. It is more popular, I believe, in old Albion."

Gowan did not look impressed. "I didn't see that elective offered. What about your core discipline?"

"I'm here as an exchange student, so am not required to choose a discipline. In fact, I lack only the completion of this year abroad, and my final exam."

Gowan looked ready to say something, then closed his mouth, as if cowed by the revelation that Dida was almost a full-fledged wizard.

Interesting, Val thought, *that he's so humble. Maybe wizards aren't all the same.*

"And I think we all know who you are, my dear," Xavier said in a respectful voice to Adaira. "Though I didn't realize you had chosen cuerpomancy. Very impressive."

I don't know who you are, Val wanted to say. *But I'd like to know why those two majitsu in the garden won't let you out of their sight.*

"My mother was a cuerpomancer," Adaira said with a soft smile. "I'd like to continue the tradition." She turned to Riga. "An aquamancer, I assume?"

Riga placed webbed hands on the table and regarded her with those frank and lidless eyes. "Like Dida, I come as an ambassador for my homeland, to facilitate the relationship between our races. Unlike him, I am just beginning my cross-discipline studies."

"And if you don't mind, how is it that you can," Adaira gestured with her palms and smiled, "survive so long outside water?"

"I have a magical endowment in place." Riga did not look offended by the question, though it was clear from her tone that further explanation would not be forthcoming.

Before anyone could ask Gowan about his background, his eyes slid away from Val and then the rest of the group, and he muttered "pyromancer" as if embarrassed by his choice.

Adaira turned to Val. "I've never encountered your accent before. From where do you hail?"

"From the North," he said. "The far north."

"Outside the Protectorate?" she asked.

"Yes."

She looked him in the eye as she brushed back a strand of hair the breeze had tossed in her face. "Interesting."

It was the kind of *interesting* that Val recognized as coming from someone who had been sheltered all her life, and longed to know more of the world. He wished lunch would hurry up and arrive. He would have looked for food somewhere else, but Gus wasn't due to return until the end of the day, and Val wouldn't have known where to go.

"A real live spirit mage acolyte," Xavier said, in an awed voice. "I hear there're only six spiritmancy students in the whole school. How did you . . . ."

He trailed off, but Val knew what he was about to say. So did Gowan, who was staring at Val with undisguised jealousy, and a touch of contempt. "What he meant," the pyromancer said, "was how did you pass the entrance exam if you can barely work with light?"

Val didn't care for Gowan's tone, but he swallowed his retort, along with his pride. He didn't need enemies. Plus, the question was valid. "I'm not quite sure."

"You must have lifted the block," Dida marveled. "I couldn't budge it."

"No one lifts the block," Gowan said. "It's a trick. It's supposed to break your will for the next two tests."

Val didn't say anything.

"Did you move the block?" Adaira asked, leaning forward in her chair. The fidgeting around the table had ceased.

Val's wheels were spinning, dissecting the angles, but he saw no reason to lie. They already knew he had passed the test. "My power increases when I get upset. I'm not sure why."

There was a prolonged silence, and then Dida slapped him on the back. "Remind me never to approach you in anger, my friend!"

The others chuckled, until Gowan said, "Especially on the Arch Bridge."

Eyes lowered. The laughter died.

"Not amusing," Adaira said.

The chef arrived with the meal, a platter of chicken and rice stewed in spiced banana leaves. He ladled out portions in silence.

"I don't understand," Riga said.

The others exchanged a glance, and Xavier said, "An Abbey student was murdered last night, on the Arch Bridge. His throat was slit with a knife."

"Which is why the majitsu are standing guard," Val murmured.

Gowan barked a laugh. "No murderer would dare step foot inside the

Wizard District. The majitsu are for her." He jerked his thumb at Adaira, who looked embarrassed. "Lord Alistair is her father."

Val gave a brief nod, as if the revelation didn't surprise him, but he felt his pulse quicken at the knowledge that he had landed in the same coterie as the daughter of the Chief Thaumaturge. *Way to lay low, Val.*

He could also tell, judging by the uneasy expressions on everyone's face, that there was more to the story of the murdered acolyte.

"He was the second victim this week," Gowan continued. "Both were first year students. Both had their throats slit."

-24-

As Farzal and his lieutenants stepped into the funicular, an imposing delver with a braided, navel-length beard herded the captives down the staircase on the right. Funnel-shaped clouds of smoke drifted upwards from various sections of Fellengard, disappearing into the darkness above. Smithies and primitive industry, Will assumed.

They caught glimpses of the city as they descended for a thousand feet to the floor: a stippled skyline of ornate stone buildings, a trio of aquamarine lakes with canals branching outward like spokes on a wheel, plazas made of inlaid gemstones and adorned with statues and fountains. Smokestacks and crenellated guard towers rose at various intervals throughout the city, and hundreds of winch and chain funiculars ringed the perimeter, depositing delvers at the entrance to tunnels or dwellings that honeycombed the cave walls. The dwellings ranged from barracks to living flats to elaborate stone mansions near the base of the wall.

Seeing the full might of the underground city sparked Will's imagination, but also incinerated his hopes. Even if they escaped the mines, which he imagined was some version of hell, how could they possibly get through this fortress of a city unnoticed, and then navigate the Darklands by themselves?

"*Lucka*, we'll never get out of here," Dalen muttered, echoing Will's sentiment.

Yasmina was slumped across Marek's shoulders. Caleb looked so despondent that Will worried if they weren't chained together, he might step off the staircase and let himself fall.

When they reached the bottom, the odors of smoke and limestone were replaced by the smell of spicy charred meat from street vendors and the salty tang of sweating workers. Pedestrians and stone-wheeled steam carriages on grooved tracks moved about the city in orderly fashion.

Instead of entering the city proper, the delver guards took the prisoners on a perimeter road made of blue marble. No one gave them a second glance. An hour later, on the opposite side of the cavern, they reached an enormous funicular set on four rails. A guard tower loomed over the machine.

The delvers herded the prisoners onto the funicular. It rumbled to life, and they descended for so long Will guessed they were now deeper than when they had begun the ascent to Fellengard. With the prisoners pressed against the side railing to absorb the view, the funicular finally came to a stop in a ruined city in another bowl-shaped cavern, vast but smaller than the one above. Instead of the wide boulevards of Fellengard, high granite walls and sinuous alleys dissected neighborhoods of rough-hewn stone, and the buildings were two and three stories high instead of six and seven. It looked as if some great battle had once taken place, because the walls and buildings were crumbling and pockmarked by jagged holes. Now and then Will saw a giant heap of coagulated stone, as if melted by a powerful fire.

The funicular came to rest next to a guard station. A sign carved into the wall read *Olde Fellengard*, and above it was another phrase written in unfamiliar script. The delver language, Will assumed.

The station exited onto a large courtyard lit by mineral lamps. Guards, prisoners, and workers crisscrossed the open space. Will spotted two more vertical trams on the periphery, and while their group waited at the station for the delver guards to fill out scrollwork, another group of chained humans ascended into Olde Fellengard on a funicular, from somewhere below the city.

Not just *somewhere*, Will thought, taking in the filthy appearance and glazed eyes of the new arrivals.

The mines.

*   *   *

A short time later, Will's posse of prisoners was shepherded into the court-yard, unchained at the waists, and grouped into fours. Will, Caleb, Dalen, and Marek were placed together. Yasmina was carried off by a delver.

"Where're you taking her?" Caleb shouted.

"To the infirmary," the delver said with a smirk.

Will didn't like the ominous implications of his tone, but there was nothing they could do. He could only pray Yasmina would receive some type of medical care.

Another delver led the four of them down a curving street to a circular courtyard with a gaping hole in the middle. The courtyard was lined with delver dwellings converted into cells, and a guard shoved Will and his companions into a barred enclosure the size of a small garage. It contained four straw mats and a bucket. The only illumination came from a mineral lamp hanging near the center of the courtyard, emitting an olive-green light so dim Will could barely see inside the cell.

The delver locked them inside without a word. After he left, Will placed his hands on the bars and tried to shake them.

Solid as the mountain itself.

"Well," Caleb said, "this is fun."

Marek eyed Will warily from the corner. Will went over and offered his hand. "Thanks for helping with Yasmina."

Marek ignored his gesture. After testing the solidity of the wall at various points, the large man slumped with his back against the wall. Dalen did the same.

Will searched deep for words of encouragement to offer his companions, but found he had nothing to say.

The delver took Yasmina five streets away, to a low rectangular building stuffed with narrow cots. Though conscious, her mind was imprisoned in a dreamlike state. The outside world felt very far away, on the other side of a one-way mirror. She barely registered the smell of urine and death in the room, the dozens of prostrate forms lying on cots, the lack of any equipment resembling medical care, or the groping hands of the delver guard.

*   *   *

Will had no idea if it was day or night. The constant, disorienting glow of the mineral lamps added to the feeling of being trapped in a nightmare phosphorescent twilight.

Not a *feeling* of being trapped, he corrected. A reality.

At some point, a delver guard led two women in chains and tattered clothing into the courtyard. Heads bowed, the women shuffled around the courtyard passing out food and jugs of water to the cell blocks, then emptied the prisoners' waste buckets in the hole next to the mineral lamp.

Dinner consisted of bread, mushrooms, and a nutty gruel. At least there was plenty of it; Will assumed they wanted the prisoners to have energy to work the mines. Despite the foulness of the meal, Will shoveled it down, and made sure Caleb and Dalen did the same. Marek didn't need any urging.

After dinner, Will lay on his side on his smelly mat, trying not to think about how far underground they were, or the bedbugs he felt crawling through the straw, or the rats he heard scuttling through the courtyard, or the cold black tunnel his future had become.

The next morning all the prisoners in the courtyard were chained in a line and marched through Old Fellengard, to a section of the city reduced to rubble. Along the way, they passed three more funicular stations and dozens of plazas lined with cellblocks. How many prisoners were down there, Will wondered? How many mines?

Down they went on a new funicular, squeezing through a narrow shaft for what seemed like miles. At last they creaked to a halt, entering a cavern far different from the grimy coal mine Will had expected.

A grotto of ethereal beauty stretched before them, filled with giant crystal shards as thick as Will and three times as tall, jutting out of the floor and ceiling and walls at crazy angles. They picked their way a few hundred yards through the jumble of quartz behemoths, then passed into an even more stunning cavern.

Formed out of some translucent mineral, the floor was a mantle of blue glass, the ceiling carved by nature into whorls that curved downward to merge with the maze of pillars and grottoes forming the interior of the cavern. He thought it looked like something created by CGI for a fantasy video game. Except, that was, for the harsh reality of the pick axes hanging near the entrance, the delver guards grasping three-pronged scourges, and the group of prisoners hacking away at one of the blue pillars.

"Shift's over!" roared one of the delvers. After filling the mine carts behind them with broken pieces of blue mineral, the prisoners stumbled to the wall and replaced their picks. Will noticed women and a few different races sprinkled among the captives.

No instructions were given, though some of the prisoners in Will's group looked experienced. Scrambling at the crack of a delver whip, Will and Caleb grabbed pick axes and started hacking at the same pillar as the previous miners.

Will ended up between Caleb and a tall man with broad shoulders and a gaunt frame, his long blond hair tied in a ponytail. Will could tell he had once been imposing. Unlike most of the prisoners, he held his head high and didn't act as if he would never see daylight again.

Well into the day's labor, when Caleb and Dalen could barely lift their picks and Will's arms ached from wrist to shoulder, he risked addressing his neighbor. The guards kept to the rear of the room and didn't seem to mind conversation, unless it interfered with the work.

"What's your name?" Will asked.

Startled Will had spoken, the man regarded him with a grim expression. "Tamás. Of the Mirgath Clan. And you, my friend?"

"Will Blackwood." He saw no harm in revealing his name. As if it would matter down here. He jerked his head to the left. "That's my brother, Caleb."

The man stared at him. "Blackwood? You're Romani?"

"Apparently." It was the first time Will had heard the term *Romani* used, and he wondered why Mala had always referred to herself as a gypsy.

"From where do you come?"

"The far North," Will said, playing along. "We were taken on our way to New Victoria."

Tamás nodded, and Will breathed a sigh of relief. He had been practicing the local accent so he could blend, and Tamás hadn't seemed to notice. It was easier in this world, he suspected, because of the lack of transport and global connections. Who knew how a villager from "the far north" would talk?

"Why New Victoria?" Tamás asked.

"We have another brother. We're trying to find him."

"I wish you success," he said, though even Tamás's confident voice bore a trace of despair. "And how is it in the North for our people? Genocide as well?"

Will paused a beat, earning a crack of a whip.

Tamás caught the confusion in his eye. "You haven't heard? I feared as much. The wizards run a fine propaganda campaign. Death squads and Inquisitors patrol the Ninth, under the pretext of searching for followers of Devla, but exterminating any of our people they encounter. And not just us—all freeholders who refuse to take the Oaths. I'm certain they're preparing the Ninth for settlement." He frowned at the pick in his hands. "With help from us."

"I don't follow," Will said.

Sweat dripped from Tamás's brow as his shoulders heaved with effort. "This blue mineral is tilectium. The wizards adapt it for use in their personal flying carriages. Gathering tilectium in this quantity . . . they've something nefarious in mind, rest assured."

"But why bother with secrecy or a propaganda campaign?" Will asked. "Who's going to stand up to them?"

"'Tis true," Tamás said, "that the Revolution was never much of a threat. But we've no choice. The Devla uprising has angered the Congregation, in the manner that a bee sting angers a cloud giant, and Lord Alistair is unlike his predecessors. He makes the steam carts run on time, as the delvers say, but there is no tolerance within his bones. The only check to his power is the perception of the people. Though the wizards don't need the common born to win a war, where would the Congregation be without its tax base, its laborers, its servants? Most common born have no love for our people, but outright genocide might not sit well."

"So he does it on the sly," Will murmured, remembering the bodies of the villagers stacked like firewood they had seen on the journey. "Like Hitler at first."

"Who?"

"No one," Will muttered.

Tamás's eyes lit with a feverish glow. "It's not just about settlement. It's the return of an *idea* he fears, Will Blackwood. Impotent the Devla uprising may be, but were it to spread outside the Romani, then who knows what might result?"

"Then the wizards would just kill everyone," Will said, "and bring in some common born from somewhere else to do their bidding."

Caleb chuckled. "Ever the sword of logic, brother mine," he said, wheezing his words out.

"Just calling it like I see it," Will said.

"You're not wrong," Tamás said, dropping his gaze and striking the tilectium with a defeated swing of the pick. "Opposing the wizards is foolish. The likely outcome is that Alistair will have his way, our people will perish in the Fens, and he will swallow the Ninth and turn his ambitions across the borders. A man such as he will never be satisfied."

"Maybe they'll surprise you," Will said.

"Who?"

"The leaders of the Revolution. Maybe they have something in mind you don't know about."

"The sentiment is a kind one," Tamás said, lowering his voice, "but I believe I would know of such a plan. Until my arrival in these accursed mines a year ago, I *was* the leader of the Revolution."

Will forced himself not to show surprise. The guards were watching. "Then why are you still alive?" he whispered. "They don't know who you are?"

Tamás shook his head. "True to form, they see only wizards as a threat."

Long hours later, after Will's muscles had turned to slush and blisters had formed on his hands, a new crop of prisoners arrived by funicular, and the delvers ordered Will's group to stop. He lowered his pick, watching Caleb's slumped form with worried eyes.

"I was brought here with my brother as well," Tamás said, leaning on his pick and flicking his eyes at Caleb. He dropped his voice so only Will could hear, the sadness of his next words radiating outwards. "He died last month."

Will balled his fists and let out a slow breath. "We have a friend they took to the infirmary when we arrived. What do you know about that?"

"The infirmary?" Tamás's smile was grim. "No such place exists. There is merely a room where the delvers wait to see if the sick are going to live or die."

-25-

Traveling on the currents of the night, the thing known as a Spirit Liege briefly pondered its existence, shadowy images of the man it used to be flickering in the synapses of its mind like an unremembered dream. As did memories of the terrible experiments that had broken that man.

It no longer knew what it was. It only knew that it had emerged in its present incarnation in a castle in the sky less than a day ago, and that it was called a Spirit Liege. That, and it knew the nature of its mission.

Find the sword born of spirit.

Kill whoever wields it.

Bring the weapon to Lord Alistair.

It would have to be careful, though. Both the wielder and the weapon handled with the utmost of care. For the sword born of spirit, the Spirit Liege had been told, was one of the few things on Urfe that could destroy it.

The Spirit Liege alighted outside Zedock's swamp citadel in the middle of the night. Drifted through the heavy curtain of air that it could no longer feel.

It could feel currents of energy, psionic signatures, astral winds, magical vibrations.

But not warmth or morning dew, pain or pleasure, the stinging slap of an icy day.

It flowed into the bottom level of the obelisk. The ghost knight guarding the fortress descended the spiral staircase, regarded the intruder with the silence of the damned, and then clanked away.

The Spirit Liege floated back and forth over the bottom level. Near the base of the stairs, it found the residual psionic signatures of the two men who had died there—one a necromancer, one a much less potent wielder of magic. Scattered throughout the room, it could also sense the faint and non-magical energies of three more humans. Even more indistinct, so old as to be useless but infusing the obelisk like a rag soaked in blood, it sensed the charred aura of death. Death and suffering.

And finally, entangled within the energy lines of one of the humans, was the magical residue which the Spirit Liege sought: the sword born of spirit.

Unlike the energy traces left by the humans, or even the two wizard born, the scent of the sword saturated the essence of the Spirit Liege as would the scent of fresh meat to a canine.

As it absorbed and catalogued the residual energy of the sword, the Spirit Liege had the thought that whatever its masters had created it to be, it and the sword were kindred things.

It followed the trail of magical currents through the swamp. Often the path would disappear, because that was the nature of residual magical energy, but the Spirit Liege would search in a wide perimeter until it resumed once again.

The trail led to a boat by the fen where the three humans had lingered, on into the marsh forest, and then to the remains of a campsite, where the humans were joined by the energies of dozens of beings. The Spirit Liege did not know this new scent. It just knew that it was not magical and it was not human.

The three humans comingled with others, confusing the Liege. It could no longer distinguish the individual human energies. But the scent of the sword was as strong as ever. Over the course of the next week, it followed the magic out of the swamplands and onto the plains, into the hills of trollkind, and all the way to a collection of fantastical rock outcroppings at the base of a mountain range.

And then, perhaps blocked by the towering mass of granite stretching to the horizon, the heady fragrance of powerful eldritch magic—the sword born of spirit—disappeared.

The eyes of the Spirit Liege glowed white in the darkness.

-26-

For his History and Governance class, Val returned to a small auditorium in the main building. Rows of cushioned chairs faced a central dais, and students from multiple coteries filled the room. Val was relieved beyond measure to be a face in the crowd.

Slipping into the back row, he squeezed between an older woman smothered in diamond jewelry and a muscular blond man draped in furs and wearing a golden helm. The professor was a pale sorceress with dark hair piled in a bun, wearing a gray robe with the traditional stole. She first gave an eloquent spiel about how wizards were the chosen ones, the cream of humanity's crop. How they were different from the common born and had a duty to uphold the Congregation's standards and ideals.

After conditioning the students for leadership, she ran through the principal duties of a wizard: governing their estates and serving the Congregation, honing their craft, providing certain services to the public, developing new magic-driven technologies.

The professor then set forth a fascinating overview of the early history of the Congregation. After describing the formative years during the Age of Sorrow and the Pagan Wars, she moved on to the first epoch of wizard rule.

Val took notes along with the other students. After the lecture had finished, during his thirty minute break, he sat near the stone fountain and highlighted the salient points in his notebook.

The Realm (British Empire) began in Year I, when the native peoples of Albion (England), led by the wild mages that roamed the island's forests, repulsed the invading Romans.

At this stage of history, wizards were a reclusive and fractionalized group.

The first King of the Realm was a druid warrior-priest (mage?)

called Taranis. The indigenous wizards refused to bow to the druid theocracy.

P.R. (Post-Realm) 105: with the help of foreign mercenary wizards, namely the Dragon Mages in service to the Hong Bàng Dynasty (which the Congregation has never forgiven), King Taranis and his druids staged an assault on the newly formed wizard council, slaughtering the entire leadership.

This initiated the Age of Sorrow. The druid warrior-priests whipped public hatred of wizards into a frenzy, and for the next thousand years, wizards were labeled heretics, marginalized, and banned from practicing secular magic.

P.R. 1175: in response to a new druid policy limiting wizard families to one child, a revolutionary group of mages called the Conclave was formed.

In response to the guerrilla acts of the Conclave, the Druid King waged a genocidal war on the remaining wizard families, slaughtering thousands.

With their numbers dwindling, the pockets of renegade mages scattered about the Realm joined with the Conclave to form a united front.

Under the leadership of Myrddin the Defender, the so-called Pagan Wars ended with a decisive victory by the Conclave in 1201, at the battle of Londyn, where a gathering of three hundred Conclave wizards defeated a force of over sixty thousand soldiers and druid warrior-priests, as well as a regiment of Dragon Mages.

After the Pagan Wars, in defiance of their former oppressors, the Conclave adopted the name The Congregation. The Conclave became the name for the leadership council within the Congregation.

The wizards allowed the Albion monarchy to remain in name alone. After the Pagan Wars, true power = wizards.

After that, the lecturer had droned on about the First Epoch and how the

Congregation had vastly improved society. Val had taken only a few more notes.

P.R. 1225: York School of Wizardry established, core wizard disciplines defined.

P.R. 1363: separatist movement of Scottish Cloud Mages crushed by Congregation. Remaining Gaelic peoples absorbed into Realm.

P.R. 1441-1449: the Teutates Rebellion, a religious uprising led by the remaining druids, roamed the countryside decrying Congregation rule, drowning non-believers in giant vats of acid.

P.R. 1450: After crushing the Teutates Rebellion, the Congregation outlawed organized religion and prohibited public worship of deities. Similar anti-religion revolts followed in other countries, mainly in the West. Theocratic castes of priest-magicians still rule most of the East, including Egypt and the Bharat Empire (India).

P.R. 1475—1850: Age of Expansion (read: the Congregation flexes its colonial muscle and kicks the crap out of Gauls, Romans, Iberians).

P.R. 1492 (eerie parallel): Discovery of New Albion by the aquamancer Grinaldus.

P.R. 1620: New Victoria established. Eventually becomes wizard power center and de facto capital of the Realm, though Londyn remains capital in name.

Queen Victoria, not just a rare wizard-born monarch but an arch-mage aeromancer, consolidated the wizards and the monarchy by joining the Congregation, ushering in the Golden Age of the Realm (which we're still in).

Note: P.R. 1981 = Present Day (36 years behind Earth, if meaningful).

A bell chimed, and Val closed his notebook. With a deep breath, he rose and tried to prepare himself for the gauntlet he knew awaited.

The time for his first spiritmancy class had arrived.

*   *   *

Most of the discipline classes were held in the main building, known as the Manor. But according to Val's registration scroll, Spiritmancy 101 was held in the Observatory. He followed the signposts through the foliage until he came to a bluish-white, star-shaped building with a domed rotunda tucked into a cul de sac. Val gaped; unless he was mistaken, the outer layer of the structure was azantite.

As he circled the building, looking for an entrance, he saw a cloaked man and then a woman with flowing silver hair fly over the foliage and disappear into the top of the thirty-foot rotunda.

The other two students, Val assumed. Using the only available entrance.

Great way to start.

He stood with his arms crossed outside the Observatory, trying to decide what to do. Was this a test? Had he failed before class had even begun?

Before he could decide on a course of action, someone unseen lifted him into the air and levitated him towards the top of the rotunda. At first he flailed, but then he gave in, realizing someone was floating him into the building. He rose to the top and dropped through a wizard chute, coming gently to rest on a circular, blue-white dais inside a rounded chamber made of black marble streaked with silver. Five wide archways led to the wings of the building. Silver glow orbs provided illumination.

Ten more suspension discs peppered the room, two feet wide and suspended three feet off the floor. The black-walled room gave the effect of floating in a void.

"I was informed you did not have full awareness of your abilities, *neh*, but they did not tell me you are unable to *fly*."

Val turned towards the speaker, a striking older woman with coppery skin standing on a larger dais. She had lustrous, waist-length black hair and intense blue eyes that sparkled like diamonds.

He remained silent and stole a glance at the other two students. To his left was a very pale and stern young man, wearing glasses and a black tailcoat. On the far right, an Amerindian woman with curved green eyes coolly met his gaze. She looked about Val's age and had silver hair that partially concealed a long vertical scar on the side of her face.

"I am Professor Azara," the older woman said, her accent an elegant lilt.

She clasped her hands and peered down her aquiline nose at her students. Val noticed her hands looked much older than her face.

"You are here," she said, "because your psionic signature is far greater than the average wizard. Not everyone with superior ability chooses to become a spirit mage, though in my opinion—" she smirked "—they have chosen poorly. Who would relinquish the opportunity to explore the outer boundaries of magic and reality, the nature of the multiverse?"

Val wondered if Alrick and the other phrenomancers would have something to say in response to that. *They seem to have explored some pretty wild places themselves.*

The room had the odorless hush of a museum. Professor Azara continued, "You are extremely privileged to have been chosen, *lah*, yet your innate abilities are only the beginning. To complete the Planewalk and reach the level of a spirit mage adept, you must possess far, far more than an elevated psionic signature. You will need fortitude. Physical and mental stamina. Invention. Imagination. Cleverness. Courage. Willpower almost beyond comprehension. And, most of all," she pressed her hands to her heart, "you will need desire. An overwhelming urge to succeed."

At least I have something going for myself, Val thought.

Her hands dropped, and her expression turned grave. "Spiritmancy is the rarest of disciplines not just because of the immense power it requires of its adepts, but because of the dangers." Val's eyebrows rose as streaks of black energy crackled at her fingertips. The energy flared, running up and down her arms, lighting her face. During the display, Val felt as if he were moving towards Professor Azara, sucked in by her gaze.

"Test your boundaries," a voice whispered in his ear as the energy dissipated, "but know your limits, for power such as this can consume you."

"By the Queen," the female student murmured in an awed voice. "Actual spirit fire."

Professor Azara's gaze lasered onto her, a stare worthy of the sternest of ballet teachers. "Lydia, was there a question in your response?"

The Amerindian woman swallowed. "No."

"Then please keep your observations to yourself. I require—spiritmancy requires—utmost discipline and concentration. There is no time for frivolity."

So it's like that, Val thought.

"My apologies," Lydia said.

Professor Azara had already turned away. She tapped a manicured nail against the side of her head. "Unlike other disciplines, our power derives not from the seen, but from the unseen. The essence of the universe. The places in between. As the aquamancer utilizes water, the pyromancer fire, the geomancer stone—so we harness spirit."

Interesting, Val thought. *Is magic simply magic, or are spirit mages harnessing some kind of undiscovered energy source? Or is there a difference?*

He was frightened, but his skin tingled at the possibilities.

"One other thing of note. Since spiritmancy is far more difficult to master than the other disciplines, you might grow frustrated when the students in your coterie advance beyond you in practical application. Learn from them, study the common core, and rest assured that, should you reach the level of an adept, then your fellow students will watch in awe as you wield spirit fire, rip holes in space and time, walk the astral plane, and summon beings from other worlds to do your bidding."

Lydia's eyes widened, and an eager light crept into the gaze of the other male student.

"We shall begin with a basic spell, but one with a multitude of practical applications. Damon—" the other male student snapped to attention like a Marine—"are you able to create a Wizard Shield?"

"Of course," he said, narrowing his eyes in concentration.

Professor Azara drifted over to him, palms extended until they stopped a foot from his body, as if bumping against an invisible barrier. "Good," she murmured, pushing against the shield. "Lydia?"

Lydia did the same, also drawing praise.

"Val? I understand you've had no formal schooling."

Val looked her in the eye. "I don't know how to form a Wizard Shield."

The other two students looked disbelieving, and Professor Azara drifted closer. "Harden the air in front of you. Imagine it is dough, and you are kneading it with your mind, pressing it into shape."

Val focused his magic, then attempted what she said. He could feel the magic trying to congeal, but it felt watery, limp.

Professor Azara reached forward and touched him on the chest, pushing through his barrier.

"Force it to harden," she said, her voice sharp. "Bend it to your will."

Jaw tight, Val poured every ounce of effort into solidifying the air in front of him, congealing it into a tangible barrier. It was a strange concept to him, but he had seen its effects before, and knew it could work.

She pressed again. "Knead, Val. Tighter. Compress the air."

It cost him great effort, to the point where he felt as if he were about to pass out, but when Professor Azara reached for him, her hand slowed just before touching his chest, as if passing through molasses. "A beginning," she said, and he felt a rush of pride and relief. He released his will, grabbing the edge of the dais to stop himself from keeling over.

"Though common to all disciplines," Professor Azara said, drifting away, "the Wizard Shield is the closest most come to using spiritmancy. True, air is utilized instead of spirit, and requires less application of will, but air is also an unseen force. The principles used to collect and harden air are similar to those used to harness spirit. We just have to reach deeper." Her smile was cold. "*Much* deeper."

She continued, "Your lesson, until we meet again: practice your Wizard Shield until it is second nature, as impenetrable as you can achieve. Analyze the process, make note of your efforts. Once I am satisfied, *if* I am satisfied, we shall begin to summon spirit."

Val spent the next week working as hard as he had ever worked—just to keep his head above water.

In his common core class, they continued refining Light, as well as introducing spells in each of the four principal elements. For fire, they used Ignite and Firesphere. Earth was Dig and Shelter, air Wind Push and Wizard Shield. Lastly, for water, came Float and Purify.

Because Val was practicing Wizard Shield every night for his spiritmancy class, he surprised everyone by excelling at that spell. He made much slower progress with the others.

While Riga far surpassed the others when working with water, and Dida had a wholly foreign skill set, when it came to the common core Adaira and Gowan were the most advanced spell workers of the group. Still, at every turn, Val could feel the jealousy radiating off of Gowan, and guessed the budding pyromancer had wanted to become a spirit mage but failed to satisfy the entrance requirement.

Unsatisfied with the progress of her three students, Professor Azara spent the entire week making them practice their Wizard Shield. After each class, feeling as if he had run a marathon with his mind, Val had Gus drop him at Falrick's Folly for dinner. After a solid meal and a few drinks, Val would stumble to his quarters to practice his spells. Most nights he turned in after two a.m., rising at dawn to make class on time. Though brutal, it was a lifestyle to which he was accustomed.

Refining Wizard Shield taught him a few lessons about the limits of magic, and he was beginning to get a handle on the energy cost of each spell. Wizard Shield was most effective in a limited space that the mage could see. Akin to using an actual shield. Much stronger and more experienced mages could wrap a Wizard Shield around their bodies, but even then, holding any version of the spell for longer than a moment was draining. Which made it great for stopping a quick attack, but far from a defensive magic bullet.

Nor could a mage cast anything else while using Wizard Shield. If Val wanted a practical tool for battle, he realized he would have to learn to employ his shield at a moment's notice—which advanced wizards seemed able to do.

Light, on the other hand, was simple to maintain. One could also cast Light as a flare, allowing the motes to slowly dissolve while moving on to cast another spell.

Like the ogre-mage had done, he thought with a shudder.

He tried without success to engage Lydia and Damon in conversation. This frustrated Val, as he wanted to probe their knowledge of the Planewalk.

Though pleasant enough, Lydia always seemed in a rush. Damon clearly considered talking to Val a waste of his time, and didn't bother hiding it. Spirit mages were supposed to focus on public service as well as wizardry, the "stewards" of the mage world, but Val recognized the signs of a good Washington power broker in Damon and even Lydia: present a civil face to the world, but do whatever it takes to get ahead.

At the end of the week, near the end of spiritmancy class, Professor Azara cocked her head as if listening to someone in her mind, then announced that all students must report to the Lyceum immediately after class.

Puzzled, Val wanted to follow Lydia and Damon, but they flew off without him. He had to suffer the daily embarrassment of allowing Professor Azara to lift him out of the Observatory. He got the sense that everyone in the Academy, especially budding spirit mages, had arrived knowing the basics of flight. As soon as he got to know one of the other students better, he planned to ask someone to teach him. He didn't want to kill himself trying to learn on his own.

He hurried back to the Manor and slipped into the rear of the packed Lyceum, where he found Adaira and Dida beckoning to him. Val waded through the crowd and slipped in between them.

"What's going on?" he asked. "It looks like the whole school is here."

"No one knows," Adaira said, craning her neck towards an empty dais at the rear of the hall.

"Perhaps they will announce a holiday," Dida said, looking as tired as Val felt. "I've never experienced a week so difficult."

Adaira brushed back a strand of hair. "That's the one thing I know they won't do."

Val was sure Lord Alistair knew what was happening, but he also knew Adaira was independent enough not to run and ask daddy.

The crowd quieted as a woman swooped into the room between two pillars, arcing above the crowd before she alighted on the dais. It was the dark-haired woman who had administered the entrance exam, still wearing a crimson robe and platinum circlet in her hair.

"Dean Varen," Adaira whispered. "Pyromancer."

"I'm afraid to report," Dean Varen said, pausing to sweep her gaze across the crowd, "that another Acolyte has been murdered."

-27-

A week after their arrival in the mines, Caleb and Will and Dalen lay on their backs in their cell, exhausted from their labors. Fine-boned by nature, Caleb looked emaciated, and Will was relieved he had lasted this long without collapsing. Caleb and manual labor went together like pork ribs and tofu.

Dalen was juggling balls of light above his head. He always practiced his magic after the last guard run.

Marek sat cross-legged by the bars, taciturn as always. So far, he had refused to speak.

"We have to think of something," Will said.

Caleb turned on his side to face him. "Eh?"

"A way to escape."

"I don't want to die here, little bro, but this place makes Alcatraz look like a Lego jail."

"I refuse to pry rocks out of a wall until I die," Will said. "I'd rather take my chances with the Darklands."

"*Lucka*, you wouldn't last a day," Dalen said. "There're things in the Darklands—"

Will waved a hand in irritation. "Yeah, yeah, you've told us over and over how terrifying it is, and I'm sure you're right. You know what I find more terrifying? Dying a slow death as a slave for the delvers."

"What do we do?" Caleb asked quietly. "Even if we manage to leave this cell, how do we find Yasmina and get past the guards? Out of the city?"

Will stood and began to pace. "I don't know. Dalen, do you have any other tricks up your sleeve?"

The colored balls disappeared, and Dalen rose to a sitting position. "There are too many guards. I can fool one or two, but not a whole city. *Aike*. If only I was stronger, knew more spells."

Will stopped beside Marek. "What about you? Any ideas?"

Marek's head tilted on a slow axis to face Will. He smirked and returned facing the courtyard.

"Just checking," Will muttered.

He kept pacing and trying to analyze the possible angles of escape. Despite his efforts, he failed to produce a single idea. Security was too tight, the situation too hopeless. If Tamás—the leader of the revolution—hadn't been able to escape after a year, what chance did they have?

Still, he knew that loss of hope equated to death. They had to keep watching, keep striving, keep believing.

He reached the end of the cell. When he turned, he saw Marek crouched in front of him, hands up and fingers twitching, as if ready to attack. "You vant to do something?" he said, stalking towards Will. His accent sounded Slavic. "Then stay prepared for vhen your time comes."

He rushed Will, this time on guard against a cheap shot, catching Will around the waist and tackling him. Caleb rose to help his brother, but Marek pushed him down as if he were a twig figure.

Marek ended up straddling Will's chest. Will executed a maneuver Mala had taught him, trapping Marek's left leg and arm and tossing him sideways. Each of them scrambled for position, ending up with their arms locked together in front of them, holding each other at bay.

The big man grinned. "That's good."

Dalen and Caleb started towards them. "It's okay, guys," Will said, trying and failing to trip Marek, instead landing with an *oomph* on his back as Marek threw him to the ground. The man was *strong*.

Marek offered to help Will to his feet, and he accepted.

"Again?" Marek asked, breathing hard as he crouched into position.

Will crouched as well, adapting his old wrestling stance to the tighter street-fighting position Mala had taught him, in order to protect his vitals. "Oh yeah."

Yasmina felt hands on her body. Calloused palms roamed her thighs, strong fingers pressed into her stomach and then higher. She moaned and tried to thrash, but couldn't find the strength.

Was she dreaming?

As she drifted in and out of consciousness, the sounds of the dying rose around her, a concerto of foghorns moaning into the night.

A heavy form flopped on top of her, a squat pale body she knew belonged to one of the delvers.

"No," she whispered. "Please."

"Just relax, lovey," the delver whispered back, holding both of her arms down with one hand, while the other reached for her shirt.

Then she felt the weirdest thing—she must indeed be dreaming—a sensation of tiny feet swarming up her legs. The padded soles were cold and dry, strange but not unpleasant.

The delver pulled on her shirt, and then he started shouting.

Beating his hands over his body, he flung himself off Yasmina and started spinning in a circle and stomping his feet.

That was when she noticed the moles.

They were everywhere: running up the delver's limbs, biting his face, tangled in his hair. Blood poured from a thousand bite wounds, and the delver ran screaming out of the infirmary calling for help, which made her chuckle even in the dream. *Ironic, that.*

Yasmina sensed eyes on her. She shifted her head to the left, a torpid movement that sapped the rest of her strength.

On the next cot over, she saw an old man with long stringy hair and eyes the color of a winter sky. He was watching her. Two moles chased each other up and down one of his arms, as if playing a game.

Surely she was dreaming.

"Did he hurt you?" the old man asked.

Yasmina smiled at the dream figure.

"I'm Elegon."

"You know who I am," she replied. "You're in my dream."

The old man looked at her sadly. "Rest, young one. I know this fever. If you can last but a few more days, it will break. You mustn't give in."

Dream apparition or not, Yasmina took his advice. She closed her eyes and let her mind drift, all the way back to Brazil, to her youth in Manaus.

Heart of the Amazon, they called it. *City of the Forest. Paris of the Tropics.*

Most people in the United States thought Yasmina—the brown girl with

the funny accent—was from Rio de Janeiro or the concrete forests of Sao Pau-
lo, because that was all they knew. They also thought she loved soccer and
samba and maybe Formula 1 racing and plastic surgery.

Yasmina didn't love any of those things. What she loved was the beauty
of her hometown, a city of two million accessible only by boat or plane, surrounded by the jungle, at ease with the natural world. She loved its tropical
rhythm and rich smells, its lush gardens and surprising sophistication. Home
to an opera house and art museums, it was once flush with the wealth of rubber
barons.

Yet most of all, she loved its fauna. For as long as she could remember, Yasmina had identified with animals better than humans. Animals did not judge,
or practice willful cruelty, or spew racial epithets.

A shy string bean of a girl mocked by her peers and even her mother for
having no figure, Yasmina had few friends growing up. From a young age, she
had sought refuge in the jungle, yet another quirk that her society-obsessed
mother did not understand.

Not until she came to the United States for college did Yasmina start to
find her way. America had its own demons, but at least she could be herself.
She was free to study her animals at Tulane and avoid the microscope of Brazilian society and love the man who didn't love her back.

Oh, Caleb.

Beautiful, kind, gentle Caleb. There her mind lingered. He reminded her
of her father, including the drinking and the gambling and the womanizing.

Still, she preferred those weaknesses to a violent man.

Her mind drifted again, to the recent past, and a sob escaped her. Her animals in her apartment back home, they needed her! What had happened to
them when she had been forced into this world?

Or had the dream begun then, with her capture by that terrifying man who
could call upon the dead? Was this a dream within a dream? Was she at home
in New Orleans, her dogs and cats and ferret by her side, trying desperately to
get her attention?

She didn't know.

She just knew she wanted to wake up.

                              *   *   *

Will and Marek began a nightly sparring routine. Caleb couldn't believe it. He asked Will how he managed to lift a finger after working in the mines all day, wondering if their parents had swapped him at birth for a Viking warrior.

"Thanks for the compliment," Will had said.

"A short, geeky Viking," Caleb clarified.

The hand-to-hand combat practice was good for Will, both for his mental health and his budding warrior skills. Marek was the polar opposite of Mala: unskilled, one-dimensional, physically powerful. While Will would have employed a different strategy in a more open setting or with weapons, he was forced to confront Marek on his own turf, and it was making Will a better fighter. He had to practice his strikes and holds and escapes on a much larger opponent, in a tight space, adapting his techniques to fit the situation. And Marek learned from him as well, grunting with respect every time Will slipped out of a bear hug or forced him to submit with a limb lock.

It was a surreal experience, their quiet and determined sparring in the silence of the ruined courtyard, lit by the eerie glow of the mineral lamps. To Will it felt proactive, a way to improve his situation and rebel against their captivity.

A few weeks later, after another twelve-hour shift in the mines, the delvers took them home on a new funicular, which was not uncommon. They ran captives into the mines twenty-four hours of the day, and scheduled funicular journeys like air traffic controllers.

The new route carried them to an area of Olde Fellengard they hadn't seen before, a section of dried up canals and stone dwellings missing their roofs. Behind them loomed a huge, intact ziggurat. The masonry was exquisite, and the top of the structure, a flat pillared roof, was sprinkled with statues and gemstone sculptures.

"Delver temple," Dalen said.

"What was the name of their god?" Will asked.

"They had many. I don't recognize this one, perhaps Mith-Kavi? My Da told me stories about the delvers of old, but that was a long time ago."

"So the delvers banned religion, too?" Caleb asked.

"The clans inside the Protectorate gave it up to avoid war with the Congregation. *Lucka*, I'm no delver expert, but from what my Da said, their two religions are crafting stone and collecting wealth."

Though albino and crueler, Will thought, the delvers of Urfe were similar in many ways to the dwarves of fantasy legend. Had delvers inspired the myths on Earth?

Of course they had.

They rounded a corner and saw a sight that caused the line of prisoners to pause, earning a crack of the whip. A few streets behind the principal barracks, recognizable by its octagonal roof, was a basin of water the size of a home swimming pool. A narrow canal flowed into the basin on the far end. Another led from the basin to the rear of the barracks.

Chained to a rock in the center of the pool, shivering with cold and hugging her knees to her chest to conceal her nakedness, was a young female with long black hair and bright crimson skin.

And horns.

And a barbed tail.

One of the delvers snapped another whip. "Keep yer arses moving! Nothing to see here."

Will saw a few of the guards making lewd gestures in the direction of the girl. She hugged her knees tighter and began babbling in a strange language.

A language which Will, thanks to his magical armband, could understand.

Free me, she said. *Free me and I can free you.*

"Um, is that a devil girl?" Caleb whispered.

Free me, please please please. Free me. Free me.

"What's she saying?" Caleb continued.

Will shushed him. "Later."

The girl's babbling turned louder, more insistent. *I'm so cold. Free me. Please. Please please please please please*

Caleb was craning his neck to look at her. "Succubi or not, she's smoking hot."

Just before the group marched out of sight of the basin, Will and Caleb turned and saw the crimson-skinned girl dipping into the water, which reached to her waist. Before she dove under, Will caught a glimpse of lithe limbs and a voluptuous figure. He also caught a glimpse of a red glow spreading outward from her hands.

"Wow," Caleb said.

Will rolled his eyes. "She looks sixteen."

"Not from where I'm standing."

Will didn't reply. He was too busy empathizing with her plight, pondering what had caused her hands to glow, and thinking about the first words she had spoken.

Free me, she had said, in a throaty, mellifluous language unlike anything he had ever heard.

Free me and I can free you.

-28-

Mala eased open the thatch door to the largest of the three huts. After sweeping her gaze around the interior to ensure she was alone, she slipped inside and closed the door, which had a crude wooden hinge and no lock.

The smell was horrific, a fetid odor of unwashed bodies. The only furniture was a reed mat in the center of the hut, lying directly on the clay-like ground, and she realized the bedding was the main source of the smell. Years of hag rot soaked into the fibers.

Mala had expected human skins hanging on the walls, animal skulls, body parts soaking in black cauldrons. But there was nothing. No toilets, no food-stuffs, no personal items. The lack of belongings was disturbing, as if the hags were . . . animals. Creatures of instinct imbued with the power of speech and rudimentary survival skills.

The other two huts looked the same. Disappointed, Mala had only one remaining option: follow the hags into the forest. She doubted that would get her anywhere, but she had found nothing in the valley to aid her escape.

If forced, Mala would gather her belongings, flee into the forest, and search for civilization. That was the last option, since she had no idea what awaited her inside those trees, whether she could reach the nearest town, or if towns even existed on this world. And once she left the valley, she risked losing the amulet—and her way home—forever.

Whispering words of courage to herself, she stopped to grab her sash and short sword from the storage house, then scouted the perimeter of the clearing.

Close to where she and the majitsu had first popped into the world, she found a well-trodden path leading into the woods.

Leaning down to eye the indentations made by three sets of six-toed hag feet, she realized the tracks were fresh, just a few hours old, and surrounded by layers of older tracks.

Crouching, her senses on high alert, Mala crept into the mist-enshrouded forest. Though brown bark comprised the trunks of the enormous old-growth trees, the ashen color of the leaves and foliage, combined with the omnipresent haze, made her feel as if she were walking through a hoary dream world, a worn-out land of fog and secrets.

As soon as she entered the woods, she felt the foreboding sense of a presence even more strongly. Like someone or something was watching her. She realized it was not coming from any one place, but all around, as if the forest were a sentient being. She shuddered and pressed forward.

The path branched a few times, but the widest trail was the one she was following. It also had the most footprints. She became one with the forest, moving at a cautious pace and attuning herself to the woodland sounds, lest the hags catch her unawares.

Mala had learned to fight and steal and survive in the dangerous underworlds of Londyn and New Victoria, becoming the youngest person ever—male or female—to gain the rank of guild master in the New Victoria Rogue's Guild. Restless and proud, longing for more adventure, she had traveled east to join the ranks of the Alazashin, a legendary group of thieves and assassins whose rite of initiation had almost killed her. Realizing a life of indiscriminate crime was not for her, she blackmailed the Grandfather of Alazashin Mountain to gain her freedom, then roamed the world as a professional adventuress, searching for objects of magical power to sell to those with means.

She had faced some of the deadliest creatures on Urfe, had penetrated the keeps of wizards who could kill with a flick of their wrist, but as she crept through the woods in this alien world, facing beings who had stuffed her and a majitsu into a cage without breaking a sweat, she felt the cold fingers of fear crawling up her spine.

No, it was more than that, she realized. Fear she could overcome. It was the helplessness that terrified her. The same feeling she felt in the presence of a powerful wizard or even a majitsu, and which she hated with all of her being: the knowledge that she could not defeat these hags, not without help.

An hour into the forest, she found them. The grotesque hags were digging around the roots of an ancient tree, rooting through the soil with their bare hands, like animals. The sense of a presence felt stronger here. Making sure to stay upwind, Mala flattened behind another tree and watched.

The hags' tree was easily the largest in the forest, larger than any tree she had ever seen. Its canopy of branches, thick and gnarled like an oak but even longer and more clustered, hid the sky from view. The aboveground roots were a nest of petrified anacondas stretching twenty yards in every direction.

As Mala watched, the largest of the hags extracted a wriggling gray worm from the soil and plopped it into her mouth.

A food source, then. But why this tree in particular? Why not something closer to the valley? Did the gray worms only thrive in this one environment? Or were they just tastier here?

Over the next few hours, Mala watched the foul creatures dig up a few dozen worms. Each hag ingested one of the slimy larva every hour or so, and the lead hag impaled the remaining worms on her necklace. As the sky darkened and the hags stood to leave, Mala slipped back on the path and rushed back to the valley, hoping she hadn't waited too long. After flinging her sword and sash into the farmhouse, she raced into the kennel and took the potion.

"What did you see?" Hazir called out, just before she shrank and climbed into the cage.

"Nothing. Nothing at all. Quiet now, they're coming soon."

Terrified the hags would return before she grew to normal size, Mala paced back and forth on the straw, pressing her tiny body against the back of the pen when she heard footsteps approaching the kennel.

Grow, Mala willed herself as the two sister hags stepped through the entrance.

Grow.

The hags slopped food into the kennels, starting with the unicorn. Sensing Mala's predicament, Hazir tried to engage them in conversation, but they didn't respond. Mala heard them move forward again. A few more steps, and they would be able to see inside Mala's cage and discover her secret.

The backs of the two hags came into view as they paused to feed the nymph cage. The woodland creature pleaded for release as Mala finally began to grow, lying flat on her back to conceal the magic, scrunched against the rear of the pen.

The hags shuffled forward. Just before they turned and saw her, Mala returned to normal size, the slop splattering her legs as it sailed between the gray bars.

The next morning, the hags varied their routine. After doling out the morning meal, they took the unicorn out of the cage, wrapped it in grey coils as the poor creature whinnied in terror, then carried it outside.

Mala was curious. She took another dose from the dwindling vial, grabbed her weapons once she returned to normal size, and followed the hags into the woods. They had taken the same path.

When she reached the giant tree and saw what the hags were doing, her stomach tightened, and she felt prickles on the back of her neck. The unicorn was bound with grey tendrils to the base of the tree, and the hags were cavorting grotesquely around the poor creature, waving their arms, jumping up and down, babbling in their strange language as they beseeched the ancient hardwood. At the end of the ritual, the lead hag whisked a talon across the throat of the unicorn, opening a vein.

The hags stepped back and watched the unicorn bleed to death, its shrill whinnying cutting through the silence of the forest like nails on chalkboard. After it expired, the hags made more cuts around the body, draining every last drop of blood onto the forest floor. Then they tore the creature apart with their hands, ripping off hunks of white flesh and stuffing them into their mouths.

Disgusted, Mala forced herself to watch, gaining as much insight into the habits of the creatures as she could. After they had their fill, the hags tossed the carcass aside and started digging for more worms.

Mala watched as long as she dared and then slunk back to the valley, repulsed but thoughtful at the behavior of the strange hags.

-29-

"Our deepest sympathies extend to the friends and colleagues of Warwick Ledden of Laketown," Dean Varen continued, speaking to the assembled students in the Lyceum. "Despite the circumstances, there is no cause for panic."

Three murders of Acolytes in two weeks? Val thought. *Seems like cause for panic to us.*

"Rest assured we have our best investigators searching for the murderer, and he or she *will* be brought to justice. In the meantime, you should avoid traveling alone at night or in isolated areas. If you find yourself in the Abbey after hours, please utilize your coterie facilities for the night, or one of the visiting dignitary suites." Dean Varen swept her imperious gaze across the crowd, a show of confidence meant to reassure the students. "That is all."

As soon as Dean Varen flew out of the Lyceum, the students dispersed, muttering in small groups. Val followed Adaira and Dida outside.

The bibliomancer's bald pate gleamed in the sunlight. His features were drawn. "Never have we had such things happen in our learning centers."

Adaira beckoned them closer to the fountain, where they couldn't be overheard. "I heard my majitsu discussing the details," she said. "They're not telling us everything."

"I gathered," Val said drily. "As in, why can't the most powerful force in the Realm figure out who's killing their students?"

"Not even spirit mages can divine the future." She lowered her voice even further. "Though at times they can peer into the past. I do know they've consulted both a necromancer and a scryer, neither of which was able to complete a reading. They were blocked."

"Blocked?" Dida echoed. "How can this be?"

"They believe the assassin possesses a magical item that prevents scrying. The wizards are sure of it."

"Could it be a mage assassin?" Val asked.

Adaira grimaced. "It's possible, though unlikely. A wizard would not need to use a knife."

"Unless he wanted to mask his intentions," Val said.

"True. Though if the assassin were a wizard of any power, they would likely target higher impact victims. Real wizards, not Acolytes. The Congregation believes this to be an act of revolution. To sow discontent and disrupt the Abbey."

Val crossed his arms. "What else aren't the professors telling us?"

Adaira glanced around to make sure no one else had approached. She needn't have bothered; when the other students noticed her, they steered well clear, intimidated by her lineage. "Investigators found claw marks on Warwick's left arm. As if the assassin had grabbed him with one hand—a clawed hand—and knifed or clawed his throat with the other."

Dida wiped a bead of sweat off the eraser-smooth slope of his forehead. "Oh my."

"As Val said," Adaira continued, "it could be a minor wizard. Or a beast under the control of a wizard. Or a human assassin with a magical glove. And there's one other . . . troubling . . . piece of information." Her eyes flicked to Dida and then Val. "The first victim was murdered on the Canal Street Bridge. Because the bridge is such an important access point to the city, both ends are patrolled, day and night."

"And no one saw anything," Val guessed. "They don't know how the assassin got to the victim."

She nodded, lips pressed tight.

Dida shifted from foot to foot, his brown face sallow. Val wondered if he had ever left the library in his homeland. "I must be off," Dida said. "Our consulate has scheduled a dinner this evening that requires my attendance." He clasped Val's forearm, and then Adaira's. "Thank you for confiding."

"Of course," she murmured, giving him a peck on the forehead. "Discretion, please."

Dida tipped his head and walked away.

"I'd better be going as well," Val said.

"Val," she said, as he turned to leave. "Do you have any engagements tomorrow night?"

The look in her eye was mischievous and bold and shy, all at the same time.

Flirtatious. Given that she was the daughter of Lord Alistair, it scared the hell out of him.

But she might know something about the Planewalk. Brushing her off could be even more dangerous to his cause.

"Nothing except studying," he said.

"Everyone needs a study break."

"Maybe," he said, and cocked a grin. "But not everyone takes one."

Her eyes were alight, not used to being toyed with, enjoying the game. "And do you skip all of your meals as well, in pursuit of the perfect Wizard Shield?"

"I can study during meals. It's sleep I don't like."

"Ah. Then I must ask what it would take to secure a dinner arrangement with someone so driven?"

"An equal or greater force, I suppose."

Her eyes staying on Val, she took a step towards her waiting majitsu. "Meet me at the Oasis Café at dusk tomorrow evening. And for Queensake, leave your notepads behind."

The next morning, Val attended a Relics class. Most of the lecture concerned the history of magecrafting, the term for the creation of magical items. As he had guessed, wizards had made the bulk of Urfe's relics, excepting a rare few taken from 'other realms.'

According to Professor Bilxao, a gnomish wizard with sleepy, rust-colored eyes, it could take months to craft a minor relic, years for a major one, and de-cades or longer for some of the legendary artifacts scattered about the Realm.

Though no mention was made of a weapon similar to Will's sword, Val pe-rused the syllabus and noticed a class two weeks hence dedicated to Major Artifacts.

He started preparing his questions.

Saturday evening. The hour had arrived for Val's date with Adaira, daughter of Lord Alistair, Chief Thaumaturge of the Congregation.

Val knew he was playing with fire.

He tried to push his worries away as he cruised down St. Charles atop

Gus's carriage, enjoying the endless ivy-covered mansions, the mild late-winter weather, and the intoxicating aroma of decaying vegetation.

He had always loved New Orleans, the way it relaxed his mind and soul. There was nothing better than a beer with his brothers on an oak-shaded patio, strolling the back alleys of the French Quarter, swaying to the sweaty rhythm of a brass band in the Faubourg Marigny, and then sleeping late and lazing by the levee the next day, watching the river drift by, warm and languorous and green.

He had often wondered why he kept returning to the concrete jungle of Manhattan. But he knew. As much as he appreciated the laissez faire of his home city, it was the buzz of New York, the compressed energy of eight million souls, that injected him like a drug, satisfying his need for excitement, his thirst for ambition and life on the edge.

As the horses pranced past the imposing marble buildings of the Government District, Val had to admit he liked the grandeur and vitality of this world's version of New Orleans. It was like New York in the subtropics—with magic.

When asked about the Oasis Café, Gus had chomped on his pipe and proclaimed it the finest pleasure garden in the city. When Val probed for details, the grizzled driver said, "Ye'll have to see for yerself, laddie. It ain't like I've been there."

As they approached the Canal Bridge, Gus veered to the right on a handsome brick street, away from the French Quarter. A succession of private manors and fancy restaurants lined the riverfront, and they found the Oasis Café tucked inside a high-walled property.

The wall was inset with swirls of colored gemstones. Val dismounted and strolled to an iron gate beneath the entrance sign, then gave his name to an olive-skinned girl in blue livery. She ran her finger down a scroll, raised her eyebrows when she found his name next to Adaira's, opened the gate, and asked Val to follow her down a pebbled path through the foliage.

The grounds of the restaurant were the most beautiful Val had ever seen. Hedgerows of vivid tropical flowers lined the main path, groves of palms and banana trees sheltered candlelit tables, oak trees dripping Spanish moss caught and diffused the moonlight.

Guided by azure glow orbs, they wound through a maze of pathways and private tables to a central courtyard that backed onto the river. The brick courtyard was empty except for a stone fountain in the center, gurgling a polychromatic stream of liquid.

Candlelit tables and divans dotted the periphery of the courtyard, shielded from the other patrons with discreetly placed foliage. Adaira was waiting for him at a table for two made of emerald quartz. He spotted a pair of silver-belted majitsu fifteen feet away, standing next to a kumquat tree with folded arms and set mouths, eying Val's approach.

When Adaira rose to greet him, he had to force himself not to gawk. Flaxen hair, unbound for the first time Val had seen, flowed in gentle waves down her back, brushing his arms as he leaned in to exchange a kiss on the forehead. Her pale skin looked milky in the soft light of the glow orbs, her eyes two circlets of sea-green velvet.

She wore an ankle-length dress that matched her eyes, slit up the side and clinging to her figure. Delicate calfskin boots brought her an inch below Val's six-foot stature. Again, her only jewelry was the black pearl choker.

"It's a pleasure to see you outside the Abbey," she said, letting her hand slip away from his arm. She gave his high-collared white shirt, dark wool trousers, and black dinner jacket an approving eye. "I appreciate a man who doesn't conform to the latest fashions."

He had noticed the other men wearing knee-high golden boots, loose shirts of fine wool with V-neck collars, and loads of jewelry. Unlike Adaira, the women seemed inclined towards flared shoulders, high waist pants, and an equal amount of jewels. Val had chosen his pants and coat because they were the only ones Salomon had provided.

He crossed his legs and rested a forearm on the table. "You look lovely."

She blushed.

"Is this a wizard hangout?"

"A wizard what?"

"Café. A wizard café."

A waiter approached, and Adaira lifted a flute glass for him to fill. "At times you employ the strangest turns of phrase," she said. "It must be quite the interesting place, your homeland."

Val took a sip from his glass. He needed to be more careful with his language. "Our customs are quite different."

"I can see that. And the way you approach magic . . . it's almost as if you're from another world."

The cocktail tasted like rose wine infused with butterscotch, too sweet for his taste. He lowered his eyes to take another sip, taking care not to betray his surprise. *Did she suspect the truth?* "What do you mean?"

She waved a hand. "Everything you do is different. Original. People are talking, you know. Both students and professors. You've made quite an impression."

Val's surprise was genuine. "From where I'm sitting, I'm a below average student struggling to keep up."

Adaira cupped her glass and leaned into the candlelight. "And from where I sit, you're an untrained mage who makes extraordinary leaps and bounds every class, whose Wizard Shield is already stronger than mine, and who lifted the gold block during the entrance exam. It's been some time since an Acolyte has lifted the stone, my father says. Nearly a generation."

A generation? Her father? "Lord Alistair knows who I am?" Val said, again masking his unease.

"He knows we share a coterie, yes."

A breeze sent the subtle spice of her perfume drifting across the table, cinnamon and sandalwood and a hint of rose. Val felt a jolt of attraction. "Because of my entrance exam or because you talk about me?"

"Both," she murmured, returning his bold gaze.

What are you doing, Val?

The waiter returned on his left, setting out a plate of artfully arranged shellfish appetizers. Behind him, the spires of the Wizard District backlit the silver arc of the Canal Bridge.

He followed Adaira's lead, using a toothpick to dip a shrimp croquette into a tangy orange sauce. The ability to blend with the etiquette of other cultures had always come easily to him.

"How do you find your discipline class?" she asked. "My father never speaks of his own spirit mage training."

"All we've done is practice Wizard Shield, which is why I'm so good at it."

Her laugh was light and genuine, with a touch of throatiness.

"It's much more competitive than the coterie," he said. "Well, except for

Gowan. He hasn't liked me from the start. I feel as if he's jealous, but why? He's far more advanced than I am."

"You don't know?" At Val's blank look, she said, "His mother is Professor Azara."

"Oh. I had no idea."

"His father was a spirit mage as well, before his death."

Val swirled his amber liquid, which Adaira called *granth*. It had complex flavors, and the taste was growing on him. "So he views himself as the family failure?"

"You shouldn't take his jealousy personally."

"He's making it personal. But I understand, I'd probably feel the same way. How did his father die?"

"Natural causes. He was much older than his mother."

"I have to confess," Val said, wondering how some mages managed to prolong their lives, "his mother terrifies me. I feel like I'm back in primary school. Grade school," he added quickly. It was a struggle not to use words unfamiliar to her culture.

She laughed again. "We call it primary school as well. I've known Professor Azara my entire life. And yes, she has a way of making one feel quite small."

The waiter brought out strips of pheasant in a plum sauce. As he watched Adaira sample the dish, Val realized the full import of what she had just told him, and he gripped the side of his chair.

Gowan was from a family of spirit mages, and he had grown up at the Abbey.

Which meant he knew something about the Planewalk.

"Something else terrifies me about spiritmancy," Val said.

Her eyebrows arched.

"The Planewalk."

"Then we are much alike," she said, with a wistful smile. "Already thinking ahead, saddled with the weight of ambition."

"If so, you hide it well."

"When one's father is Chief Thaumaturge of the Congregation, one is born into ambition. And discretion."

The waiter refilled their glasses. Val was buzzing from the granth.

"But are you ambitious by nature?" he asked. "Irrespective of your family? And if so, for what? Your legacy? Philanthropy? Power for power's sake?"

She took her time responding, and when she did, he saw a whirlpool of emotion in her eyes, and knew he was dealing with a complex woman. Young and innocent to the ways of the world, but complex. Layered and clever.

"All three," she said.

"You said your father never speaks of his education, but has he ever spoken of the Planewalk itself?"

She cocked her head, and he knew he was pushing it. "You seem like a brave man—is the thought of the spiritmancy trial that oppressive?"

"I wouldn't call myself brave. More that I'm someone who likes to know his enemy before he engages."

She took a long sip, considering her response. "No, he's never spoken of it. Not that I can remember."

Disappointed, Val was forced to move on. "I'm sure I'll discover more in due time," he murmured.

"Enough talk of the Abbey, no?" she said, smoothing her dress. "We came here to escape. Tell me more about you."

"Me?"

"I shall rephrase," she said. "Tell me *anything* about you."

Val chuckled to mask his discomfort at the topic. "I come from the far North, have brown hair and blue eyes, and look much better in formal wear than I do in leather vests."

Her eyes twinkled, but she didn't bother with a response, just kept looking at him over her glass.

Tough woman. Val ran his thumb along the rim of his flute glass. "I . . . have trouble talking about myself. There, that's an answer, isn't it?"

"Why?" she asked. "Is it such a serious topic?"

He looked away, then gave a candid answer that surprised himself. "I suppose because I see the world in layers of gray. Myself as well. My choices in life. It makes it hard for me to express exactly who I am, even in my own mind. So how I can talk about it with other people?"

He thought she would scoff at his response, or not relate to it, but she leaned forward into the candlelight and said, "That's the most honest answer to that question I've ever received."

He didn't know if it was Adaira that had made him open up, or the fact that he was in a different world. Whatever the reason, it was as far as he was prepared to go. He unleashed his most charming grin and said, "And how many men have you asked about themselves?"

Her level gaze told him she knew he was diverting the topic. "I suspect not as many women as you have."

He took a sip and didn't deny it.

"Do you have siblings?" she asked.

His heart surged through his throat at the question. "Two younger brothers," he said, forcing away the grief and rage simmering just beneath the surface. "And you?"

"No. I wish I did. You love them very much, I see?"

Val swallowed, not trusting his voice, realizing he had done a poor job of concealing his emotions.

It was unlike him.

A cymbal clashed, and he jerked his head up. Adaira clapped once in delight and slid her chair next to his, facing the courtyard. The colored water in the fountain sprayed skyward, and a band of troubadours strode into the courtyard, strumming their instruments as they belted a folk tune.

More delectable courses arrived during the performance, until Val thought he would burst. Waiters in white livery refilled his glass as soon as it was half empty.

"Why cuerpomancy?" he asked Adaira, leaning close to be heard.

He felt the hotness of her breath as she leaned in to respond. "My mother was a cuerpomancer, and I wish to honor her memory. It's also the discipline most focused on philanthropy."

Val remembered the enormous sum Mala was forced to give a cuerpomancer for helping Marguerite. He kept his expression blank.

"I know what you're thinking, but after the Pagan Wars, cuerpomancers improved mortality rates in the Realm by almost a third. And they helped arrest the Black Plague."

"So why is it so expensive to find a cuerpomancer these days? Shouldn't there be a few free clinics in the city?"

She scowled. "Cuerpomancers now charge so much for their services, and restrict entry to so few, that it's become a haven for the powerful and greedy. I'd like to change that."

Okay, then. This woman is full of surprises. "I'm betting you'll succeed."

A troupe of acrobats in masks and patchwork clothing cartwheeled into the courtyard. As the troubadours switched to a rhythmic beat, the acrobats began performing impossible feats: somersaulting dozens of feet into the air, flying in tandem across the courtyard, juggling assorted props using only their minds.

Adaira noticed Val gawking at the performance. She smiled. "Gypsy troupe. Low-level magicians."

"They're amazing."

"Aren't they?"

She slid her hand over his, and he squeezed it in response. They held hands as they watched the performance, which was backlit by bursts of colored water from the fountain.

"I don't see many gypsies around New Victoria," he said.

Adaira waved a hand. "Oh, I'm sure these are sponsored."

"Sponsored?"

Her mouth curled, and he berated himself for asking what was probably an obvious question. "Talented performers are saved from the Fens by sponsors," she said, "who speak for their debts. Better some than none, no?"

Better that none go to the Fens at all.

Yet he didn't judge too harshly. Unlike his brothers, who tended to have doe-eyed visions of the world, Val understood that Utopia was a myth, and some things could never be fixed. It was a depressing fact of life, but there would always be haves and have-nots, on every world.

The acrobats filed out. A squat Indian man wearing a brown robe and turban, with a beard curled like a French horn, strutted into the courtyard. A slender woman in a midnight blue dress covered in stars followed him in. The fountain quieted as they performed a series of sleight of hand tricks.

"There's something I wanted to discuss with you," Adaira said, without taking her eyes off the performers. "The acolyte murders. Unless something is done, I'm afraid there will be more."

"You don't have faith in the investigators?"

"They've had no success thus far," she said.

"Won't the wizards step in?"

"They're watching, trust me. But if an item that can shield its wearer from scrying is involved, what is there to do? Ward the entire city?"

The crowd clapped as the two magicians finished their opening routine. The man raised his hands above his head, calling for attention. When the crowd quieted, he twirled his wrists in midair, and the woman began dancing towards him with a sinuous rhythm. While she advanced, he produced a stoppered bottle from his robe.

"We have something the investigators do not," Adaira said.

"What's that?"

"Bait."

Val paused with his glass halfway to his lips. "Ourselves, you mean."

"Is it not in our own interest to act? Self-preservation?"

"That's not how I would term chasing after a murderer."

"We're the strongest coterie at the Abbey. The future leaders. I feel we have a duty to act before others are harmed. I'd like to involve the rest of our group, but," she hesitated, "I'd like you to propose it."

"So it doesn't look like the daughter of the Chief Thaumaturge is giving orders."

A short nod. "I'd quickly offer my support, of course."

The woman in the star-filled dress danced faster and faster, a tornado of movement, twirling so rapidly it had to be magical. As the turbaned man approached her, the tops of her fingers dissolved into a fine mist, followed by her hands and arms and torso, then finally her head and legs. The crowd gasped as the man directed the mist into the bottle, then stoppered it.

"And we do this how?" Val asked, distracted by the stunning performance. Had that woman really turned into smoke? "By conducting our own investigation? Walking the streets at night, searching for a fight we might not win?"

He gave Adaira credit for bravery, if nothing else. With a constant guard of majitsu, she was in no danger, and didn't need to step outside of her comfort zone.

"I thought we would begin with an investigation," she said. "A new perspective on the evidence."

Val's eyes flicked to her silver-belted guards. "What about your father? He would never agree to this."

"He cannot forbid that of which he does not know."

The Indian man accepted the wild applause with a series of bows. As he moved to exit, he tripped over the edge of the fountain and dropped the bottle, shattering it on the bricks. After gawking in disbelief, the performer tried in vain to grasp the mist as it drifted skyward, releasing a cry of anguish as it seeped through his fingers.

Adaira gasped. A shocked hush overcame the crowd. The swami rent his hair and collapsed in a heap, weeping on the bricks of the courtyard as the essence of his partner dissipated on the night breeze.

Adaira gripped Val's hand and jumped to her feet, but there was nothing to do. Val lowered his eyes, dismayed by the turn of events. The swami lurched to and fro like a drunkard, bellowing his grief. Just as his anguish became unbearable to watch, the fountain erupted, and his mouth opened impossibly wide. The woman in the blue dress flew out of his distended jaws, somersaulting and then landing high atop the colorful geyser of liquid, balancing on the water as she bowed.

After a moment of stunned silence, the crowd roared its approval. Adaira sagged into her chair before clapping, and Val let out a long breath.

"He fooled me, I must admit," she said, wiping a tear from her eye and then intertwining their fingers as she peered up at Val. Her hair brushed against his forearm, giving him goose bumps. "So will you help me?"

"No," he said, having already decided that it was not in the best interest of his brothers to risk his life chasing down a murderer. This beautiful scion of privilege would have to prove her worth to her father in another way. "I'm sorry."

She looked as if she thought he was joking, then withdrew her hand and turned away. Val took another sip of wine and sampled the passion fruit mousse, which was delicious.

It was time to talk to Gowan about the Planewalk.

-30-

"Drink."

The voice had come from Yasmina's left. She shifted her head and saw the old man with long hair and wintery eyes. In his hand was a cup of water, held out as an offering. He was sitting up on his cot. The two moles snuggled in the tattered folds of his cloak, watching her.

Her brain had cleared. It was an odd sensation, like waking up from a coma or a very long dream.

Only she was still in this strange world, chained to a cot in the death ward of an underground city full of albino dwarves. The dream—the nightmare— was all too real.

She struggled to a sitting position and took the cup of water. It tasted like nectar from the gods. "Thank you. I'm Yasmina."

"Your fever broke last night," he said. She remembered the old man saying his name was Elegon. "Once a Breakbone Rash takes hold, not many recover."

Light-headed and weak, her body felt wrung out by the hands of a giant. She looked down and noticed that the signs of the blue rash had almost disappeared.

"How long did it last?" she asked.

"Two weeks. You are strong."

She put a hand to her mouth. "My friends, do you know—"

"Hush, child," he said. "They're probably in the courtyard cells. The delvers have no reason to harm them, as long as they stay fit. They need their workers."

"Caleb isn't strong. He won't last."

"Maybe he'll surprise you. No one knows what one can endure," he gave her a pointed look, "until one is tested."

She shuddered at the memory of the journey through the Darklands, the days and nights blurry with fever. The moles in Elegon's lap started to play, and she looked up. "You did that, didn't you? Ordered the moles to help me."

He nodded, gravely. "I didn't order—I requested."

"How?"

"I'm a wilder. As, I believe, are you."

She gave him a blank look.

"You're not aware, are you?"

"I don't know what a wilder is." She looked down, cradling the empty cup in her hands. She didn't know anything about this world.

He seemed surprised. "A wilder is a roamer, a traveler and steward of the land, who can communicate with animals."

She swallowed. "You speak to them?"

"I communicate. Have you never," he said gently, "felt a kindred spirit with the creatures of the wild? Felt as if you could speak with them and they would understand?"

"Sort of. I've always felt more comfortable around animals."

Elegon gave a small smile, as if he had already known.

"But nothing like you did," she said. "That's . . . magical."

He arched his eyebrows. "Have you ever made an attempt to communicate with them? *Really* tried?"

"I . . . suppose not."

"There are precious few wilders. Your gift is very rare, my dear."

"But how do you know?" she asked. "That I can . . . communicate?"

Elegon looked down at the two moles. They started chirping, and his whiskered face broke into a grin. "Because they told me."

The two moles ran down to the floor and then up Yasmina's legs, all the way to her face. They nuzzled her cheeks before coming to rest in her lap.

Maybe, she thought, the fever hadn't broken after all.

If what this man said were true—and she couldn't deny what she was seeing with her own two eyes—then she had to assume that whatever affinity she had with animals in her own world was somehow magnified here.

Or was it?

A delver came around with jugs of water and bowls of thin gruel. Yasmina forced it down. When the jailer left, she said to Elegon, "Why are you helping me?"

"Because that's what a wilder does. Helps those in need."

She turned the information over in her mind. "Can you not use the animals to help you escape?"

He drew his cloak tighter and coughed. He couldn't seem to stop, and ended up doubled over in his cot. She tried to help him, but she was too weak to rise, and had to sink back down. When the coughing trailed off, Elegon said, "Yes, my dear, I could escape these chains. But where would I go? More important, I was dying when they found me, and my time in this life is short. The Darklands would swallow me within hours."

Yasmina reached out and took his hand. "How does one become a Wilder?" she asked, sensing this was the question he wanted to hear.

"The only true training is to commune in nature, among the animals. "But here," he said, raising his hands and waiting for the moles to scamper into his open palms. "Let us begin to understand them."

The next morning, when Will and the others were sent to mine the blue cavern, he managed to position himself between Caleb and Tamás. He liked the gypsy leader and had some questions.

"Theoretically," Will said as he swung the pick, his back and biceps glistening with sweat, "if we were to escape this hellhole, how would we return to New Victoria? I was captured east of the Ninth. I don't know the way."

Tamás grunted. "Escape?"

"You know, if a nuclear explosion rips off the top half of the mountain and the Navy Seals send in a team to extract us."

Tamás stared at him, and Will barked a laugh. If he didn't manufacture some levity, he knew the mines would drive him insane.

"You've never fantasized about escape?" Will asked. "As impossible as it is?"

"Every minute of every day."

"Well, there you go. I like to dream out loud."

Tamás chuckled. "I appreciate your spirit, my friend. We'll escape together, perhaps. You'll be my guest in Freetown. It's a better place for you than New Victoria."

"Except my brother's not there."

"Ah yes, the missing brother." He swept a palm around the mine. "The lucky one, eh?"

"Yeah," Will mumbled, remembering his last image of Val, overwhelmed by skeletons and zombies in the cemetery outside Zedock's house.

They had drawn the attention of a delver, and Will lowered his voice and swung the pick harder. "But if you did escape and were going to New Victoria, how would you get there?"

"A dreamer with intent, then?"

"I have a potent imagination."

Tamás shrugged. "I would still travel to Freetown. Cross the lower end of the Dragon's Teeth, find your way to the coast, then hire a Yith Rider to take you across the Great River. Or, if you lack funds, accompany one of our trading caravans."

"What's Freetown like?" Will asked.

Tamás's eyes grew distant. "A place of great beauty, my friend. Where men are free to live as they see fit, create their own destinies, worship how they please. A place where no one lives in fear of the Inquest, or is forced to tithe their entire income to the Congregation."

"Sounds like Texas," Caleb said under his breath to Will.

"We saw something strange yesterday I wanted to ask you about," Will said. "A humanoid with red skin and horns and a tail, chained to a rock behind the barracks. She was, um, a female."

Tamás swung harder at his section of tilectium. "The darvish? An abomination."

"Is she really that bad? She just looked terrified. And sad."

"Not her. What the delvers have done to her."

"I don't understand," Will said. "Why is she chained up?"

"You've never seen a darvish before? Of course you haven't. Almost no one outside the Darklands has. They're a very old race, if not *the* oldest. Ancient enemies with the delvers. A raiding party must have captured her somewhere deep."

"Deeper than here?" Will asked.

"Legend has it that long ago the darvish fought an epic battle with the delvers. The darvish race was almost annihilated, and driven to the very center of Urfe."

"Is it just me," Caleb said, again too low for Tamás, "or are these darvish sounding more and more like the inspiration for the devil?"

Will wiped sweat off his brow. "So . . . what's up with the water torture?"

"They use her to heat water for the barracks," Tamás said. "If she doesn't perform, she'll die of cold."

"They're keeping her chained naked to that rock to heat their bath water?" Will said grimly. "For how long?"

"For as long as I've been here. For as long as the tenure of my cell mate, as well."

"Which is?"

Tamás eyed him as he swung. "Seven years."

"Good God," Caleb said.

Will's stomach fluttered with rage. "That's why her hands glow? She produces heat that way?"

"I assume so. I've no idea the extent of her abilities."

"Why doesn't she burn the chains?" Will asked.

"They must be magical. The geomancer lives on the top level of the barracks."

Caleb's swing faltered, slipping off the edge of the tilectium. "Geomancer?"

Tamás smirked. "A Congregation wizard. Working in tandem with the delvers."

"And taking his nightly bath with water heated by a slave chained to a rock," Will said, unable to stop thinking about her appalling fate. "What do they feed her?"

"I once saw her pluck a fish from the basin," Tamás said, "and eat it raw."

Will spent the rest of the shift swinging his pickaxe in double time, imagining he was taking aim at a delver.

Free me, he kept hearing in his mind.

Free me and I can free you.

"We've got to try," Will said. "If we can just get our hands on my sword, we can use it break her chains. Then we find Yasmina and let the darvish girl lead us out of here."

He was sitting cross-legged in the cell after their shift, addressing Caleb, Dalen, and Marek. Thick callouses had formed on Will's hands, the muscles in his forearms looked like grapefruits, and his blond hair brushed his eyes.

"That's assuming a thousand things," Caleb said. His hair hung past his shoulders, and Will thought he looked like a Hollywood actor starving himself for an indie role.

"Even if it works, then what?" Caleb continued. "You want us to risk our lives just because this darvish claimed to nobody in particular that she could free us? Free us *how*? She didn't do a very good job saving herself from capture. And what if your cursed armband of Babel is lying to you? What if she's really telling you to bring her a steak and some French fries?"

"What if she's not?" Will said softly.

Caleb started to say something else, then fell silent.

Marek gave a slow nod. "I vill go vith you. It is better than rotting in here."

"If she can guide us through the Darklands," Will said, looking at Caleb and then Dalen, "she may be our only hope."

"Or she might take us straight to hell," Caleb muttered. "Look, of course I want to get out of here. I just think we need more of a plan. And before we do anything, I want to see Yasmina. We have to know she's able to go with us."

"I agree with that." Will said. "But if her condition is worsening, getting her out of here is her only hope."

"Let's just find her."

Dalen interlocked his fingers and placed his hands on his knees. "*Aike*, Will, none of this matters if we can't escape this cell. And you haven't told us how we're going to do that."

Will frowned and looked away. He hadn't figured that one out yet, either.

"We might be able to help with that," said a voice, followed by two shadows materializing in the near-darkness outside their cell.

Not just any voice, but a familiar female voice.

Yasmina.

-31-

Val realized he had turned down the prom queen. Adaira ignored him the next week, though he kept catching her glancing at him out of the corner of her eye.

But he had bigger problems to worry about, such as keeping his head above water in wizard school, avoiding the supernatural killer picking off his peers, and navigating the mysterious Planewalk so he could find his brothers.

He had gotten nowhere with Gowan. In addition to the pyromancer's jealousy of Val's acceptance into spiritmancy, Gowan had a crush on Adaira, and word had spread that Val and Lord Alistair's daughter had been seen together at the pleasure garden.

Gowan refused to study with him, and Val had no other leads. He had scoured the Abbey library, the Hall of Wizards, and the Museum of History, but none of them mentioned the elusive spirit mage exam. He had twice returned to Bohemian Isle, and both times Alrick's door had been shuttered.

On Friday morning, Val walked into the coterie house to find Adaira slumped into a chair, eyes red. Dida eyed him as he entered, then looked away. Gowan was staring straight ahead, and Riga had yet to arrive.

"What happened?" Val asked, looking around the group. "Dida?"

"Another murder has occurred," the bibliomancer answered, more somber than Val had ever seen him. "The victim was Xavier."

Though Professor Gormloch pressed on with class, it was a gentle session, and he let them go early. Xavier's empty dais loomed beside them like a fresh grave.

After class, the five of them met on the rooftop for lunch. No one touched the food.

"He had children," Adaira said. "A boy and a girl."

Val had been thinking of that himself.

Adaira's fingertips pressed into her temples. "We have to do something."

"A memorial service?" Dida offered.

"Of course," she said, eyes flashing. "But something more. He deserves justice."

"Justice?" Dida echoed.

Adaira was staring in the direction of her father's blue-white spire. "I'm going to find whoever's doing this. I'm going to find him and stop him." She looked them in the eye, one by one, though her gaze slipped away from Val. "Who will help me?"

The bibliomancer rested his palms on the table. "Xavier was my friend," he said quietly. "I shall assist you."

"Thank you," Adaira said, then turned to Riga, the question unspoken.

"I am sorry," the kethropi woman answered. "My consulate would never approve, and I fear my magic would be of little assistance to you. Please, if there is any way I might help from afar, let me know."

Adaira pressed her lips together and nodded.

"I'll help," Gowan said. "I'll find the bastard and burn him."

Val had the feeling Gowan wanted to impress Adaira more than he wanted to find Xavier's murderer. Or maybe, since he couldn't be a spirit mage, he was desperate to stand out from the crowd.

Or maybe you're too cynical, and the guy just wants to help.

Whatever the reason, this was an opportunity for Val to get closer to Gowan. Not only that, but Xavier had been Val's friend. Though he doubted they would actually find the murderer, with all of them sticking together, it would lessen the danger quotient.

Adaira covered the pyromancer's hand with her own, and Val could see his Adam's apple bob. "Thank you, Gowan. Your prowess will be a most welcome addition."

The pyromancer glowed at the compliment, and she removed her hand. After glancing at the clock on the wall, her eyes flicked to Val. "I propose that those who are interested meet here after discipline class. We'll discuss how to proceed."

When Val landed on his floating dais inside the Observatory, joining Lydia and Damon for the afternoon spiritmancy class, he raised his hand before Professor Azara could begin. It was time to expedite matters.

Her imperious gaze leveled on him. "Speak your mind."

"I'd like to know more about the Planewalk. I feel it's never too soon to begin preparing."

Damon coughed a laugh, earning a glance from Professor Azara that silenced him like a muzzle.

"Val's intentions are not misplaced," she said to Damon. "And it would behoove you to emulate his habits, since he has made the most progress in class. Despite the fact—" this time her piercing stare was for Val —"that he still cannot fly."

Val clenched his jaw at the rebuke. He was all too aware of that fact, and wished Professor Gormloch would hurry up and teach that skill. Val wanted to practice on his own but it was all he could do to keep up with his studies.

"By design," Professor Azara continued, "the Planewalk is a trial that one cannot prepare for. Nor is outside assistance allowed, either from magical items or from other students."

"How do we know when we're ready?" Val pressed.

She whipped her gaze around. "You're ready when the faculty deign you so, *nish*? Since the inquisitive mood is upon you, you should know that historically, no more than two graduates per year attempt the Planewalk." Her chin lifted, her posture straight as a flagpole. "Only one time have both students succeeded. Often neither does."

"They . . . perish?" Lydia asked, with a twitch of her thumb.

"One may choose to abort the test at any time, but some choose to continue rather than face failure. Now, then. Today is an important day. You've done well with your Wizard Shields, and we are ready to begin summoning spirit fire. Or at least to attempt."

Val caught his breath. *Summoning spirit.*

"Beware," Professor Azara continued, "that until you have mastered summoning spirit fire in class, you must not attempt it at home. If it escapes your grasp, you or those around you could perish."

Val shifted on the dais. He remembered the black energy he had seen crackling at the fingertips of Professor Azara, the power he had sensed. He felt flushed, as if someone had turned up the heat in the room.

The Professor clasped her hands behind her as she paced. "We began with Wizard Shield for a reason, as the process of summoning spirit fire is analogous. Analogous—but one must reach deeper with spirit than with air. *Much* deeper. Concentrate as if forming your Wizard Shield, then choose a point of reference—I suggest a fingertip—and focus your will on that point. Pretend you are splitting apart this invisible point until you feel it opening. An act of great finesse. Once a crack is managed, you must fill that invisible space with your will, as much as possible. *Shove* your will inside. This is where strength is important. Quite literally, none of the other acolytes at this school are able to summon spirit fire—they have not the raw power. We believe that you can, which is why you are here, but whether we are correct, and to what degree, remains to be seen."

After that daunting opening monologue, they spent the rest of the class attempting to call forth the mysterious energy of spirit. Val absorbed Professor Azara's instructions, but try as he might, he failed to produce a spark.

His only consolation was that the other two failed as well.

"You may practice opening the doorway to spirit—finding the crack—at home," Professor Azara said as class ended. "But no more than that. If you do succeed in creating an opening, you must not, under any circumstance, infuse it with your power."

When Val returned to the coterie's rooftop patio, only Adaira had arrived. Her hair was tied in a braid, and she was dressed in leather breeches, a cotton blouse, and a thin, pale blue traveling cloak. Val had untucked his white dress shirt, leaving the high collar unbuttoned.

He sat across from her. In a neutral tone, she said, "Xavier changed your mind?"

"That, and other things."

"Such as?"

He decided not to answer, not wanting to lie to her if he didn't have to, instead meeting her gaze and letting her imagination go to work.

Her gaze softened, and she put her hand over his. "I'm glad you're here."

Dida interrupted them, plopping down beside Val in a camel hair dinner jacket. Gowan arrived soon after, his heavy frame settling next to Adaira, the wool shirt and trousers matching his dark curls.

A butler brought out cold cuts, cheese, bread, and fresh pineapple juice. "As I've told Val," Adaira said after they started eating, causing Gowan's jaw to tighten, "I've talked to the majitsu in charge of the investigation."

She relayed to Gowan and Dida what she knew about the first two murders. "And Xavier?" Val asked. "Where did his murder take place?"

"On the periphery of the French Quarter. Close to the site of the first murder, and not far from the Canal Bridge."

"Were the details the same?"

Her eyes moistened, but her voice was venomous. "He was stabbed in the back. Similar claw marks on the body. It happened in an alley, between two busy streets. No witnesses have come forth."

Val frowned. "What was Xavier doing in an alley in the French Quarter?"

"His lodging was nearby. I assume he chose it for reasons of thrift."

"What do you propose?" Dida asked.

Adaira leaned forward. "Someone saw Xavier leave the Abbey library near midnight, placing him in the French Quarter not long after. The first murder was estimated to occur at a similar time." She took a deep breath. "I propose to walk the quieter streets of the French Quarter near midnight, with the rest of you close by, ready to assist."

"That's a terrible plan," Val said. "Either we'll be too far away to help, or too close for the murderer to appear."

"I have something in mind. An item that can keep you close but unseen."

"Such as?" Gowan asked.

"A Sphere of Veiling."

Gowan frowned. "None of us is advanced enough to cast such a spell."

"I'm aware of that. It would involve a trip to the Goblin Market."

"Hardly a place for acolytes," Gowan muttered. "Not to be presumptuous, but do you not have access to an item that might help?"

You should be more presumptuous, Val thought. *She might like you more.*

Adaira's voice turned cold. "I remind you that we're not yet wizards. And quite obviously, I cannot ask for my father's assistance in this endeavor. He has also restricted my access to our family's magical possessions until I pass my discipline exam. I would ask the same of you, Gowan. Or are your family's items restricted to spiritmancers?"

Gowan looked as if he had been pole-axed. Adaira relaxed her stare. "Forgive me," she said. "That was unfair. We're all on edge."

Gowan swallowed, and Val almost felt sorry for him. "It's fine," the pyromancer muttered as he looked away. "It's the truth."

"When do you wish to leave for the Goblin Market?" Dida asked.

Adaira pushed her plate away, eying the declining sun. "Now."

-32-

Caleb sprang to his feet. "Yasmina! Thank God you're okay!"

Will watched with a lump in his throat as they embraced through the bars of the cell, reaching up to cup each other's faces. The person standing beside Yasmina, an old man with wild hair and snowy eyes, was holding a skeleton key.

"I'm relieved beyond words to see you," Will said to Yasmina, "but get us the hell out of here."

The old man unlocked their cell. "This is Elegon," Yasmina said. "After my fever broke, he helped me escape."

"How?" Will asked. There were murmurs from some of the other cells, prisoners wanting to know what was happening.

"With a little help from some friends," Yasmina said, with a mysterious glance at a mole scurrying inside the sleeve of her companion's cloak. "I'll tell you later, okay? Elegon thinks if we can reach one of the tunnels, there's a small chance we can escape into the Darklands. After that—" her eyes slipped away—"our chances aren't good."

Will noticed Elegon glancing at Yasmina with kind but sad eyes, as if he knew a harsh reality of which she was unaware. Will wasn't sure why, but he already trusted the old man.

"I've got a better idea," Will said, "but I need my sword."

He quickly told them about the plan to enlist the help of the darvish. Elegon leaned against the cell, nodding sagely. "An interesting idea, if you can free her."

"It's settled, then," Will said. "Let's go."

Caleb peered into the darkened courtyard. "Now?"

"What about the other prisoners?" Dalen asked. A few cellblocks close to theirs had noticed what was going on, and were clamoring for release.

"If ve free all slaves," Marek growled, "delvers hunt us down. If ve go alone, maybe not worth the trouble."

Everyone was looking at Will. He mashed his hands together, trying to decide what to do, remembering the prisoner the tuskers had stuffed into a pot. It was a damnable choice. Still, it was not his to make. Everyone should have the right to choose their own destiny. "Marek's right. If we free everyone, our chance of a stealthy escape goes way down." He ran a hand through his hair, took the key from Elegon, and unlocked the next cell over. "But I can't leave them."

"Good choice, little bro," Caleb murmured.

To Will's surprise, only one of the four prisoners left the cell, a red-headed woman with tribal tattoos covering her face. The other prisoners watched her leave with disbelieving stares. "Where will you go?" one asked. "It's certain death out there."

"Better death than captivity," the woman said.

"Aye," Marek agreed.

"Free whoever wants to leave," Will told her. "After that, you're on your own."

She clasped his hand, forearm to forearm. "Thank you," she said, then hurried to the next cell over.

The six companions crept through the silence of the ruined delver city. They knew the way to the barracks, but it took time to peer around each blind corner and pile of rubble for signs of a guard. Will knew the exit tunnels and the funiculars were swarming with delvers—a problem they would soon have to confront—but the interior of Olde Fellengard was quiet. It must be what passed for nighttime.

The octagonal roof of the barracks came into view. As they approached, the party kept to the intervals of darkness between the hanging mineral lanterns, eyes straining for signs of a sentry.

"Two by the door," Dalen whispered, pointing out a pair of shadowy forms near the front entrance of the barracks. Delvers, each carrying a shield and a war hammer.

A large courtyard fronted the barracks. The party slipped behind the last building before the open space, and Caleb pointed out a flat-roofed structure on the left. "That's where they took our gear when we arrived. I've got no idea if it's still there."

"There's only one way to find out," Will said. "Dalen, can you provide a diversion?"

"I'll do my best."

"Do better than that. Caleb, as soon as Marek and I engage, you're on."

Caleb swallowed, palmed the sliver of tilectium he planned to use as a lock pick, and started creeping through the shadows towards the equipment room. Will prayed his brother was up to the task.

And then, as the group made a rough plan of attack, he prayed that *he* was.

As Dalen wove his hands through the air, an emerald mist started to form. The illusion took the rough form of a delver girl, albeit a green and insubstantial one.

"You're getting better," Will murmured.

Dalen blew out a breath, and the illusion drifted in view of the guards. Will heard them gasp, and Dalen pulled his creation back behind the wall.

"Help," Yasmina cried, in the voice of a little girl. "Help me."

Will heard boots slapping on stone. He exchanged a look with Marek as the party backed against the wall. Once the delvers rounded the corner, Dalen disintegrated the illusion, stunning the guards with a flash of green light.

Will and Marek pounced.

Will jumped behind the shorter opponent before he could react, reaching around the delver's neck for a rear chokehold. He didn't have the confidence that one punch would silence him, and couldn't risk sounding the alarm. The delver gasped and bucked. Out of the corner of Will's eye, he saw Marek pummel his opponent with a huge roundhouse to the temple, dropping him to the stone floor.

Will's opponent couldn't breathe or cry out, but he swung backwards with the war hammer and landed a glancing blow on Will's shoulder. He gritted his teeth and bore the pain. If that had been a direct hit, it would have crushed his shoulder blade.

The delver started flailing, stumbling around with Will clinging to his back, tightening the chokehold. Will hung on like he was riding a mechanical bull. He had badly miscalculated the strength of his opponent.

The delver tried to hit him with the hammer again, but this time Will jerked straight backward, dropping them both. He landed hard on his back and lost his grip.

The delver's cry of "Intruders!" came halfway out of his mouth before Marek shattered his jaw with a blow from the other delver's war hammer. Marek's next swing crushed the guard's head like a burst water balloon, spattering Will with gore.

They all froze, subjects of a still life painting, waiting for more guards to come spilling out of the barracks. When no one appeared, Will turned to see Caleb's shadowy form slipping through the door of the equipment room. "*Move,*" he said, helping Marek pull the dead bodies behind a pile of rubble. "Caleb's inside."

Will took the other war hammer, joining the others as they rushed across the street, Yasmina holding the wheezing old man by the arm.

When they entered the equipment room, Will saw what he had feared: a huge room stacked with piles of weapons and armor. Swords, shields, crossbows, buckles, helms, halberds, knives, and a hodgepodge of medieval armaments littered the storehouse.

Caleb was slipping his leather vambraces on his forearms. "I got lucky with these, but I haven't seen your sword."

Will swore. The sword was their only chance to free the darvish girl, and it could take them hours to sift through these stacks.

Dalen stopped and stared, then began walking towards the back wall, waving his hands as he went.

"What is it?" Will asked.

Dalen held up a finger for silence, maintaining a course for the back wall.

And then he stepped right through it.

"Come," he called out. "It's an illusion."

Will led with a hand out, feeling nothing but air as he stepped right through the illusory barrier. The others followed him in. On the other side, they found a much smaller room with weapons and armor hanging from orderly hooks on the wall. Rows of wooden chests filled the center of the room.

"I noticed the light hitting that wall wrong," Dalen said. "A little trick my Da taught me."

With a surge of hope, Will spotted his scabbard hanging on the wall to his left. He walked over and drew his sword, dropping his hammer in favor of a tooth-shaped shield. Marek picked up a larger shield and a flail with a spiked ball as big as a grapefruit.

Caleb was bent over a chest, checking it for traps. "We might need some funds if by some miracle we survive this mountain."

"Leave it," Will said. "We need to hurry."

"Just one sec, I've almost—"

There was a loud click. Three darts shot out of the locking mechanism, embedding themselves into Caleb's chest. "Caleb!" Will cried, rushing to his brother, who was looking down at his chest with a mixture of dread and disbelief.

Moments later, shouts carried into the room from outside.

Delver shouts.

Marek looked from the chest to the street outside, then back at Caleb. "Fool!" he said. "It vas a silent alarm."

Caleb tore the darts out of his chest, biting his tongue so he wouldn't scream. Will felt frozen by the turn of events. *This is all falling apart.* He forced himself to shake off his sense of impending doom, and said, "We have to reach the darvish girl. It's our only chance. *Go!*"

Caleb stumbled, already pale from whatever poison the dart had injected. Will pulled him along as they fled the storeroom. Yasmina picked up a knife on the way out, Dalen took a short sword, and Elegon seemed happy to find a knobby walking stick topped with a bronze owl.

When they exited the building, the street was full of delvers streaming out from the barracks, and Will felt a wave of despair.

We were so close, he whispered to himself. *So close.*

One of the delvers pointed at Marek, who stood a head above the others. "There they be! Take them!"

Will spun one way and then the next, trying to decide what to do. If they ran, the delvers would cut them down. If they surrendered, their captors might or might not let them live, but they would certainly take steps to ensure an escape attempt never happened again.

"They'll kill us all," Dalen said in a defeated voice, as the delvers raced towards them.

Caleb gripped Will's hand. His palm felt clammy and a sheen of sweat coated his forehead. "It's been real, little bro. Sorry I'm a failure at being a thief, too."

The first delver was twenty feet away, battle hammer raised. Dozens more followed in his wake.

"Will Blackwood!"

The shout, from a familiar voice, came from the main avenue leading to the barracks.

Will turned and saw a swell of prisoners rushing towards the courtyard, with Tamás in the lead. "Will Blackwood! We are with you!"

He realized Tamás was aiming for the barracks, to arm his people.

"Dalen!" Will screamed. "Another diversion! Marek, watch our backs! Everyone else, help me!"

Marek faced off with the lead delver, while Dalen created bursts of light to confuse the next wave. His spells barely slowed them, but the delvers were forced to turn and confront the greater threat of hundreds of freed prisoners bearing down on them.

Will dashed back inside and gathered a pile of weapons in his arms. Caleb and Yasmina followed suit, and they began launching weapons across the street to the prisoners. Tamás noticed and directed a group of his men towards the storeroom, forming an assembly line of weapons. The skirmish quickly turned into a pitched battle. The delvers were better armed and organized, but the prisoners fought with the furious desperation of those who had nothing to lose.

Caleb eyed the top of the octagonal building. "What about the geomancer?" he asked, fear coating his words.

"He must be absent," Dalen answered. "Or we would know by now."

More and more delvers poured into the fray, racing in from all angles, and Will knew it was a matter of time before the prisoners were overwhelmed.

Tamás dashed to Will, who was backed against the door of the barracks. "If I know you at all, Will Blackwood, then this is not the extent of your plan."

"This wasn't my plan at all," Will said, looking for a way to escape the chaos. "I want to free the darvish and flee into the Darklands."

Tamás grasped Will by the arm, catching his breath from the battle. "Clever." He surveyed the rapidly deteriorating scene. "It must be a small group to succeed."

"I know," Will said in monotone, thinking of the likely fate of the other prisoners.

Tamás gripped his shoulder in understanding. "The delvers will give them a chance to lay down arms. They need workers. And if these people choose to die fighting rather than live as slaves, that is their choice. A valiant one."

Will blew out a breath. "Can your men cover us?"

Tamás's smile was bright and cold. He exchanged words with two of his closest men, who started ordering the fighters to make a push away from the barracks. Will gathered the others, and they fled in the opposite direction from the melee, towards the imprisoned darvish girl.

No one followed, but when they rounded the next corner, three oncoming delvers stood in their way. Marek, Tamás, and Will engaged them with a fury. The delvers were wily fighters, tough and skilled, but Tamás proved to be a vicious opponent, using a pair of scimitars to cut his delver down and then rush to Will's aid. The delver fought like a cornered badger, but Will held him off while Tamás slipped behind him and ran him through.

Rising from the shadows behind the remaining delver, Dalen stabbed the smaller opponent in the back with his short sword. The delver arched in pain, and Marek ended the fight with a skull-crushing blow from his flail.

Dalen stared down at the dead delver in revulsion, and Will sensed it was the first life he had taken. Will squeezed his shoulder and pulled him along. It was only a few months ago that Will had felt the same. And it hadn't gotten much better. "Two streets to go. We're almost there."

Caleb was short of breath, growing paler by the minute. Yasmina had to pull Elegon along. Will wondered what they were going to do with the old man if they needed to sprint. *Too much thinking*, he told himself. *Just act.*

With the sounds of battle ricocheting through the night, the screams of the dying a constant stabbing reminder of the choice Will had made, the party turned a corner and saw the basin of water.

The darvish girl was poised atop the rock, straining to determine the source of the fighting. When she saw them, she jumped into the water, covered her nakedness with her hands, and started babbling.

Free me, she said. *Please oh please free me. I will die here. Free me. Free me. Free me.*

"Delvers!" Tamás cried. Will turned to see eight albino warriors rounding the corner and rushing down the street.

Will grimaced. Eight was too many. He tossed his sword to Caleb, who he knew wouldn't participate in the battle. "Free her," he said.

Tamás gave Will one of his scimitars in replacement. It felt awkward, but it was all he had. To Will's surprise, Elegon raised his walking stick in a defensive posture and stepped next to Tamás. From his stance, he looked like he knew what he was doing. "Be strong, my friends. Help is on the way," the old man said mysteriously.

For some reason, the sound of his voice imbued Will with courage. Yasmina stood beside Will, Dalen beside her. Though Will loved them for their bravery, he pushed them both behind him. They wouldn't withstand the first onslaught. "Do what you can with your magic," he said to Dalen. "Yaz—help protect Caleb if anyone breaks through."

And then the delvers were on them. They bore down on Will and his companions with a roar, weapons raised, eight strong and experienced fighters in battle formation. Will felt as if he were going to vomit, but he gave a war cry of his own, drowning his panic in adrenaline.

Tamás yelled at them to push out of the courtyard and into the street to clash with the delvers, so they wouldn't be surrounded. The delvers squinted off Dalen's bursts of light, and Will blocked the first blow from an opponent with an upraised shield, though it pushed him back and vibrated his arms. He swung with the scimitar and missed badly, leaving him off balance. It was a completely different feel from his sword. The delver took a swing and Will jumped back, feeling air *whoosh* by his face.

Marek matched his opponent blow for blow, then drove the delver backwards with a snap kick to the chest. Tamás and Elegon each faced off against two opponents. Tamás was a wizard with his blade, spinning and whirling, keeping the delvers at bay but not managing to advance. Elegon used the superior length of his six-foot long walking staff to fend off his opponents, even cracking one of them on the back. The other delver met the walking stick in midair with the blade of his battle-axe, but Elegon's weapon held firm. The delver grunted in surprise, and Elegon swept out his legs.

It wasn't enough. The delvers managed to push them into the brick courtyard in front of the basin, where the rest of their fighters could enter the fray.

Will wanted to protect Dalen and Yasmina, but his opponent was experienced and enormously strong. It was all he could do to stay alive.

The delvers kept pushing, forcing Will and his companions to backpedal. One of the delvers rushed around the flank to reach Dalen. If he cut the young illusionist down, Marek's back would be exposed.

Out of the corner of his eye, Will saw Elegon stumble and go down. The delvers left him and swarmed Tamás. The revolutionary roared, but Will lost sight of him as he focused on his own opponent. The bearded delver facing him grinned, swatted away a blow from Will's scimitar, and then hit Will's shield so hard he dropped it and stumbled to a knee.

Will dove backwards as the delver's hammer came down for the killing blow, striking brick instead. As the delver raised his weapon again, a flash of crimson came between them. With an ululating cry, the darvish girl whirled into the fray, pushing against the delver's chest with both hands. Will watched in shock as the palms of her hands glowed a deep golden-red, like coals stoked in a fire, and the delver's tunic burst into flame.

One of the delvers surrounding Tamás broke away and rushed the darvish girl. She flicked her tail, and the barbed tip whipped into the delver's back, tearing out a chunk of flesh. The pale humanoid screamed and dropped, writhing as if poisoned.

Will and the freed darvish tore into the circle of delvers surrounding Tamás. As she burned another warrior, Tamás spun and delivered a vicious backhand sweep with his scimitar, catching him across the neck.

"Will!"

Caleb's voice, crying out from behind him. Will turned. Caleb tossed him the sword. Will dropped his hammer, caught the blade, and ran to Marek's aid, thrusting the sword into the spine of the delver Marek was fighting. The delver fell and twitched on the ground.

Tamás, Marek, and the darvish girl faced off against the last three guards. The darvish's opponent looked particularly skilled, so Will rushed to help her, busying her opponent with his blade while she slipped behind him. She jumped on the delver's back and placed her hands on either side of his face, and his head exploded into flame. The delver roared and tried to shake her off, but she gave a cry of rage and pressed her hands deeper. He thrashed and screamed as his flesh melted, but she held tight, flames framing her face like a vision of demonic beauty. Not until the delver's head was a charred lump of pudding did she step away, letting the corpse collapse at her feet.

Will felt nauseous, but he also buzzed with bloodlust. Marek had dispatched his opponent, and Tamás's scimitar slipped through the final delver's defenses, slicing open his abdomen like a piece of ripe fruit.

"Elegon!" Yasmina cried.

She rushed to cradle the old man's head in her hands. Blood poured from a gash in his side, near his heart.

He thrust the owl-tipped walking stick at her. "You're a wilder now, my dear. My legacy passes to you."

She ignored him. "You'll be fine. We'll get you some help—"

He cut her off. "I was dying before the battle started. You must leave me."

Will heard a strange sound behind him, gentle swishing across stone, and turned to see one of the strangest sights he had ever witnessed: seven giant moles, each the size of a full grown pig, scampering towards them from the other side of the basin. The faces of the creatures resembled star-shaped pieces of rubber protruding from their fur. The party cringed as they approached, but the moles stopped a few feet away and rested on their clawed forelegs, as if awaiting a command.

Elegon sighed. "Ah, they've come." The two tiny moles scampered out of his sleeve, and he patted them. "Thank you, my friends."

Will heard more noises, this time booted feet and shouting from a group of delvers.

Tamás's voice was grim. "Reinforcements are near."

Will whipped around to face the darvish girl. "When I first saw you, you said that if we freed you, you would free us. Is that true? Can you help?"

He had no idea if she understood his words, but he thought she would understand the pleading, helpless look they were all giving her. If she couldn't get them out of Olde Fellengard, they were doomed.

Her lips moved, forming a breathy language of crackling embers and whispers on stone. Will's armband translated. *I shall do my best.*

The girl's hands returned to their normal color as she climbed onto one of the giant moles and waved for everyone to follow. Elegon protested, but Tamás and Marek lifted him onto one of the creatures.

With everyone gripping the fur of a mole, the darvish girl pointed to her left, deeper into the city. Just as the moles began to move, their stiff gaits reminding Will of a mechanized toy, a large group of delvers came into view, shouting and pointing towards Will and his companions.

In the lead was Farzal.

"We'll get ye!" Farzal roared, one hand stroking his curly beard beneath a wicked grin, the other hand hefting a battle-axe. "We'll get ye and flay ye alive!"

-33-

Tonight is the night.

Mala estimated she had two remaining dosages of the Potion of Diminution. One for her and one for the majitsu. For better or for worse, her fate was about to be sealed.

She had a hunch and a plan, depending on what happened in the forest that night. If her hunch was wrong, her backup plan involved fleeing deeper into the woods, hoping against hope she survived long enough to find a town—and most likely never seeing her home world again.

Two hours after the sun went down, once reasonably sure the hags were asleep, Mala undressed and squeezed her clothes through the latticework opening. No matter the outcome, she wasn't going back inside that filthy cage. Not ever. She would drink her own poison first.

She emptied two more drops, slipped the vial through, and shrank to the height of two inches.

After climbing out and returning to normal size, she donned her clothing and strode to the majitsu's cage. He was next in line to be sacrificed in the forest, though she hadn't told him what had happened to the unicorn. Her plan depended on his ignorance.

"This ends tonight," she said. "I'll be back for you an hour before dawn."

Hazir snarled. "What do you have planned? Are we not working together?"

She could hear the distress and frustration in his voice, and she smiled to herself. *Let one of the vaunted majitsu feel fear for once.* "I've come to believe the hags are weakest just before dawn," she said. "Weak enough that we might be able to overcome them."

"Might?"

"Have you a better option?"

He grasped the gray coils of his prison. "Tell me more."

"When I return."

"Where are you going?"

"To find my weapons."

She left him peering at her through the bars. She was too nervous to relish his discomfort. Her plan was insane, and she didn't even know if it was viable. But it was time to find out.

A starless night oppressed the valley. Mala padded inside the storehouse, this time taking her magically enhanced short sword, her boot knife, and the curved dagger she kept sheathed on her corded leather belt, alongside the pouches. She tied on the weighted blue sash, slipped on her rings and bracelets and choker of intertwined bronze, then ran her fingers over her nose stud and her earrings, feeling whole again. Finally, she touched the bare space between her breasts where the circular amulet hanging from a silver chain used to fit.

The Amulet of the Planes.

Eyes flashing with anticipation, short sword and curved dagger in hand, she entered the woods in a predatory crouch.

The nighttime sounds in the valley were magnified a thousand fold inside the forest. Insects screamed their nocturnal concerto, the throaty shrieks and cries of larger predators tracked her progress. What strange creatures roamed these woods, she wondered?

Mala's eyes strained to follow the path as she walked, her blades at the ready. Progress was slow, but when she finally reached the clearing with the hags' favorite tree, she stopped to regard the gargantuan sentinel.

You're the presence I sense throughout the woods, aren't you? The deity of this wretched place. You control the forest, accept the sacrifices, produce the worms that give the hags their power. Worms fed by the soil beneath your roots, rich with the blood of magical creatures.

Mala strode to the base of the tree, sheathed her short sword, and began to dig with her dagger. Fearful of other predators, she worked as fast as she could, but it took long hours before she finally collected a handful of the wriggling gray worms.

There was only one thing left to do. As she pinched one of the worms between thumb and forefinger, cringing as she prepared to swallow, she wondered if she would be returning to the valley to fight the hags at dawn, or instead leaving her world behind and running for her life, deeper into the alien forest.

-34-

Before Val could protest, Adaira took flight towards the Goblin Market, followed by Gowan and Dida. When they realized Val wasn't with them, the others hovered in place and looked back.

"Is something wrong?" Adaira called out.

"I haven't learned how to fly," Val said evenly.

Gowan snickered and crossed his arms in midair.

"I'll have my driver take me," Val said. "He's waiting outside the coterie."

"I believe I can carry you," Dida said. "The market is near, no?"

"We can do better than that," Adaira said, swooping in to hover just above Val. "If you can move the exam stone, you can fly. I've seen you perform Wind Push in class. Taking flight is the same principle. Push against the ground, and the force of the air pressure will lift you up."

While the depths of his powers still drifted out of reach, Val could now cast lesser spells on command. He took a deep breath and tried what she said, focusing his will on pushing against the ground instead of forcing air away in a concentrated space, like a typical Wind Push spell.

To his surprise, he thrust ten feet straight into the air, much faster than he expected. It was so simple he chided himself for not thinking of it before. After wobbling in midair, he dropped and crashed onto the table.

He limped to his feet and scowled as he saw Adaira trying not to join the others in laughter. "You forgot to tell me what to do when I get up there," he said.

"Instead of using the ground, continue pushing against the air beneath you, or beside you, depending on which direction you wish to go. It takes much less effort."

"How do I land without killing myself?"

"Surely one as sharp as you might formulate the principle?"

He could tell she hadn't quite forgiven him for denying her request at the pleasure garden. He thought about it and said, "I can slow my descent by pushing against the ground or the air beneath me. Reversing the spell."

Her lips pursed. "Very good."

"Um, you might want to watch over me the first time."

She smirked and rose higher. "You'll do fine."

Val gathered his will and his courage, then pushed against the ground with his mind, shooting himself skyward. Dida clapped as Val rose past them. "Bravo, my friend!"

Val kept soaring until he was a hundred feet into the air. As he started to fall, he did as Adaira said, creating a localized Wind Push with the air beneath his feet. It wasn't as easy as thrusting off the ground, but after a number of attempts, he managed to control his descent. Once he got the hang of it, he put his arms in front of him like Superman and flew higher, amazed.

Because it was not Val's way, he resisted the urge to whoop out loud, but he was buzzing with his newfound power. *I could get used to this.*

When the others caught up to him, they flew as a group towards the river. The view of the city below was mesmerizing.

"Remember," Dida said, "you're vulnerable while flying. No other spells can be cast, unless one releases the spell and drops into free fall."

"That's why it's not taught to First Years," Adaira added, "though we all know it. It's also very draining, especially at the learning stage."

Val nodded, already feeling the effects. Gowan, he noted, had nothing to add, and did not look pleased that Val had picked up the skill so quickly.

When Val turned towards Adaira, he performed two accidental somersaults before righting himself. She giggled.

"What about your majitsu?" he asked her.

"They're waiting outside the front entrance. As far as they know, I'm studying in the coterie house all night."

He cast a nervous glance behind him, and then they were skirting the edge
of the Wizard District, taking care not to fly too close to any wizards in flight
who might notice Adaira. The city an open dollhouse below, Val reveled in the
wind rushing through his hair, the overwhelming sense of power and freedom.

From above, the Goblin Market resembled an ant colony, a seething line
of chaos on the river side of the French Quarter that extended a mile to the
east, and all the way to the Canal Bridge to the West. Val descended in fits and
starts, unable to make a smooth transition. Finally he realized it was akin to
the motion of letting out a car clutch on a steep hill, allowing himself to fall
while pushing against the air beneath him. It became easier as they neared the
ground, the solid surface providing a better counterweight.

Though he stumbled upon landing, he kept his feet, earning praise from
Dida and Adaira.

Not a perfect ten, Val thought to himself, but not bad. Not bad at all.

A six-foot wall cordoned off the market from the rest of the city. As soon as
they passed through the creaking wooden gate that marked the entrance, eying
the *Goblin Market* sign painted in red letters, Val felt as if he had stepped into
another world. Another world in the *other* world, that was.

The canvas roofs of the grimy tents and stalls created a canopy over the maze
of narrow lanes. Buyers and shouting vendors filled every inch of the bazaar,
pointing and snarling, babbling and bartering. An onslaught of smells wafted
to Val's nose: exotic perfumes and incense, coffee and grog, animal dung and
roasting meats and unwashed flesh.

Gowan's hands were clenched at his sides. Dida looked astonished but not
uncomfortable, taking it all in with curious eyes. Adaira put up a good front,
but her mouth was tight, and Val knew that if she had ever been here before, it
had been in the sheltering company of her majitsu.

He recalled what Gus had once said to Val and his brothers. *Behold the
Goblin Market, laddies. They say anythin' your black hearts desire can be found
within.*

Anythin'.

Jostled and harangued by vendors, Adaira clenched her jaw as they pressed
through the crowd, seeming to know where she was going. Val kept a constant

watch for danger, as well as one hand clenched around the gold coins in his pocket.

His mouth dropped as he realized the Goblin Market was not a misnomer. Short, wart-covered, tusk-faced bipeds manned some of the stalls, along with lizard men, a few albino dwarves, humans of every shape and color, and even a troll that loomed above the crowd, hawking spiked clubs and animal skins from his cowhide stall.

They passed traders selling every imaginable product: foodstuffs, oils, carpets, clothes, weapons, armor, and household goods mixed in with the more bizarre items: dragons' teeth, basilisk scales, water nymph tears, homemade elixirs, magical items of dubious origin.

After wading for half an hour through the labyrinth of stalls, Adaira stopped in front of a canvas yurt with no wares displayed, no vendor waving his arms out front, no buyers crowding the entrance flap. The incongruous calm of the yurt felt sinister, as if the chaos dared not encroach.

Adaira lifted the flap and slipped inside. Val and the others followed. Deceptively large, the yurt reeked of perfumed oils. A rack of weapons stood to their left, a cabinet full of stoppered bottles and curios to their right. Silky blue curtains separated two sections in the rear corners.

A glow orb hung from the apex of the yurt, emitting a feeble light, and it took Val a few moments to notice the lean man dressed in a black robe sitting in the shadows at the back of the enclosure, legs crossed lotus style, arms resting on his knees.

Not a man, Val realized, noticing the flat nose and manicured pincers that served as fingers, the leathery scales patterned like the back of a copperhead, and the slender tail coiled behind him.

Something else.

"Yesss?"

Gowan let the flap close, sealing off the street noise. Val felt uneasy in the presence of the strange humanoid.

"I'm Adaira Inverlock."

"Ah yesss. Alissstair'sss child. You have been here onssse before."

"Yes." She flashed a handful of gold. "Might I have an audience?"

He put a palm out and lowered it. "Sssit with me."

With Adaira in the lead, Val and the others moved closer to recline on an exquisite crimson carpet. Up close, Val noticed the yurt owner's tongue was forked, and that a burn scar obscured the entire left side of his face. Unlike other lizard men Val had seen in the street, with their ridged brows and extended jaws and heavy builds, the features of this reptilian being were sinuous and sleek.

A snake man.

He took a teacup off the table beside him, the silk sleeve slipping to reveal a scaled forearm. He offered another cup to Adaira. She accepted, surprising Val.

"What isss your desssire?"

"I have need of two things," Adaira said. "Information, and an item. A Shadow Veil. Can you assist?"

He gave a supple roll of his neck, then called out in a language consisting of a string of hisses with differing pitches. The curtain to Val's left parted, revealing a cushioned interior. A female version of the snake man stepped into the main section of the yurt, exchanged hisses with him, pulled a cloak over her head, and slunk through the front flap.

"Ssshe will procure the easssier of the two requestsss," he said, then nodded on an upward diagonal. "The information you wisssh?"

"Three acolytes have been murdered recently," Adaira said. "Are you aware of this?"

"Of courssse."

"Do you know who the murderer is?"

The snake man made a sound akin to a rasping chuckle.

"Has there been any talk in the underworld?" Adaira pressed. "Rumors about the identity?"

The snake man waved a hand in front of his lap. The movement reminded Val of the weaving of a cobra. Adaira got the hint and placed a handful of gold coins in front of him.

Again the rasping chuckle. Adaira grimaced and put two more handfuls beside the first.

"And for the ssshadow veil?" he asked.

"When it arrives," Adaira said evenly.

The forked tongue flickered. "You are brave to venture out without the usssual protection."

"We can protect ourselves just fine."

The snake man flicked his shrewd yellow eyes around the group. Val felt a chill when they rested on him. "Yesss," he said again, though Val detected subtle notes of both sarcasm and menace.

"It's kind of you to be so concerned with our welfare," Adaira said, with her own dash of sarcasm, "but what are these rumors for which I have so dearly paid?"

"It isss rumored that one of the Alazassshin hasss arrived in New Victoria."

Adaira swallowed before speaking. "I see. And this is the murderer? A professional assassin?"

He spread his palms. "You know that the Alazasssshin operate under the ssstrictessst code of sssilence."

"Then how did the rumor start?"

"When the murderer is unssseen, and ssskillful, the comparissson is inevitable, no?"

"No," Adaira said. "Use of the Alazashin requires enormous funds, and usually involves a high-profile target. Why students?"

"Ssstudentsss, but ssstill a blow to the Congregation. To the reputation of invincibility."

"Who sent the assassin?"

"I do not know."

"I paid for more than comparisons which I myself could have drawn," Adaira said. "Surely there is more?"

Another flick of the tongue. "The murderer isss not known to the underworld of New Victoria. The Alazasssshin iss the logical choisse."

"Because you would know if it was someone from here?"

He gave a slight bow in response. "There isss one other thing. A sssighting."

"Someone saw him?" Adaira asked, leaning forward. "Why didn't they come forth—ah, another criminal. Of course."

Another bow. "A thief it wasss. Waiting on the Canal Bridge for victimsss to passss. He ssspeaksss of a winged man who ssslew the wizard boy."

"A winged man? What does that mean?"

"Wingsss black and sssilent like the night. Coming and going on the breeze. Leaving behind a victim."

"Where can I find this thief?" she said. "Can you arrange a visit?"

"I am afraid I cannot raissse the dead."

It took Adaira a moment, and then she leaned back. "Someone—probably the Alazashin—killed him for spreading the rumor."

The flap rustled. Val turned to see the snake woman gliding into the tent. She set a black-wrapped bundle the size of a baseball in front of her employer, then retreated behind her curtain.

"A time-releassse Shadow Veil. The mossst potent you will find outssside the magic shopsss which, judging by the nature of the visssit, I asssume you wish to avoid."

Adaira placed another handful of gold coins in front of the snake man. "Is this enough?"

Never ask that, Val thought. First principle of bartering.

The snake man's lips, thin as toothpicks, lifted at the corners. "Almossst."

She added more to the pile. He used a black-lacquered pincer to push the package across the carpet to her. "It wasss a pleasssure doing busssinesss with you. And, ah, if you will, I would prefer if thisss visssit remainsss our sssecret. It would be unfortunate if your father were to learn of it. It might affect the businesss relationship you and I have fossstered."

"You have our word," Adaira said.

"Yesss."

On their return through the Goblin Market, thinking the snake man might be of value in the future, Val asked, "Who was that?"

"Sinias Slegin. A serpentus, obviously, and one of the most knowledgeable figures in the New Victorian underworld."

Dida shuddered. "An unnerving chap, isn't he?"

"Consorting with a serpentus," Gowan muttered. "A vile race."

"A necessary evil," Adaira said, hefting the round package.

"What does the involvement of the Alazashin mean for us?" Val asked. "How powerful are they?"

Gowan gave him an incredulous look. Val had weighed staying silent, but decided information was more valuable than discretion.

"Not so powerful that the four of us should not be able to overcome a single assassin," Adaira said. "Especially with the element of surprise offered by a Veil of Shadows."

Gowan muttered something under his breath, and Dida stroked his chin. "But what if the assassin attacks before we're able to assist?"

Adaira tossed her braid. "I'm not without defenses of my own. My Wizard Shield will be ready." She reached into a pocket and produced two pairs of silver handcuffs. "I've also brought these."

"Wizard cuffs," Gowan murmured. "Excellent."

Val wondered how the wizard cuffs worked, but decided he had admitted enough ignorance for one conversation.

"I wonder what was meant by a winged man?" Dida wondered.

"Perhaps he has a magical item that provides flight and an undetected arrival," Adaira said. "We already know he possesses an item that resists scrying."

"Could he be non-human?" Val asked.

"The Alazashin accept members from all races."

Gowan's voice was grim. "Perhaps he's a wizard after all. And too powerful for us to overcome."

"A wizard assassinating a student?" Adaira scoffed. "No wizard from the Realm, not even a gypsy, would stoop to such a level. And for the rare few countries where a wizard assassin might exist, such as a Dragon Mage, this would be seen as an act of war by the Congregation. Far too risky. And again, a wizard would not use a knife."

"And *again*," Val said, wondering what a Dragon Mage was, "he wouldn't unless he was trying to conceal the fact that he was a wizard. As you said, it would be considered an act of war. Do the Alazashin employ wizards?"

Adaira shook her head. "Never. It's against their code."

"There's a first time for everything."

Adaira stopped at the entrance to the market. "Your concerns of a wizard assassin are valid, and would be cause for rethinking our strategy, or even our involvement at all." She glanced around, then said, "There's something of which you're unaware. The Congregation keeps constant wards in place on the Canal Street Bridge, to guard against magical incursions. They were never tripped. If an assassin were using magic, the wizards would know."

*   *   *

They lingered in a booth in a quiet, upscale pub with brass finishings on Canal Street, awaiting the assassin's preferred hour. They refined their strategy as they waited, though Val kept quiet for most of the evening, not having much to add. Instead he dwelled on the dangers of the plan.

The involvement of an Alazashin was not something he had planned on. He could only hope the assassin never showed, and that he could convince Gowan to divulge information on the Planewalk before Adaira grew weary of her vigilante crusade.

An hour before midnight, they stepped into the French Quarter, a few blocks from the madness of Bourbon. After ducking into a deserted alley, Adaira unwrapped the package from Sinias and handed Gowan a black sphere the size of a billiard ball.

"I'll wait around the corner," she said. "The three of you will need to link hands as you crush the veil. The ones I've seen before affect a ten foot diameter."

She left the alley. Val and Dida grasped Gowan by the forearm. With a nervous swallow, the pyromancer held the sphere aloft and squeezed it. It crumbled into a fine powder which swirled in the air around them. Val watched as their bodies slowly disappeared, dissolving into the artificial well of blackness.

"A strange sensation," Dida whispered. "We should stay connected as we walk, or we might lose contact."

Val couldn't see his own hands, making the spell even more potent than his Ring of Shadows, which he was keeping to himself. He still had the Amulet of Shielding as well, though he had no idea if any charges remained.

They stayed twenty feet behind Adaira as she wound through the cobblestone streets and alleys of the French Quarter, walking slow enough to give the assassin an opportunity, yet with enough purpose to deter casual thieves. Quiet, lit by the occasional glow orb, and lined with wrought iron balconies and closed shops, this residential portion of the French Quarter was not too dissimilar to the one on Earth.

"Gowan," Val whispered. It was odd having a disembodied conversation. "Yes?"

Val didn't know of any way to broach the subject, other than with flattery. He also thought Gowan would be less rude in the presence of the bibliomancer.

"There's something I've been meaning to ask you. I'd appreciate any advice you could give."

Gowan grunted in reply.

"I'm terrified of the Planewalk, and was wondering if you had any tips. For the future, of course."

Gowan's voice was bitter. "I wouldn't know anything about that. The knowledge is restricted to spirit mages."

"Have your parents ever spoken of it?"

The bitterness deepened. "Not with me."

So far, it was going about as Val had expected. What he was about to propose, however, was the clincher. It was a low blow, but one which he knew would tug at Gowan's wounded pride. "I was thinking . . . and maybe this is inappropriate, but from what I understand, if one completes the Planewalk, one can become a spirit mage even without completing the proper course of study."

Gowan waited a long time before responding. "And?"

Val poured humility into his words. "I was thinking perhaps you and I . . . could train for the Planewalk together. It would help both our skillsets, and who knows, perhaps one day you might decide to give it a try."

"Don't be absurd. The Planewalk can be fatal, and requires years of training as a spirit mage."

Val could sense the gears turning, and he could tell from the hint of excitement in Gowan's voice—suppressed, but there—that Val had struck a nerve. He knew Gowan would dwell on the proposal, and also knew he would never consent in Dida's presence. To make the conversation look more natural, Val said, "The offer's good for you too, Dida, though I know you'll be returning home when the year is over."

"I wouldn't dream of such a thing," Dida said, and Val could tell he thought the conversation an odd one. "I'm quite content with my chosen discipline."

"Quiet, now," Gowan said. "If the assassin is out, he might have sharp ears."

Val fell silent, replaying the conversation in his mind, abuzz with the possibilities. Most of all, he kept remembering what Gowan *hadn't* said—that he had no idea where the secret entrance to the Planewalk was located.

Gowan knew where it was. Val could feel it.

They followed Adaira as she turned a corner near the river, entering an alley rife with the odor of dead fish. The secluded byway grated at Val's nerves. As she stepped aside to avoid a pile of refuse, Val saw a fluttering in the sky, at the edge of his field of vision. He looked up and gripped Dida's arm.

Twenty feet above Adaira's head, an enormous bat-winged creature, its furry humanoid body as large as Gowan and its membranous wingspan easily fifteen feet across, was floating silently downwards.

At the same time, a group of thugs emerged from the other side of the alley, fronted by a man in a black sash and a woman wearing a green and yellow patchwork coat.

The woman was holding a gnarled ebony staff and hovering two feet above the alley, drifting towards Adaira with the ease of a seasoned wizard. A quick glance told Val that the winged man had fled or taken cover.

"Don't be scared, lassie," the black-sashed man said to Adaira. He was dressed in a threadbare brown suit, scratching his stubbly face with one hand and grasping the hilt of a sheathed sword with his other. "This won't hurt too much."

-35-

With Farzal and his delvers in pursuit, the darvish girl wove through the heart of Olde Fellengard, guiding the giant moles to the edge of the ruined city and inside an abandoned house littered with broken dishes and discarded clothing. After throwing on a pair of breeches and a leather shirt meant for a large male delver, she hurried Will and the others through the back door and into an alley.

A hundred feet away, a fissure cleaved the narrow lane in two, Will guessed from an earthquake or a geomancer's spell. The darvish aimed straight for the crevasse, and the moles stepped lightly down the near-vertical slope until it intersected with a tunnel twenty feet beneath the buildings. There were no mineral lamps. Darkness loomed in either direction.

The darvish girl spoke, and Will's armband translated. *We must hurry. The delvers know of this place, too.*

Will relayed her words as their mounts scampered forward. Within seconds, the darkness was so complete he couldn't see the velvety fur of the mole he was clutching.

"I hope she knows what she's doing," Caleb muttered, pain lancing through his words.

"How's your chest?" Will asked.

"Like a group of scorpions are throwing a stinging party on it."

"Hang in there."

Caleb didn't answer.

Not long after, they heard the sound of delver boots pounding down the tunnel behind them. It felt to Will as if the moles were lurching to the left or the right every few feet, following new tunnels, but he had no way to be sure. He desperately wanted to communicate with the darvish girl, ask her where they were going and if they had a chance to succeed, but he dared not talk.

The sounds of pursuit faded, but the party maintained its silence, in case the delvers or other predators were lying in wait.

Up ahead, a green glow appeared like a blot of color in his mind's eye. Even with the moles as guides, fleeing through complete darkness was terrifying, and Will welcomed the approaching light.

When they emerged into an intersection of delver tunnels lit by mineral lanterns, Will saw no sign of their enemy—and Elegon was dead.

Slumped across the front of his mole, it looked as if he were resting, but when he didn't respond to Yasmina's voice, she lifted his head and Will noticed the sightless eyes.

"No," she moaned, cradling him to her.

Tamás checked his pulse and tried to revive him, but it was too late. Will bowed his head; in the short time he had known the old man, he had sensed a brave and gentle soul.

As Yasmina wept over the body, Will glanced back at Caleb and saw him clutching his mount with a white-knuckle grip, sweat pouring from his face. He looked much worse than when they had entered the tunnels.

The darvish girl was waving them forward. *Come. This is not a safe place* to *stop.*

"Wait," Will said. He jumped off his mole and got her attention, then pointed at Caleb. He went over and lifted his brother's shirt to expose the three dart wounds that formed a triangle on his upper chest. The area was red and inflamed.

Caleb made a feeble protest about not having time to fool with the wounds, but Will cut him off. "Can you do something?" he asked the darvish girl, knowing she understood the situation.

With a worried look, she jumped off her mole and went to Caleb, giving the wounds a critical eye and gently stroking his face. He shrank from her touch, and Will skipped a breath, expecting his brother's head to burst into flame. But nothing happened, and she smiled at Caleb and pressed the back of her hand to his forehead.

Caleb gritted his teeth as sweat dripped from his brow. She took off his shirt and, after gently probing the inflamed area, held the shirt up to his mouth. Will was confused, and then he understood.

Whatever she planned to do, it was going to hurt like hell.

Caleb swallowed and bit down on the shirt. Will took his brother's hand and said, "You ready?"

"No."

"It'll only hurt for a second."

Caleb cracked a weak grin. "Liar."

He clutched Will's hand as the darvish girl's palms started to glow. It took a few seconds for them to reach the golden-red color, and then she spread her fingers and placed her palms on Caleb's chest.

His back arched and his face contorted, and he moaned and bit down hard on the shirt. A tear fell from the darvish's eye as the hairs on Caleb's chest curled and blackened from her touch. Will choked back his emotions as his brother's fingers dug into him.

It was over in seconds. The darvish removed her palms, eyed Caleb's blistered chest, swallowed, and nodded.

Caleb swooned, but Will encircled him with his arms and eased him onto the mount. Yasmina, still weeping and gripping the back of Elegon's cloak with one hand, urged her mole forward so she could grip Caleb's hand and help keep him upright.

*   *   *

Not half an hour after fleeing through the twists and turns of the lantern-lit tunnels, they heard voices and the clang of metal up ahead. The sounds increased in volume, as if approaching a factory. Will was nervous and didn't understand why they kept moving towards the noise.

It is the only way, the darvish said, as if reading his mind. *The entrance to the Darklands is near.*

The tunnel spilled into a walkway that circumnavigated the top of a cavern hundreds of yards wide, sprawling beneath them like a gargantuan fishbowl of stone. Groups of prisoners mined veins of minerals in the walls or heaved wheelbarrows to the center of the cavern, where teams of delvers worked to assemble the exoskeletons of giant ships. Sapphire blue rods and panels—tilectium, Will realized—supported the wooden bases.

"By the Queen," Tamás swore. "They're making war machines."

"How will they get them out?" Will asked.

"They'll disassemble them, or float them down the river and have the geomancer open the mountain."

Will looked closer and glimpsed a river on the far side of the cavern, hidden by the half-built ships.

Dalen caught his breath. "There he is."

In the center of the activity, hands thrust forward in effort, was the unmistakable sight of a wizard, head held high above the collar of his cloak, working to fuse a pile of mined tilectium into a flat panel.

Hurry, the darvish said. *With me, along the edge. We are very exposed.*

Will sent back a telepathic reply of *no crap*. "Dalen," he said in a low voice, "can you shield us along this walkway?"

"I can try," he said. A moment later, Will noticed the forms of the moles and their riders blurring into shadow. "We should be fine," Dalen muttered, "as long as the geomancer doesn't look up."

"Alchemancer," Tamás corrected, as he watched the mage work. "A very good one."

It was at least a hundred yards across the cavern to where the pathway re-entered the tunnels, and it was the longest journey of Will's life. The moles slowed to a walk, creeping forward on their broad clawed feet. The limited movement helped preserve Dalen's illusion. Will had no idea how the moles knew to slow down, but his eyebrows rose when he saw Yasmina whispering to her mount.

Halfway to the end, Will risked a glance down.

Then he wished he hadn't.

Not only was it a thousand foot drop off the walkway, but the cavern was swarming with delvers. If one of them looked up for too long, Will knew the shadow illusion would shatter, and the alchemancer would summon a wizard wind or crack the walkway under their feet, sending them plummeting to their death.

The exit tunnel, wide and unguarded, loomed in the distance like the portal to heaven. The portion of the walkway leading to the tunnel had split, and the moles had to leap over a four-foot gap to reach it. It didn't seem to bother them, until the last mole, the one carrying Will, missed the landing with its back foot. It slipped and quickly righted itself, but a small piece of rock broke off and fell away, crunching into the floor of the cavern below.

Time seemed to stop. Will didn't dare look down to see if anyone had noticed. *Rocks fall in caverns all the time,* he told himself. Urging his mole onward, he tucked his body into the huge rodent as it raced forward, steps behind the others.

No alarm sounded, and they didn't pause until reaching the safety of the lantern-lit tunnel, which stretched before them as far as they could see. Spurred by the waving hands of the darvish girl, the moles scampered down the wide tunnel. No sounds of pursuit came from behind, and Will gave a silent prayer of thanks.

After a few hundred yards, the tunnel sloped downward, ending at a rune door guarded by two delvers, who scrambled for their weapons when they saw the moles and riders bearing down on them.

Tamás raised his scimitars in preparation. "The entrance to the Darklands," he breathed.

Marek lifted his war hammer, Will drew his sword, and the darvish girl stood on her mount, balancing on the balls of her feet.

Before anyone could react, one of the delvers grabbed a horn off the ground and blew a resounding series of notes. The clarion call echoed through the tunnel. Somewhere in the distance, another horn sounded in response, sending a chill down Will's spine.

The delvers rushed to meet the charging moles. The darvish girl somersaulted over the two sentries, while Tamás and Marek jumped off their mounts and met them head on. Will rushed to Marek's flank, and the darvish girl came up behind the delver fighting Tamás. She set his clothing aflame with her hands, and Tamás cut him down. Will and Marek struck the delver they were fighting at the same time, Marek providing the death blow.

"What about the rune door?" Tamás asked, wiping his blades on the tunic of the dead delver at his feet. "How do we get through?"

The darvish girl stepped in front of him and placed her hands on the smooth surface of the door. Her palms started to glow, and after a minute or so, the rock softened and her hands pushed a few inches into the door.

"King's Blood," Dalen murmured.

"Hurry," Tamás urged.

The stone around her hands glowed brighter and brighter, until the entire door melted into a molten pudding. She pushed, and the door collapsed inward.

The darvish stumbled with the effort, and Marek caught her. He made sure not to touch her hands, but they had lost their glow, and she looked pale and exhausted. The party returned to their moles and leapt over the ruined portal, into the mortar-less stone tunnels and arched ceilings of the Darklands.

As they raced away, another horn sounded behind them, this time longer and with a more ominous tenor.

Will saw the darvish girl tense and grip her mount. "What is it?" he asked. "What's that horn mean?"

Tamás rode up beside him, his jaw tight, a tendril of blond hair hanging loose in his face. "It means a war party is coming."

A few minutes down the corridor, Will said, "How many?"

"If I judge the horn correctly, it's an elite search party," Tamás said. "Thirty of their best warriors."

Dalen was kneading the backs of his hands. "*Lucka*, we saw their secret cavern and they don't like it one bit. Will the alchemancer come with them?"

Tamás snorted. "A Congregation wizard sullying his hands chasing the common born through delver tunnels?"

"Dalen isn't common born," Will said.

Tamás glanced at Dalen but didn't reply, and Will could tell he either didn't trust the fledgling illusionist, or think much of his abilities. Or both.

Dalen released a breath, unconcerned with the slight, and Will shared his relief that the wizard might not come after them. He glanced back at Caleb, who was hunched over, face twisted in pain. Will started to ask if he was all right, and then stopped. His brother had just suffered a localized third-degree burn. *Of course he isn't all right.*

"If they catch us," Tamás said, "they won't need a wizard. Thirty fighters is far too many for us too overcome, and they'll be prepared this time."

"Aren't the moles faster than they are?" Will asked, as their furry mounts bounded through the tunnel, star-shaped faces twitching.

"They won't stay with us much longer," Yasmina said. "We're a heavy burden to them, and they have to return to their burrows."

Caleb lifted his head to stare at her. "And you know this how?"

"I just . . . do."

Will pondered the cryptic nature of her response. Yasmina looked different to him, as if she had both hardened, yet also become more serene. The hardened part he understood—an ordeal like hers would either kill you or strengthen you—but the new tranquility surprised him. Had Elegon imbued her with some sort of supernatural power?

He urged his mole forward, parallel to the darvish girl. He could feel a gentle warmth radiating out from her body. "Thank you."

Her tail twitched, and her return smile lit the tunnel. Will placed his palm on his chest. "I'm Will Blackwood."

She looked confused, and he repeated his name. Her eyes brightened, and she put her palm on her own chest. *My name is Lishavysginthkoth.*

Will chuckled and said, "How about Lisha?"

Her black hair swished as her head made a sinuous rolling motion which, coupled with her smile, Will took for approval. He wished the armband worked both ways, though he had the feeling she understood basic English, the common tongue in the Realm. Maybe she had picked it up from the delvers. "Where are you taking us? Can you help us reach the outside?"

We are journeying to my home. My people know a path to the surface, an ancient way. We will guide you.

"I hope so," he muttered, not wanting to think about wandering the

Darklands alone. But her words raised a brittle hope, and for the first time in many weeks, he felt as if the smothering cloud of depression had started to lift. Then a faint note from the horn of the delver search party sounded behind them, his stomach churned, and the cloud returned to spit freezing rain in his face.

Lisha glanced back. *We must not falter. It will take us two days to reach my people.*

Will heard her, but it took him a moment to process the words. Two days of constant pursuit, two days to reach an uncertain fate with the darvish.

Two days in the Darklands.

-36-

Val glanced skyward again. The descending winged creature had disappeared. He could only hope it had retreated with the appearance of the street gang, and wasn't circling behind them for another approach.

The leader was not the same man who had killed Mari, but Val's stomach still clenched with rage at the sight of the black sash. It clenched even tighter, this time with fear, at the sight of the gypsy wizardess in the green and yellow patchwork coat drifting closer to Adaira.

"I warn you," Adaira said, "to back away."

The wizardess cackled, put her feet on the ground, and raised her staff. Adaira put a palm out, Val heard a rush of wind, and the man in the black sash tumbled backwards.

"She's a wizard, too," someone called out.

"Not nice, girlie," the wizardess said, unaffected by Adaira's spell. She curled a gnarled finger, and Adaira started drifting towards her. Adaira struggled, but couldn't stop the forward motion, as if caught in a tractor beam.

The leader scrambled out of the garbage pile in which he had landed, pulling fish guts out of his hair. "We've seen yer face before," he said, "in the scrying pool. Yer the daughter of Lord Alistair."

The men behind him, perhaps a dozen strong and all wearing black sashes, shifted at the news. "Ye know how much she's worth?" one said. "Buy a castle on St. Charles, we will."

"Ye'll buy nothing but whores and grog," said another, followed by a rough laugh.

A burly man with an eye patch stepped forward. "I say let her go. Lord Alistair will kill us all fer this, if 'e finds out."

The black-sashed leader laughed. "We're already dead. Take 'er alive, Leega," he said to the wizardess. "And no need to be gentle."

"I've heard enough," Gowan whispered. A spark appeared in the darkness beside Val, from the flint igniter all pyromancers carried. The spark expanded with a pop, forming into a sphere of fire that whooshed down the alley, striking one of the thugs in the chest and setting him ablaze.

"There's more of 'em!"

"Leega!" the leader cried. "Light!"

Adaira fell to the ground in a heap, and the wizardess made a sweeping motion with her staff that caused the alley to burst into light, negating the effect of the Shadow Veil.

"Three of 'em!" one of the black-sashed men cried.

"Wizard whelps," the leader said, "hiding in the shadows. Men, hold 'em off while Leega takes the girl."

A few of the men raised their bows, the rest stones or bottles. They took aim at Val, Gowan, and Dida. Val raised his Wizard Shield alongside the others, deflecting the projectiles, but they were forced into defensive position and unable to attack. A full-fledged wizard would not have been so helpless, he knew. Still, it chilled him that these black sash gypsies were not more afraid.

Out of the corner of his eye, Val saw Leega resume pulling Adaira towards her, and wondered what would happen when she caught her. Adaira was squirming and trying to use her magic to escape, but Leega was too strong.

As he used Wizard Shield to deflect the missiles, Val tried to think of a spell that might turn the tide. Gowan fired off another two fireballs in between the rounds of projectiles, but the thugs were ready for them, and dove to the side. Val tried a powerful Wind Push, but all it did was drain him and toss a few of the gypsies into a heap, from which they brushed off and recovered.

The barrage of missiles grew thicker, Val grew weaker, and he worried they would have to leave the alley or risk losing their Wizard Shields. He desperately needed more spells in his repertoire, more access to his well of power, more magical endurance. The four of them were far from being real wizards, and might pay for their hubris with their lives.

Dida stepped forward. "Create a Wind Push, both of you. On my count. One, two, *three*."

Val had no idea what Dida was doing, but he followed the more experienced mage's instruction, putting everything he had into a Wind Push that, along with Gowan's, tumbled the entire group of gypsies backwards. Only Leega held firm, still drawing Adaira to her. The two women were less than ten feet apart, Adaira fighting to free herself while Leega cackled and twirled her staff.

Dida ran three paces in each direction, tracing his finger in the air as he went, creating the outline of a translucent blue square the size of a garage door. When finished, he whispered an unfamiliar word, then ushered Val and Gowan behind the barrier. Val took a leap of faith and obeyed, just before a volley of arrows struck the magical wall and bounced off.

"Well played!" Gowan shouted, stepping just to the side of the blue wall and releasing another Firesphere. It was smaller than his others, but caught one of the black-sashed men on the leg, engulfing him in flame.

Dida had given them a defensive gift, but they were still trapped behind the Rune Shield, their magic growing weaker. Val watched, helpless, as Adaira drifted to within five feet of the sorceress, and then three, and then one. Leega crowed and reached for her neck, her hand expanding into a set of pincers large enough to take Adaira by the throat and drag her away.

The leader stalked towards Adaira holding a short sword. Val had a flashback to Mari, and started to run to Adaira's aid, but another volley of projectiles pinned him behind Dida's magical barrier. Val seethed in frustration.

"Get ready to leave, laddies," the leader said, producing a rag in his other hand. "A whiff of this and she won't remember 'er name."

Leega reached for Adaira's throat with her pincer. As soon as the enlarged claw made contact with Adaira's choker, arcs of black lightning leapt out from the piece of jewelry and swarmed over the gypsy sorceress. She disintegrated in an instant, flesh and bones turned to dust.

Val stepped back in shock.

Spirit fire.

Adaira looked as surprised as everyone else, but she recovered in a hurry, whipping out the silver handcuffs and tossing them at the hands of the leader. They encircled his wrists and tightened. She tossed the other pair at his feet, and he toppled over.

The remaining thugs were stunned by the sudden turn of events. Gowan hurtled another Fire Sphere, Val put everything he had into a fierce Wind Push, and Adaira poured her fury into a spell that caused the skin of the black-sashed gypsy nearest her to erupt into boils that burst and oozed pus. He screamed and tried to stumble away, but Adaira raised a hand and he flew headlong into a wall, his skull crunching into the bricks.

The rest of the men scattered into the night. Gowan walked over and planted a foot on the leader's chest. He started babbling, and Adaira cast a spell that muted his speech.

Val saw the fire in her eyes, and he glanced at the broken, boil-ridden gypsy crumpled at the base of the wall. *Maybe Adaira's not as sheltered as I thought.*

"What shall we do with him?" Gowan asked, nudging the leader.

"We'll leave him on Canal," Adaira grimly said, "for the Guard to find."

Val pointed at her choker. "You didn't know, did you?"

Adaira swallowed and looked at the pile of dust at her feet, the remains of the sorceress. She pressed her lips together and shook her head.

Val took her hand. "Looks like your father didn't leave you unprotected. The necklace must react to danger."

She squeezed his hand and then touched the choker gingerly with her fingers, as if afraid it would erupt again. "It was a gift for my debutante ball."

"What's the significance of the black sash?" Val asked, thinking of the man in the green top hat snuffing Mari's life like dampening a wick.

"Gypsy street gang," Gowan said, and spat. "Vermin."

"The mercenaries of the Revolution," Adaira added.

Val wanted to question the leader, but it would be too awkward in front of the others. He quelled the urge to stand the man up and thrust his face against Adaira's choker, instead giving him a kick to the face that snapped his head to the side and glazed his eyes.

I'll find you, he said, an image of Mari lying in a bloody heap crowding his mind. *If it's within my power, I'll find you.*

*   *   *

They floated the leader a few streets over to Canal, leaving him in a heap on the side of the road for one of the Protectorate patrols to find. After that, they returned to the safety of the coterie for a nightcap. Everyone needed a stiff drink.

As they retired to the rooftop, surrounded by the beautiful spires, Val told them about the winged creature he had seen. None of them had any idea what it was, and Gowan's expression was disbelieving.

"I'll supply an anonymous tip to the investigator," Adaira said. She shook her hair loose from her braid and slumped in her seat. "That was a strong rogue wizard," she said, the waver in her voice betraying her frayed nerves from the encounter. "If she hadn't grabbed my choker . . . ." She took a deep breath. "Unrest is growing. In the past, one such as she would never show her face so near the city center."

"But have measures not been taken?" Gowan asked. "Travel restrictions, checkpoints, village patrols, executions?"

"That's why unrest is growing," Val said drily.

"But why?" Gowan questioned, as if truly perplexed. "They have no hope of prevailing."

"Loss of hope is a powerful motivator."

No one responded. Dida looked uneasy, as if uncomfortable embroiling himself in the problems of a foreign land. "I was outside the History of the Protectorate Museum yesterday," he said. "A woman in a gray caftan immolated herself in front of a crowd. She bore three blue dots on her forehead."

"The Devla Cult," Adaira said, sparking Val's interest. He had been wondering about the import of that scene on Bohemian Isle. "As if belief in a fictitious pantheon is not foolish enough, the followers of Devla believe in a single deity who they believe will lift their people out of misery."

"They should work to lift themselves," Gowan said, "rather than entrust in a mythical being."

Adaira murmured her agreement, but Dida kept a neutral expression, causing Val to wonder about his belief system. He found the prevailing atheism of the Realm fascinating. A culture that had no problem believing in magic, but which eschewed the concept of the divine?

But he understood the reasoning. The wizards believed religion to be antithetical to their survival, and had implanted an atheistic belief system into the psyche of the people. It reminded him of the repression of religion by the Marxist-Leninist states back home.

Which hadn't gone over too well.

Then again, they didn't have a wizard oligarchy in charge.

"I believe we should proceed more intelligently against this foe, whatever it is," Adaira said.

"I second that," Val muttered, though he had been hoping she would abandon her mission.

He had to admit, however, that he didn't relish the thought of that winged black thing dropping down on him on his way home one night.

"Do you think the black sash gypsies could be involved?" Val asked.

"I suppose it's possible," she said. "If they had a wealthy enough backer."

"Your proposed course of action?" Gowan asked.

"We need to discover the nature of this creature Val spotted," Adaira said. "It can only be the assassin. And once we determine what it is, we kill it. Before it kills us."

-37-

Soon after Will and the others passed through the rune door, they entered a cavern with a swift stream flowing through it. Yasmina asked them to wait at the water's edge, then started to lift Elegon's body off the mole. Will and Tamás helped her ease the fallen wilder off the mount and into the stream.

Yasmina held Elegon's hand before she let go, murmuring her goodbyes and then watching the body drift through the cavern and into the mountain. Without a word, she drank from the stream and rinsed her face, then used Elegon's walking stick to push to her feet.

Caleb lay on his back to ease the searing pain. After everyone drank their fill of water, they carried on. Every thirty minutes the delver search party would sound a long note on their horn, trying to break the morale of their quarry.

And the strategy was working, at least for Will, until the moles put enough distance between them for the sound of the horn to fade away. He felt a whisper of relief, right until they reached the next underground stream and the moles stopped moving.

Yasmina dismounted and stroked the head of her mount. "They won't go any further. They're exhausted and have to return to their families."

Will felt the edges of panic creeping in as everyone dismounted. It had only been a few hours since the last horn blast. Surely they couldn't outpace the delvers on foot.

The moles wriggled their star-shaped facial protrusions, lapped from the stream, then squeezed through a hole in the wall and disappeared. Lisha noticed the party's defeated expressions and began talking.

The dwarves will outpace us, but I have a few tricks. We must not delay. Come.

Will relayed the message, and no one needed any urging. They walked for what felt like half a day, until blisters formed on the soles of their feet and Will felt light-headed from hunger. Caleb was feverish with pain and barely managing. Everyone took turns supporting him with an arm.

Even Dalen was quiet on the journey. It was unspoken that the party needed to conserve every ounce of energy if they hoped to survive.

At one point, after walking alongside a shallow sump the rich green color of wet grass, Lisha left to find food. She said the present tunnel continued in a straight line and that she would soon return.

Still, it was a nerve-wracking journey through the eerie, mineral-lit terrain without their guide. They all remembered the terror of the battle with the darrowgars, and the lake monster that had come to claim the bodies. Who knew what else was lying in wait in the Darklands?

Lisha returned without incident, running back with her arms full of freshly killed fish. Everyone tore into the cold flesh, spitting out bones and finishing every last morsel. It wasn't pretty, but it gave them the energy to keep walking. Will estimated they had been traveling a full day, and wondered how they would last for another. He knew the delvers wouldn't stop to rest.

An hour later, they heard the deep boom of the horn again. The sound was far in the distance, barely audible, but the party exchanged glances of fear.

The delvers were gaining ground.

*   *   *

So far, the scenery had been a blur of uniform, downward-sloping tunnels, but after passing through a series of intersecting corridors, Lisha guided them into a cavern with a waterfall so high they couldn't see the top.

Follow me, the darvish said. *Take a deep breath and do not panic.*

Another horn blast, much closer, sounded behind them. Lisha waded into the pool below the waterfall, the water churned black from the falls, so cold it snatched Will's breath away when he entered.

Just before the darvish girl reached the plunge point of the waterfall, she dove beneath the surface. Will looked back to make sure everyone was with him, then took a deep breath and followed her down. She dove deep beneath the waterfall, so deep Will's ears started to hurt. When he saw the rocky bottom, he wondered what she planned to do—and then she disappeared.

After a moment of shock, he swam over and realized she had slipped into a narrow fissure. Will checked on Caleb and then pulled himself through, hoping Marek could fit through the hole.

Will kept expecting to pop out into a cavern, but the hole kept going, so long his lungs quivered inside him. There was no light, and he had to feel his way along the wall. At times a fish would brush against his face, and he quelled the urge to panic. It was one of the most unnerving things he had ever done, diving blindly into this lightless hole miles underground. What if Lisha had grown tired of helping them, and was leading them to a watery death?

At last his fingertips broke the surface, and he plunged headfirst into another waterfall that landed in a pool of water twenty feet below. He lost his form and ended up belly flopping, swimming to the side just before Marek squashed him. The others plopped into the waterfall soon after, Yasmina holding Caleb by the arm.

The cavern was filled with phosphorescent mushrooms that emitted a faint blue light. Everyone stood shivering by the edge of the water, ears cocked for another horn blast. Lisha looked the most miserable of all, and Will wondered how long it would take her internal heat source to recharge after melting the rune door.

We have gained time, she said, *but the delvers will find us. They will listen to the stone and know what we have done. Our only hope is to reach my people.*

"How long?" Tamás asked, after Will translated.

Half a day's journey to the Great Chasm. My people live at the bottom. The delvers will not follow us down.

Twelve hours, Will thought. Twelve hours and they would survive, at least for another day.

I do not know if we will make it before the delvers catch us.

"You can stop talking now," he said.

Will expected Lisha to keep them off the grid, but after navigating natural pathways through the caverns for another half hour, they stepped through a hole in the wall and back into the delver tunnels. Will wondered if her people had made the hole in the wall and why they weren't continuing through the undeveloped portion of the Darklands, but the darvish girl offered no answers.

He had a thought. "Yasmina, if you can communicate with the giant moles, how about calling up some more? We could use a few right now."

He thought she would scoff at his half-joking request, but instead she said, "Elegon said to beware of calling for animals in the Darklands, unless you knew exactly what to do. I am not yet ready," she said, looking both confident and embarrassed by her own speech.

"O-kay," Will said. "Yasmina . . . was Elegon some type of ranger?"

"A what?"

Yasmina used to join Caleb when he teased Will about his love for fantasy. She was very much a real-world kind of girl.

That was, until she left the real world in the rearview and started talking to giant moles.

"Someone who roams the outdoors, is good with animals. Usually a caretaker of the land."

"He called himself a wilder," she said. "And yes, he was very attuned to animals." Her eyes drifted. "It was . . . magical."

Yasmina was acting strange, but she had been through hell and back, and Will was just happy she seemed alive again. He could quiz her later.

The scenery turned spectacular, taking Will's mind off the fact that his brother was in extreme pain, they were all wet and shivering and probably catching some rare form of pneumonia, his legs felt like they had refrigerators tied to them, and they still had a fifty-fifty chance of being caught by the search party and flayed alive by Farzal.

The tunnel floor merged into a natural rock path that ran alongside an inky, narrow lake for at least a mile. Violet phosphorescent minerals in the walls provided natural lighting. The ceilings were low, just above Marek's head, and they had to weave through thousands of stalactites and stalagmites crisscrossing the long cavern like the jaws of some vast stone beast.

After that, they used a rope already in place to rappel down a cave with the smooth sides and funneled shape of a nuclear reactor. At the bottom, the tunnels resumed, only to spill into another walkway that wound through a series of formations made of black marble and scooped out in the middle, like half-cleaved giant pearls.

The combination of tunnels and fantastical natural caverns continued, awing Will with their beauty. He felt as if he were inside a Jules Verne novel, exploring unknown realms far beneath the surface. The sense of wonder continued until the tunnel dead-ended at a platinum-colored rune door, and the feeble but chill-inducing notes from a delver horn sounded in the distance.

Everyone looked anxiously at Lisha, but she made no move to place her hands on the door.

This rune door is special, impervious to our fire. The delvers are quite aware of our abilities.

"That's great," Will said, then relayed the message.

"You tell us this now?" Marek snarled. "After ve reach a dead-end?"

But Lisha was already moving. She approached the door, turned, and marked off fifty paces, ending at a non-descript portion of the tunnel. She put her hands up, and then stepped right through the wall.

Will's jaw dropped, and Lisha poked her horned head back into the corridor.

Many ages ago, when the tunnels were built, our people employed a wizard. Or shall I say, she said, producing an impish grin and flicking her eyes at Caleb, who she had been eying with gratitude the entire journey, *we seduced one.*

As the party stepped through the illusory wall, Will put his hands out and felt solid rock on either side of the opening. The tube-shaped passage continued for fifty feet. Lisha pushed on the wall where it dead-ended. A concealed door swung open on silent hinges, and they stepped into a natural rock

passage, twenty feet down from the other side of the rune door. The entrance
to the hidden passage swung shut behind them, indistinguishable from the
wall.

Tamás whistled, and Will said, "Nicely done, Lisha."

The delver horn sounded again. Dalen tensed.

We are close, the darvish said. *This is neutral ground. But I have no more
tricks.*

Will pointed at the portion of the wall concealing the invisible doorway,
then shrugged and pointed at the rune door. "How will they know?"

*Unless they brought a wizard, they will not discover our secret. But they will
listen to the stone, and know to open the rune door and follow.*

"What does she mean by listening to the stone?" Will asked, after relaying
Lisha's words.

"I'm uncertain," Tamás said. "I only know that delvers can somehow communicate with the stone, perhaps sensing faraway vibrations."

The 'neutral ground' was a series of natural rock passages, at times so tight
they had to crawl on their bellies or squeeze their bodies through cracks and
fissures. There were no mineral lamps, but Dalen figured out he could create
bursts of light using the glow from Lisha's fingertips. After one of Dalen's spells
lingered and dissolved into scattered motes of light, Lisha would warm her
palms for another burst. It wasn't much, but it allowed them to see.

The sound of the delver horn drew closer, and then closer still.

"How far?" Will asked, gripping his sword at his side.

Lisha didn't answer.

The tight passageway opened up into a maze of wider, intersecting tunnels.
They debated making a run for it, but Caleb and Dalen were too spent. Will
had to admit he wasn't sure how far he could have run either. They stumbled
forward as best they could, the stronger members of the party pulling the
weaker ones along.

The next horn blast echoed through the cavern. Will looked over his
shoulder in panic, sure the delvers were right behind them, yet only darkness
loomed. He willed his legs forward, dragging Dalen with him. Marek and Yaz
supported Caleb.

They turned a corner and saw an awesome sight: fifty feet ahead, the passage widened even further, ending at a staircase that plunged into a vast abyss, extending as far into the distance as he could see.

Lisha's voice brimmed with excitement. *The Great Chasm! We have only to descend to my people.*

Will translated. The party raced forward with a burst of adrenaline. Will's intuition told him that if they could just reach the staircase, the delvers wouldn't follow them down.

Halfway to the chasm, a familiar voice sounded from behind. "Lookie lookie. Six humans and a darvie girl, all by their lonesome. A merry chase ye led me, indeed ye did."

Will whipped around, his blood curdling at the sound of the voice. Farzal stood thirty feet away, hands on his hips and a wide grin splitting his beard. He had donned a helmet and a bronze breastplate with red insignia, hammer in hand, his battle axe gleaming from a hook on his belt. A cadre of delvers stood behind him, the ones in front holding crossbows aimed at Will and his party.

There was no way they would reach the stairs in time.

Will heard a twang, and saw an arrow speeding towards Lisha. Just before it struck her, it exploded into a net that ensnared her within its strands. She screamed and struggled and tried to burn her way through, but the magical netting held tight.

"Tis a pity how close ye were," Farzal said. He flicked a wrist, and the delvers behind him bristled. "Take the darvie with us, and kill the rest."

-38-

Though the delay failed to register, since time did not exist in the same manner for a being merged with spirit, it took the Spirit Liege nearly a month to track down the trail of the sword.

For weeks it roamed back and forth, drifting on currents of spirit, popping in and out of dimensions, until at last it found a clue: a trace of congealed spirit lingering in the campsite of a group of tusked humanoids.

Yes, the Spirit Liege thought, cloaked in spirit as it drifted silently past the perimeter guards, *the sword was here*. That or another being like the Spirit Liege had passed by, or the wart-covered creatures had been in possession of an arcane item of similar power.

Both unlikely.

It waited until the camp was asleep, then drifted into the center, where the leader, an enormous specimen of its kind, snuffed and snorted in the throes of slumber.

Acting on instinct, as the Spirit Liege did not yet know the full extent of its powers—it suspected not even its makers did—it placed its hands on either side of the bulbous head. The Liege's hands grew even less substantial, until they were wisps of blue smoke that soaked into the tusker's head, worming into his brain. It absorbed from memory that the creature's name was Grilgor, that it was called a tusker, and that, yes, the humans who carried the sword had been in this camp not long ago.

But memories were fickle things, inchoate. Nor were the pathways of spirit an easy read, even for a being such as the Spirit Liege. The current location of the sword remained a mystery.

The Liege sent the wisps of spirit deeper, until they found Grilgor lounging in the mysterious realm of the dream world.

"Eh?" Grilgor said in the tusker language. He was in a hypnagogic state, neither awake nor asleep. "Who's there?"

Though the Spirit Liege whispered its words, they sounded inside Grilgor's head as if they had boomed from the mouth of a titan. "The sword. Where is it?"

Confusion crept through Grilgor's fear, and the Spirit Liege realized the stupid creature might not have realized the true nature of the weapon. It caused images of the humans who carried the sword to drift into the tusker's head.

The images sparked a memory, and the Spirit Liege watched from inside Grilgor's mind as the humans entered a cave in the company of a group of shorter humanoids, one of whom was carrying the sword. The Spirit Liege recognized the landscape around the rock fissure. In its previous incarnation, it had gone there once before.

After gaining what it sought, the Spirit Liege congealed its hand as it pulled out of Grilgor's head, just enough to rip out the tusker's memories.

The Spirit Liege flew through the night, straight to the cave it had seen in

Grilgor's mind. After a brief search, it found the invisible wards which shielded the entrance from detection—but which had no effect on the Spirit Liege.

Once inside, the scent was clear.

-39-

Mala hurried back to the kennel after ingesting the gray worms, hoping she hadn't lingered too long in the forest. She thrust the vial with the last drops of the Potion of Diminution at Hazir. "It's time."

He held the vial in his hands, eying it with suspicion. "You could crush me with your heel after I drink this."

"I gave you my word," Mala said evenly, "and that's the chance you'll have to take. Now hurry! The hags rise at dawn."

The majitsu pressed his lips together, stuffed his robe through one of the holes in his cage, then drained the last of the potion. He shrank to the height of Mala's index finger and climbed out.

The other creatures were fast asleep. Mala paced nervously back and forth inside the kennel, waiting for Hazir to return to full size. She had to suppress her desire to bring his fears to fruition and squash him like a cockroach. Without him, she knew she was no match for all three hags, even if weakened.

Even with her secret advantage.

The potion wore off just as the first rays of dawn brightened the horizon. After tying on his robe and silver belt, Hazir followed her outside. "What now?"

"I've come to believe the hags are dependent on the gray worms for their magic." The majitsu's eyebrows raised, but she said, "I've no time to explain. If I'm wrong, then we will likely die. But if I'm right . . . we might have a chance."

"Your proposal?"

"We attack while they're weak, after the long night has lessened their powers, before they've had a chance to eat and replenish their magic. We attack *right now*."

Hazir looked in the direction of the three huts, then back at Mala. His eyes gleamed with a cold, vicious light as he balled his hands into fists. "I see no better time than the present."

Side by side, they strode towards the mud and thatch dwellings, heading for the largest of the huts first. Take out the leader and destroy their will.

Just before Mala and Hazir arrived, one of the smaller hags stepped out of the hut right in front of them, covering her mouth as she yawned. Mala and Hazir didn't look to each other for support or discussion. They simply attacked.

Mala stabbed the hag through her gut with the short sword, while the majitsu flew forward and pummeled her with strikes and kicks, so fast and powerful the hag gurgled her last breaths before she slumped to the ground. Hazir had crushed the hag's skull with his blows, and her insides spilled forth as Mala ripped her short sword out of the creature's stomach.

She turned to see the other two hags emerging from their huts. The smaller one stiffened and extended her hands to release twin streams of gray tendrils towards Hazir. The missiles were slower and thinner than usual, and when Hazir bladed his hands and swiped them in midair, they split apart and fell to the ground.

Mala's spirits soared at the validation of her theory. The hags were weaker. They had a chance.

Instead of joining the attack, the larger hag reached for her necklace and tore off a handful of worms. She rushed to plop them into her mouth, but Mala was twirling her sash in anticipation, and she let it fly as soon as she saw the hag reach for her choker. The sash struck the hag in the throat, the weighted ends twirling around her head and thudding into the side of her face. She let out a strangled cry and dropped the handful of worms, clutching her ruined cheekbone.

Out of the corner of her eye, Mala saw Hazir leaping at the smaller hag. The majitsu batted away another round of gray projectiles as he approached, then doubled his fists and leapt forward. He struck the creature in the chest, propelling them both through the mud wall of the hut.

As Mala sprinted towards the larger hag, the creature recovered and fired off two ropy strands of gray magic, then reached for more worms. Mala ducked and rolled under the lethargic missiles, choosing not to reveal her new weapon unless she had to. She recovered in time to whip her boot dagger at the hag's hand holding the worms, spearing her through the palm from twenty feet away.

The hag roared and dropped the worms, stomping her feet in anger and clutching her injured hand to her chest. Mala experienced a shiver of fear at the raw physical power of the creature, but she pushed through it, whipping out her curved dagger as she approached, then slicing downward with both dagger and short sword.

Just before her blades cut through the hag, the creature caught Mala in the chest with two more gray strands, hurtling Mala backwards and then slithering around her. Mala freed a wrist just before she was cocooned, working furiously to saw through her bonds. They were much weaker than usual, and she was able to cut her way through.

But not before the hag ate a handful of worms.

With a triumphant cackle, the creature swallowed the wriggling invertebrates and shuddered as the power of the forest coursed through her. As Mala prepared for the next round of missiles, sure to be faster and stronger than before, the hag stepped forward and raised her hands—and then Mala saw a blur of movement rushing towards the hideous creature from behind, right before the hag's chest exploded.

Hazir retracted his fists, ripping backwards through the ruined body, smiling wickedly above his gore-streaked hands. The hag collapsed at his feet, the light in her eyes extinguished.

"I commend you," the majitsu said, eying the bodies as he reached for the amulet still clasped around the hag's neck. "Had you not been common born, you would have made a good majitsu."

"I'll take the amulet," Mala said coldly. "I know how to use it."

"Do you think I've never seen an amulet such as this before?" His grin was mocking as he undid the clasp. "I just depress the back and rotate, no?"

"We had a deal."

"I promised to grant your freedom if we returned to Urfe. And so I would have. But I'm sorry to say you won't be coming with me."

He stood with the amulet grasped in his right hand. When he reached up with his left to maneuver the device, Mala extended her hands, releasing twin ropy tendrils from her fingertips that shot towards the majitsu too fast for him to react. The magical strands struck his wrists and wrapped his body in a bundle of gray coils.

He toppled over, cocooned by the powerful tendrils, gasping as Mala picked up the amulet. "How?" he spluttered. "*How?*"

After she gave a mocking grin of her own, he continued, "You found the worms in the forest, didn't you? You found them and ate them yourself."

"How astute you are," she replied, the memory of the foul experience returning in a rush: standing alone before the tree, feeling the strange power of the forest surge through her after she swallowed a dozen of the wriggling larva. They were disgusting, but she had felt the magic oozing out of her, swimming in her veins. Just in case, she completed a successful test run with the gray strands, which seemed to naturally coil around whatever they came into contact with.

She stalked towards the majitsu with the amulet grasped in her hand. Hazir said, "You promised, gypsy. You promised to take me with you."

"Yes," Mala said, "and so I shall."

With a flick of her wrist, she stabbed him through the heart, twisting the blade of her short sword as Hazir's eyes dimmed and then closed. Wary of some majitsu trick of which she was unaware, she decapitated him to be sure he was dead.

As mortal as I am, she murmured.

She freed the rest of the imprisoned magical creatures. Without further delay, not wanting to spend another second in that creepy gray world, she depressed and rotated the amulet while holding onto the head of the dead majitsu, keeping her promise to the last.

-40-

The members of Val's coterie spent the weekend searching for information on the winged assassin. Val and Adaira scoured the Wizard's Library, a beautiful, curvaceous building of colored glass and mosaic tile near the Sanctum. Dida paid a visit to the staff of the Bestiary, and Gowan made inquiries at the New Victoria museums.

No one at the Bestiary had heard of such a creature, and Gowan's search came up empty. The closest mention Val and Adaira could find in the library was an ink drawing of an eagle-man reputed to have been created by a menagerist. Even if real, the wings of the eagle-man were separate from the body, and Val was sure the wings he saw were membranous, attached to the arms and clawed hands.

Though Val had already checked the Wizard's Library for information on the Planewalk, he searched again while he was inquiring about the winged creature. While he was at it, he kept a lookout for information on his father.

No luck on any of the fronts. Val was growing frustrated.

"Perhaps someone in the Goblin Market might have knowledge of the winged creature?" Dida offered, as they gathered before class.

"Maybe," Adaira said, "but I've got a better idea. If there's someone in New Victoria who has encountered one of these creatures somewhere around the world, and lived to tell about it, then they're likely a member of the Adventurer's Guild. After Londyn, New Victoria has the largest chapter in the Realm."

"Are non-members allowed access?" Val asked.

"No," she said, "and since our mission is discreet, we can't get a special dispensation from the Council. But there is a pub near the Adventurer's Emporium—a popular outfitter for their Guild—infamous for the exploits of its patrons. The pub is called The Gryphon's Beak."

"Yes," Gowan said, "I've heard of this place. It's frequented by some of the most well-traveled adventurers in New Albion."

"Wednesday is Myrddin Day," Adaira said, "and I've functions to attend every night this week. Gowan, I assume your family does as well?"

The pyromancer nodded, and Adaira gave Val and Dida an apologetic expression. "The longer we wait, the more victims there will be. Would the two of you be able to take a night off from your studies?"

Before Val could protest, Dida said, "I'd be delighted. I haven't explored the city enough during my stay."

"I can spare an evening," Val said, annoyed at the prospect of another wasted night, but not wanting to alienate the group.

"Excellent," Adaira said, her turquoise gaze lingering on his.

*　　*　　*

The week's History and Governance sessions expanded on the timeline presented during the first week, drilling down into the minute details of the Age of Sorrows and the Pagan Wars. Terrible atrocities had been committed against the wizard families: inquisitions, torture, burnings, slaughters of entire clans and wizard outposts.

Val finally got the Relics class he had been waiting for, the one dedicated to major artifacts. It was more of a history class, discussing how certain artifacts had helped shape the course of events. While traditional armies and methods of war existed, the trump factor was the strength of the wizards and artifacts each country or kingdom brought to bear.

Disappointingly, they spent most of the class discussing only two artifacts: the Eye of Yidni, an orb whose function Val gathered was similar to a magical, three-dimensional GPS map, providing invaluable information on advancing troops; and the legendary Coffer of Devla, a type of Pandora's Box for armies that could reputedly sway the entire course of wars. Devlan mystics, of course, claimed the power of the Coffer stemmed from their deity, while Val's professor scoffed at the notion and claimed that, if it existed at all, it had been constructed by an ancient wizard of unknown origin.

Just before class ended, Val raised a hand. "Have you heard of a sword that can cut through magic?"

Val thought the professor would chuckle or dismiss his question, but instead he said, "You must be referring to Zariduke. 'Devourer of magic,' in the native gypsy tongue. Also called Spiritscourge or Spiritwell. Yes, I would certainly place this item in the category of major relics, though its existence has never been confirmed. The Coffer of Devla, for instance, appears in numerous ancient texts."

Val tried not to splutter his next few questions. "Who made the sword? What was its purpose?"

"Most scholars attribute the crafting of the sword to Salomon the Lost—" the Professor made a wry face—"though of course the details of *his* existence are up for debate. As the legend goes—and I do *not* consider the Gypsy Canticles historical texts—that after the astral wind stole Salomon's son, he decided to journey to the furthest reaches of the multiverse, searching for the source of magic itself—Devla, in gypsy vernacular—to demand his son's return. To aid his journey, Salomon locked himself in his tower and forged a weapon of pure magic, one that could cleave through spirit itself. Legend holds that he spent a hundred years crafting Zariduke."

"What," Val swallowed, "does the legend say happened to it?"

"According to the Canticles, when Salomon failed to find his son after a thousand years of searching—hyperbole and rounding off years are of course common mythological themes—the arch spirit mage became so distraught he tossed the sword into the Place Between Worlds, leaving its fate to the astral wind. I'm curious; where did you hear of the legend?"

Val swallowed. "Just something I read."

On Thursday night, Gus left Val and Dida on a cobblestone street fronting a row of brick buildings in the commercial district, near the edge of the Guild Quarter. The Gryphon's Beak was wedged between an apothecary and Lareck's Alchemical Supplies, just down from the Adventurer's Emporium.

Val was exhausted from his studies and decided to make the best of it, hoping for a good meal and a fine ale. He always enjoyed the company of the good-natured bibliomancer.

Opening the pub's heavy oak door released the smell of wood smoke and worn leather. The Gryphon's Beak was a cavernous establishment with groups of men and women standing with beer steins at high tables spread throughout the room. A huge inset grill, laden with roasting meats, filled half of the rear wall, and a square wraparound bar dominated the center of the establishment. Above the bar hung a slew of pennants, flags, and coats of arms.

The patrons represented a variety of races, and looked the part of adventurers: riding boots and breeches, capes and cloaks, vests and tunics. Everyone had one or two weapons by his side. Val felt an edgy aura emanating from the crowd of swashbucklers: these were people who traveled the Realm for adventure and profit, who lived and died by the sword.

Dida tripped over the doorstep, drawing a few raucous laughs. Val caught him. "Way to make an entrance."

"Pardon me," Dida said, blushing. "I am rather clumsy at times."

"I've never noticed."

"No?" Dida said, then caught Val's sardonic grin and laughed. "Yes."

They waded to the far side of the bar, squeezing past a boisterous group of lizard men and a table of heavily armed dwarves with hard stares. Val found a pair of empty stools in between a muscular brunette with a longbow strapped to her back, and a well-dressed, slender man with a goatee. He looked more merchant than rogue.

The slender man stuck his hand out to Val. "Wynsom Kilnor," he said, with a mellifluent British accent. " 'Tis a pleasure."

"Best check your purse," the brunette said to Val, grinning. "Wynsom might have already snatched it. As you can see, I prefer at least two bar stools 'tween us."

"Tsk tsk, Carmena," Wynsom said. "A lady shouldn't exaggerate."

"I'm exaggerating, all right. In the *other* direction."

Val and Dida ordered mugs of house ale and introduced themselves as students at the Abbey, drawing the interest of the other patrons.

"Budding wizards, is it?" Wynsom said. "Good show, that. Could use a wizard on my next outing. I'm after the gold in the Blackdown Hills, just across the border with the Ninth."

"Wizards have better things to do than chase rumors of gold with a cutpurse dandy," Carmena said.

Wynsom cocked an eyebrow. "Do they? Why don't we ask them? The Gryphon's not a wizard pub, so what's your game, gents?"

"We're looking for some information," Val said, pausing to imply they were willing to pay for it. He described the winged creature, and asked if they'd ever seen or heard of anything similar.

"That's a strange one," Wynsom said. "Can't say that I have."

Carmena bit into a turkey leg, tearing off a piece of gristle. Her wrists were as thick as Dida's biceps. "Neither me."

The word spread around the bar. After another few rounds and a string of interesting but fruitless conversations, and a delicious platter of fire-crisped antelope, Val was ready to call it a night when the bartender, a swarthy bald man covered in red tribal tattoos, sidled up to Val.

"Never heard of such a creature meself," he said, with an Australian accent. "But the man you want to talk to," he pointed at a burly, one-armed, older man sitting alone near the fire, "is there." The bartender smirked. "If you live to use the information, that is."

Val noticed the older man's beer mug was half-empty. "What's he drinking? I'll take one. And two more for us."

The bartender poured three ales, two golden and one red. He slid them across the bar, and Val left a generous tip.

"Obliged," the barkeep said. "His name's Rucker. I'd advise against making any sudden movements."

"Thanks," Val murmured.

With Dida a step behind him, Val approached the grizzled adventurer's table, noticing the corner was devoid of patrons in a wide radius. Stuffed animal heads and knick knacks from around the world covered the mahogany wall behind him.

Rucker's face was so scarred and weathered it looked like a piece of chewed meat. His gray hair was tied in a ponytail, and he wore a battle-notched, black leather breastplate with a grey sleeve. A shorter sleeve covered his stump. Two weapons hung from his hip: a serrated hunting knife and a wide sword curved on one side, like a flattened meat cleaver.

Val set Rucker's beer on the table. The gnarled warrior looked up, eyes flashing, and caught Val's wrist in a bear paw of a hand. "I don't know ye."

"I'm Val, and this is Dida. We're—"

"Students at the Abbey."

Val started. "How did you know that?"

Rucker snorted. "Everything about ye screams wizard whelps." He was looking at Dida, and his eyes narrowed as he studied Val's face and clothes.

Val pressed forward, unnerved by Rucker's piercing stare. "We have a question. The bartender said you're the most knowledgeable adventurer in the bar."

Rucker grunted. "In the tavern? Try all of New Victoria. Which sort?"

"Sorry?" Val asked. Rucker still had his wrist pinned to the table. The man had to be at least sixty, but his grip felt like a bear trap.

"Which sort of wizard pups are ye? What discipline?"

"I'm studying spiritmancy, and Dida's a visiting bibliomancer from—"

"The Kingdom of Great Zimbabwe," Rucker finished.

Dida's eyebrows lifted. "How did you know?"

"Do ye look Zulu? Ghanaian? No, that curved nose of yers is pure Shona. A biblio, eh? Useful skill, if ye ever manage to leave the library."

"You know about bibliomancy?" Dida asked, even more amazed.

Rucker gave him a bored look, then turned to Val. "Yer either brave or foolish, trying for spiritmancy. Ye must have some talent, though."

"Could I have my wrist back?" Val asked.

"Not till ye tell me where yer from, outsider. And who sent ye."

"I'm from a village in the North. I doubt you've heard of it."

"Try me."

"Talinmar, just outside the Protectorate."

"Surname?"

"Kenefick."

The old warrior leaned forward as he pulled on Val's wrist, jerking him halfway across the table. Rucker smelled like beer and a worn saddle. "Lie to me again," he said with a snarl, "and we'll both 'ave one arm."

Val's shoulder felt like it was about to slip out of the socket. He tried to keep his cool, but his mind was spinning. Clearly the man had been around the world, and from the look of it, he would carry out his threat if Val gave another false answer.

He decided he had no choice but to tell the truth. "Another world," Val muttered.

"I know that already," Rucker said. "Which one?"

"You've never heard of it."

"*Which one?*"

"Earth."

Rucker ran his tongue across his teeth. "Who sent ye?"

"No one. I don't even know how I got here. That's the truth."

Sort of, Val thought.

"And yer a wizard on yer own world, and think spiritmancy might get ye back?"

Val nodded.

Rucker let him go, looking him over as if judging his intent. "Never heard of this world of yers," he said, "but there's plenty of 'em out there."

Val rubbed his wrist and took a long swig of beer. Dida was looking at him with eyes like dinner plates. Val would have to figure out something to tell him.

Rucker downed his beer, then started on the one Val had brought. "Well? What do ye want? I don't join parties anymore."

Val placed a stack of five gold coins on the table, then folded his arms. Quick as a rattlesnake, Rucker smacked the coins off the table. They clattered to the floor near a group of bearded Vikings, who noticed where they had come from and then pretended not to.

Rucker snarled again. "Don't insult me, boy! I've got more gold than ye'll ever see, and I work for no man."

During the course of his law career, Val had rubbed shoulders with CEOs and politicians, and he was now studying magic with people who could summon spirit fire and lay villages to ruin.

Not many people unnerved him—but the man in front of him did.

He forced a measure of calm into his voice. "I was going to offer to pay you for information. Nothing more. I apologize if I've offended you."

Rucker's face relaxed, and he returned to his beer. "At least ye have the stones to stand there."

"We're attempting," Dida said, "to identify a creature."

"A creature, eh? What sort?"

Val described what he had seen, and Rucker gave him a long look. "Were the wings flapping?"

"No. It looked like it was drifting downward on an air current."

"And the body, was it long and slender like a man, or squat like a delver?"

Val had no idea what a delver was. "Definitely similar to a man. With limbs attached to the wings, and clawed hands."

"Wings black, with grayish underside?"

"Yes."

"Tipped with claws? Not the hands, but the wings?"

"I didn't notice."

"Pronounced ears?"

"Yes."

Rucker leaned back, looking at Dida and then Val. "Boys," he said, "ye've seen a werebat." He shook his head. "Don't know what one's doing on the continent—I've only seen one in all my years, in Kalingaland." He leaned forward. "I suggest you do everything in yer power to avoid it."

"A werebat—a man that can turn into a bat, and back again?"

"That's what a were-creature is, ain't it? Killing machines, they are. The instincts of a bat, with the size and intelligence of a man. Ye've got a real problem on yer hands, if a werebat's got yer scent."

"What do you suggest?" Val said.

He chuckled. "Leaving town."

Dida put his hand on his chin. "Is it a true lycanthrope," he asked, "or the creation of a menagerist?"

Rucker wiped his mouth as he considered the question. "Impossible to be sure, and besides, they say the first lycanthropes were menagerist creations, from the ancient temples. Then there's the lycamancers, rare as black azantite. Who knows? All ye need to know is what they're capable of."

"Which is?" Val asked.

"Flying predators with the speed and skill of a hawk, hearing better than the Queen's best hunting dogs, fangs and talons that can shred a man in seconds."

"And what if," Val said, "they were also one of the Alazashin?"

Rucker leaned back, regarded Val with a disbelieving stare, and then slapped the table and brayed, spraying flecks of beer in their faces. "Then boy, like I said, ye've got yerself a real problem. Ye might want to go right on back to this Earth."

Val put his palms on the table. "Could you kill it for us?"

"*Could* I? Perhaps, with the right gear and team and planning. *Would* I?" he asked rhetorically, grasping the hilt of his sword with an easy grace that made Val take an involuntary step back. "As I said, I'm not for sale. And it ain't my fight."

"How did you kill the other werebat?" Dida asked.

"Who said I killed it? It followed our party through the jungle for a week, picking us off one by one. We holed up in some ruins until it got bored and went away. We never saw it again."

"That's comforting," Val muttered.

"Didn't 'ave a wizard with us, mind ye. I'll give ye a tip, though, before ye leave me to my cups. When I returned to the village, I asked the elders about the damnable thing, and they said a family of werebats had plagued the jungle for decades, raiding the villages when they got hungry. Didn't know how they got there, but they gave me a few nuggets of information. Told me something the infernal creatures avoided like the rat plague, and another they couldn't resist."

Like any good storyteller, Rucker paused long enough to pique Val's interest. "If they're in bat form, cold rain will turn 'em human," Rucker said. "Messes with their flight pattern and body temperature. And if for some reason you wanted to draw one close before you turn it," he said, with a gleam in his eye that suggested that would be his plan of attack, "then ye'll want to use a mint orchid. They can't resist 'em."

"A mint orchid," Val repeated, committing it to memory. "Where can we find one?"

Rucker gave a predatory grin and held up a brass amulet attached to his belt, flipping it open to reveal a miniature earth-colored globe showing the rough outline of North America. With a squat finger, he rolled the globe until it displayed the unmistakable image of the Indian subcontinent.

"Right about there," he said. "The jungles of Kalingaland, a few thousand leagues east of here. Shouldn't take you more than a few months travel."

-41-

As the delvers prepared to attack, a deep-throated battle cry sounded from behind Will's party. The delvers hesitated. Will turned to see five male darvish bursting out of the Great Chasm, riding saddled darrowgars. The thong-clad males were seven feet tall and powerfully built, their horns curved forward and much longer than Lisha's three-inch nubs.

While the delvers fumbled to re-aim, the darrowgars pushed off the lip of the chasm and leapt high into the air. Each of their darvish riders raised diamond-shaped shields attached to their forearms, and employed their weapons: five-foot long gray tubes with the diameters of tennis ball cans. Palms glowing, they aimed the strange tubes at the delvers, and balls of molten lava shot forth, exploding into flame when they hit a target.

The delvers managed to release a volley of crossbow bolts. All but one of the darvish blocked the bolts with their shields, but the unlucky one bellowed and fell to the cavern floor, clutching the middle of his chest.

Yet the damage from the lava weapons, fireball after fireball after fireball, was devastating. The front line of delvers ignited into a mass of smoke and flame, obscuring the vision of their archers, creating chaos in the ranks, dropping smoking corpses to the floor. After the darrowgars touched down from their initial leap, they darted up the walls and onto the ceiling, creating moving targets and exposing more delvers to the lava tubes.

Will tore his vision away from the spectacle and raced to free Lisha. He hacked away at the magical netting, ripping a hole for her to slip through, then joined Marek and Tamás as they rushed into the fray, hoping to end the battle before the delvers had a chance to regroup. The initial darvish attack had decimated their ranks and caused mass chaos, but at least a dozen still stood.

The darvish seemed to have either spent their weapons or exhausted their internal heat source. The four remaining warriors leapt off the darrowgar, drawing pitchforks from scabbards slung on their backs, whipping their barbed tails back and forth. They were twice the size of the delvers.

Pitchforks? Will thought. *Really?*

The delvers formed a tight circle and fought like wolverines. Will watched in horror as Marek took a blow from Farzal that cleaved through his arm at the biceps. Marek bellowed and fell, and Dalen and Caleb rushed to drag him from the melee. Tamás stepped in to protect them, while Will labored to keep up with his skilled delver opponent.

The darvish fared better. Out of the corner of his eye, Will saw them dispatch delver after delver, blocking axe blows with their diamond shields, jabbing with their pitchforks, whipping their tails around to stab the delvers in the side. When one of the darvish's pitchforks got stuck in a shield, he picked up an axe and sliced through a delver torso, almost cleaving him in two. The darrowgars joined in as well, snapping at their hated enemies.

Will's own opponent was fierce, and he started to push Will backwards. Farzal outclassed Tamás as well, which panicked Will. The leader of the delvers kept flashing his evil grin, and Will knew that if either he or Tamás faltered, they would both pay the price.

Farzal was pushing Tamás towards the edge of the chasm. Though Will's arms ached with exhaustion, he roared and redoubled his efforts, weaving his sword back and forth, blocking his opponent's axe swing and probing for an opening, too often striking the delver shield or whipping through empty air. The delver was stronger than Will, well-trained, and more experienced. Will knew he had to make this fight messy if he hoped to survive.

Images from Mala's lessons dashed through his head, implanted through long hours of practice.

Lesson the first: always be aware.

Lesson the second: strike first, and with intent.

Lesson the third: cheat.

The next time their weapons clashed, the delver tried to smash Will with his shield to off-balance him. Will let him, pretending to stumble to a knee. He raised his sword in mock fear of the coming blow, but as the delver swung his battle-axe, Will spun to the side, tripping his opponent with a two-legged scissors maneuver that Mala had taught him. The delver lost his balance and fell. Will jabbed upward with his sword, just underneath the ribcage, slipping through his opponent's defenses and running him through. The delver's weapon fell from numbed fingers, his surprise at Will's maneuver the last emotion that registered in his eyes.

Tamás teetered on the edge of the chasm, with Farzal bearing down on him. Will sprang to his feet. "Farzal!" he screamed, swinging his sword at the delver leader's back.

Farzal was forced to turn and block Will's swing. When he did, Tamás regained his balance and thrust forward with a scimitar. The delver leader was quick as a mongoose and managed to block the blow, but Tamas's second strike slipped through, piercing Farzal's side. Still the delver fought, grunting through the blow and spinning away, kicking Tamás in the gut and then meeting Will's swing so hard that Will lost his grip on his sword, and it clanged to the floor.

Farzal sprang forward, a demonic gleam in his eye. Will dove for his sword as the delver leader raised his axe for the killing blow, but before he could swing, a pitchfork exploded outward from his chest. The darvish wielding the weapon lifted Farzal high into the air, and their tormentor gurgled his last few breaths before the darvish pitched him off the edge of the chasm.

Will snatched his sword off the ground and whipped his head around. Two more darvish warriors stood near the center of the cavern, surrounding Lisha and capping their weapons with gray basalt lids.

Marek lay gasping on the floor, his left arm a bloody stump. The rest of Will's companions were alive and unharmed.

The delvers were all dead.

*   *   *

The darvish immolated their fallen companions and left the delvers where they lay. Will sat in a circle with the others near the edge of the Great Chasm, awaiting their fate while Lisha argued with the male warriors. Marek was in rough shape, lying on his back while his stump bled. None of them knew what to do about it. Marek had rebuffed their efforts to console him.

"What could they be discussing?" Dalen asked.

"I'm sure they're deciding whether or not to kill us," Caleb answered, gasping in pain as he eased onto his back. The journey had opened up the burn wound, and blood seeped down his chest.

Yasmina rose and walked towards one of the darrowgars. Caleb gasped as he raised to his elbows. "Um, Yaz, I don't think that's a good idea."

She ignored him and knelt next to one of the salamander-like creatures. It eyed her, then bowed its head and let her stroke its neck.

O-kay, Will thought.

"By the deuce, surely they won't kill us," Dalen said. "*Aike*. We just saved one of their own from enslavement."

"And brought the delvers to their doorstep, causing the deaths of three of their people," Tamás snapped.

Will tried not to think about their fate, fumbling nervously with his scabbard until Lisha returned. She spoke to Will.

They do not want to help you. Though our races once traded goods, that was many ages ago, and now there is great fear and mistrust.

Will looked away, wondering how many hours they would survive in the Darklands without Lisha to guide them.

But I convinced them, Lisha said. *They appreciate what you have done, and saw your courage in the battle with our sworn enemy. At the bottom of the Great Chasm lies our city, as well as an ancient route to the surface. I will guide you myself.*

"Thank you," Will said, whooping and then embracing her. "Thank you."

In his joy at the news, he forgot about her heat source. But as he pulled away, he realized that her outside body temperature was not much greater than someone with a fever.

She smiled, sensing his confusion. *There is nothing to fear, unless I wish to harm you.*

Will relayed the news to the others. One of the male darvish took an earth-en jar out of a bag tied to a darrowgar saddle, and gave it to Lisha. She applied a brown paste that smelled like ground mushrooms to Marek's wound. The bleeding stopped, and he groaned and curled into a ball.

This will help seal the wound. Lisha turned towards Caleb. *If my savior wish-es, this will prevent infection and speed his recovery. But it will burn.*

My savior? Will thought. He had been the one with the idea to free her; Caleb had just caught the sword. But Will was used to that. Caleb could pee in a corner and women would find it noteworthy. And if Lisha helped ease his pain and lead them to the surface, then she could worship his brother all she wanted.

Will told Caleb what Lisha had said. Caleb grimaced and nodded. Lisha held the back of his head in one hand, and with a strained smile, looked him in the eye while she applied the paste.

Caleb's howls of pain echoed through the cavern.

The Great Chasm was immense beyond imagining, an ocean drained of water set miles beneath the earth. The party traversed a staircase so precipitous Will had to keep his eyes focused on his feet to keep from getting vertigo. He pre-tended he was in Caleb's bar as they walked, knocking back a plate of wings and a pitcher of Abita.

After providing Will and his companions with water and a bag of mush-room wafers for sustenance, then wrapping Marek's stump with a roll of gauzy material, the male darvish rode at the head of the group. They gave Lisha, Yas-mina, and Marek each a darrowgar mount as well. The big man bore the jour-ney with a stoic heart, grunting and favoring his stump, but Will could only imagine the pain he was suffering. Caleb, at least, seemed to be doing better, after the initial onslaught of agony from the salve.

As the battle adrenaline faded, the reality of a two day walk with no sleep and little food reared its head, and Will wondered what the darvish would do if one of the walkers collapsed. He and Tamás were holding up, but Dalen and Caleb stumbled forward as if drunk. Will kept a hand on his brother's shirt, afraid he would misstep and plunge into the chasm.

Silence and oppressive darkness defined their descent. One of the darvish carried a glow stick that provided a circle of weak illumination at the front of the group. Long hours later, a reddish light appeared far below, glowing brighter as they approached. Will also noticed that the air had warmed and smelled faintly of sulfur.

"Is that hell down there?" Caleb muttered. "If so, I hope it has a La Quinta."

"With a pool," Will said. "And an Outback next door."

"What are these things, a La Quinta and an Outback?" Dalen asked, causing the brothers to cackle and Yasmina to give a musical laugh.

As they continued to descend, the temperature increased until sweat dripped from Will's brow. Breathing became a chore, and the sulfurous odor grew stronger. Just as he began to wonder if he could stand any more heat, the red glow coalesced into one of the strangest and most wondrous sights he had ever witnessed.

Set in an immense, oval-shaped cavern at the bottom of the Great Chasm, the tops of the darvish city's crimson arches appeared first, towering structures which spanned hundreds of feet. Further down, thousands of smaller arches and domed buildings emerged, connected by suspension bridges at varying heights, the structures composed of a variety of colors: red and gold and tan, silver and pink and green.

The base of the city was a layer of porous rock carved into streets and plazas, and darvish filled the public spaces like swarms of red ants. Beneath it all, bubbling through in fumaroles and short geysers, pooled into lakes and directed into canals, was a sea of molten lava.

Will caught his breath at the sight. The walls of the cavern surrounding the city ran bright with veins of magma, illuminating the darvish metropolis with a beautiful glow. He realized the entire city must be made of igneous rock and hardened lava—thus the different colors—and marveled at the time and creativity it had taken for the darvish to shape it.

Lisha dropped to her knees. A tear dropped from her eye. *Is it not the most beautiful sight you have ever seen?*

"It is," Will murmured in reply. "It truly is."

We are the last of our kind, she said. *This is our only remaining city.*

Her words made Will sad, and he wondered how the delvers had managed to get the upper hand over the centuries, when six darvish had just destroyed an entire war party.

With machines and cruelty, he thought. *The hallmarks of a successful civilization.*

They halted beside a side tunnel leading out of the Great Chasm. Lisha started waving her hands and arguing with the male darvish. The largest one threw his hands up, then jumped off his darrowgar and stalked down the staircase in his knee-high golden boots.

The other two males followed his lead, leaving the mounts behind.

The air of our city is too hot for you, Lisha said. *We can descend no further. My companions are not pleased, but I persuaded them to leave the darrowgars. This tunnel leads to the surface. On foot, it is a rigorous three-day journey to the nearest source of water. I fear some of you would not survive.*

Will did not disagree, though he was sad not to see the darvish city up close. With a final glance at the fiery metropolis, he mounted his darrowgar and entered the tunnel, exhausted beyond belief, wary but ready for the final leg of the journey through the Darklands.

-42-

Instructing Gus to pick him up early, Val paid a visit to the Wizard Library before class. He was surprised to find a listing for *mint orchid* in the catalogue, and he tracked the reference to the floramancy section on the third floor.

Next to a window overlooking the Hall of Wizards, Val found the book he was seeking: a recent edition of a tome entitled *Botany of the Bharat.*

He checked the index and flipped to page 346, a third of which was given over to the mint orchid: a flower which resembled an emerald lotus hanging from a silver stalk. Val perused the entry, learning that the mint orchid was highly attractive to most genera and species of the chiropteran order of mammals.

Bats.

As he expected, the last line in the fifth paragraph informed him that the exceedingly rare mint orchid was native to the humid forests of Kalingaland.

That line was marked with a tiny numeral, however, and Val felt a tingle of excitement as he read the footnote: *Successful cultivations of mint orchids have been reported in the Port Nelson Botanical Garden, the Royal Arboretum in Londyn, and in the private collection of the floramancer Wellesey Kilmore, of New Victoria.*

When he arrived at the coterie house, Val found Dida waiting for him by the front door, the exact scenario Val wished to avoid. He knew what the bibliomancer wanted to talk about.

"A moment, if you will?" Dida said.

Val was tempted to push past and ignore him, but he considered Dida a friend. "Sure."

"Are you really from this place called Earth?" Dida asked. Val didn't answer, and Dida continued, "The knowledge is safe with me, if that is your worry. I'm merely curious, as I've never met anyone from another world. We hear about the journeys of the spiritmancers, but none of us . . . I am simply curious."

Val looked him in the eye, and found that he trusted his classmate. It was better to confront the issue headlong before the bibliomancer shared the knowledge with others. "I am, Dida. Please, no one else can know. It's extremely important."

"Of course, my friend—you have my word. And is it so different from Urfe, this other world?"

"Yes and no. Some things are different almost beyond belief, but it's still filled with people just like you and me. Families with the same hopes and concerns."

"I see, yes. How did you arrive?"

Val scrambled to find something to say. "I'm here for the same reason as you," he said, dodging the question. "I was sent as an emissary, to learn and interact. Just in secret."

Dida gave a slow, thoughtful nod. "I'd very much like to see your world. Perhaps one day, we might visit it together?"

"I'd like that," Val murmured.

*   *   *

After class, Val discussed his find in the Wizard Library with the others.

"Wellesey Kilmore was a professor at the Abbey known for his brilliant experiments with plant life," Adaira said, excited. "I read about him in sixth form. When he retired, he moved to an island in Bayou Village to establish a private garden. He was called the menagerist of floramancers."

"Is he still there?" Val asked.

"I believe he died a few years ago, and I've no idea what happened to his estate." She crossed her legs, her mouth curling into a determined smile. "But we're going to find out."

Adaira informed them that a trip to Bayou Village, a community of eccentric nature lovers just outside the city limits, would require a full day, and that they would have to wait until the following Sunday, as she had functions to attend. Both Dida and Gowan were busy the weekend of the planned excursion, so Adaira and Val decided to trek to Bayou Village by themselves.

Val was frustrated, as he was hoping to corner Gowan about the Planewalk. He grew even more frustrated over the next two weeks, when Gowan brushed him off whenever Val offered to introduce him to spiritmancy. Val had come to believe that Gowan knew he didn't have the power to become a spirit mage, would always be bitter about it, and would never attempt the Planewalk.

Which meant he was going to have to find another way to pressure Gowan to reveal what he knew.

In the meantime, Val poured everything he had into preparing himself for the upcoming trial, studying and practicing his magic to the point of exhaustion. His cross-discipline studies accelerated, and he began catching up with the others, earning sour stares from Gowan and looks of admiration from the rest.

During the Friday spiritmancy class before the planned trip to Bayou Village, Val found himself again trying to produce a spark of spirit fire—the only thing the class had been doing for weeks. No one had succeeded, and Professor Azara kept watching over them with folded arms, murmuring words of wisdom as they struggled.

Find the smallest point possible. Split that in half, then half again. Deeper, now—deeper, deeper, deeper. Reach, students, reach. Reach until it burns, until you quiver from the effort, until your mind feels ready to explode into a million shards.

Val stood on his dais, shaking from exertion and lack of sleep, determined to reach the source of spirit. He broke off staring at his fingertips and closed his mind to the Professor's voice, closed it to everything except the raw power he knew seethed within him, waiting to be unlocked.

Dig, Val. Dig as you have never dug before.

He squeezed his eyes shut and imagined a ball of energy inside his head. He kept shrinking that ball with his mind, forcing it to an unimaginably small size, ever smaller, ever denser, infinity in a thimble, in a speck of dust, in an atom, squeezing so hard he felt a blood vessel pop in his eye, didn't matter, had to keep going, *smaller smaller smaller smaller smaller*

Val fell off the dais at the same time he saw a flash in his mind and felt his power ripping apart the air around him. In a panic, he lashed out with his mind to stop his fall, trying to push against the floor with a limited Wind Push. Instead, three arcs of black lightning erupted from his fingers, two of them narrowly missing Lydia and one of them striking an invisible shield protecting the air around Professor Azara. The shield crackled with lines of black energy as it absorbed the bolts.

Val landed on his back on the floor, the fall knocking the air out of him. Despite gasping for breath, he felt giddy from the rush of endorphins the magic had released, a triple shot of pure adrenaline.

He struggled to his knees, dizzy, still trying to catch his breath as he saw the astonishment flickering in Professor Azara's eyes, the look of undisguised jealousy from Damon, and the pale visage of Lydia cringing on her dais.

"I'm sorry," Val finally managed to say as he took a step towards Lydia, realizing he had almost killed her. "I didn't know. I'm sorry."

Dazed, Lydia took a step back and swallowed.

"Again," Professor Azara said evenly. "This time with control. I'll erect a Spirit Shield."

Val tried again, swooned from the strain, and remembered no more.

He woke in the infirmary, to the welcome sight of Adaira sitting in a chair by his bed, smiling as Val blinked sleep from his eyes. She was wearing a V-necked blue dress and calfskin boots, most of her hair in a topknot, a few strands spilling across her chest.

"You don't look too worried," Val said, "so I must be okay."

"I heard what happened in class—the entire school knows—and I hurried over. The nurse says you fainted from exhaustion."

"That . . . might be the case."

"Tsk tsk." She pressed a hand to his brow as if feeling his temperature. "You must take better care. You're killing yourself."

He managed a weak smile. "I'm still alive, aren't I?"

"And let's keep it that way, shall we? Full-fledged spirit fire in the first month?" Her eyes gleamed. "Impressive."

A soothing warmth spread from her hand to his forehead, then flowed through his bloodstream and invigorated him. "Are you practicing cuerpomancy on me?" he asked, wondering how much of the tingling he felt was magical, and how much was a response to her touch.

"Indeed," she said, checking his pulse and then feeling his forehead again.

"Thanks," Val said. "You didn't need to come here."

"Actually, I did. I have something for you."

"Is that right?"

She handed him a gilt-edged envelope. Curious, he opened it and saw an invitation to a dinner party on Saturday night—the next evening—at an address on St. Charles. His eyes roved downward, then clamped onto the name of the host.

Lord Alistair, Chief Thaumaturge of the Congregation.

"You're my date for the evening, if you're willing," Adaira said, her smile expanding like a cloudless sky. "I trust you can attend?"

"Lord Alistair, eh?" Gus cackled the next evening, clamping down on his pipe as the horses trotted down oak-lined St. Charles Avenue. "Movin' up in the world, ye are. *All* the way up."

"I'm just his daughter's date for the evening," Val said. "Nothing more."

"Ye just remember the little people when yer livin' at the top o' one o' them spires, laddie." He turned and pointed the pipe at Val. "Now let's hear ye practice again."

Val started talking in his best imitation of the accent of the Kenefick clan of Talinmar Village. Claiming residual exhaustion, he had skipped his Relics class to spend the entire day with Gus's relatives in a poor section of town, absorbing the speech patterns, watching the body language, and inquiring about the customs of the Kenefcks. He wasn't about to have a repeat of the Rucker experience; Lord Alistair marking him as a fraud would be a disaster, and might even land him in the Fens.

Val didn't ask Gus what he had told his family, appreciative of the fact that no one asked any questions. Most likely, the salary Val paid Gus kept his family in good stead, and they weren't about to jeopardize the income.

As dusk approached, Gus reined in the horses outside a beige stone mansion that covered half a city block. Two live oaks shaded the front of the residence, their moss-laden branches extending to the bay windows and portico balconies jutting outward from the house.

Thickets of topiary demarcated the front lawn, as well as fountains streaming multicolored liquids. Remembering the magical defenses secreted within the landscaping of Lord Alistair's fortress in the Wizard District, Val stepped nervously along the pebbled path, taking care not to touch anything. Two majitsu watched with folded arms from a balcony.

"Don't forget where ye came from," Gus said in a low voice, cackling as the horses trotted away. Val chuckled at Gus's double entendre. He was a shrewd one.

Adaira opened the door before Val could knock, looking resplendent in a full length silver dress with crimson trim that accentuated her slender waist. Her hair was unbound, kept back with a golden circlet.

Gus had helped Val purchase a dinner jacket for the occasion, guiding him to a tailor on Canal. Val felt comfortable in formal attire; he was used to bespoke suits and thousand dollar accessories.

"My my, what a handsome gentlemen has appeared," Adaira said.

He bowed and offered his arm. "Surpassed, by far, by the beauty of his escort."

She beamed and led him through the stone foyer, down a hallway covered in oil paintings, then past a succession of lavish rooms to a dining hall dominated by a diamond chandelier.

Three wizards Val knew on sight, and two he didn't, were seated with their consorts at a long table of polished mahogany: Professor Azara, Dean Varen, a petite and beautiful blond woman wearing a high-waisted white dress and matching tiara, and a handsome dark-haired man dressed in a brown suit with coattails, fingers glittering with jeweled rings.

At the head of the table loomed Lord Alistair, wearing a sleek, blue-white robe with a high collar and buttons down the front. Except for a gloved hand, he wore no jewelry other than a thick azantite bracelet. He and Professor Azara were the only two present without a consort.

Lord Alistair swept his palm outward, ushering Val and Adaira to the table. "Welcome, Val. My daughter speaks very highly of you. As do," his eyes flicked to Professor Azara, as if sharing a pleasant secret, "your professors."

Val knew in an instant he had been invited to this dinner party not just because of Adaira's attentions, but because of the future promise he saw reflected in the eyes of the elder mages. He had seen the same look in the eyes of the partners who had conducted his first evaluations at his law firm.

The wizards wanted to groom him.

Val gave a half-bow, working hard to calm his nerves. "I'm honored to be here," he said, with just the right notes of humility and confidence.

More greetings were made. Adaira introduced the blond woman as Kalyn Tern, High Aeromancer, and the dark-haired man as Braden Shankstone, High Cuerpomancer.

"I must confess," Kalyn said to Val, her eyes sharp, "I was expecting a different accent from someone from the far North. My family is from Whiterock Junction, a few hours south of Talinmar."

"Ah, yes," Val said, switching to the soft and elongated vowels he had heard the Keneficks use, "perhaps you would prefer if I talked more in the manner of my forebears?"

Kalyn nodded and gave the hint of a cold smile, as if Val had just passed a test which could have been unfortunate for him to fail. Kalyn continued, "I see that, like myself, you've chosen to adopt a more neutral accent in your professional life. It's for the best, lest your city-bred peers," her gaze warmed as it swept the room, "judge you for your provincial ways."

The room chuckled, and Val breathed a huge sigh of relief. He couldn't have started with the Talinmar accent, of course, or Adaira would have found it suspect. Kalyn had provided the perfect opening.

A dinner party of this caliber, Val knew, was akin to war. So he went into battle playing the part of the aspiring wizard, affording his elders the respect they deserved, silent for most of the meal, chiming in when necessary to let everyone know he possessed the requisite intelligence and ambition to one day join them as a peer.

Of course, being from another world made it hard to blend, but Val was a master of assimilation, and he chimed in with cogent observations whenever he had an opening. He had already learned the dining customs of this world by watching Adaira at the coterie.

He could feel everyone observing him, evaluating, judging. When Adaira mentioned the growing incidents of unrest tied to the Devla Cult, he felt the air in the room stiffen. The elder mages seemed to exchange a collective glance, and Lord Alistair addressed Val. "Tell me, if you were a member of the Conclave, what action would you take in response to this cult?"

Val felt his palms grow warm as the attention of the room shifted his way. He met Professor Azara's implacable gaze for an instant, and he said, "A difficult road to navigate. If the response is too weak, the cult will be emboldened, and attract new members. And if the Congregation reacts too strongly, one risks alienating the more . . . moderate . . . factions of society."

There were murmurs of agreement. Kalyn said, "What would you propose, then? Leaders cannot afford to occupy the middle. Hard choices must be made."

Val liked Kalyn least of all—the woman's every word was calculated, and he sensed an animosity towards him. Maybe he was being paranoid.

"True," Val said, as his lessons from *History and Governance* flashed through his head. He thought he knew what they wanted to hear. "The Congregation is extremely powerful. Yet despite this power, wizards are still—and always will be—in the vast minority. Religion is akin to an infectious disease, and we must never allow it to regain a foothold. The common born must believe that *we* are their hope for the future, for a better life. A movement like the Devla cult must not just be defeated, but *discredited*. Not allowed to be martyred. Best of all if the cult self destructs from within, demonstrating the disastrous results of a return to a superstitious belief system."

Braden nodded his approval, and Lord Alistair leaned forward, the most engaged Val had seen him.

"Goad them," Val said. "Trick the cult into an act of violence that puts in-nocent lives at risk—common-born lives. Plant a mole that destroys the lead-ership from within. Challenge their prophets to display the power of their non-existent god, to feed the poor with their religion." He spread his hands. "Of course, the Congregation could scorch the Realm and wipe the Devla cult from existence. But a far better outcome is to use the cult to bolster your repu-tation. Secure the will of the people for the future."

Val leaned back and reached for his wine glass, resisting the urge to glance around the table for validation. He saw Adaira's hands tense in her lap, could feel all eyes on him as they waited to see how their host would respond.

"Bravo," Lord Alistair said slowly, raising his glass, "to a most measured and intelligent response."

Everyone toasted, Val felt a trickle of sweat roll down his back, and the con-versation turned to more mundane matters. After a time, Val excused himself, asking for the washroom.

Adaira led him up a wide staircase, pointing down a hallway at the first landing. "It's the second door on your left," she said, squeezing his hand. "Ex-cellent showing. You impressed them."

On his way down the hallway, Val passed a study lined with floor to ceiling bookshelves. On a hunch, he peered down the corridor in either direction, then stepped inside and perused a few of the titles, all of which pertained to the history and use of magic.

Lord Alistair's personal library, he realized. A potential gold mine.

He wondered if the library was warded, and debated slipping on the Ring of Shadows. He discarded the idea, reasoning that if the wards or one of the mages caught him using the ring, then he would really be in trouble.

Scanning the titles as fast as he could, he padded across the thick rug, know-ing he should get back to the dinner party.

There.

The title jumped out at him like a striking cobra: *Manual of Pedagogy for Spiritmancers*.

His heart slapped against his chest. Ears cocked for sounds of an approach, he checked the index.

Walk of Planes......... 257–258.

With trembling fingers, he flipped the gilt-edged pages and read the entry on the Planewalk.

As established in 1325 P.R. by a joint effort of the spirit mage thaumaturgical coalition, at the behest of Lord Myrddin and in furtherance of the need for a more rigorous and uniform standard of entry, completion of the Walk of Planes became a prerequisite to initiation as a spirit mage. Designed with the help of the renowned spirit architect Corinn Leginthius, this final and most rigorous hurdle is a test of each applicant's ability to work with spirit, as well as a measure of fortitude, will, and mental constitution.

According to coalition regulation 17.5k, the only instructions to be meted to students attempting the Planewalk are the following: (1) Utilizing solely the student's individual reserves of spirit, the Spirit Bridge must be walked in a continuous motion until the portal is reached; and (2) stopping or leaving the Spirit Bridge will result in certain oblivion.

Due to the high number of past casualties, it is recommended that a member of the faculty oversee each attempt at the Planewalk, such that the prospective spirit mage, should he or she feel unable to push through or remain attached to the Spirit Bridge, may conclude the test at any time by accepting the assistance of the elder mage. Incomplete negotiation of the Planewalk will terminate the student's candidacy. Note, however, that according to recent regulations established at the Council of Highridge, a student who has failed his or her attempt at the Planewalk may choose to undertake another Discipline Exam. This exception is exclusive to spiritmancy students.

It is further recommended that the entrance to the Planewalk remain under the sole jurisdiction of the spirit mage faculty, lest any unfortunate accidents result.

Pedagogical suggestions for navigation of the Walk of Planes include the following: rigorous application of

A voice from behind interrupted him. "Are you seeking a particular tome, or just browsing?"

Val whipped around. Standing at the entrance to the library, petite arms crossed against her chest, eyebrows arched in suspicion, was Kalyn Tern.

-43-

Riding the darrowgar through the Darklands was a surreal experience. Unlike the precipitous descent into the Great Chasm, the lithe creatures sped through the rough-cut tunnels and hollowed-out lava tubes, climbed walls to avoid piles of rubble, leapt over crevasses, darted through low passages with their riders hugging them tight.

"All this time, I thought the darrowgar were the monsters," Caleb said.

Yasmina stroked the back of her mount. "I believe this species—note the shorter tails and more powerful legs, made to carry riders—has been domesticated by the darvish."

"Ah," Caleb said. "So we could have been eaten after all, back in the first battle. Speaking of combat, you're becoming quite the warrior, little brother. I saw you hold your own with that delver."

"Becoming?" Tamás said. "I believe he has arrived."

A tingle shot through Will. It was praise he had been waiting for his entire life. "I'm still learning," he said. "Nowhere near as good as you."

"We shall work on that," Tamás said. "I recognize natural ability when I see it. In what style have you trained?"

"Um, the shotgun mercenary style."

Caleb grinned. "The try-not-to-die-while-training-with-hottie-adventuress style."

Tamás looked bewildered by both answers.

As they crossed through an intersection of passages, Dalen peered nervously to each side. "*Lucka*, I hope there's nothing out there that can catch a darrowgar. My Da told me a story once about an evil menagerist banished to a cave, who found his way to the Darklands and continues his experiments to this day."

Will appreciated a potent imagination, but seeing as they were far off the grid in the Darklands, with little protection, he wished Dalen would shut up about his Da.

Despite their fears, the old darvish tunnels remained silent and empty, an unending procession of earth and stone and cooled magma, until Lisha called a halt in a cavern of exquisite beauty.

A stream of translucent water spilled into a lake filling most of a huge grotto, the water shimmering against a beach the color of green algae. Even more stunning were the thousands of glistening silver strands hanging like strings of diamonds from the cathedral ceiling.

Glowworms, Lisha said to Will. *Trying to attract their prey. It is beautiful, no?*

It was beautiful as long as their prey was tiny insects, he thought, and not a party of adventurers.

We will stay here for the night. The darrowgar will help protect us. I will forage for food.

Will plopped down on the eerie green beach, famished and exhausted. Dalen's light source faded, but the silken strands lit the cavern with a silver glow. Everyone drank greedily from the lake and separated to wash. Lisha returned with an armful of mushrooms, caught fish from the lake by spearing them with her tail, and cooked them with her palms.

The darrowgars slept in a circle surrounding the party. Lisha said they would keep watch. After dinner, Will collapsed in a heap, out cold as soon as he closed his eyes.

Nature's call woke Caleb from a deep sleep, and he padded across the beach to relieve himself, the glowworm strings lighting his way. A darrowgar turned its angular head to watch him.

It was a bizarre but beautiful place, this underworld fantasy land, and Caleb wished they had time to explore it. Without the monsters, of course. He loved new and unusual things, but he had never been much for danger. Will had inherited that gene. The youngest Blackwood wanted to be a hero, while the eldest was shooting for Emperor of the Universe.

Caleb just wanted to enjoy the New Orleans nightlife, chow down on

Cajun food, listen to tunes, travel when he could afford it, and spend some quality times with friends. It was the Caleb Way. The Tao of Caleb.

When he zipped up and turned to go back to camp, Lisha appeared like a ghost in front of him. Caleb jerked backwards and lost a few years of his life, but the darvish smiled, pressed a finger to her lips for silence, and moved closer.

Really close.

She reached up to caress his cheek. Glossy black hair framed her oval face, those smoky eyes and long lashes drawing him in.

This is not a good idea, Caleb. Not even remotely.

He knew Yasmina would be hurt if she found out, but, surprising to him, it was another woman who gave him the most pause. The memory of Marguerite's touch still burned hot within him, much hotter than he thought it would, much hotter than he cared even to admit. Yet Marguerite was gone, dead or halfway across the world, a fading fever dream of passionate nights and shared laughter amid a doomed journey that had taken the lives of half their party.

He could counsel himself all he wanted, but Caleb had as much willpower with beautiful women as an alcoholic with an open bar full of top shelf liquor. Lisha took his hand and led him to a sandy alcove hidden in the recesses of the cavern. The glowworm threads provided just enough light for him to make out her features, but he couldn't see the camp, and knew no one else could see them.

She started to kiss him, and he stopped her. "How old are you?" he whispered, sensing by her interactions with Will that she understood most English. Lisha's tail and horns didn't bother him, but her age did.

She gave him a confused look and then smiled in understanding. She leaned down and drew a number in the sand.

Seventy-three.

Caleb stared at the number and then hiccupped a laugh. "Is that young for a darvish?"

She shook her head.

"Old?"

Another shake. She drew another number in the sand. One hundred and fifty.

"That's how long your people live?" he asked.

She nodded, smiled, and drew him close again. This time he didn't resist, stunned that Lisha was a middle-aged woman.

Whatever they did down in Darvish Land, Caleb thought, they sure knew how to do *this*. She was as passionate a lover as the heat source pulsating within her suggested. When she got too excited, she had to remove her palms before they burned him, but Caleb didn't mind the extra effort.

Not one bit.

Yasmina woke and reached for Caleb. After dinner, though they had yet to kiss, they had fallen asleep in each other's arms for the first time in a very long while. It felt nice, she had to admit.

Of course it felt nice, she chided herself. *He always feels nice. That isn't the issue.*

Maybe, just maybe, the journey and this world had changed him. Made him more at peace with himself and the universe.

Because that was the real issue with Caleb, she knew. The middle Blackwood brother was uncomfortable in his own skin, haunted by his own perceived inadequacies and the empty mysteries of the universe. So he plugged the gap with gratuitous behavior.

With things that made him feel good.

Yet she had sensed a change on the journey, a higher self-awareness from staring death in the face. She understood his pain, his yearning, his empathy, and she loved him all the more for it—if only he could balance.

If they made it out of this insane world alive, then maybe they could take baby steps in the right direction.

When she didn't feel Caleb beside her, she sat up and looked around, concerned. It wasn't like him to wander off alone and put himself in danger. The darrowgars ringing the camp didn't look worried. Maybe he had gone to relieve himself.

She wouldn't be able to relax until she found him, so she stood and took Elegon's owl staff—her staff, now—in her hands. She hadn't told the others, but when she was carrying the walking stick, she could see in the dark and hear better than normal. As if the staff granted her a modicum of the abilities of the extraordinary avian, the great horned owl, whose insignia the staff bore.

She stopped to stroke the neck of a darrowgar, and leaned down to whisper her question into the animal's ear. She still did not understand why she could communicate so well with animals or how it even worked, but with a mournful look, as if reluctant to respond, the darrowgar swung its head towards an alcove nestled in a far corner of the cavern.

Yasmina padded down the beach. As she drew closer, faint murmurings emanated from inside the alcove. The murmurings coalesced into recognizable sounds of passion, and her night vision confirmed what she had suspected.

She lingered for a moment, watching Caleb make love to the darvish woman, then slowly returned to her sandy bed, laying on her back and staring at the glowing strands of silver.

When Will woke the next morning, feeling as refreshed and alive as he had in months, he sprang to his feet, ready to finish the journey.

The others rose one by one. Will noticed Yasmina giving Caleb the cold shoulder. He also noticed Lisha making calf eyes at Caleb, and they both had a glazed, satisfied look in their eyes.

Surely not, Will thought.

They climbed atop the darrowgars and set off again, climbing steadily uphill the entire day, through endless miles of darvish tunnels. Though everyone except Yasmina seemed in better spirits, the party was quiet for the most part, not wishing to disturb whatever might be lying in wait in the Darklands.

The darrowgars started to tire, causing Yasmina to worry for their welfare, but Lisha urged them forward until they emerged from a long tunnel into a field of underground boulders, piled hundreds of feet high. The darrowgar sprang up the tower of giant rocks until they came to a stop near the apex, exposing a sight Will had thought he might never see again.

A sliver of golden daylight peeking through.

-44-

As Mala drifted alone through the impossible hues of the Place Between Worlds, stubbornly clutching the head of the slain majitsu, she pondered the wondrous mystery of it all.

What *was* this place? It was the stuff of dreams and legend—this she knew. But was it the essence of reality itself? Was it natural, an innate part of the multiverse, or had someone made it? And if so, who? Ancient beings, elder spirit mages, entities from another universe? Or was the myth of Devla, the creator god of her people, to be believed after all?

Had this place existed since time eternal, had it witnessed the birth of her world? Was the concept of infinite being even possible? Wasn't there always a beginning?

Though Mala had seen more magic than most, she considered herself a grounded woman, attuned to the harsh realities of life. But this place, this wonder of wonders, stoked the embers of mysticism in the hardened adventuress, a tingling of supernatural awe that left her humbled.

Especially now that she wasn't being chased by a murderous majitsu.

She forced away her thoughts and considered her predicament. She should have asked more questions of the fence who sold her the amulet, for she had no idea how these portals worked. Where would the doorway to Urfe deposit her? She assumed she would return where she had left, which she wanted to avoid at all costs. She had no desire to face another majitsu or find out whether Zedock had returned home.

What if there was another way? She had heard that certain magical items, especially those rare few made by an elder spirit mage, such as an amulet of the planes, could be manipulated by thought alone.

Would thinking about a place she desired to go suffice? What about some-*one*, instead? It couldn't hurt to try, she decided. It was better than the alternative, appearing uninvited in the home of an angry necromancer.

The keening of the astral wind rose in the distance as she retraced her journey through the Place Between Worlds. Despite the harried nature of her first visit, she had made sure to remember the way to Urfe, lest she be lost forever. As she drifted closer to the filmy portal, streaked with the familiar blues and browns and greens of her world, she thought of a place far from New Victoria, a place where she could rest while deciding on her next course of action. Hedging her bets, she also thought of a warrior, someone in whose arms she wouldn't mind recuperating for a few days, though that was all it would be. Mala belonged to no man.

The portal to Urfe neared, and then it was a few feet away. With the astral wind keening behind her, Mala tossed the head of the majitsu through, fulfilling her promise, and then extended her arms and dove into her home world.

-45-

Val's mind whirled, trying to think of a clever excuse to tell Kalyn. He had been so focused on reading about the Planewalk he had forgotten that he was an uninvited guest in Lord Alistair's library.

He closed the book and slipped it back onto the shelf. "Just browsing on my way back from the restroom. I'm fascinated by the history of magic, and this is a superb collection."

Can she read the title from afar? Does she suspect what I'm trying to do?

Val started for the door. As he passed the aeromancer, she said, "Talented you may be, but you're not yet a wizard. It would behoove you to treat a dinner invitation at the house of the Chief Thaumaturge with the proper respect."

Val gave a half-bow. "You're of course right. Forgive me. I meant no harm."

"Some of us wonder at your lineage, you know. 'Tis quite strange for the family of a mage as promising as you to pass unnoticed. I don't recognize your surname; are you parents not members of the Congregation?"

"Only my father was wizard born, and he didn't have the aptitude," Val lied. "My parents were as amazed as everyone else when my . . . strength . . . manifested."

"And how did it manifest?"

What does she know? Can she tell if I'm lying?

"My parents and I were walking in the mountains one day. An earthquake caused an avalanche above us, with no room to escape. Without thinking, I pushed back with my mind–and moved a few tons of snow and rock."

"I see," Kalyn said, and he met her icy stare with a cool gaze of his own, giving her no reason to doubt him.

He walked past her as he left the room, feeling eyes on his back as he descended the staircase.

The dinner party ended without further incident. After the other guests left and Lord Alistair retired to his study, Adaira invited Val to the garden for a midnight stroll. Once he agreed, she grabbed two glasses and a dusty bottle of granth and led him into the topiary.

They strolled hand in hand along the pebbled path, slipping among the hedgerows and colored fountains, stopping in an open-air rotunda draped with bougainvillea.

She sat beside him on a curved bench and poured the granth. The perfumed air tickled Val's nostrils. Insects droned in the background, the moon a silver bauble above.

"This granth is delicious," he said, and meant it. It tasted as good or better than the finest liqueurs back home.

"It's my favorite," Adaira murmured. "From an estate in the Ninth."

They drank in silence, soaking up the night. When she finished her glass, she caressed his cheek with the back of a finger. "I'm glad you came. I know it was a difficult gathering. You were more than up to the task."

"I enjoyed the challenge," Val said. "And for the most part, I enjoyed the company."

Adaira's face scrunched. "You must mean Kalyn. Yes, she can be difficult. But she's well-respected on the Conclave, an extremely powerful aeromancer."

"I've no doubt. And Braden?"

"My father's chief advisor. I would say his protégé, but I know he longs for a spirit mage to claim that title."

"Are there none available?"

"He has not been impressed with the recent graduates. Along with Dean

Groft, my father is the most powerful mage of his generation, and I suspect he is looking for someone with . . . similar ambition." She moved to caress the side of his neck. "I must confess, I had an ulterior motive for inviting you tonight."

He lifted his eyebrows.

"I wished my father to approve of you. And not because he's seeking a protégé."

"Oh?" he said, with playful ignorance. "Why, then?"

Her finger moved downward, tracing his lips, sending a current of electricity arcing through him. "Because *I* approve of you."

She took his face in her hands and leaned in to kiss him. He met her halfway. Adaira was a natural kisser, playful and passionate, though he could tell she was inexperienced. He returned her passion, keeping just enough of himself in reserve to increase her desire.

When she pulled away, her voice was husky. "Shall we walk?"

Val stood with her, relieved. The attraction was there, but he was uncomfortable in her father's garden, with the majitsu lurking about. "Let's."

They held hands again, and he could feel the heat in her palms. When they reached the front gate, she put her arms around his neck and leaned in to whisper in his ear. "You didn't expect to stay the night, did you?"

"Of course not," he said, letting his lips brush her ear.

Her voice thickened. "Though who knows what the future might hold?"

"Not even a spirit mage."

She gave him a lingering kiss on the forehead before pulling away and raising her voice. "I'll see you tomorrow morning in the coterie, then?" she said. "For our study session?"

"I'll be there."

Hand in hand the next morning, Val and Adaira flew off the coterie roof and towards the Adventurers' Emporium, where Gus and his carriage waited to take them to Bayou Village in search of the mint orchid.

"You don't think your majitsu will be suspicious?" Val shouted, as the wind rushed by. Flying over the city was an intoxicating experience.

"They think I'm studying all day in the coterie again," she replied, her green silk jacket flapping in the wind above leather boots and breeches.

"How far is Bayou Village?"

"By carriage? Two hours, perhaps. You should know the body of another acolyte was found this morning. I expect an announcement on Monday."

Val grimaced. "Where?"

"The French Quarter again. The body was lying in a gutter outside a brothel."

"Any chance the wizards will close the school?"

"Never. They are far too proud. I do know they've initiated majitsu patrols in the French Quarter and Government District."

They landed next to the carriage. Gus helped Adaira climb aboard, his eyes wide the entire time. Val slid in next to her, feeling a shiver of attraction as she looped an arm through his. A dose of reality followed the shiver, cooling him off like a dip in a freezing mountain stream.

Val liked Adaira. A lot.

But even if they found this mint orchid, he had no intention of chasing after the assassin again. According to the book in Lord Alistair's library, the spiritmancy faculty knew the location of the Walk of Planes, which meant Professor Azara knew.

And Val was betting Gowan knew as well.

Regardless of what happened at Bayou Village, it was time to move forward. Every moment his brothers were missing was a sword thrust to his gut.

"Whether we find this orchid or not," Val said, "we should meet with the others tomorrow night. Decide what to do."

Adaira leaned her head against his shoulder as they trotted down Magazine Street. "Yes," she said.

Gus carried them through the western portion of New Victoria, past the Garden District and the stables and a series of parks along the river. They turned north to skirt the enormous Fifth District Protectorate Army barracks, then west again through a residential neighborhood that merged into miles of tenement sprawl, ending at another portion of the watery Fens.

Val observed Adaira's reaction as they circled the southern edge of the horrific swamp ghetto, littered with rotting wooden planks and the hordes of wretched souls who lived atop them. A few "lucky" exiles huddled around stick and canvas tents, or sat on wooden crates and puffed on homemade pipes packed with opium-laced tobacco. Most of them just withered in the humid air, riddled with disease and surrounded by swarms of mosquitoes.

As they drew closer to the edge, Val noticed a woman with deep black skin and mini dreadlocks tending to the wounded on one of the larger platforms. A blue tribal tattoo snaked around the woman's arms and torso. "Allira?" Val whispered to himself, as the woman dabbed a cloth into a jar and applied the paste to a leg covered in festering sores.

Adaira's mouth tightened. "A horror you are spared in the North, I trust?"

"Poverty's everywhere," Val said, distracted. He wanted to call out to his old companion but dared not in front of Adaira. Even though Allira didn't speak, it would be an awkward reunion to explain. "But not like this."

"It's the children who are the tragedy," Adaira said softly, watching as a group of naked children scampered through a pile of refuse, drawing perilously close to the ridged back of a crocosaur. "The adults have made their choices."

Really? Val thought. *Because no adult he knew would choose a life like that.*

He didn't kid himself that the poor deserved to be poor, at least on any moral scale, but neither did he sugarcoat the inevitability of poverty. Not because some people deserved it, but because human greed would always ensure inequalities.

Those born into privilege, he had learned over the years, had an amazing capacity for rationalizing the plight of the needy.

Leaving the Fens sprawling to the horizon on their right, the carriage followed a rutted lane through a pine forest, until it ended at a tract of marshland dotted with pastel wooden houses integrated into groves of cypress. Gator-choked canals dissected the watery channels and islands of marsh grass, and the residents poled through the swamp in canoes and pirogues.

"Bayou Village?" he guessed.

"Aye," Gus said.

"Who lives here?"

"Artists, philosophers, a few outcasts with means, mostly those who want to live a life close to nature," Adaira said. "It's quite romantic, though I fear I'm a city girl at heart."

"Nature is for weekend getaways," Val agreed. "Any idea where to look?"

"My childhood nanny retired here. She'll be delighted to see me." Adaira leaned forward and thanked Gus for the ride with a peck on the forehead, causing him to blush, then waved for Val to follow her into flight. "I've visited her once before," she said as they soared above the collection of quaint residences, pointing at a lemon-colored tree house shaped like a boat.

They landed on the 'prow,' a deck-like area with a table and two chairs. A rope ladder led to a canoe tied alongside the house. A slim older woman with curly gray hair rushed up a ladder to greet them, hugging Adaira tight.

"What an unexpected treat, my dearie! How are ye?"

Adaira introduced Val to the woman, who she called Aunt Ilsa. After a few minutes of small talk, the former governess brought out tea and pastries.

"What brings you to our little oasis? Of course I fancy a random visit, but my intuition tells me ye've another purpose."

Adaira smiled. "As always, your intuition is astute. I've taken on a class project that involves gathering a mint orchid. A book in the Wizard Library tells me this species might be found in the private garden of Wellesey Kilmore—are you familiar with him? He's a floramancer of some repute."

Aunt Ilsa clucked. "Of course. Wellesey was our most famous resident. Being a wizard and all."

"Was?"

"He disappeared years ago, dearie. At least half a decade."

Adaira's mouth opened and then closed. "Where did he go? Does anyone still tend his garden?"

Aunt Ilsa's eyes clouded. "Wellesey lived alone on an island a few miles inside the swamp. No one knows where he went, and the few people who ventured onto his isle to see if there was anything to salvage . . . well, they never returned."

"Never returned?" Val echoed.

She held her palms up. "No one knows what happened on that island, but Wellesley came here to experiment." She patted Adaira's hand. "I don't meddle in the affairs of wizards. I believe common born should be common born, and wizards wizards."

"Can you point the way to his island?" Adaira asked. "We'd like to fly over."

Aunt Ilsa hesitated. "I'd prefer if ye didn't. Not even the crocosaurs swim near it now, and I'd never forgive myself if something were to happen. Your father . . . ."

"We'll be safe," Adaira said. "I promise. Just a glance from above."

After a few more protestations, Aunt Ilsa reluctantly gave them the directions. Adaira hugged her, but it didn't relieve the worry swimming in the older woman's eyes.

"I wonder what happened to Wellesley," Adaira asked as they flew northwest over a vast swamp lake.

"No idea," Val said, "but there's his island."

From above, it looked just as Aunt Ilsa had described: a landmass with six narrow inlets encroaching on one side, like a six-fingered hand. A thick jungle canopy, lusher and more tropical than the rest of the swamp, covered the island.

"Shall we?" Adaira asked.

Val descended in response, until they were hovering a hundred feet above the surface. From that distance, they realized the island was a seething mass of plant life so dense and overgrown it resembled a nest of snakes. The diversity of color and species was startling; every tree and bush and flower looked different than the next. Only the green, ropy vines that seemed to proliferate on the island, draping the ground and other plants, looping from tree to tree, had any uniformity.

Val pointed out the top of a stone chimney rising out of the jungle near the middle of the island. "That must be Wellesley's old house."

They drifted closer, until the outline of a modest bungalow took shape, smothered in thick vines. "I wonder what happened?" Adaira murmured. "If he left, where did he go? And why so sudden?"

Val breathed deeply, enjoying the heady floral scent. Despite the beauty, the island made him nervous, as if something alien lurked amid the trees and vines, waiting for them to step foot on the surface.

Lucky for them, they didn't have to.

He folded his arms as they hovered. "How in the world are we going to find a single orchid in this jungle?"

Adaira gave a knowing smile and took a stoppered bottle from a pocket of her breeches. "I made a little purchase at the New Victoria Magick Shoppe. A potion of enhanced smell." She unstopped the bottle and downed the potion. "As long as the mint orchid smells like mint, we should have no trouble."

After a few moments, she sniffed the air, her eyes widening. "This is amazing. I can smell *everything*. There's jasmine by that oak tree, fennel and rosemary and lemons on the breeze, iris and lily coming from behind the house, a *thousand* different smells."

She drifted towards the house, pointing out a patch of greenery near the front door. "Mint for the kitchen, as I suspected. We'll need to range further."

They flew in lazy concentric rings radiating out from the house, allowing Adaira to test each section of the island with her nose. Though Val still had plenty of energy, it was the longest time he had spent in the air, and he was tiring. He understood why Adaira had suggested taking the carriage to Bayou Village.

"I have to ask," he said, "why we didn't go to the Magick Shoppe for the Shadow Veil that night?"

"Too expensive," she said, distracted by her task. "I have only a small allowance, and could barely afford this potion."

Val thought of the chests full of coin in Salomon's Crib. *I could have helped with that.*

Halfway between the house and the northern shore, Adaira stopped moving and breathed in deep draughts of air, her nose twitching. "There," she murmured, and dove towards the trees.

Val followed, landing next to her in a thicket of vines and hibiscus. Adaira waded through a clump of yellow bushes to a group of orchids with elegant silver stalks growing alongside a fallen log. Hanging pendulously from the stalks were emerald flowers similar to an upside down lotus, with pulpy red centers.

True to the name, the orchids smelled strongly of mint, enhanced with notes of vanilla. As he helped her harvest the flowers, placing them in a cloth bag she had brought, Val heard a whisper on the breeze.

Elpwkemstr

He started. "Did you hear that?"

"Hear what? My nose is limiting my other senses."

"It was strange. Like a whisper in my mind, or a voice floating on the breeze."

"What did it say?"

"It sounded like gibberish."

Adaira gave the jungle a nervous glance, then closed the bag and tied it. "This should be plenty. Shall we leave?"

"Definitely."

Val kept an eye on the jungle as he drifted upwards, Adaira a few feet beside him. He heard her laugh and say, "We can play later, silly."

Elpwkemstr

Before he could ask what she was talking about, she shrieked at the same time something tugged on his leg. He whipped his head down and saw a vine wrapped around his ankle and another snaking upwards from the undergrowth, attaching to his other leg. He tried to jerk his away, but the vines were too strong.

Elpwkemssssttttrrrr

"Adaira!" He yelled.

"It has me, too!"

Instead of bringing him to the ground, the vine carried Val ten feet to the left, where another vine wrapped his waist as the original fell away. As he started to panic, the whole jungle came alive, a continuous stream of writhing vines that rose up to carry him and Adaira towards the center of the island.

She thrust her palms downward, slicing through the vines attached to her leg with cuerpomancy, but as she freed herself and tried to fly higher, more vines ensnared her, wrapping her faster than she could cut them away.

"I can't get free!" she screamed.

Val craned his neck as he struggled. He saw the stone chimney poking out of the jungle a few hundred yards away. For whatever reason, the vines seemed to be taking them to the house. Was it possible Wellesley was still alive?

Elpwkemssssttttrrrr

"What's that voice?" she asked, her voice shrill. "What's it saying?"

"I don't know," he yelled back.

Elpwkemsstr elpwkemsstr

They drew close and closer to the center of the island. Adaira tried a fire sphere, causing the vines holding her to curl away, but a dozen more ensnared her. Val tried desperately to think of a spell that might free them, and finally decided to conserve his remaining energy until they knew the end game.

The front of the house came into view. He paled when he saw the vines covering it rising and falling in a regular rhythm, over and over, as if breathing. He had the sudden insight that the mass of vines covering the island was a single organism, an experiment by the floramancer gone horribly awry.

Elpwkemsstr elpwkemsstr

Was the damnable thing trying to communicate with us, Val wondered? What does it want?

Or was it just hungry?

The front door had long ago been ripped off its hinges, and the vines thrust the two of them inside the house. What he saw next caused his stomach to lurch and his throat to tighten with panic. A sinkhole had swallowed most of the floor, and at the bottom lurked a bulbous green plant with a circular maw of teeth, at least fifteen feet in diameter. Dozens of vines of all sizes, some as thick as flagpoles, snaked out from the maw, writhing as Val and Adaira drew closer.

Elpwakemstrelpwakemstrelpwakemsstrr

Adaira screamed again. Val spotted something in the corner of the room, something he had to look at twice to believe.

An intact human skeleton sitting upright at the kitchen table, the bones held together by a nest of tiny vines.

Elpwkemstr elpwkemstr elp wke mstrrrrrr

And then he got it. He understood the twisted dynamics in play, the sentient nature of the plant, its confusion over Wellesley's death, and the meaning of the words they kept hearing.

Elpwkemstr

Help wke mstr

Help wake master

"Adaira!" he shouted, as they approached the edge of the sinkhole. "On three, I want you to punch through the ceiling, then free yourself and fly straight up as fast as you can. *Don't stop.*"

"Why will that work? What are you doing?"

The vines carried them above the maw of the plant monster. Below the buzzsaw of razor-edged teeth, the pink flesh of its gullet throbbed in anticipation. "Trust me," Val said, with confidence he didn't feel. "Are you ready?"

"Just hurry!"

"One . . . two . . . three!"

As Adaira used Wind Push to blow a hole in the ceiling, rattling the entire structure, he used his magic to levitate the bones of what he knew used to be Wellesey Kilmore.

Mstr, the vines whispered as the skeleton drifted across the room. *Msstrr!*

The vines holding the skeleton intact slithered away, and Val felt his own bonds loosening. He drifted Wellesley's skeleton to the right, holding the bones together with his will, positioning it ten feet above the gaping mouth of the plant creature.

As soon as he felt the vines holding him slip away, forcing him to use magic to stay aloft, he dropped the skeleton into the open maw.

Msstrrr . . . noooo!

As every loose vine rushed to cradle the falling bones, Val exploded upward, following Adaira through the hole in the ceiling, using every ounce of his power to speed his flight.

When he risked a quick glance back, he saw an army of vines shooting skyward, grasping for them. Adaira managed to soar out of reach of the plant creature, but the closest vines shot skyward and caught Val by the ankles, yanking him down. He tried to accelerate away, but the vines were too strong.

"Adaira!"

She turned and flicked her wrist downward, cutting through the vines holding Val's ankles. He flew higher, but two more vines shot up and took their place. Adaira cut those, too. In the intervals between cuts, Val kept surging skyward, gaining foot by foot. He was tiring quickly, but Adaira and the threat of death urged him on, and he finally flew high enough to escape the grasp of the vines.

Breathing hard, they extended their arms and flew as high and as fast as they could.

They didn't stop until they reached Bayou Village.

Val landed hard, then stumbled to his feet. His whole body ached from the escape and the day of flying. Again he marveled at the bone-throbbing physical exhaustion the prolonged use of magic entailed, not to mention the mental fatigue.

As Gus clicked the horses into action, Adaira collapsed into Val's arms. The bag of mint orchids was tied to her belt. "I've never been so frightened," she said. "If you hadn't figured it out . . . ."

He stroked her hair. "It took both of us, working together. You need to teach me the spell that sliced those vines."

"It's a simple cuerpomancy spell. A matter of focusing power in a small enough place to strip through the tissue."

"Remind me not to make you angry. Or any cuerpomancer."

"Once you master Spirit Fire, you needn't worry about dealing with plant creatures. It was sad, wasn't it? The poor thing just missed its master."

"I'm wondering if that *poor thing* didn't kill Wellesley."

She frowned. "He was a powerful mage. I suspect his heart failed him, with no one but his creation to bear witness."

They rode in silence for a while, until Val leaned forward, elbows on his knees and hands clasped. "We need to give this mint orchid to the investigators, Adaira. We've risked enough already, and from what I've heard about this assassin . . . it's too risky. We're not full mages yet."

Adaira stared straight ahead, then surprised him by biting her lower lip and agreeing. "You're right, but Gowan and Dida have a vote as well. It should be a group decision."

"They'll agree with me."

When they reached Canal Street, Adaira flew towards the coterie house after a long kiss and a promise to meet with the others after class the following evening.

Val watched her fly away, feeling a stab of regret at the imminent loss of the relationship. How deep his feelings might run, he didn't know, because he wouldn't let himself go there.

The endgame had arrived, and it didn't involve Adaira.

"Playing with fire, ye are," Gus said, startling him.

Val took a moment to respond. High above the velvet-draped entrances of the restaurants lining Canal Street rose the spires of the Wizard District, javelins of color punctuating the charcoal hues of dusk. "Some fires have to be extinguished before they burn too bright," he said.

"Aye."

-46-

Will led the way as the party squeezed through a pile of loose rocks and found themselves standing in a field comprised of boulders and glassy black obsidian, interspersed with hardy shrubs whose variegated leaves sparkled green, red, and gold in the morning sun. An old lava field, he thought.

Dalen and Caleb gave whoops of joy, Marek cracked a smile, and Yasmina looked dazed. Tamás fell to his knees, and Lisha had to shield her eyes from the morning sun. For a long moment, Will stood in place with his face upturned to the sky, basking in the sweet warmth, the smells and colors of the surface, the knowledge that he was a free man once again.

"The air is crisp," Tamás said, choking up, "with the youth of spring. And the colors . . . I never thought I'd see them again."

"Any idea where we are?" Will asked.

Tamás turned, eying a forest just visible to their left. A line of stippled peaks crowned the horizon in the other direction. "I'd wager those peaks are part of the Dragon's Teeth."

"The Rockies, I'm guessing," Will said to Caleb in a low voice.

Caleb rubbed his eyes in the sun. "That narrows it down to a few million square miles."

"The Dragon's Teeth extends to the Great Northern Forests and beyond," Tamás continued. "We must travel west to reach the Barrier Coast, then south for Freetown."

Lisha started speaking. *I do not know the surface world*, Will translated. *My people have maps, but they are no longer taught in our schools.*

Tamás looked at Dalen and then Marek. "Where do you call home, my friends?"

"The Third," Marek said. "I vas hunting for my family's dinner, and the tuskers—" he spat—"captured me alone."

Dalen looked down at his feet, then forced a smile. "I'm just an adventurer, out for fame and fortune. I'll go wherever the winds take me."

"They why not accompany us to Freetown? All are welcome, and you can resolve your next course of action from there."

"I've always wanted to see the Barrier Coast," Dalen murmured. Will thought he looked both pleased and relieved at Tamás's offer, as if afraid he would be turned away.

Marek pondered the idea, then looked towards the mountains and grunted. "To the forest, then."

"To the forest," Tamás agreed.

It took them half a day to clear the lava fields and reach the woods, a pristine landscape of conifers, gushing streams, and moss-covered rocks. They padded across pine needles and drank greedily from the streams, though as the day wore on, the need for food and shelter grew pressing. Just as they decided to camp for the evening and forage for food, Yasmina pointed at separate plumes of smoke barely visible through the trees.

"A small town, from the looks of it," Tamás said.

"Good eyes, Yaz," Caleb said.

She didn't respond, and Caleb looked away.

Will had expected Lisha to return to the Darklands once they emerged, but she stuck with them, spending the entire day a few steps away from Caleb. He looked like he had no idea what to do. Will could tell his brother was fond of Lisha, but hardly in love.

Typical Caleb, Will thought. *Confrontation is not in his vocabulary.*

As they started towards the smoke, Dalen hesitated, wringing his hands. "This town . . . I am not a citizen."

Tamás stalked towards Dalen as if he were going to rebuke him. At the last second, he laughed and clapped him on the back. "My friend, we're in the Ninth Protectorate. *No one* is a citizen." His face darkened. "That's not entirely true. Spies abound, and colonies of loyalists live along the Great River."

"I thought so," Dalen muttered. "But I wanted to be sure. No more mines."

"No more mines," Tamás agreed.

Despite his exhaustion, hunger, and the growing chill, Will felt a warm glow of friendship towards his companions.

*   *   *

As dusk bled to night, the forest broke, exposing a settlement sprawled along the bank of a swift river. The radiance of the moon illuminated wide dirt roads lined by attractive timber-and-stone dwellings. The party shivered in the cooling air, and Will eyed the smoking chimneys with envy.

They emerged close to a two-story inn with a peaked roof. The door opened and three patrons emerged, revealing the glow of a hearth and the sound of laughter from within.

Will almost salivated at the thought of a seat by the fire, a warm bed, and a hot meal not comprised of gruel. "That place looks perfect. Too bad we don't have any money or clean clothes."

Caleb cracked his knuckles and eyed the three townspeople strolling towards the town center. "I could, you know, follow them and try to help relieve them of their reliance on material possessions."

"More likely you'll get caught picking their pockets and land us in jail," Will said, remembering the incident in the armory.

"You're probably right," Caleb said, and Will regretted his words. Ribbing his brother came naturally to him, but he knew Caleb felt useless in this world.

"I saw a cave not far back," Yasmina said. "We can shelter there for the night."

"There's no need to risk a theft, or to sleep another night on stone," Tamás said. He started walking towards the river. "Come."

Will realized he was heading towards a collection of colorful wagons parked a few hundred feet outside town, alongside the river.

Of course, Will said to himself.

Gypsies.

Instead of the harsh reality of most of the Romani people back on Earth, this was the gypsy camp of Will's fantasy-fueled imagination: a circle of stout wagons painted in bright colors and festooned with beads and ornaments, open wagon doors revealing candlelit interiors warmed by silk wall hangings and exotic carpets, lean men and dark-eyed women lounging in the spaces between the wagons, drinking from jugs and telling stories, breaking into dance and song.

The sight brought a stab of memory as he remembered the night Mala had let her hair down and danced around the fire. He still wasn't sure what to think of her mock-seduction.

Not that it mattered anymore. He sighed heavily and followed Tamás to the wagons.

A group of men stepped forward to meet them. Tamás told them the truth: that they had been waylaid by slavers, managed to escape, and were in need of food and shelter.

One of the women pointed at Lisha. "And that? From where does that come, and why is it with you?"

"Her name is Lisha," Tamás said evenly, "and she was also a prisoner. She helped us escape at great personal risk."

The gypsies huddled for a few minutes among themselves, and though the group eyed Lisha with suspicion, one of the men broke from the circle and clasped Tamás by the arm. "You are Roma, yes?"

"I am."

"Then you and your fellow travelers are welcome here. The snows have melted, and we head east. If you wish to join us, we will find room. There are always extra tasks for willing hands."

Tamás embraced him. "Thank you, friend. We head west in the morning, to Freetown, but we're grateful for the night's lodging."

Though it was freezing, Will and the others bathed in the river, feeling the need to wash away the stench of slavery. The troupe outfitted them in basic clothing: wool trousers, boots, colorful cotton shirts. They also fed them and gave them blankets and two large tents to share, one for each gender. Will was moved by their generosity.

After dinner and a round of homemade stout, Lisha, Marek, and Dalen collapsed in their tents, Lisha taking refuge from the cold under a pile of blankets. Tamás had disappeared into one of the wagons, and Yasmina headed off into the forest, rebuffing both Caleb's and Will's efforts to follow. Will knew she wasn't about to share a tent with Lisha, but worried where she would sleep.

Then again, Yasmina had changed, and for some reason he couldn't quite explain, Will sensed he didn't need to worry about her.

After relieving himself by the river, he returned to find Caleb sitting on a blanket near the bonfire, an earthen jug on the ground beside him. One of the men was strumming a lute, two women danced in tune, and another dozen were sprawled around the fire. The camp smelled like incense and smoked meat.

Caleb waved him over. Will grabbed a free jug, sat beside his brother, and waved a hand. He recalled how Mala had pegged Caleb as a gypsy the first time they had met. "You're home, aren't you?"

Caleb grinned and took a swig. "Damn skippy."

"Listen man, I was just yanking your chain earlier. With those bracers and your rogue skills, you're really coming along."

Caleb spluttered into his beer, his face darkening. "Rogue skills? Good god, Will, after all we've been through, you still think this is a D&D club."

"Hardly," Will said quietly. "It's just . . . ." He broke off, unable to find a diplomatic way to boost Caleb's confidence.

"Let me help you," Caleb said. "What you're trying to do is find a way to convince me I'm not as useless as we all know I am. Listen, little bro, don't be a buzz kill. What you don't get is that I don't *need* to be a hero. I don't even need to be brave. Pacifist, remember? I just—" he broke off and stared at the forest—"Yasmina gets it. God, I screwed up there, Will."

"Yep."

"You know about . . . ." He glanced at Lisha's tent.

"She's following you around like a starving puppy."

"Yeah," Caleb muttered.

"You must be really good at what you do."

"I—" Caleb threw his hands up—"she threw herself at me, Will. She's seventy-three, by the way. Middle-aged."

Will was stunned.

"And it's not like Yaz and I have been together recently. I've apologized and tried to talk to her about it, but she won't even look at me."

"Listen, you're a complete ass with women, but you've got to stop being so hard on yourself about everything else. Yasmina's right about that. You're your own worst enemy."

Caleb slapped him on the back of the head, causing Will to spill his beer. "Drink up, orc-lover. I don't know about you, but tonight I'm happy to be alive. Happy and shocked beyond belief."

"I'll drink to that." Will took a long swig and then lay on his back, staring at the heavens. His greatest dream had been to discover what lay beyond the stars, and now that he had found out what it was, it terrified him beyond belief.

But it was still wondrous.

"You've realized you haven't had a panic attack on the journey?" Caleb said.

"It's hard to be panicked when you're a slave imprisoned ten miles underground by a race of evil albino dwarves. The panic comes before all of that."

"True."

Will pushed up on his elbows. "For whatever reason, fate has given us a second chance. Let's make the most of it and find a way home."

"I'll drink to that."

"Home, is it?" Tamás said, stepping into view.

Will froze. How much had he heard? "We have to get back to New Victoria as soon as possible. To find our brother."

"I still maintain the fastest route is through Freetown." Tamás squatted and unfurled a canvas map showing a rough sketch of the Ninth Protectorate. He jabbed a finger at a spot in between two mountain ranges. Will guessed the location he had pointed out was roughly southeastern Idaho. "Our new friends tell me we are here," Tamás said, moving his finger an inch west on the map. "There's a Yith outpost nearby, if we can reach it. With a Simorgh Rider, it's a two day journey to Freetown."

A simorgh, Will knew, was a legendary bird from Persian mythology. Just how many myths and legends from back home had started on Urfe? While he pondered that train of thought, Caleb asked a more practical question. "What do you mean, *if* we can reach the outpost?"

Tamás jabbed the map again, this time pointing out a narrow valley that looked like a blade of grass slicing between two mountain ranges, just before the Rider outpost. "That's the Valley of the Cursed. And with the threat of snow still alive, it's the only way through."

-47-

By the time Val had dinner at his local pub, returned home, and made his way to the rooftop patio to contemplate his next course of action, he felt reconstituted, his wellspring of power renewed.

His plan was to use the Ring of Shadows to follow Gowan home the next night, after the group discussion about the mint orchid. Once he discovered what Gowan knew about the location of the Planewalk—whether the pyromancer wanted to tell him or not—Val was going to attempt the spirit mage trial straightaway, in case Gowan decided to turn him in.

So tomorrow night it is.

Val had brought his father's staff to the rooftop. He leaned on it as he took a deep breath of humid air.

The Planewalk. The Walk of Planes.

After tomorrow night, would he be reunited with his brothers? Or would he perish in the gauntlet that awaited?

Val set his staff aside and extended his hands. He concentrated on the empty air at the end of his fingers, a pinprick of space, and he pushed until it burned, reaching for the fabric of reality and then tearing at that fabric with his mind, forcing, splitting, ripping, diving deep inside until he felt as if his mind would burst out of his skull, deeper and deeper. Still he needed more, so he pushed and he pushed and pushed pushed pushed pushed pushed

Val shuddered and stumbled backwards as he felt the same rush he remembered from spiritmancy class, the feeling that he had just torn a tiny hole in reality itself, had unlocked a power that flooded him with dopamine and made him feel as if he could lift the world on his shoulders.

It was, Val thought, the closest thing to a religious experience he had ever felt.

And it was getting addictive.

He shoved his will into the crack he had opened, infusing it with power. Darkness coalesced at his fingertips, blacker than deepest night, the dark energy gathering and emitting tiny silver sparks. Val labored to breathe, exhausted by the effort, watching the weird flames lick the air.

He thought he would have to focus on keeping the energy contained and not kill himself, but it was the opposite: despite the whiplash of spirit fire he had produced in class, it now took everything he had to keep the spark alive.

He wasn't nearly strong enough, not to truly summon and command spirit fire.

But he was strong enough to do what he needed to do.

Closing off the conduit was easy; he simply stopped pouring energy into the crack he had opened. After the spirit fire extinguished, he collapsed against the stone wall.

It had taken him a month of exhaustive study and practice to produce a few minute sparks, and the effort drained his reserves. He couldn't imagine the power needed for real application. But that was what training was all about, he mused, whether law or sports or the practice of magic: harnessing your natural talent, enhancing it to the breaking point, bending it to your will with sweat and tears.

He rested his elbows on his knees and caught his breath. It took longer to recover than he wished, hours, but when enough of his magical energy returned, he slipped on the Ring of Shadows, grabbed his staff, and took flight into the starry sky.

There was one thing left to do on his final night in New Victoria.

After slipping the Ring of Shadows on his left index finger, Val arced high above the city, keeping well to the side of the Wizard District to avoid the magical defenses in place. Though he was allowed night access, he didn't want anyone to know he was out.

Soaring past the Government District to the north, he flew over the Spectacle Dome and a two-mile stretch of crumbling tenements, then slowed as he entered the Gypsy Quarter, a maze of soot-blackened buildings and weed-choked cobblestone streets, hushed by the omnipresent threat of violence. The once-proud section of the city which his father had long ago called home.

The section of the city in which Mari had been murdered.

Val flew as high as he could while still able to observe the ruffians lurking about the streets. Every time he saw someone, he flew in for a closer look, staying above the light of the handful of cracked glow orbs, shielded by the power of his ring.

After hours of scouring the streets, he finally saw him: the cornstalk-thin leader of a ragtag group of gypsies, green top hat sitting cockeyed on his head, dressed in colorful rags with a black sash tied loosely around his waist. One of his arms ended at a stump.

Val flew towards the closest tall building, a brick tenement with shattered windows and a flat roof. He landed softly on his feet, then walked along the edge until he spotted the gypsy leader on the street below. When he found him, Val used Wind Push to lift the man into the air, bringing him soaring towards his position.

As the black sash leader shouted and waved his arms, his followers stood in the street and pointed. Val needed to finish this before they found a way onto the roof. He hoped they hadn't picked up a mage since they had last met.

After depositing the leader roughly on the roof, Val stood ten feet away and took off his ring, relishing the look of shock on his face. "Lost, me friend?" Val asked, repeating the words the black sash gypsy had said to him just before sticking his knife in Mari's gut.

The man tried to sound brave, but Val heard the tremble in his voice. "I know ye, don't I? The one with the staff." His voice cracked at the end of a nervous chuckle. "So maybe yer a wizard after all. What do ye want?"

"You know what," Val said.

"I can get yer gold. I'll have it tonight."

"What I want, you don't have to give. So I'll take a life in return."

Along with the shouting, Val heard footsteps climbing a metal ladder, probably a fire escape. The black sash leader produced a desperate grin, his rotting teeth poking through like nuggets of coal. "Let's make us a deal, eh? I can get women, more women than ye need. Every night, delivered to yer door."

"She told you to walk away," Val said. "You should have listened."

He extended a palm and thrust the man high into the air, positioning him above the street. The sounds of climbing drew closer.

"Wait," the man begged, flapping his arms as if he could fly himself back onto the roof. His hat fell off, exposing a bird's nest of limp yellow hair. "Don't do it, I beg ye."

"She didn't want to die, either," Val said softly. With an explosion of will, he thrust the gypsy leader straight down, accelerating him faster and faster during the hundred foot fall.

Right before Mari's murderer crunched head-first into the cobblestoned street, Val stopped his descent and flipped him around, letting him crash land hard but alive. His legs broken, the man screamed and pulled himself to the side of the street, casting fearful glances up at Val.

Two more of the black-sashed gypsies burst onto the roof. Val blew them back with a Wind Push. Nearing the end of his energy reserves, he slipped on the Ring of Shadows and flew off into the night. Unsure what to expect after the first act of premeditated violence in his life, he realized he didn't feel satisfied, or guilty, or relieved.

He just felt cold.

Val collapsed onto the rooftop of Salomon's Crib. After catching his breath, he climbed down the collapsible metal ladder into the kitchen, then descended the pantry stairs into the cellar.

He needed a drink.

While Val felt nauseous in the aftermath of the encounter, it was not due to the fate of the gypsy leader who had killed Mari and who knew how many others in cold blood. In Val's mind, the man had deserved to die, and Val had cut him a break. At least he wouldn't be walking the streets any more.

He entered a cellar lined with casks of real ale, the temperature cold enough to keep them preserved. Val had no idea how Salomon kept the cellar cool, or maintained a cellar at all in a city with an average elevation below sea level.

But the underground cellar was the least of the mysteries swirling around the arch spirit mage.

After gulping down a mug of ale, Val leaned on the wall with his free hand—and felt the wall move.

He jumped back, watching as the wall performed a slow rotation, stopping at a forty-five degree angle to reveal a hidden room. After dragging a cask of ale over to block the new doorway, in case it decided to close on him, Val stepped inside, curious but wary.

The rectangular room, two hundred square feet at most, was made of rough stone. There was no furniture, but hanging from the walls on short wooden hooks were hundreds—if not thousands—of silvery-blue keys about the length of a smart phone.

Keys that looked exactly like the one Will had described receiving from Salomon, and which had transported the brothers to Urfe.

Upon closer inspection, Val noted that each of the keys had long blades with serrated edges, similar to keys back home. And each of them had a different cut.

Val took a step back, the implications tightening his stomach. Was each of these keys a portal to another world? Had Salomon made them all?

Just before he left the room, Val noticed a plaque hanging above the secret passage. *In my Father's house are many dwelling places.*

The phrase sounded familiar. As he refilled his mug and climbed the stairs to the kitchen, Val tried to recall where he had seen it. Then it hit him, causing him to stop and grip his mug.

The phrase was a verse from the Bible.

What the hell?

Val paced the kitchen, thoughtful and unnerved, then climbed to the rooftop again, feeling the need for a dose of fresh air. As his head broached the lip of the trapdoor, he saw an old man with wispy gray hair watching him climb, causing Val to miss a step and spill his beer.

Dressed in a worn tweed coat and stained white dress shirt, looking for all the world like a disheveled college professor, Salomon's silver eyes glittered as he watched Val climb the ladder.

"Such a pleasant evening, eh?"

"Shut up," Val said. "Take me to my brothers."

"My my, so different from your siblings, aren't you? How do you rate my ale? I spent a good bit of time with the Trappist monks in the seventeenth century, you know. The seventeenth century of your world, that is."

"Are you going to help me or not?"

"Ah . . . yes . . . well . . . the thing is, as I told your youngest brother, I have decided not to be an active participant."

"A participant?" Val snarled. "*Participant*? This isn't a game, you crazy old man. I'm stuck in a barbaric fantasy world, I don't even know if my brothers are still alive, I just broke the legs of a man who killed my friend—" Val put his palms to the sides of his head and squeezed his eyes shut—"What are those keys doing in your cellar? They're portals to other worlds, aren't they? Are you God, Salomon?"

Salomon laughed, and then started coughing. "God? I? What an absurd notion. I—" a wave of sadness crashed across his features, and his eyes drifted, as if he had gone to another time or place. "No, my boy, I am hardly God."

Val remembered the story Alexander had told him, about a legendary two-thousand-year-old spirit mage named Salomon who traveled the multiverse looking for two things: his lost son, swept away by the astral wind; and proof for the existence of God.

Val walked to the edge of the roof, crossed his arms, and stared out at the city. He had so many questions he didn't know where to begin, and he knew Salomon was toying with him, playing at some game Val couldn't begin to fathom.

"Do you know where the entrance to the Planewalk is?" Val asked, knowing that he did.

Salomon didn't answer.

"Tomorrow I'm going to find it. If I live through the trial, I'll attempt to take the Pool of Souls to my brothers."

"You aren't ready," Salomon said.

"Doesn't matter," Val said, still not looking at him. "I have to help them. Unless you'd like to? I know you can, if you want to."

More silence.

"Can one of the keys in the basement get us home, if I bring them back here?"

"You have already utilized that key."

Val turned. "Then make another. But you won't, will you? Not unless it suits your purposes, which it obviously doesn't, because for some reason you want us here, don't you?"

Salomon's eyes were sad.

Val took a step closer. "You know that son you lost? The one who's driven you to stay alive for a few thousand years and travel the multiverse trying to find him? The unbearable sadness you feel, the *guilt*? The rest of us can feel that, too, Salomon. *I* feel that, for my brothers. Just so you know."

"No," he said quietly, "you are not like them at all. You're more like your father."

Val turned away, the sight of the black-sashed gypsy's legs crunching into the ground flashing through his mind like a splice from a horror film. "My father was a wise, kind, and gentle man. He was nothing like me."

"My boy, your father was all of those things. You saw the side of him he wanted you to see, as all children do."

"I suppose you knew him?"

"Oh, yes."

Val snorted. "What don't you know?"

Again the mournful eyes. "Many things. *Many.*"

"What is magic, Salomon?"

The silver eyes twinkled. "Sorry?"

"What *is* it? Where does it come from?"

Salomon's eyes went distant, like an absent-minded professor working through a problem. "I've performed quantum-wave brain scans which have isolated the region of the interdimensional cortex activated during the use of magic. It is the same area triggered by psychic phenomena on your world. Wizards born on this world, of course, have a much greater capacity to harness this power. Yet these scans, advanced as they might seem, are limited. Psychic phenomena is far too simplistic an appellation for what is occurring. The source of magic lies deeper still, emanating from an . . . unknown . . . source. What exactly magic is and from where it originates, why mages possess different affinities and have varying levels of power, I've not yet discovered." He blinked. "Does that help?"

"No," Val said. All he had gathered was that even Salomon didn't understand the true nature of his power. *That's why they call it magic*, Val supposed. "So what do you want?"

"Your father once stayed here, you know. In the very room in which you now reside. In fact, he left something for you, in case you ever happened to find this world and decided to undertake a magical education of your own. Your father, of course, also studied at the Abbey."

Val pressed his lips together. "What did he leave me?"

"Before you rest tonight, check the floorboards underneath your bed. But, my boy—" Salomon stared at Val, the elder mage's overgrown eyebrows curling like tongs under the sloping forehead, his strange eyes reeling Val in with the mesmeric power of a snake charmer—"since your father is not here, and I feel some duty to his legacy, I believe I should repeat my advice that you are not ready for the Planewalk." The eyes drew closer, enlarging, making Val feel as if he and Salomon were occupying the same space. "Not as you are."

It took an effort of will, but Val jerked his gaze away, glancing down at the orb-lit streets of Uptown, a maze of golden-hued canals.

When he looked back up, Salomon had disappeared.

-48-

When Will woke the next morning, he spotted Yasmina sitting alone by the river, legs crossed and wringing out her hair. As he approached, a badger gnawing on a root at Yasmina's feet glanced up and bared its teeth at him.

O-kaaay.

She calmed the badger, then gave Will a warm smile and greeted him as if it were normal to have a wild badger for a companion over morning coffee. He chatted with her for a few minutes, happy to see her animated and trying to probe the nature of her new powers, but she kept deflecting his questions. He suspected she might not even know.

Before they left camp, Tamás told the troupe who he was, which caused a great commotion. After an impromptu celebration at the return of the leader of the Revolution, the entire camp gathered to see the party off, stuffing clothes and food and supplies into packs, and thrusting them at Tamás.

As Will and the others made their way out of town, the villagers stared at Lisha and muttered, causing her to shrink into her cloak. Caleb put his arm around her, and the rest of the party glared back at the townspeople.

Three days to the Valley of the Cursed, the gypsies had said, and the trail was hard to miss: when the twin ranges come into view, head for the pass that divides them.

Will had asked Tamás about the valley. *A place of last resort*, the revolution-ary had said. *Home to freaks, genetic mutations, the creations of rogue menag-erists. A place where the lost, the insane, and the criminal live out their lives apart from accepted society. We might pass through the Valley of the Cursed unmolested, or we might have to fight our way through.*

The alternative? Will had asked.

The alternative was a month long journey to the next closest Rider outpost, through lands infested with trolls, tuskers, roving gangs of slavers, and who knew what else.

The group opted for the quicker route.

Rested and well-fed, the party's spirits increased as the morning wore on. Despite the looming dangers, they had overcome so much that it was hard for Will not to feel optimistic. Back when he had longed for adventure, sitting in his Papasan with only the heft and mystery of a polyhedral die for company, this was *exactly* what he had dreamed of: strapped with gear, traipsing through an old-growth forest with air so fresh it felt alive, an illusionist and a rogue and a couple of trained fighters by his side, on their way to the Valley of the Cursed, no less.

He allowed himself a few minutes of pure, unadulterated pleasure at the thought, because he believed in wallowing in the pleasures of life, and then he reined himself in.

Keep it real, buddy. Keep it real or you'll end up with your head stuck on a pike, as dead as Hashi and Fochik and Alexander and Charlie.

Oh, Charlie.

He missed his godfather dearly, almost as much as he missed Val. Two an-chors for his life that this world had taken from him. Not to mention Mala and Dad, neither of whom Will could think about without feeling a lump in his throat.

After making camp the first night, an hour before dusk, Tamás drew Will aside. "I promised to assist with your training, if you still have an interest?"

"You bet."

They retrieved their weapons and cleared a space near the tents. After a quick sparring session to assess Will's abilities, Tamás began to instruct him in classic Romani swordsmanship: an elegant style full of sweeping strokes of the blade, clever parries, and circular foot movement. Though Will recognized some of the core principles from Mala's teachings, the execution was night and day. Mala preached economy of movement, pure and simple. Everything she did, every half-step and twitch of the blade, was designed to maximize positioning and damage.

Will had seen Tamás in action, so he knew the style worked, but he also knew he was not in the presence of genius, as he had been with Mala. It made him wonder where she had gleaned her knowledge, and how much of it was her own amalgamation of styles.

"You learn fast," Tamás said when they took a break, both of them exhausted by the effort.

"My first teacher was very gifted. I didn't deserve to be her pupil."

His eyebrows lifted. "Her? And who was this extraordinary swordswoman?"

"Her name was Mala."

Tamás paused with his water skin halfway to his lips. "Surely you don't mean *the* Mala? Of the Kalev clan?"

"Um, I guess. Short, hot, long scar from her nose to the top of her forehead? Extremely dangerous and a bit intense?"

Tamás's eyes widened. "How did you come to be taught by Mala?"

"It's a long story. Do you know her?"

"Aye," Tamás said with respect, though Will sensed an underlying layer of animosity.

"You two weren't . . . ."

Tamás laughed. "No, no. Though I appreciate a spirited woman, I also prefer to keep my head on my shoulders." He leaned on his sword and returned to his water skin. "Mala is Romani royalty, my friend. The daughter of the Catalan clan leader."

"Why did she . . . leave her clan?"

"Her parents—most of her immediate clan—were killed in a raid near Londyn. A raid ordered by the Congregation."

"Ah."

"I'm unsure of the details, but Mala was very young when she was orphaned, and had to fend for herself on the streets."

"You don't seem too fond of her," Will said.

Tamás shrugged. "She wants nothing to do with the Revolution. She turned her back on her people."

"Maybe she just wants to be left alone. It sounds like she had a pretty horrific childhood."

Tamás finished drinking and picked up his scimitar, locking gazes with Will. "We no longer have the luxury of choosing to be left alone, Will Blackwood. Not anyone who chooses not to bow to Lord Alistair." He spat, and then attacked with a vengeance. Will fought back as best he could, but Tamás knocked him down, and stood with his sword pointed at his chest.

Will tensed, but Tamás helped him to his feet, his eyes full of passion and warmth. "You should consider such things, my friend. We're in desperate need of good fighters for the cause."

The next morning, the party passed through a series of small villages. Whenever a townsperson noticed Lisha, they started muttering and making finger signals as if warding off evil spirits. Will could tell it was starting to bother the poor darvish woman. He tried to ask her how long she planned to stay with them, but either the language barrier was too great or she chose to avoid the question. She seemed content to follow along behind Caleb.

After lunch, the forest curved around a hill and they got their first glimpse of the Valley of the Cursed: a sliver of green on the horizon, poised between two jagged mountain ranges. The party spent a moment in silent contemplation of the sight, then pressed forward.

As evening approached, they found themselves traversing a broad meadow with a stream running through it. Yasmina stopped to shield her eyes from the sun, then announced the approach of a group of humans. Will assumed the owl-tipped staff had something to do with her enhanced vision.

To be safe, Tamás hurried them off the trail and into the woods surrounding the meadow. Will peered between the trees and watched a line of people in gray caftans pass, walking single file beside the stream. All bore the same marking: three bright blue dots forming a triangle on their foreheads.

"Followers of Devla," Tamás said in a low voice.

"Who?" Will asked.

"While gypsies worship many different deities, they are all manifestations of Devla, the one true God."

"The god of vengeance," Dalen muttered.

"The god of all things," Tamás corrected, "vengeance among them. While gypsies are not known for their piety, the Devlan take their religion seriously. Especially since the rise of the Prophet."

"Every world has its crazies," Caleb whispered to Will.

"The Prophet?" Will echoed, unable to help himself. He couldn't stand being in the dark.

"Has his name not spread to the north?" Tamás asked. "It seems to have spread everywhere else."

Marek grunted. "Aye."

"We don't get much news in our village," Will said.

"Long before the Realm was established, Devlan prophecy held that the Prophet would herald the arrival of the Templar—the fist of Devla—a true cleric who will lead our people out of bondage."

"*Lucka*, history is full of charlatans claiming to be the Prophet," Dalen added, "but there hasn't been a true cleric in the Realm since the Pagan Wars. And the Congregation, of course, despise the Devlans and claim there has *never* been a true cleric."

"Aye," Tamás said. "'Tis no secret that Alistair wishes to eradicate the order."

"Are you afraid of them?" Will asked. "Is that why we're hiding?"

Tamás shifted to get a better view of the approaching people. "Unless they are protesting wizard rule, the Devlans are known to be kind and gentle, and seek only the peaceful spread of their religion. They can be unpredictable, however, if they feel their god has been slighted." He glanced at Lisha. "I'm unsure how they would react to our darvish friend."

Will peered more closely at the line of people as they exited the meadow. "They look more like refugees than warriors."

"The Devlans count a small number of wizard converts among their numbers. I would not wish to run afoul of one."

"Ah," Will said. "Me neither."

*　　*　　*

After a lunch of cold rabbit stew, courtesy of the gypsies, the party entered the foothills of a mountain range. They passed through the smoking ruins of a village, bodies stacked in neat rows by a stream, similar to what Will and the others had seen on their way to the mines. The sunny blue sky was a jarring contrast to the massacre, and Will had to choke back his bile. Tamás stared at the pile of corpses for a long time before walking away with a clenched jaw.

Not an hour later, after they topped a small knoll, Yasmina put a hand up. "Tuskers," she said, staring with undisguised hatred at the copse of fir trees at the base of the hill, "with a group of prisoners. They're heading right towards us."

The party slipped behind a group of boulders. Dalen looked stricken. "Slavers? We have to run!"

"How many?" Tamás asked grimly.

Yasmina strained to see into the woods. Will thought he saw a rustling through the trees in the distance. "Ten. With four prisoners."

"A small party," Tamás said. "It's possible they're responsible for the village."

He looked at Marek, and they exchanged a nod. Will noticed and said, "Count me in."

Caleb put his hands to his head. "Jesus, Will."

"Those poor people are headed to the mines," Will said, "or worse. We can do something about it."

Caleb lowered his voice. "It's not our fight."

"Today it is," Will said, as a line of chained humans, heads bowed in submission, came into view.

Tamás squeezed Will's shoulder. "With the element of surprise, I believe we can manage ten tuskers without casualty. If we're shrewd in our tactics."

Lisha was staring at the tuskers with a tense, vicious light in her eyes. *Yes.*

Will knew Caleb had a point, but he didn't care. He couldn't sit there and watch the tuskers herd another group of people to the mines. Not if he could do something about it.

As they devised a quick plan of attack, the tusker party started up the knoll, pulling the slaves behind them. Will grew jittery with anticipation, dopamine pouring into his nerve endings. His knuckles turned white from squeezing the hilt of his sword.

When the wart-covered creatures reached the halfway point, Caleb stepped into view, whistling to himself. The tuskers eyed him like a Happy Meal. Caleb froze as if he had just seen them, then took off up the hill. The tuskers shouted and followed.

As the first two tuskers came into range, passing right by where the party was hidden, it happened all at once, fast and hard like most battles. Dalen threw a flash of light into the lead tusker's eyes, disorienting him, while Lisha dropped down from a tree and set the second on fire with a thrust of heated palms.

The burning tusker screamed. Tamás, Will, and Marek rushed into the fray, storming down the hill with battle roars to increase the perception of a larger enemy. All three of them cut down a tusker on the first wave. Dalen cast a replication spell on Yasmina, causing three tall Brazilian women wielding quarterstaffs to enter the fray, further panicking the slavers. Will and Caleb had argued vehemently to dissuade her from fighting, but she insisted, and Will had to admit she could hold her own with the staff, albeit with the help of Dalen's illusion.

What else had Elegon taught her?

Lisha leapt onto the back of another tusker and ignited him, Will pressed forward with his fellow warriors, and the fight was over before it began. Nine tuskers dead and one pinned on the ground by the tip of Tamas's sword. The success of the attack shocked Will, and he realized with a surge of pride that in a fair fight, he was now a match for a tusker. Not a match—better.

The human captives looked stunned, then started cheering as Yasmina found a set of keys and freed them. It was one of the best feelings of Will's life.

Tamás used the tip of his sword to raise the tusker to his feet. "You must be touched by the gods," the revolutionary said, his blond hair menacing his face, "because today you get to live. But go: go back from whence you came and tell whoever sent you that this despicable practice is finished." He smacked the foul creature on the back, then sent him scurrying with a kick to the rear. "Spread the word, tusker," Tamás roared. "Tell them our people will not be enslaved!"

Will and his companions guarded the freed prisoners during the night, then accompanied them to the next village. The townspeople welcomed them with open arms and vowed to help them return home.

The villagers did not, however, welcome Lisha. Despite the goodwill the party incurred for killing the slavers, they were hustled out of town for consorting with the darvish woman. And in the next village, a dilapidated collection of brick and straw huts, an old woman stumbled into the muddy street and hurled epithets at Lisha. A crowd gathered and started throwing stones, forcing the party to flee town yet again.

"I guess there're bigots on every world," Caleb muttered as they ran. "Superstition, religion, rich, poor, wizard born and common born—I can't stand any of it, man. All it does is divide us."

Will felt a rush of warmth for his brother, because he knew what he said was true. No matter the circumstance, Caleb would welcome a stranger of any color or race with open arms. He might have his faults, but he was a kind and gentle soul, one of the few people Will had ever known with no prejudices.

They stopped for lunch and Lisha caught trout from a river. After a quick training session—Yasmina and Marek had started to join in, the big man slowly learning to fight with one arm—they returned to the forest. It broke to reveal a shattered landscape of rock fragments, stunted cinder cones, geysers and fumaroles with smoke pouring out, sagebrush, and crater-like impressions. In the distance, Will saw a red glow emanating from one of the cinder cones.

Caleb swiveled to take in the Jurassic landscape. "Are there lava fields in the Rockies?" he asked Will.

"Maybe we're in Yellowstone," Will said, "though I think that's on the other side. Or maybe this world's just different."

They started along the edge of the forest, skirting the blasted region, until Will turned and saw that Lisha hadn't moved. He went back to her.

"What is it?" he asked.

I know this place. I can return home from here.

Will didn't respond. He sensed she had more to say.

I can accept the differences of the surface world, but it appears they cannot accept me. Can you please tell the others? I wish to say farewell.

It was so abrupt. Will's first instinct was to persuade her to change her mind, but then he saw the pain and finality of her decision reflected in her eyes. If villagers were stoning him for being different, he wouldn't stay, either.

He hugged her tight. "Thank you for saving us. If you ever need anything, come find me, and I'll do everything in my power to help you."

Thank you, friend. You gave me life again.

Will told the others of her decision. One by one, everyone except Yasmina embraced the darvish girl who had led them to the surface. Yasmina said a curt goodbye and stood off to the side.

Lisha's eyes watered as Caleb whispered into her ear and held her close. Their embrace lasted long moments, causing everyone to move on and leave them in peace. Will watched over his shoulder, a hollow feeling inside him, as Caleb wiped an eye and walked slowly back to the party, leaving Lisha to cross the lava field alone. She climbed into a cinder cone and disappeared.

The rest of the afternoon walk felt somber, muted by the loss of Lisha. As daylight waned, the party rounded a cluster of rocky hills, crested a ridge, and gazed upon an awesome sight below: a slender emerald valley slicing between two mountain ranges so steep they looked sheared by scissors. A trail led down the other side of the ridge, right to the start of the pass.

"The Valley of the Cursed," Tamás said. "We'll camp here tonight, and enter at first light."

-49-

Mala materialized in a sloping wooded glade. The unmistakable details of her home world, the lush greens and browns of the forest, the trill of birdsong and a heady aroma of fresh air and loamy soil, almost brought her to her knees. Like most gypsies, her clan had traveled throughout her youth, and she did not think of any one place as her own.

But she did have a place to long for, she realized. Urfe itself, in all its terrible beauty and wonder, was her home.

Relieved not to see Zedock's citadel but expecting to land somewhere near New Victoria, she knew with a glance that this forest was taller, less dense and humid, than the woodlands of the Fifth Protectorate.

The Barrier Coast, she guessed.

Needing to gain her bearings, she shimmied up a large spruce to better understand her surroundings. Near the top, after watching a red-crested eagle—another sign of the Barrier Coast—leave its perch as she climbed, she found a sturdy branch and gazed upon the land.

Half a kilometer to the north, she spied a fast-flowing stream that made her salivate. She had never desired a bath in cool waters, followed by a flagon of honey grog and a platter of fire-crisped meat, quite so much. Turning eastward, she gasped in delight when she saw the muscular sprawl of the ocean in the distance, just a few kilometers away. On the shoreline of the curving bay, downhill from her position, rose a familiar sight. A large encampment of beautiful domes and spires that brought another swell of relief, as well as a surge of pride.

This was a stroke of luck, she realized. Against all odds, her interdimensional journey had brought her closer to her ultimate destination. That brought thoughts of the map she had discovered in Leonidus's Keep, and a stab of worry that her sojourn in the Place Between Worlds might have affected her belongings. After she climbed back down, she made sure all her weapons and jewelry were intact, then checked the contents of her Pouch of Possession, a magical canvas bag whose holding capacity far exceeded its size.

When she withdrew the scroll, she unrolled it and checked to make sure it was intact, handling the thin parchment as carefully as a robin's egg.

It was just as she recalled. The map, the runes, the legendary tomb of the sorcerer king.

She knew why Leonidus must have sought it out—to aid the Revolution—but she desired the map for a very different reason. A frisson of excitement coursed through her. If the map was real, and her adventurer's intuition screamed that it was, then that which she had longed for her entire adult life might be within her grasp.

A vivid flashback rocked her on her heels. The attack on her clan while the morning dew was still fresh, the giant red-bearded man with cruel eyes and a black robe belted in silver, her father hiding her under their wagon with tear-filled eyes and a whispered goodbye. The screams of her clansmen that haunted her dreams to this day.

Killing Zedock's arrogant majitsu had felt good. Empowering. Yet she had caught him unawares and harnessed the magic of a strange world. The warrior-mage whose head she craved was far more powerful, perhaps the most terrifying majitsu who had ever lived. A man named Kjeld Anarsson who had risen to great power in the Realm, and who most would consider untouchable.

And so he might be.

She started walking towards the stream. Yes, she knew the nature of her next adventure. For once, she was seeking something for herself. She could assemble a team, but why not let the gullible Council engage one for her, on the promise of the other relic the existence of the map implied?

The Coffer of Devla. Fools they were. Chasing after a myth, resting their hopes on a god whom had either never existed or had long since abandoned them.

The desire to set forth on the quest tingled through her, a song to her gypsy soul, giving her a sense of purpose she had not felt in a very long time. She almost felt young again, both empowered and burdened by the youth she had lost.

First things first, she thought as she stumbled to the stream and stripped off her clothes.

Bathe.

Find grog and food.

Crawl into warm bed and collapse.

-50-

Val raced downstairs, shoved his bed aside, and found the loose floorboard. He caught his breath as he reached inside and extracted a black vellum notebook.

Dad.

Trembling with emotions he had kept suppressed for a very long time, he opened the first page and saw his father's name, written in his tight, elongated scrawl.

Journal of Wizard Studies
Dane Blackwood

Val flipped through the worn notebook, which contained observations and tips on the spells his father had studied during his three-year tenure at the Abbey. His father's first year had consisted of a coterie class, a spiritmancy class, and History and Governance. He had even chosen Relics as his elective.

Just like Val.

Hoping against hope, he was disappointed to find that the journal ended with his father's graduation. There was no mention of the Planewalk.

Val stayed awake the entire night and devoured the spell book cover to cover. He paid attention to the tips and absorbed the wide range of spells from the other disciplines, as well as the far fewer spirit mage spells, such as Spirit Radiance, Mind Whip, Spirit Door, and Moon Ray. There were descriptions of higher level spells introduced at the school, but which his father had not yet mastered: Create Portal, Stasis, Astral Cord, Gravity's Kin, Spirit Skin, Stargaze, and Spirit Storm.

With dawn came gummy eyes and fuzzy thinking. Val allowed himself a few hours of sleep, then rose and prepared a pot of coffee, drumming his fingers as he thought.

Salomon had made an appearance for a reason. Val's guess was because of the Planewalk. The good news was that Salomon must think Val was on the brink of finding the entrance.

The bad news was that he thought Val was going to die in the attempt.

His father's spell book was a nifty addition to Val's repertoire, but it wouldn't help with the Planewalk. Not this soon. He would need weeks or months—maybe years—to learn those spells.

He paced the house, pausing in front of the tapestry in the common room portraying two wizards facing each other on a rock bridge spanning a bottomless chasm. Two fortresses, one silver-blue and one gold-and-crimson, stood on either side of the bridge. One wizard held an azantite staff, the other an orb of roiling darkness. Swirls of color ignited an inky sky, and bizarre creatures dotted the landscape.

Was the tapestry a vision of the past? The future? Another world or dimension?

Or just a piece of art?

Whatever it was, Val had the feeling the imagery was important—perhaps even a depiction of Salomon himself.

Back to the Planewalk.

You're not ready, Salomon had said.

Val rolled his eyes. *Thanks for pointing out the obvious, old man.*

Yet Salomon being Salomon, Val figured he probably knew he was going to attempt the Planewalk regardless of what anyone said.

You're not ready. Not as you are.

Not as you are, Val repeated to himself.

The phrase had meaning, he could feel it.

What was he supposed to become?

The spell book might help transform him, but not in a day. No, he needed something else. Something that would render him more powerful. Make him something more than who he was at this stage of his development.

Rubbing his chin as he thought, he looked across the room and noticed the cabinet on the other side, the one that contained the enormous chest of gold and gems he had been using to fund himself.

A slow smile crept onto his face.

Holding a canvas bag stuffed with coins and gems in each hand, having to use a bit of magic to carry the load, Val entered the New Victoria Magick Shoppe.

Not as you are.

Expecting a creaky wooden shop filled with overflowing shelves of potions and arcane magical trinkets, he instead saw Saks Fifth Avenue for the wizard set. A marble foyer heralded an atrium with a glass ceiling, filled with flower-beds and statues and artwork displayed on easels. Groups of wizards conversed at a sunny café in the middle of the indoor courtyard, screened by potted banana trees.

Gemstone archways lined the perimeter of the circular room, leading to alcoves arranged by wizard discipline. To his left was a ruby archway for pyromancers, displaying a Rod of Fire in a glass case near the entrance. Val checked the price and whistled. Five hundred gold pieces.

He passed a sapphire entrance for aquamancers, amber for geomancers, diamond for aeromancers. *How much are those archways worth?*

He didn't see an alcove for spiritmancy, but opposite the foyer, a black-and-white marble archway opened up into the largest room of all, which seemed to contain a potpourri of items not endemic to any one discipline.

Lugging his sacks inside, Val approached the counter clerk: a stern, red-headed woman wearing a high-necked gray blouse. He said, "Do you carry any items useful to a spirit mage?"

The woman replied in a slow, controlled voice, as if speaking to a child. "Spirit mages are not allowed to craft magical items for public sale. It violates their code."

Oh. "In that case, where are your most expensive items?"

The woman looked down her nose at him. "Each Discipline Vault maintains a collection of rare pieces. There is also this vault's Thaumaturge Case."

Val affected his best look of disdain. He was already tired of this lady's attitude. "Which is where?"

She smirked and looked him over, as if to say, *you're not dressed for this place.* "We require proof of funds before viewing the Thaumaturge Case. The least expensive item is one thousand gold pieces."

Val lifted the two sacks and plopped them on the counter, spilling a few gold coins in the process. "I trust you can hold these for me while I browse? It might help if you start counting."

Eyes wide, the woman bit back her remark and waved over a man in a tuxedo. He bowed and led Val through another archway in the rear, this one warded by sigils and isolated by a silver curtain.

On the other side of the curtain, he saw a collection of glass cubbyholes embedded into the far wall. A diverse range of items was displayed, eighteen in total. Each item bore a descriptive plaque underneath.

He approached the first case. The clerk stood discreetly behind him. The case contained a green and black feather as long as Val's forearm. The plaque read: *Rakha Feather. Allowance of magical flight of forty-eight hours duration. 1,100 gold pieces.*

Useful, Val thought, but not for present purposes.

The next case contained an onyx crown. *Coronet of Achen-Tur. Enables telepathic communication with most varietals of undead. Five thousand gold.*

Val averted his eyes. *No thank you.*

He saw a ring that could turn the user into a jaguar; a salve that rendered human skin as hard as stone; a hand-held piano-like instrument whose notes could summon and control serpents; a bottle of misty vapors which, when released, could detect invisible wards. The cheapest item he saw was the Rakha Feather, the most expensive a human eye preserved in an amber brooch which claimed to allow the mage to see through walls, among other things. When the eye blinked at Val, he shuddered and kept moving, pausing in front of a case containing three vials of blue-white liquid. The vials were tiny, the size of a thimble. *Spirit Water. Restorer of magical energies. Six thousand gold pieces.*

"Tell me about this one," Val said.

The clerk looked startled he had spoken. "Ah, yes. Each vial of spirit water replenishes a wizard's store of magical energy."

"I can read, thank you. Restore as in entirely?"

"I believe that is the case."

"The effect is instantaneous?"

"So I am told."

"I thought spirit mages couldn't craft magical items?" Val said.

"Spirit water is technically a hybrid creation, crafted jointly by a spiritmancer and an aquamancer. Because it has such practical utility, it was, ah, granted a special exemption by the Council. It is extremely rare, however, and most difficult to produce. One of our best-selling items when in stock."

"I'll take it."

It turned out Val had brought nearly seven thousand gold pieces worth of coins and gems. After using the remaining thousand to purchase a pair of wizard cuffs, he dismissed the obnoxious counter clerk with a smile, then flew back to Salomon's Crib with his purchases.

Midday. He needed to move. After a quick meal, he donned a pair of woolen pants, a white shirt with a high and frilly collar, and a light cloak—his typical outfit for the Abbey—and then packed a leather satchel with his father's spell book, the spirit water, wizard cuffs, and two handfuls of gems and coins. He tucked his Amulet of Shielding underneath his shirt, slipped the Ring of Shadows in his pocket, drank a glass of ale for courage, and made the last minute decision to leave his father's staff and spell book behind. They would be awkward to explain if something happened. After saying goodbye to his abode, he shut the door behind him.

On his way to the Abbey, he flew to the street corner on St. Charles where Gus gave city tours. The driver was parked on the corner, chomping on his pipe.

"How's it, lad? Didn't think ye had plans today. Ye be needin' me?"

Val nodded. "If you don't mind."

"I'm always here for ye."

Val was pensive as Gus drove him through the city. Despite the insanity of it all, he had been on Urfe for months: long enough to make friends, start to fall for a woman, embrace the rhythm of this world's life. He had learned magic, redefined his concept of reality, and born witness to terrifying, beautiful, impossible things. It was all about to end, and he wasn't sure how he felt about it.

But that was all irrelevant right now. The only thing that mattered was helping his brothers.

"Drop me at the Hall of Wizards today, Gus."

"Aye."

When they arrived at their destination, Val said, "I won't need your services for a while. Maybe a very long while. Listen, I want you to know I appreciate everything you've done for me." He dug into his satchel and handed Gus a handful of gems. "For you and yours."

Gus's mouth fell open, and he had to catch his pipe as it slipped out of his mouth. "This here is too much, I can't—"

Val clapped him on the shoulder and walked off. "Goodbye, my friend."

"Thank ye, me boy! *Thank* ye! Ye know where to find me!"

Val stepped between the enormous red-gold columns and into the Hall of Wizards, where hundreds of statues of mages filled the open-air interior that somehow never got wet and maintained the same pleasant temperature. Each statue bore an actual wizard's stone, worn as jewelry or embedded into a weapon. The flash of color from the gemstones provided a sharp contrast to the somber gray statues.

Val was pretty sure that after death, these mages had somehow been frozen in stone. The details were too life-like for anything else. Were they still alive in some way, he wondered? This world's version of cryogenic stasis?

At the rear of the Hall, a garage door-size plaque displayed the names of a few dozen wizards, along with their specialty. Each plaque bore a dash instead of a second date, implying the wizards on the plaque had gone missing—or something else had happened. He stopped to regard the second name on the last row.

Dane Blackwood
Spirit Mage
1850–

He paused for a moment of silent contemplation, telling his father how much he missed him and promising to do his best to keep his brothers safe. Val bowed his head, wondering who his father had really been, wondering why he had never returned to his homeland, wondering what he would think of Val's choices in life. After lifting his head to press his fingers to his lips and then against his father's plaque, he wheeled and left the Hall of Wizards, choked with emotion, heading for the coterie house to meet the others.

It was time to finish this.

Val entered the cottage and found Adaira, Gowan, Dida, and Riga already on the rooftop. "Sorry I'm late."

Adaira eyed him curiously. "Where were you today?"

"I wasn't feeling well."

Adaira let the silence marinate, as if to say, *you look fine now*. "The professors don't look kindly on absences."

"I know. Just a vicious stomach bug this morning. It passed quickly."

Her face softened. "I'm sorry to hear that."

Val eyed the bag of mint orchids at the foot of the table, forcing himself not to look at Gowan. He truly hoped the pyromancer cooperated with him later in the evening, but he had the feeling he wouldn't.

And then it was going to get ugly.

"I just told the others of our decision to involve the investigators," Adaira said. "I wasn't sure if you were coming."

"We agree it's for the best," Dida said.

"I'm glad," Val murmured.

"Excuse me for a moment," Gowan said, "I need to use the washroom."

He left, and Val said, "How'd he take it? I had the feeling he . . . really wanted to bring in the murderer."

"We all did," Adaira said. "But he understood the danger."

"The mageworks have begun," Dida said, pointing at the sky.

Val turned his head and saw a pyrotechnic display lighting the sky above the Wizard District. "What's that?"

"Queen's Day tomorrow, silly," Adaira said, and Val mumbled a reply about studying too much.

As they watched bouquets of color explode above their heads, brighter and with far more intricate patterns than the best fireworks back home, Val cursed and wondered how long the display would last. What if Gowan stayed here all night to watch?

"It's marvelous," Riga said.

A latticework of color filled the sky, then broke apart and fell like raindrops towards the ground. When the drops hit, they bounced back up like comets streaking in reverse, higher than before, forming a new pattern. Despite his wish to get on with his plans, Val was transfixed by the stunning display.

"Where's Gowan?" Dida asked. "He's missing quite a show."

The pyromancer had been gone quite a while, Val realized. He flicked his eyes around the patio, and realized what was missing at the same time Adaira voiced it.

She pushed away from the table. "The bag of mint orchids—he took them!"

"Let's not rush to conclusions," Dida said. "Perhaps he's downstairs."

Val ignored him and ran to the stairs, Adaira and the others right behind. They searched the bottom level of the coterie and found no sign of Gowan.

"All this week," Riga said slowly, in her gravelly voice, "he wanted me to practice water spells with him. I thought nothing of it. He claimed he was weak on aquamancy . . . ."

"We told him what Rucker said about werebats and cold water," Dida said. He pressed a fist to his mouth. "Oh my."

Val cursed. They had all underestimated Gowan's wounded pride and ambition. And now he had to find his classmate before the assassin struck, killed Gowan, and ruined Val's chance of locating the Planewalk.

"Everyone is watching the mageworks," Adaira said. "If Gowan takes the mint orchids to the side streets, he will be the only target."

"Which is what he's counting on," Val said, already heading for the door.

The four budding mages took flight under the exploding sky, soaring past the wall of the Wizard District and then drifting over the darkened streets of the French Quarter. As Adaira had guessed, thousands of people were lined up on Canal and Bourbon near the Goblin Market, where they had better views of the mageworks. Except for a few rooftop gatherings, the interior of the quarter was eerily silent.

"How long will the celebration last?" Val asked. "I've never witnessed the New Victoria version."

"Hours," Adaira said.

Starting at Bourbon Street and working their way towards the river, they drifted above the seedy lanes and alleys, looking for Gowan's telltale red cloak.

It didn't take them long. Halfway through the quarter, they spotted him skulking through a trash-strewn alley, hands in his pockets, the bag of mint orchids open and tied to his belt.

"What are those other two pouches he's carrying?" Val asked.

Adaira's face was grim. "Water skins. He aims to force the werebat to shift form. Come."

As they prepared to descend, a shadow stepped off a rooftop and drifted down behind the pyromancer, black wings spread so wide they obscured him from view.

"Gowan!" Adaira screamed. "Behind you!"

He turned just before the werebat landed, stumbling backwards as the winged creature whirled to see who had screamed. Val and the werebat locked eyes, and Val saw a furry gray head and a body the size of a burly lumberjack, its arms and legs attached to the razor-tipped, membranous wings. The terrifying vision caused a wave of fear to crash over him.

Gowan roared and threw the two water skins at the werebat, bursting the leather covers with his mind and propelling the water straight at the assassin. The werebat flew on a backwards diagonal faster than Val would have thought possible, avoiding the stream of water and then flying straight back at Gowan, incisors bared.

A spark appeared in Gowan's hands, and a Fire Sphere burst into existence and shot towards the werebat. The creature folded its wings and spun like a tornado, avoiding the missile. It swatted Gowan with one of its wings, ripping his cloak and thrusting him into a wall.

The creature started towards the battered pyromancer, then changed its mind and shot into the sky, seeking to escape. Val and the others raced towards it, but it was faster in flight, a streak of dark lightning.

A flash of mageworks illuminated the sky. As the assassin flew towards the river, Riga extracted a silver stopper from the inside of her cloak. She emptied a stream of liquid as she flew, and it formed into the shape of an arrow and shot towards the werebat, almost too fast for Val to follow.

The creature saw the water coming and dodged to the side, but the water arrow under Riga's command followed it like a heat-seeking missile, striking it full in the back.

Before their eyes, the werebat shifted form, plummeting towards the ground as it blurred into a hulking man dressed in black and holding a dagger in each hand. His wings remained long enough to manage a rough landing in an alley, and all five classmates touched down behind him.

Fully human, the assassin whirled and threw two daggers, one at Gowan and one at Riga. Both erected wizard shields and blocked the attack.

The alley dead-ended behind the killer. With a quick glance, he eyed the sheer brick walls and the five advancing wizard students, then produced two more daggers and sprinted right at them.

Gowan threw another Fire Sphere. The assassin slid underneath it. When he regained his feet, his form was blurring again, his face contorted with pain as fur erupted from his pores and the skin on his back elongated to form membranous wings.

Val had wondered why he was running straight at them, but when the assassin regained his form and leapt straight into the air, Val realized he sought to gain momentum for a quick flight while he shifted.

It was too late. Before the werebat could escape the alley, Val tossed him against the wall with a Wind Push. Someone else picked up the attack and pinned him against the bricks in a spread-eagle fashion, which allowed

Gowan's next Fire Sphere, weaker than his first two but still potent, to strike the creature in the chest. The werebat shifted to human form again, screaming as he burned.

Val and the others watched the assassin's hair blacken and curl, his skin melt off his hands and face. Adaira bladed her hand and completed a slow horizontal sweep, her face contorted with effort as the assassin's jugular ripped apart. He clutched his throat and collapsed, his lifeblood soaking into the pavement.

"For Xavier," Adaira said. "And the others."

"For Xavier," Val murmured, and meant it.

He didn't show it, but he was shaken at how easily Adaira had ended the assassin's life. Not just at her show of nerves, but how frail the human body was, and how poised a cuerpomancer was to exploit those weaknesses.

Riga stared down at the corpse with an unreadable expression. Dida put his arm around Gowan, who looked pale. "Are you injured, my friend?"

"I'm fine," Gowan muttered. He passed his hand over the corpse, quelling the flames. Adaira spread her fingers, and the remaining tatters of the assassin's shirt flew off his body, exposing a tattoo of a curved black dagger still visible on the burnt skin. A series of miniature runes formed the tattoo.

"The Alazashin, as we suspected," Adaira said. "The rune dagger is one of their symbols."

"Why did he keep his clothes when he turned?" Val asked.

"His ability to change his nature must have been the result of a temporary spell or object, not a true case of lycanthropy."

"Should we not have tried to ascertain his purpose?" Dida asked.

"The Alazashin take a strict oath never to reveal their employer. They never break under torture, not even for a cuerpomancer." Adaira stepped closer to the body and severed the head with another, more prolonged, swipe of her hand. "But if I hurry, there are other methods to compel the dead to speak." She took off her cloak and spread it on the ground. With the toe of her boot, she rolled the head onto the fabric and wrapped it inside.

That's some kind of woman, Val thought.

"I'll take this to my father, and he will know who to consult. He'll be furious with me, but that's far less important than discovering the perpetrator behind these murders. The rest of you should return home. And Gowan—I will inform my father of your instrumental role in the assassin's demise."

Gowan tipped his head, swallowing his disappointment at not dispatching the assassin himself. "Thank you," he whispered.

Just before she flew off with the macabre bundle, Adaira's eyes lingered on Val's, questions and attraction smoldering in her gaze.

As soon as the rest of his companions flew in separate directions to return home, Val slipped the Ring of Shadows on his finger and soared upward, following Gowan through the night sky.

-51-

The smell of sage and juniper infused the breeze as the party descended the precipitous ridgeline the next morning. Will kept staring at the Valley of the Cursed with a mixture of dread and fascination.

When they reached the rocky mouth of the valley, which looked much wider from ground level that it had from the ridge, Tamás gathered everyone close. "Needless to say, be on your guard. I've heard stories of travelers who have passed through the valley unharmed, and stories of those who . . . have not."

"I've heard them, too," Dalen said, his beige eyes wide and roving the woods. "Tales of escaped murderers who prey on those foolish enough to pass through the valley. And worse, much worse. Owlbears and garloths and insects as big as humans that drag you to lairs beneath the earth and—"

"Thanks for all of that, Dalen," Will said. "Imagination engaged."

With a last glance at the serrated peaks looming on either side, they entered the woods on a path of beaten earth and pine needles that led straight into the heart of the valley. It all seemed quite normal to Will. Endless copses of firs, aspens, pine, and spruce. Birds chirping, a caressing breeze, oxygen that didn't poison their lungs.

Still, the forest had a feel to it. Perhaps it was Will's preconceived notion of the dangers awaiting them, perhaps it was something else, but he couldn't shake the feeling of being watched as they trekked through the valley.

Yasmina had joined Tamás at the head of the group. Growing more confident with each passing day, as if born to be a wilder, she listened to the wind

and the insects, and every now and then a squirrel or some other forest creature would run beside her for a spell, chirping away.

Will decided to have a frank chat with her. "Hey," he said, catching up with
her long stride. "Do your forest friends tell you anything about this place?"

He was half-joking, but she responded with solemn eyes. "They are wary
here. There are always predators in the wild, but these woods . . . I sense alien
things here, Will. Things I cannot describe."

"Do you mean *E.T.* aliens, or alien as in strange and unusual?"

A ladybug landed on Yasmina's staff, and she eased it away as the corners of
her mouth upturned. "I'm no wizard, Will. And no, I don't believe most of the
creatures here mean us harm. They're just curious and . . . ashamed. Yes, that is
the best word." Her eyes grew sad. "Ashamed of what they are."

"But some mean us harm."

She gave a careful nod as her gaze returned to the forest. "Some, yes."

Each time the trail branched, Yasmina and Tamás conferred on the direction
to take. Tamás was clearly at home in the outdoors and seemed to have an innate sense of direction, and Will had no idea how Yasmina was helping. Maybe
the squirrels were feeding her information.

Around mid-morning, Yasmina and Tamás stopped walking and cocked
their heads to listen. The party crowded forward, though at first Will didn't
notice anything. Then he saw a rustling in a bed of waist-high wildflowers, just
off the trail and violent enough to signify a creature of some size, or a group
of creatures.

The party backed away slowly, weapons raised, as three animals crawled
out of the wildflowers and raised the hair on Will's arms. Long and low-slung,
about the size of crocodiles, the creatures were covered in foot-long bristles as
sharp as daggers, had curved beaks like a parrot, and each sported eight feet
that looked quite capable of running down two-footed prey. They were gnawing on wildflowers as they waddled, and when they opened their mouths to
chew, Will saw four interlocking incisors, reminding him of vampire fangs.

"Let's hope they're vegetarian," Caleb whispered.

"I don't think those six-inch long pointed teeth are for the wildflowers,"
Will whispered back.

Following Yasmina's lead, everyone stilled as the things meandered across the path and into the forest on the opposite side. Not until the bizarre creatures disappeared from sight did the party breathe a collective sigh of relief and move forward.

They lunched on the bank of a small brook, huddled together, trying to eat as quietly as possible. After devouring cold provisions provided by the gypsies, they washed the meal down with water from the stream, then resumed the journey.

The next incident was even more disturbing. Tamás had dropped back to confer with Marek, leaving Yasmina alone up front. Caleb tried to engage her, but she rebuffed him. As Dalen regaled Will with stories he had heard about the Barrier Coast, an eight foot tall praying mantis dropped out of the sky, as silent as a pin falling on a cushion, and landed right in front of Yasmina.

Will froze in horror as the thing raised up on two sinewy rear legs, antennae poking skyward, its serrated forelimbs crossed against its chest. Instead of compound insect eyes, it stared down at Yasmina with twin yellow orbs, and its thin mouth twisted as it tried to communicate with a series of garbled sounds.

No one knew what to do. The creature looked as if it could tear Yasmina limb from limb, so Will didn't want to spook it. He cringed as Yasmina took a hesitant step forward, then reached up and placed her hand on a back that looked like body armor in the shape of a leaf.

The mantis tipped its head downward. More incomprehensible sounds issued from its mouth. Its face balled in frustration when Yasmina didn't respond, though her touch seemed to calm it. After a few moments of mute companionship, it vaulted without warning thirty feet into the air, landing on the branch of a spruce. It jumped again, disappearing high into the canopy.

Will and Caleb rushed to Yasmina, whose hands were shaking. At first Will thought it was from fear, but then he saw the flash of pain and anger in her eyes.

It was empathy that had rattled her.

As the day wore on, Will's sense that someone or something was watching grew stronger, and he didn't think it was the praying mantis. Sadly, he got the feeling that the insect-man had tried to communicate and, when he failed to make a connection, moved on.

He decided to broach his worries to the group. "Anyone else feel like we're being watched? Yaz, have you seen anything?"

"No," she said, "but I feel the same."

"I was hoping you wouldn't agree," Will said.

"*Lucka*, what if something's waiting for nightfall to attack?"

Tamás grimaced. "We need to find shelter, someplace to defend ourselves."

They decided to press forward as fast as they could, hoping to find a cave, a hill, or a body of water to put their backs to.

What they found was even better—or so Will thought. "Am I seeing things, or is that a house up ahead?"

They drew closer. In the center of a large, overgrown clearing, a storybook house of stacked stone came into view, complete with gingerbread trim, a chimney, arched windows, and an unkempt front yard surrounded by a wooden fence.

"It's full of weeds," Caleb said. "No lights, no smoke in the chimney, and that fence is falling apart."

"Aye," Tamás said. "It appears abandoned."

They circled to the rear and saw three smaller structures attached to the house via enclosed stone tunnels. *Above-ground tunnels?* Will thought. *Weird.* He also noticed a stack of rotting firewood beside the house.

To be safe, they knocked on the door.

No answer.

A heavy dusk had settled over the valley, and the sense of being watched increased with each passing minute. Will peered nervously into the woods.

"It appears we have no choice," Tamás said.

Dalen crossed his arms against his chest. "I don't know what this place is, but it's better than sleeping in these woods."

"You clearly haven't read the Brothers Grimm," Caleb muttered.

Tamás tried the door. It creaked open. The party filed inside with weapons drawn, not relaxing until they had explored the main structure. It was empty, though to Will's trained contractor eye, he could tell it had once been furnished, due to the dents and scuff marks on the wooden floor. Whether the inhabitants had packed up and moved on, or looters had stripped the place bare, he had no idea.

Heavy doors in the rear of the house, secured by iron bars and clasps with the padlocks missing, guarded the entrances to the three stone tunnels. After removing the iron bars, Dalen created a ball of floating silver from the weak moonlight, helping the party navigate the twenty-foot long tunnel on the left. They needed to ensure they were alone in the compound. Will felt claustrophobic in the odd passageway, and again wondered at its purpose.

The corridor led to a square stone room with five sets of manacles, each of varying size, mounted on the walls. In the middle of the room, a thick, four-foot iron chain was bolted into the floor.

After staring at the ominous chamber, they returned to the main house and followed the stone tunnel on the right, which led to a similar room. More manacles, another floor chain. A feeling of oppression infused the room, as if the ghosts of whatever had been imprisoned there still lingered.

Yasmina looked increasingly distressed. When the party traversed the middle tunnel and saw what it contained, she gasped and covered her mouth.

Spaced about the room were five cast-iron pods, standing upright and bolted to the floor. Each pod had clasps and hinges on the side, and the doors had swung outward, reminding Will of suits of armor sheared in half. Dark stains covered the insides of the pods.

A bronze operating table was attached to the far wall. Above it, an assortment of hooks and chains hung from the ceiling at various heights. Empty shelves stood on either side of the table. Will could imagine the knives and other tools of vivisection that must have once filled the room.

Yasmina looked faint. "What is this place?"

Dalen's face had paled, and Marek was standing by the door, arms crossed and bearded face grim. Tamás surveyed the room with hooded eyes. "The workshop of a menagerist. A rather primitive one, but effective, I'm quite sure."

"What—" Yasmina swallowed—"is a menagerist?"

"A wizard who fuses different species together," Will said. "A Doctor Moreau—a mad scientist."

"The discipline began with good intentions," Tamás continued, "seen as a way to improve the quality of domesticated animals. But it has always attracted the wrong sort of wizard, and was banned for good reason."

No one liked the idea of spending the night in the house of a menagerist, even if abandoned, but camping in the forest was too risky. They barred all the doors and returned to the common room, huddling on the cold stone floor as they finished the last of their provisions. The next day they would have to hunt or forage.

The nighttime sounds of the forest penetrated the stone walls: the monotonous buzzing of insects, the hoot of an owl, the mournful howl of a canine. Just as Will was about to find a corner of the room to sleep, Yasmina rushed to the window.

"There's something out there," she said. "Moving through the woods."

Will hurried to the window and saw a figure with leathery skin and a long, misshapen face creep out of the woods and into the clearing surrounding the house. Clad in animal skins and wielding a club, the creature looked like a smaller version of the hill trolls, except it had two heads and two extra arms sticking out of its chest. Each head swiveled in a different direction to observe the meadow, and the muscular arms took turns holding the club, tossing it back and forth.

Will clenched the windowsill, palms sweating, as the others gathered around. The monster stopped to sniff the air. It cocked its head as if listening, then waved one of its arms forward.

Five more of them stepped into the clearing.

And then five more.

Twenty came in total, spread out around the house, creeping towards the door and windows. Any one of them looked like more than a match for Tamás or Will.

"*Lucka*," Dalen said, his voice tight.

"My God," Caleb whispered, "*look* at those things."

Will whipped his head towards Yasmina. "Is there anything you can do? Call for help from your friends?"

Yasmina shook her head without looking away from the window. "I don't know how. Not here."

"Away from the windows," Tamás said. "They might have projectiles."

Caleb backed towards the center of the room. "What about one of the dungeon rooms? Hole up there and take them one by one?"

"We'll be trapped with no exit," Will said. "They could come inside or just bar the doors and starve us to death." Tamás nodded in agreement.

One of the creatures beat against the door with his club. The boom reverberated throughout the room.

"Dalen," Tamás said, impressing Will with his calm, "perform as usual. We make our stand here, as they come through the door."

They didn't even have that luxury. The door toppled inward at the same time the windows shattered, and the monsters poured into the room with clubs raised and murderous gleams in their eyes. Will, Marek, and Tamás formed a rough triangle around the others, though Will had no illusions of victory.

Just before they engaged, a man dressed in ragged pants and a purple, shopworn, hooded velvet cloak appeared in the middle of the room, between Tamás and the first two-headed creature. He popped into existence as if by magic, and Will assumed that was exactly the origin. The hood shielded the man's face, and his fingers were swathed in white bandages, like a mummy. From the side, Will saw him shuffling a pack of playing cards.

As soon as the man appeared, he took a calm look around the room. "What'll it be, I see?" he said, and thrust a card into one of the hands of the nearest four-armed monster. The creature, as surprised as Will by the sudden appearance, took the card out of reflex—and then turned to dust. The next monster in line reared back, and the man flicked another card at it. The card morphed into a frog, which proceeded to land on the head of the creature and bound onto the fireplace.

After a moment of confusion, the monsters resumed their attack, and Will didn't have time to ponder the absurdity of what he had just witnessed. He parried the blow of the first club, but the monster followed it up with a backhand from one of his other arms, which caught Will on the shoulder and spun him halfway around. The creature grabbed him with yet another arm, holding him in place as he swung the club again. Will moved into the swing, as Mala had taught him, and head butted the nearest of the two heads. The monster stumbled back, and Will planted a side kick to his stomach.

Before he could follow up, another monster stepped forward, and Will had to fend off another club swing. Two more creatures pressed him, but Yasmina ran forward swinging her staff. Even Caleb entered the fray, sneaking behind one of the monsters and knocking him on the back of a head with his bracers.

The two-headed monster fighting Yasmina knocked her staff away, then picked her up with two of its arms. She screamed and tried to wriggle free as the monster raised its club with a third arm. Will bellowed but couldn't free himself to help her, and no one else was close enough. He watched in horror as the club swung downward, but just before it struck Yasmina, a long green appendage snatched the club away, then jerked the two-headed creature straight into the air. Yasmina fell to the floor, and Will saw an eight foot tall praying mantis—he had no idea if it was the same one—behead Yasmina's attacker with a vicious swipe from a serrated forearm. It tossed the body aside and picked up the next one, who met the same fate.

The two-headed creature fighting Will broke away to take a swing at the praying mantis, but the weapon bounced off the leaf-shaped carapace. The mantis reared, its head brushing the ceiling, then held its forelegs high and wide. It released a blood-curdling battle cry, causing Will to cringe, and the two-headed monster nearest the enraged insect man fled the house. The mantis followed, bounding across the clearing with huge steps and cutting his opponent down from behind.

Will whipped around to see who needed help. Tamás and Marek were squared off against opponents, and the man in the moth-eaten velvet jacket was running around trying to hand playing cards to the remaining two-headed creatures. One of the cards disintegrated a monster, another turned into a bouquet of flowers which the man stopped to smell. A third card produced a gray ooze that clung to both faces of one of the creatures, causing it to roar and run away, raking its eyes with its hands.

One of the monsters almost caught the card-wielding man in the chest with a club swing, but right before Will's astonished eyes, the man disappeared and then re-appeared five feet away, behind his opponent. He stuffed a playing card into the animal skin tunic, just above the shoulder blades, and the monster winked out of existence.

The man grabbed his own chin, face cocked in a quizzical smile. "I'll say. What a jolly new thing, that. A tat for a tit, a tit for a tat."

Between the rampaging mantis man and the card-wielding lunatic, the remaining invaders must have decided there was easier prey to be found, because they broke off the attack and fled into the woods.

Humming to himself, the man in the purple cloak turned to face the party.

His hood was so voluminous Will couldn't see his face. The bandage on one of his hands had started to unravel, and Will looked down. It looked like the hand of a normal white male, until he saw one of the fingers disappear and then reappear a moment later, and then half of his palm do the same. As if parts of the man's hands were blinking in and out of existence.

The hooded figure took a step in one direction, and then the other, muttering to himself. Finally he plopped down on the stone floor, crossed his legs lotus-style, and started humming another tune.

"I believe the creatures have fled," Tamás said, running to each of the windows to peer outside.

"Not all of them," Yasmina murmured.

Will saw her gaze focused on a space between the trees. He stepped closer to the window and noticed the camouflaged form of the praying mantis staring back at them. "I'll be back," she said, moving for the door. Will and Caleb moved to stop her, but she held them back. "It's okay."

Caleb kept an eye on her as Tamás squatted to face the new arrival, though the gypsy leader kept a healthy distance.

"Thank you," Tamás said.

The man in the purple cloak looked up, startled. "What? Oh, that? Just a blit of blat. A good morning to skin the cat."

Dalen looked hesitant, then decided to sit next to Tamás. "But it's not morning."

The man peered outside as if surprised. "It was for me," he muttered. "Disturbed I be."

"What's your name?" Dalen asked.

The man cackled and held a card out. "I call myself The Dealer, if I may. I've no idea what others say."

Dalen shrank from the card, and the man flipped it over, revealing the Jack of Spades. Then he shuffled the deck and tucked it inside his cloak, as adept as any street magician.

Will found it disconcerting not being able to see the man's face. Did he keep it hidden because of what Will had seen of his hands? What *was* he? Besides completely insane?

"Are you a mage?" Dalen asked quietly. "Is this your house?"

"No no no," the Dealer said, laughing. "Oh no no no. No no no. No no. No."

"But your powers . . . ."

"Don't know what I am. Do you know what you be? A heart, a mind, a spirit, all three?"

Fair question, Will thought. He took a seat next to Dalen, and the Dealer's eyes latched onto Will's sword as he slid it back into its scabbard. "Where did you get that? Did you make it? Pull it out of a hat?"

"It was my father's."

The dealer reached out with a bandaged hand. "I would like very much to—no, I wouldn't." He retracted his hand. "Yes, I would. No, I wouldn't. Oh, but I could. No, no no no."

Will put his hand on the scabbard. "Would you like to see it? Do you know anything about it?"

"Know anything—do I know anything about—" He doubled over in laughter, the folds of the cloak rippling. "Oh, you're quite the wit. Inside that sword I'd fit."

"Thank you again," Will said. "For saving us."

The dealer waved a hand. "Bah. It was the mantis, you see. I owed him a favor and paid the fee." He stood. "And with that, I take my leave from thee. Perhaps we'll meet again, tee hee."

He withdrew the deck again and started tossing cards above his head. The first two missed him and hit the floor. One turned into a beetle and scuttled away, while the other bounced high as if made of rubber, punching a hole through the roof and soaring into the night sky.

The third one nicked the Dealer in the head, and when it touched him, he disappeared.

Yasmina didn't return until the next morning, bleary-eyed and sad. Will asked her where she had spent the night.

"Talking to the mantis man. He's the only one of his kind, and very lonely. He doesn't know how he came to be. He sometimes has flashbacks of terrible experiments."

"Talking?" Caleb asked.

Yasmina didn't look at him when she responded, and her voice was cold. "Communicating. Unlike some, he's very loyal, and will watch over us until we leave the forest."

Caleb looked away.

"Does he know who that man was?" Will asked.

"Someone who came to the forest recently and has strange powers. That's all he knows."

They discussed the Dealer's appearance, but no one had any idea who he was, other than perhaps a wizard who had lost his mind. They just knew he was unpredictable and dangerous in the extreme, despite having saved them.

Each of them took a turn on guard duty for the rest of the night, but neither the two-headed monsters nor the man in the velvet cloak returned.

"We should be off," Tamás said, as soon as they gathered in the morning. "I've no wish to spend another night in this forest."

Everyone wholeheartedly agreed. They hustled out of the house, had a breakfast of berries and water from a nearby stream, and returned to the main path. As they walked, Will felt the familiar feeling of being watched, but this time the sensation was not an uncomfortable one, and he sensed the mantis man nearby, escorting them on the final leg of their journey.

They pushed hard throughout the day, stopping only to forage for mushrooms and berries. While the light snack left Will craving a cheeseburger, or at least a couple of fresh trout, they decided not to take the time to hunt. They wanted to put the valley far behind them.

The only oddity they saw on the second day was a group of squirrels with bat wings that flew into the trees and picked up nuts with their feet. The party cleared the forest by nightfall, and when they stood atop a knoll and took a final look at the dangerous woods, Will glimpsed the mantis man standing on a branch just inside the forest, watching them leave. Yasmina mouthed a sad goodbye.

Tamás turned to point at the shadowy bulk of a mountain looming above them, the tip of its peak lost in the dim light. "Greybeard Mountain," he said. "One of the ancestral homes of the Yith—the Simorgh Riders. Tomorrow my friends, Devla willing, we fly to Freetown."

-52-

Gowan's flight pattern was wobbly and slow. Val knew he was drained from the fight with the werebat. Producing fireballs from a tiny spark consumed a massive amount of energy, a fact Val had learned from trying it himself.

The mageworks ended with a finale that lit the night sky like a million rainbows exploding from a cannon. Humid night air rushed through into Val's face as he followed Gowan through a city marked by revelry. Crowds of people poured into the streets of the French Quarter and the Government District, though once they crossed into the more residential streets of Uptown, the hordes thinned.

Val suddenly remembered that Gowan was the son of Professor Azara. If things turned sour, he didn't want to be anywhere near the home of his powerful teacher. His plan needed an immediate tweak.

"Gowan!" he called out, slipping off the Ring of Shadows and speeding up to fly alongside the pyromancer. "You forgot something."

"Val?" Gowan said in surprise, slowing his flight and turning.

"I've been following you, trying to catch up."

Gowan's eyes were suspicious. "I wasn't flying that fast."

"I'm exhausted, too," Val lied.

"What is it that I forgot?"

"My request to teach you spiritmancy. You've been avoiding me."

Gowan flew in silence for a moment. "And?" he said, arcing towards St. Charles.

"I know how badly you want to be a spirit mage. I know you fear the Planewalk, and so do I. Let's do it together. Tonight. Right now."

Gowan's chuckle sounded half-mad. "You don't understand, do you? I haven't the power."

"Then take me there," Val said. "Help me."

"What? Have you gone insane?"

Again, Val was well aware of what Gowan *didn't* say.

He never denied knowing the location of the Planewalk.

"I have to use the Pool of Souls," Val said, deciding to tell the truth. He wanted to avoid a fight, and hoped Gowan would understand the gravity of his predicament. "Two people very dear are lost to me. I have to find them, and it's the only way I know how."

He turned his head to give Val a disbelieving stare. "The Conclave will never let you use the Pool of Souls. Not even if you survive the Planewalk."

"I know," Val said quietly, as they veered towards Napoleon, a wide avenue with mansions almost as grand as those on St. Charles.

Any of those houses could be Gowan's. Val had to hurry.

"Do you actually think," Gowan said, his lip curling, "that I would help you defy my mother? Increase my shame even further?"

"Just tell me where the entrance to the Planewalk is, and no one will ever know. I give you my word."

"And I bid you goodnight. Don't bring this up again in my presence."

"Gowan," Val said, reaching for the wizard cuffs, "I'm not asking."

"Wha—"

Val threw the wizard cuffs at him before he could finish his sentence. The magical bonds held the pyromancer's wrists tight, though they did not affect his ability to fly or cast spells.

"Take these off, you pagan!" Gowan commanded. "What are you doing?"

"I know your magic is almost spent," Val said. "I conserved mine during the fight." He used Wind Push to propel Gowan towards the ground. The pyromancer tumbled through the air, managing to right himself at the last minute, but Val dove into him, tackling him on the cobblestones. Gowan scrambled away, huffing and jerking in vain on the cuffs, while Val stalked towards him.

"I have to know where the Planewalk is," Val said. "And I know that you know."

Gowan snarled, somehow lit his igniter stick with his hands bound, formed a Fire Sphere, and sent a ball of flame spinning through the air.

But Val was ready. He put up his Wizard Shield as soon as he saw the spark, placing it halfway between them to dull the heat. The fireball hovered in midair, useless, unable to advance. Both of them strained with effort, Gowan trying to propel the missile forward, Val working to keep it at bay.

Val was growing weaker by the second, but he knew Gowan was weaker still. The pyromancer looked clammy and drained in the light of the glow orbs above the street, but he clenched his teeth and said, "You shouldn't play with fire against a pyromancer."

The fireball disappeared, Val heard a series of sharp cracks, and then bolts of golden fire were streaking at him from ten different directions, formed from the glow orbs Gowan had just shattered.

Val had a strong Wizard Shield, but he didn't yet know how to protect himself on all sides. Instead he had to deal with each bolt one by one. He whirled, putting up magical barriers as fast he could, but the last missile got through, striking him in the shoulder.

There was a sizzling flash of blue. Val reeled, expecting to burst into flame, but nothing happened. He looked down and saw the Amulet of Shielding glow blue and then crack underneath his shirt. It must have had one last charge.

Val looked back at Gowan and produced a wicked smile, concealing his own relief.

"How can that be?" Gowan gasped, taking a step back. "You're not strong enough to absorb that."

"I don't think you have any idea how strong I really am," Val said, as he stalked towards Gowan. He put his hand out, and the igniter flew into it. Val threw it on the ground and crushed it with his foot.

The pyromancer tried to fly away, but he was so weak he could barely get off the ground. Val used Wind Push to hold him in place against the wall. "No more games. Tell me where the Planewalk is."

Gowan raised his bound wrists. "Release me at once."

Val took a step forward. "I don't want to do this. Last chance, Gowan."

"Are you mad? Perhaps you have a modicum more strength in reserve than I do," Gowan panted, "but you're not strong enough to force me."

Val took out one of the vials of spirit water, broke the seal, and drank the contents. The viscous white-blue liquid slid down his throat like mucus. As soon as he swallowed, he felt his energy pouring back in, filling up a well deep inside him, in the mysterious ether where the magic lived.

"Spirit water," Gowan breathed, both frightened and amazed.

Val reached deep inside. In the chaos of the moment, the magic wouldn't come at first, but he gritted his teeth and thought of his brothers, pouring every ounce of emotive power he had into tearing apart the void. When he felt the barrier rip, flooding him with sweet release, he shoved magical energy into the gap.

Spirit fire swarmed on the fingertips of his left hand, black lightning sparking inches from the pyromancer.

Gowan shrieked and pressed his head against the wall. Fear and jealousy vied for supremacy on his face. "How did you—by the Queen, you wouldn't dare! My mother will impale you on the Sanctum!"

"I'll be dead or gone before your mother finds out. But you'll never tell her anyway, will you? Your shame would be too great." Val used his free hand to grip Gowan by the neck. "Where's the Planewalk?"

Gowan still refused to answer. Val brought the spirit fire right up to Gowan's face. Val didn't feel a thing, not even heat, as if the spirit fire were under his control yet a separate thing entirely. It was unnerving.

His power was waning fast, however, and he had to convince Gowan before the spirit fire disappeared. Val himself wasn't sure how far he was prepared to go. "Trust me," he said, "when I say I will do *anything* to help my brothers."

Val reached forward, spirit fire swarming at his fingertips. Gowan hesitated a final time, looked into Val's eyes, and rushed to get his words out. "The Observatory. The end of one of the hallways is an illusion. Step through and you'll see a staircase. At the bottom is the entrance to the Planewalk."

"How do I get through? It has to be warded."

Gowan whipped his head back and forth, trying in vain to escape.

"Tell me!" Val roared, thrusting his palms an inch from the pyromancer's eyes.

"You have to use spirit to open the door," Gowan whispered. "That *is* the ward. No one but a spirit mage is strong or foolish enough to attempt the Planewalk."

"Stand up," Val said. "You're coming with me."

Gowan's eyes popped. "No, I can't, my mother—"

"Stand up! If you're telling the truth, I'll let you go when we arrive."

Gowan lurched to his feet. "I swear by the Queen I've told you the truth. Please, if she finds me—"

"Turn around."

"Please," Gowan said, a sob escaping him as he complied. "Don't."

Val extinguished the spirit fire, picked up a loose rock, and bashed Gowan in the temple at half-strength, dropping him to the ground. He had only wanted to ensure he wasn't lying. After finding Gowan's pulse, sure he would be fine, Val slumped to the ground in exhaustion.

No time for that. He pushed to his feet with a shudder. Though he knew Gowan would be too proud to inform his mother of the incident—and probably expected Val to perish during the Planewalk, thus eliminating any evidence of his own role–Gowan might send an anonymous message. So Val had to keep going. Right now.

Shaking with exhaustion, he somehow found enough strength to use Wind Push to lift himself into the air, and cut a direct path to the Observatory.

-53-

The scent of the sword grew stronger as the Spirit Liege drifted through the maze of stone. Strong residual memories told it that humanoids called delvers had built these tunnels beneath the mountains, and that he was in a place called the Darklands.

It noted with interest that the Darklands were the closest thing it had experienced on Urfe to the solitude of pure spirit. Similar to the vast emptiness of the nether realms, it sensed old things—very old things—living in the nooks and crannies of the Darklands, deep beneath the surface.

But it kept to the delver tunnels and avoided these entities, a few of which might even match or surpass its own powers.

And these entities, in turn, had the good sense to avoid the Spirit Liege.

Onwards it drifted, to the massive city of Fellengard and then down into the mines, draped in spirit, following the scent of the sword from an empty courtyard cell to a deeper region of the Darklands. The humans must have had help, it thought, escaping the grasp of the delvers and fleeing into the bowels of Urfe.

Deeper still it went, past the limits of delver territory and into a chasm so enormous it made the Spirit Liege feel adrift in spirit. Here it would like to linger. A glow appeared below, like a distant star, but just as the lava city manifested, the trail of the sword reemerged, leading back into the tunnels.

Finally the Spirit Liege emerged onto the surface, tracking the sword through a series of human settlements and then to a narrow valley wedged between a pair of mountain ranges. It entered a wood rife with strange magic, and found a stone house where the scent of the sword was very strong. It had just been there, the Spirit Liege realized. Days, if not hours.

But there was something else. A spirit residue similar to its own, from a being belonging both to this world and to the world of spirit. Different from itself—not quite as pure, as if the formation or process or whatever had been done to them was interrupted—but the kinship was remarkable.

The Spirit Liege had a brother. Out in the world.

The missing sibling.

Lord Alistair, it thought, would want to know.

This other being was no longer present, and the Spirit Liege returned to the scent. It followed the sword out of the valley and to the base of a mountain that touched the clouds, confident it would have its prey by nightfall.

-54-

It took Will and the others most of a day to ascend the first half of the steep mountain trail. The crisp elevation chilled them to the bone and left them gasping for breath. Eager to reach the top, they pushed through the fatigue and hunger until they could make out the shadows of majestic, amber-colored avians circling the peak, their shrill cries piercing the sky.

As they drew closer, Will stared in fascination at the powerful birds. Lithe and graceful like small dragons, though feathery instead of reptilian, the simorghs wheeling above his head and perched on the craggy summit possessed beautiful crimson wings and long tails that fluttered behind them as they flew. Four squat, taloned limbs helped them leap off the ground and could no doubt rend an enemy to shreds.

Roughly three quarters of the way up the mountain, a quartet of sentries stepped out from behind a boulder with crossbows trained on the party. "Hail, travelers!" the woman in front said. She wore knee-high boots, baggy trousers made of a thick canvas material, and a furry white jacket with feathered shoulder pads that extended a foot on either side.

Tamás crossed his arms against his chest and bowed. "Hail, Riders of the Simorgh. We come with goodwill to the ancestral lands of the Yith, seeking assistance with a journey."

The four Riders looked impressed at Tamas's gesture, and returned his bow in kind. After introductions were exchanged, two of the sentries led them to a collection of huts built into the mountain, hidden among the crags and outcroppings.

One of the Yith, a tall man wearing a coat made of simorgh feathers, knew Tamás by sight and embraced him. The Rider's name was Esseni, and he was the chieftain of Greybeard Mountain. On the ascent, Tamás had explained to Will that each Yith tribe claimed a particular mountain as its home.

Inside Esseni's thatched hut, a deal was negotiated with Tamás while the others waited outside, warmed by an herbal tea. They were fed hunks of spicy meat with bread, and Will began to feel himself again.

After dinner, a pair of sentries accompanied the party to the summit, where three Riders waited to carry them through the night on the first leg of the journey to Freetown.

Behind the elaborate saddle for the Yith Riders fastened around the shoulders of the simorghs, each bird had two extra saddles attached to its back with leather straps. Tamás and Yasmina saddled together, as did Marek and Dalen, and Will and Caleb. Over the last few days, Will had noticed Tamás looking at Yasmina with obvious interest.

When everyone was secured, the simorghs sprang into the air, a sensation unlike anything Will had experienced. He could feel the power surging through the thick body, and felt sorry for any creature caught in the iron grip of its talons.

As the avians circled higher, he noticed something odd: what looked like a human shadow drifting up the mountain, a few hundred feet below the Riders watching from the summit. Caleb distracted him, pointing out the last dreamy hues of sunset glazing the horizon, and when Will looked back to search for the shadow, it had disappeared.

It must have been a trick of the light.

They stole what sleep they could on the backs of the simorghs, tucked into thick blankets provided by the Yith Riders. Just before dawn, they touched down on another Yith mountain, trading simorgh mounts in the semi-darkness, gobbling down vegetable pies.

By mid afternoon, after crossing a smaller mountain range, they saw the canvas of the ocean stretched out in the distance. They veered south as they neared the water, soaring over a region of lakes and dry golden hills, then racing above emerald ridges that sloped down to the water, dyed with swaths of wildflowers. Settlements appeared both on and off the coast.

The simorghs slowed as they approached an impressive sight: thousands of colorful tents and pavilions, many of them as tall as small buildings, populating a wide strip of land between a half-moon bay and a line of steep hills covered in fog. To Will, it looked like all of the world's circuses had convened at this one spot.

"Freetown," Tamás said, able to speak over the wind once the simorghs slowed to drift downwards. As the ground rose to meet them, Will saw a crush of people and wagons filling the gaps between the tents, as well as more permanent structures: inns, shops, smithies, the whole gamut of commerce expected for a settlement that large. He even saw a few wizard towers poking skyward, topped with circular balconies instead of spires. As they flew over one of the towers, Will noticed the roof was fashioned in the likeness of a wheel.

"I thought the Roma wandered by nature," Will said, as the simorghs descended towards a square of red and gold patterned mosaic tile, surrounded by whimsically painted wooden buildings.

"We do," Tamás said. "While Freetown is a permanent settlement, most of the tents you see, especially the smaller ones, come and go throughout the year, trading throughout the Ninth. There are similar cities up and down the coast. Occasionally we venture into the other protectorates, though in the last few years that has become a dangerous undertaking."

Yasmina was leaning sideways to get a better view, her long hair streaming behind her. "It's breathtaking," she said. "Like a fairy-tale city."

"We're quite proud of it," Tamás said, and Will could hear the emotion in his voice at seeing his homeland. It gave him a stab of longing of his own, wondering when he would see New Orleans again. The revolutionary swiveled to regard Will and Caleb, pointing north of the foggy knolls hedging the city. "In that direction lies the Blackwood Forest."

Will felt goose bumps spread along his arms as he stared down at the cluster of shaggy hills. Was he looking at the birthplace of his ancestors? Did their father truly hail from this mist-draped forest, so far from their own world?

Caleb put his hands on Will's shoulders from behind, his soft squeeze all that needed to be said. Will felt incredibly grateful he was able to share this moment with his brother, and wished more than anything that Val could be there as well.

The simorghs touched down in the central square, an entire city block filled with minstrels, vendors, street magicians, and pedestrians. Families and friends dressed in Romani attire strolled arm in arm, fathers holding children on their shoulders to see the performers, mothers pointing out dresses to their daughters. It wasn't just gypsies. Will saw humans of all sorts, dressed in a variety of fashions, as well as a smattering of other races.

Close to where they landed, an elaborate fountain spewed amber-hued liquid from a dozen spouts. People bent to collect the beverage in cups and mugs.

"Is that what I think it is?" Will asked.

Tamás grinned. "Once a month, the municipality provides free ale from sunrise to sunset."

Caleb looked as if he had just won the lottery. He clapped Will on the back. "I think I'm home, little brother."

A crowd gathered to observe the simorghs. Children pointed in awe at the regal creatures and the elaborate jackets of the Riders. Someone noticed Tamás, and within seconds a huge cheer arose from the crowd, which turned into a roar and a much bigger crowd. Before Will knew it, the square had filled with legions of people celebrating their leader's homecoming.

Tamás stood on the back of the simorgh and called for silence, his long hair streaming in the breeze behind him. He gave a speech describing their journey and his companions' role in his escape. Near the end, he pumped his fist in the air. "The Congregation thought they would break me, but we are not so easily broken! I have returned stronger than ever; *we* are stronger than ever! The Revolution lives, and I refuse to rest until every clan in the Realm is safe from the horrors of slavery and the Fens, until the bonds of all those who desire freedom are broken!"

It seemed as if the whole city erupted into a wild, spontaneous celebration, feting Will and the others almost as much as Tamás. Will heard numerous cries of "The Revolution Lives!" and "Death to Tyrants!"

The square crackled with energy, alive with music and dance. Will and the others feasted on food and drink brought to them in a continuous stream by everyone from elders to street vendors. A few hours later, long after the Yith Riders and their mounts had returned skyward, Will and his companions had barely moved from the spot where they had landed.

Tamás waved for the core group to gather close. "You must all be very weary. Let me accompany you to an inn I've selected for your stay, after which you may continue in the festivities if you wish, retire to your rooms, stroll along the beach—whatever you desire. Tomorrow we will reconvene and discuss the future. But for now, my friends—" he was almost overcome by emotion, and took a moment to compose himself—"I thank you from the bottom of my heart for making this return a possibility. We will never forget your service. As they say in our homeland, there are no friends among Romani. Only family."

Everyone exchanged emotional embraces. Will picked Tamás up in a giant bear hug and thrust him skyward by the armpits, initiating a new round of cheers and drinks from the crowd.

It was slow going, but Tamás led them through the crowd to a two-story wood and thatch guesthouse a block off the square. It had the cozy feel of an English country inn.

"The best tavern and guesthouse in Freetown," Tamás said. "The proprietor is expecting you, and your rooms and meals will be provided for as long as you wish to stay."

They all thanked him. Just before he left, he cast a longing glance back at Yasmina, who had declined his invitation to return to the crowd.

Dalen and Marek stumbled upstairs. Yasmina did the same, exchanging a warm hug with Will and giving Caleb a cold nod.

The brothers climbed the stairs to their own room, which sported wooden ceiling beams, bearskin rugs, two cozy beds, and a view overlooking the celebration raging on the square. Will plopped onto the bed. "I'm spent."

"Let's get a nightcap," Caleb said.

Will recognized the gleam in Caleb's eye that meant his nightcap would last until the last drink was poured. While his body felt like Jell-O, Will couldn't deny that he was wired from the excitement. "Yeah, sure."

"Good man," Caleb said, clapping him on the shoulder. "Tamás would be embarrassed if we didn't show support for the local brew."

Will chuckled and led the way to the common room, a sprawling medley of dark wood, worn leather furniture, and tables filled with chattering patrons. The brothers found a place in the corner, next to the fire. Hundreds of empty beers mugs hung on pegs from the walls. Moments after they sat down, a starry-eyed waitress brought out steins of house-made ale. "You're the fellows flew in with Tamás!"

Caleb cocked a grin. "I'm Caleb, and that's my brother Will."

She took their order and gave him a lingering gaze, swaying as she walked away. Will pointed at his brother. "Keep it out of the room, you hear me? I'm not going to spend my first night in a real bed in months listening to my brother get busy with a bar waitress."

"What if there aren't any more rooms?"

"Not my problem. Find a woodshed."

"Can't you be a team player?" Caleb's mouth opened to say something else, then closed. "Besides," he murmured after a pause, "you might want to rethink that rule."

"What are you spouting about?" Will said.

He turned to see who Caleb was staring at, sure it was another in an endless string of bosomy barmaids, and then Will's world shifted on its axis.

Climbing down the stairs to the common room with her self-assured sway, lithe and smooth-skinned as ever, jewelry flashing and curved eyes dancing, was the woman of his dreams.

A woman he thought was lost to him forever.

Mala.

-55-

The star-shaped Observatory came into view. Val flew through the circular opening atop the rotunda. After ensuring the building was empty, he soared down the first of the five black marble hallways, encased in the silence of the empty corridor.

Glow orbs ignited and dulled as he passed. When he reached the end of the hall, he pushed against the marble, testing for an illusion. It didn't budge.

He tried the other four hallways with similar results. A surge of panic overcame him. Had Gowan been lying?

Val took a deep breath. He didn't think so. The pyromancer had genuinely feared for his life. Val returned to the end of each hallway again, this time testing the marble walls with magic, just enough to push through a soft illusion. From his classes, he knew illusions could engage all of the senses, not just the visual.

As he stood with his hands against the end of the middle passage, probing with his magic, he felt the barrier lose its integrity, become less substantial. Val kept pushing, and was able to step through the false wall.

And into a stone passage.

The new corridor was short and almost completely dark. It ended at a set of wide granite steps, so old they were spotted with age, leading downward. A hint of residual light from somewhere, he wasn't sure where, allowed him to inch along. Val took the staircase at least fifty feet down, wondering how such an underground structure could exist in New Victoria, sensing the false wall had transported him to another location, maybe another dimension.

When he finally reached the bottom, he found the source of the illumination: a wall of darkness sprinkled with twinkling stars.

The wall looked insubstantial, as if he could step right through, but when he tried to push his hand into the blackness, it felt as solid as the ancient steps he had just traversed.

Step through and you'll see a staircase, Gowan had said. *At the bottom is a doorway, the entrance to the Planewalk.*

This was it, he knew. The entrance to the walk of planes.

You have to use spirit to open the door.

Val placed his hands on the edge of the barrier. He attempted to split it apart in the same way he reached for spirit fire, but felt heavy resistance. The barrier was dense, denser than anything he had ever experienced, and was going to take a far greater influx of power than he was used to. Was it even possible for him to do this? Was this a task for elder spirit mages alone?

He gritted his teeth. He was about to find out.

Reaching as deep as he ever had, pouring every ounce of power he possessed into forcing the doorway open, he felt the essence of the wall start to give. He balled his fists and pushed harder. It could be done. He knew it could.

The problem was, his store of magical energy was drained from using Spirit Fire against Gowan. Val could feel the entrance giving way, but not enough for him to make it through.

He reached for another vial of spirit water. It pained him to use one of the remaining two, but if he never got inside, the trial would be over before it started.

Keeping his will pressed against the wall of stars, holding open the sliver of space, he opened one of the remaining vials and swallowed the slimy substance. Another surge of energy coursed through him. He pushed even harder.

Though he couldn't see anything, he could *feel* the entrance opening. Using his magic to grip the crack he had opened in the black doorway, he formed a mental image of prying it apart with his fingers, and thrust it open.

Accompanied by a flash of silver light that robbed his vision, Val felt his entire body vibrate and then dissolve at an incredible speed, every molecule jerked forward. It lasted the briefest of moments, an instant in time—just like when he had gone through the first portal to Urfe with his brothers, using Salomon's key.

When Val opened his eyes, he was standing on a ray of bluish-white light the width of a balance beam. Thick darkness hovered all around, as if he were suspended in a patch of starless space. At the end of the ray of light, perhaps a hundred feet away—it was hard to judge distance—loomed a doorway-size portal the same color as the beam.

One hundred feet. How hard can this be?

Val tried to take a step, and the room spun around him.

He was falling off the beam, the blackness revolving as if attached to an out-of-control carousel. He reached up to right himself, but his arms wouldn't move, or his legs, or his fingers. If he didn't do something quickly, he was going to plummet into the blackness. Into the Void. And he had the innate understanding that he wouldn't be coming back.

In desperation, he tried to use Wind Push to right himself on the beam. The room rotated back to normal, and he regained his balance. He didn't think it was that particular spell that did the trick, but rather *thinking about* standing upright. He tried it again, and confirmed his suspicion: movement responded to thought. He could rotate the angle of the beam just by using his mind.

Having regained his balance, he tried to move forward, but frowned when he couldn't advance. He turned to look behind him and blanched; the beam extended in a straight line as far as he could see, with no sign of the stone staircase.

Keep calm, Val.

As he debated what to do, a gust of wind caressed his cheek. Though curious, he was too focused on reaching the portal to ponder it. He tried using Wind Push to move forward. No dice. As he pondered what to do, the strange wind grew more forceful, creating a high-pitched keen as the intensity increased.

Val remembered what he had read in the library of Lord Alistair.

The Spirit Bridge must be walked in a continuous motion until the portal is reached. Stopping or leaving the Spirit Bridge will result in buffeting by the astral wind and certain oblivion in the realm of spirit.

Well, that wasn't good.

The force of the gale strengthened. Growing desperate, Val searched for a solution as the wind howled in his ears and pounded him on the beam, threatening to sweep him away.

It's a spirit bridge, he thought. *Maybe it has to be walked with spirit.*

He reached for his magic. Though still difficult, it was easier to access in this place. He tried to propel himself forward along the beam, using spirit as an energy source.

It worked! He moved a foot forward, and then another, and then another.

The wind abated with each step, until it died away and Val's confidence returned. He had figured this out!

Twenty steps later, a fifth of the way to the portal, the thickness of the spirit barrier increased, until he felt as if he were moving through molasses.

A test, then.

He pushed harder. The increased exertion helped, but he was unable to advance more than an inch or two. The astral wind returned, tickling his cheek. Fear arced through him, and he blew out a breath, pushing with body and mind.

It took him long minutes of extreme exertion to break through. When at last he passed the invisible barrier, he was so drained he was feverish and shivering, as if he had succumbed to the flu. When he stopped to catch his breath, the spirit wind picked up.

He had to keep going.

Push, Val.

Moving forward had become much harder, as if he were walking underwater with weights on his feet. Each step became heavier than the last, consuming his final reserves of energy.

When he was halfway to the portal, without warning, he walked right into a filmy invisible substance, like a curtain of gauze. The blackness around him exploded with color.

Similar to the sight of the Grid he had glimpsed when gazing with Alrick, spirals and vortices and multi-dimensional patterns of color extended in all directions, as far as he could see, whorls and pathways and oceans of color, planes and helixes and spirals, hues so brilliant he had to shield his eyes. As he took in the awesome spectacle, a gust of astral wind hit him so hard that he flew off the beam.

In a panic, flying sideways into the rush of color, he reached for the beam with his hands.

And missed.

He was floating away. The astral wind picked up, whistling like an oncoming train as it readied for another assault. Forgetting where he was, Val flailed for the beam with his hands, drifting further afield. He finally remembered to use magic to propel himself towards the Spirit Bridge, which had almost blended into the polychromatic background.

A gust of wind hit him just as his fingers grasped the surface of the blue-white beam. He clung with his magic to its solidity as the wind increased in force, buffeting him with the power of a hurricane.

When it finally abated, Val collapsed onto the walkway. He couldn't move. His magic was spent.

Shivery with exhaustion, he knew what he had to do. The spirit wind had already picked up again. Terrified even harder tests lay ahead, he consumed the last vial of spirit water. As soon as it slid down his throat he felt renewed, and he took a step forward, determined not to waste another second. He passed through another of the filmy barriers, and the colors disappeared, replaced by blackness. The portal loomed closer than ever, less than thirty feet away.

Prepared to face whatever final challenges were thrown at him, he pushed grimly through another of the gauzy barriers, this one slipping over him like a wetsuit, and then he was in his living room, ten years old, clapping with joy at the new bike beneath the Christmas tree.

"It's all yours, Val," his father said. "Go ahead, try it out."

Val turned from his father, whose warm smile beamed at him from his easy chair by the bay window, to his mother, her slim arms holding little Will in her arms, Caleb hugging his knees at her feet.

"Your father's been so excited to give it to you," his mother said.

Val's smile outshone the blinking lights on the Christmas tree. He ran to the bike, admiring the sleek red form, the new wheels, the streak of lightning down the side. Grinning the entire time, he took it out to the driveway. His father watched as Val tested the gears, then eased the bike onto the road.

"Look, Dad!"

"I see you, You're a natural."

He felt a lump in his throat at his father's words of praise. As he took off down the street with the wind in his hair, a feeling of utter happiness overcame him, the joy and freedom of youth coupled with the security of being loved by his family. Val tore through the neighborhood, the wind at his back propelling him forward, so fast he could barely hang on, then faster and faster, lifting him into the air as his father screamed for him to stop, spinning him in circles, out of control, he couldn't stay on the bike, *the astral wind*, some submerged part of his brain screamed, *you have to keep moving*. He pushed and the image switched to his brothers sitting in the living room after Dad's death, so young and vulnerable, he had to protect them, he was the oldest brother and that was his duty and Dad was gone and not coming back and Mom was in an institution and it was all on him and it was never enough and he could never be enough and the pressure was more than he can could bear, even more than this awful wind—

The anguish, the stab of emotion, made Val remember where he was. It was all so real that leaving the past behind was like a knife to his gut, but he blocked out the impossible images, his beloved brothers with him again, and he returned to the beam of spirit and the terrifying nothingness surrounding it, the astral wind whipping so fiercely he could barely hang on.

He took a step forward. The wind abated a fraction.

Another step, and the images returned. Different. This time a succession of girlfriends, from his youth to law school and beyond, smart and pretty girls but never enough for Val, he broke their hearts one by one not because he was cruel but because of the impossible standards which he could not even meet for himself. They came at him in a rush, pleading, calling, asking him to stop and chat, come back to bed, don't leave them in the Void.

He pushed them all away and moved closer.

Skeletons and zombies came at him from all sides, pouring out of graves and mausoleums. Caleb was clutching at his shirt. Will was beside him, chopping down the undead with his sword. Val had to protect them. He lifted his staff, but shook his head in denial as he swung at the approaching fiends.

It's not real.

A skeleton lunged for him, and Val set down his imaginary staff and closed his eyes.

The blow never came. When he opened his eyes, the skeletons and zombies had disappeared. Another step forward, this one excruciatingly slow, wading through wet cement.

Next it was Mari, holding his arm as they stepped through the neon-soaked streets of New York City, the night they had traveled through the portal.

Stay with me, she said. *This is real, Val, this isn't an illusion. You're on the Planewalk, after all. The walk of planes. Of course there's an alternate world where I can live and your brothers are safe and sound back home. Why would you not choose this? All you have to do is let go.*

She smiled and took his hand, holding her stomach in the exact place the black sash gypsy had stabbed her. *Don't let me die again, Val. It's up to you. Just let go.*

Choking back a sob, he flung away the images and took another step. The last one had gotten to him.

Because what if it *was* true? What if he could choose one of these alternate realities, one where Mari and his father were still alive, his mother not catatonic, his brothers safe at home? Would he do it, even if it meant living in a slightly different reality?

Oh, how he wanted to. So very much.

But he couldn't. Even if those things were true in some other place, it didn't mean Mari wasn't dead in *this* world, or that his brothers didn't need his help *here.*

Anything else was just a selfish solution.

He took another step.

The blackness returned.

And the portal was right in front of him.

When Val tried to push forward, he encountered another barrier, a congealing of spirit. Exultant at his progress, he reached for his reserves of power, ready to force his way through this last invisible wall.

Nothing.

He reached deeper, gathering his will and pouring it into parting the veil of spirit standing between him and his goal. He felt the hint of an opening, the darkness giving way.

But only a fraction.

Val sagged, panting from the effort. He was running dangerously low on magic, and the door had barely budged.

The astral wind howled.

He had to move. Standing in place was a death sentence. Stray gusts whipped his hair, and he could feel the kinetic energy of the wind as it gathered around him, ready to surge forward and thrust him off the beam.

If Alrick spoke the truth, then the Pool of Souls—the path to his brothers—lay behind this final portal. There was no more spirit water. No help from outside. Just Val and whatever last reserves he could dredge from the bottom of his dried-up well of power.

He roared, pouring everything he had into a final push of magic. "I am Val

Blackwood, spirit mage," he screamed, "and . . . I . . . WILL . . . FIND . . . MY . . .
BROTHERS!!!"

The crack inched wider. He shoved even harder, past the breaking point,
his whole body quivering with effort, feeling as if his heart would explode, and
then he pushed harder still, shrieking his rage, roaring at the barrier to open,
fighting not with magic but with sheer force of will, daring the universe to
deny him access to his family.

He felt the veil of spirit give a few more inches, and he knew this was his
chance. Using his last ounce of magic not to force the barrier wider but to try
to slip through the veil, he closed his eyes and flattened his body, propelling
himself forward with his mind.

At the end of his effort, he lay on his stomach, face pressed against the floor.
He wasn't sure what had happened, but he thought he must have failed.

Wait—the floor?

He realized the wind had died. In disbelief, he opened his eyes and found
himself lying face down on a natural stone floor. The Spirit Bridge and the
surrounding blackness had disappeared. The portal was right in front of him,
inches away.

He gathered the strength to push to his knees, realizing he was in a high-ceilinged cavern lit by a dull orange glow. Keeping his eyes on the portal, as if it
might reach out and pull him through, he edged around it and saw a pool of
viscous silver sunk into a basin on the other side. The liquid was shimmery,
tinged metallic blue.

The Pool of Souls.

He looked inside and saw a rush of images, people and places from his past.
His law firm, middle school, friends from summer camp, judges, checkout
clerks, random people he had seen on the street.

No more tests. No more games.

He concentrated on his brothers, and a series of images from his past shim-
mered on the surface of the pool: Caleb's bar, their family home, vacations
to the Gulf Coast. Going on instinct, Val tried to push his thoughts to the
present. The images skipped forward as if by remote control, until he saw his
brothers in a cozy tavern with a group of people he had never seen before,
dressed in the clothes of Urfe. Everyone looked rushed, as if something were

happening outside, and Val had the sudden knowledge that the image was real, happening in the present. Right that instant.

"Will!" he cried. "Caleb!"

To Val's shock, his brothers froze at the sound of his voice. They had heard him!

He called out again, joyous, and they responded. Called out for him to come. Giddy with joy and relief, he started to dive into the pool, when his body was jerked backwards by an unseen force.

"Val Blackwood," a stern and familiar female voice called out, "you are under arrest by the Conclave of High Wizards."

The faces of his brothers blurred and then faded, replaced by a jumble of images inside the pool. "No!" he cried. He fought to return to the pool and dive inside, but he was too weak too resist, and even if he could, he was being held in midair by a power much greater than his own.

Two majitsu drifted forward, each taking him by an arm. Behind them were three wizards he knew on sight: Professor Azara, Kalyn Tern, and Dean Groft. The Dean's burnt orange eyes radiated sadness, and Kalyn Tern bore a triumphant grin. Professor Azara looked disappointed and impressed and upset, all at the same time.

"Did you not consider that we would have wards alerting us to a breach of the Planewalk?" Kalyn asked. "Unauthorized use of the Pool of Souls—or the attempt thereof—is considered an act of treason. According to Council by-laws, the penalty for such transgression is immediate imprisonment, followed by execution. Since all of us have witnessed the attempt in person, I see no need for a hearing. Dean Groft, if you will?"

The dean's melancholy gaze bored into Val's own. The elder spirit mage flicked his wrist, and a portal opened between Val and the Pool of Souls. Inside the portal, Val saw a cube-shaped room with honeycombed walls the color of azantite. Kalyn raised a hand, and the majitsu tossed Val through the portal, where he landed in a heap on the floor.

The gateway closed, sealing him inside the cell, leaving him to choke on his failure. He could sense the immense power of the wards shielding the room.

Wards he could never hope to break.

-56-

Mala looked the same as the first time Will had seen her lounging on the wall outside the Minotaur's Den, shaking him and his brothers down in black leather pants, calf-high boots, a lace-up leather vest, and a crimson sleeved shirt. Will was surprised to see her without her pouches or her blades, though her weighted blue sash was tied to her waist, and he was sure she had a dagger or two concealed.

"Mala!" he shouted, jumping up and wading through the crowd. "You're alive!"

Cool as ever, she turned towards the sound of her name, her expressive lips parting in surprise when she saw him. "Will the Builder?"

The sound of her voice sent a shiver of attraction coursing through him. Her eyes were as fascinating as he remembered, expansive in her narrow face, sensuous violet orbs that looked far older and harder than they should.

Then his eyes continued past her, noticing what he should have seen from the start: the sight of the muscled behemoth descending the stairs behind her, pausing when she paused, putting a protective hand on her back. He was about six foot six, annoyingly handsome, and moved with the easy grace of a fighter.

Will tried to shake off his disappointment, failed miserably, and embraced Mala as she stepped into the room. "How . . . I thought you were . . . what happened to you? You were fighting a majitsu!"

Mala patted his cheek, causing another shiver. "You doubted me?" she asked, her tone half-mocking as always.

"Not even you . . . where did you disappear to?"

"Someplace where the odds were more even," she said.

"How long have you been back?"

"Let us say that where I was, time did not pass in the same manner."

The man behind her grunted and touched her elbow. She shook him off. "I heard Zedock suffered the fate of his undead creations. Did you play a role in that?"

"We killed him," Will said, experiencing one of the most satisfying moments of his life when Mala's eyebrows lifted with admiration. In the past, he might have gushed and stammered out an explanation, but he had been through a lot in the past few months.

A *helluva* lot.

So he looked her in the eye and said, "It seems we both have a few stories to tell."

Mala eyed him back, lips parted in a half-smile, eyes unreadable. "It appears we do."

With that, she swept past him and settled into a table in the opposite corner, along with her strapping companion. Will returned to his own table, feeling both unbalanced and more alive by her proximity—the way Mala always made him feel.

"Why did I think anything would be different?" he asked Caleb. "I'm just a mark to her, someone who hired her to do a job. Now she's back in her element, frolicking with Studlord the Barbarian while she waits for her next adventure."

"Want another round?" Caleb asked.

"Yes."

"Done feeling sorry for yourself?"

"No."

Caleb raised a finger to signal the waitress. "You've noticed all the women in this room looking over here, right?"

"Yeah. They always do. At you."

"True. But news flash, it's not just me anymore."

Will waved a hand, dismissive, though when he glanced around the room he noticed his brother was right. A lot of attractive females were glancing Will's way. Still, when it always came to women, he had always had a one-track mind.

When the beers arrived, Caleb rubbed his hands together and took a greedy sip. "Enjoy it while it lasts."

"Enjoy what?"

"Unrequited desire is a beautiful thing, Will. Once both people are on board it becomes something lesser. Like marriage."

Will pulled his eyes away from a stunning redhead who was smiling at him. He found himself comparing her unfavorably to Mala, which annoyed him. "It may not always be equal in the beginning, but I refuse to believe true love works like that. I think it's just the opposite. That it can't be true unless both people are in the same place." He jabbed a finger at Caleb. "You have a warped perspective."

"And you base your grandiose ideas on what? You've never been in love with someone who loves you back."

Will looked him in the eye. "Neither have you."

Caleb opened his mouth, then closed it.

"You may be an expert on seduction," Will said, "but if your heart hasn't been broken, then you've never been in the game."

Caleb's eyes lowered, and Will kept a beady eye on Mala and her companion as they shared a few rounds of drinks and then headed upstairs. Mala looked right at Will just before she disappeared, eyes challenging, lips curving upwards at the ends.

Was it a signal that he was supposed to run after her and fight for her love, even if he got tossed in the street? Or was she mocking his efforts, for daring to think they were in the same league?

Or did it mean nothing at all?

For once, he was on pace to outdrink Caleb.

The next morning, Will woke with gummy eyes and a headache. After he stumbled to the wash area and doused his face with water, there was a knock at the door. "Will? Caleb?"

Dalen's voice. Will opened the door to find the spry illusionist squinting at his disheveled appearance. "*Lucka*, Will. Tamás wants to meet for lunch. Should I tell him you're unwell?"

"I'm fine. We'll be down soon."

He roused Caleb, and they made their way to the common room where Dalen, Marek, and Yasmina were sitting around a circular table with Tamás and three people Will had never seen before: an older man in a patchwork cloak of fine material, and two young men about Will's age and dressed in local attire, both with long hair and brown eyes. They were obviously related. Though Will was sure he had never seen them before, they looked familiar.

Tamás greeted the brothers with forearm clasps. "Will and Caleb, please meet Armando, my brother in law and an aquamancer of no small repute."

Will tried to conceal his astonishment as he greeted the gypsy wizard in the expensive cloak, and then Tamás dropped an even greater bombshell. "And these two ruffians are the sons of a dear friend. Their names are Lucas and Mateo Blackwood—making them, I'm quite sure, your kin."

Will realized why the two brothers looked familiar—they both looked like younger, less clean-cut versions of Val. Will tried to speak, but could only stare at them in shock. Were these truly the descendants of his father's family? Will's *cousins*? He had to talk to them and find out everything he could about his father, his heritage.

"A pleasure," Mateo said. "From which Blackwood line do you hail—the southern or northern forest?"

Before Will could manage a response, a chorus of alarmed shouts rose from outside. Tamás exchanged a look with Armando and pushed away from the table. Everyone followed them to the door as the shouts grew in volume. Just before they left the tavern, Will heard a faint voice calling his name. He couldn't tell from where the voice was coming. It sounded garbled, as if underwater or filtered through a voice modulator.

"Willl," the voice rippled, louder this time. It was a voice Will would know anywhere, even distorted. "Calebbb."

It was the voice of his oldest brother.

"Val?" Will said, spinning in a circle. When he didn't see anyone, he tried shouting. "Val! VAL!" There was no response, and Will spun to face Caleb. "Did you hear that?"

Caleb's face was pale. "Oh yeah."

Val's disembodied voice called their names again, more insistent.

"Val!" Will shouted. "Where are you?"

An ephemeral image of their brother appeared in the air right in front of them, as if they were looking at an image on a projector screen. Val was standing in front of a shimmery pool of silver-blue water, about to dive in. Before his older brother could take the plunge, Will watched in horror as something yanked him backward.

"Val Blackwooood," an unseen voice called out from across the ether, still sounding like it was in an echo chamber, "you are underrr arrest by the Conclave of High Wizardsss—"

The voice cut off mid-sentence, along with the image. Will ran back and forth across the common room, shouting his brother's name until he was hoarse.

There was no response. Will knew that whatever connection had been forged was now severed. But he had seen him—Val was alive!

Will was breathless with emotion, but before he had time to dissect what had happened—Val was under arrest? By *wizards*?—Dalen darted back into the inn and was pulling Will and Caleb outside, towards the central square. The sky darkened with an approaching storm, and a crowd of people had gathered to observe the arrival of three giant wood-and-metal flying ships. To Will, the contraptions looked like a cross between a blimp and a flying sailboat.

Sapphire blue rods and panels supported the wooden exoskeleton, two enormous sails caught the wind and propelled the ships forward, and battalions of men in armor lined the sides. Standing on the raised front deck of each ship, behind the metal railing, was a group of men and women dressed in high-collared shirts and cloaks, staring down at the city with what Will knew were haughty expressions.

Congregation wizards.

The crowd of people pointed and shouted in confusion at the approaching ships, unsure what to make of them. Will knew exactly what they were, because he had seen them being assembled in the tilectium mines beneath Fellengard.

"Disperse!" Tamás screamed at the crowd, as Will and the others picked up the cry. "DISPERSE!"

The crowd started to comprehend the danger just as the ships settled a hundred feet above the square, under a clump of grey clouds, and twin bolts of lightning shot from the fingertips of one of the men standing at the prow of the middle ship. As storm winds billowed his cloak, lightning lanced into the nearest wizard's tower, shattering it in a spray of wood and glass. At the same time, two pyromancers cast a rapid succession of Fire Spheres the size of boulders. The missiles slammed into buildings and canvas tents, igniting them and spreading flames through the city. From one of the other ships, an aeromancer whipped up a tornado and whisked it into the central square, making Will and his companions dive for cover as the funnel cloud tossed people and stalls like matchsticks.

Terrified, the citizens of Freetown scattered in all directions, unsure whether to seek shelter or flee the city. Lightning scoured the streets, hail the size of melons rained from the sky, fires raged throughout the town. Will unsheathed his sword and turned first one way, then another, unsure what to do.

Armando snarled and soared into the sky, coming to rest on top of one of the wizard towers. He whipped his hands as if conducting a symphony, and a wall of water rose from the direction of the ocean, funneling into a battering ram high above the city, shooting straight towards the underside of one of the ships. Just before impact, three wizards rushed to the side of the ship and linked their powers to burst the massive stream of water. It exploded and rained down on the town.

Screaming his rage, Armando channeled a giant water elemental that burst out of the ocean and attacked one of the ships with beating fists of water. The elemental scooped up a line of armed men and tossed them off the ship, the fighters' blows sinking harmlessly into the creature's watery form. Just as Will got a surge of hope, a tall woman in a blue-white cloak turned towards the water creature, extended her arms, and unleashed a bolt of crackling black energy that disintegrated the water elemental upon impact.

What in the hell, Will thought, was *that*?

The same woman made a motion with her hand like opening a sliding door, then stepped forward and disappeared. She reappeared next to Armando on top of the tower. He reared, but before he could cast a spell, more black fire shot out of her fingertips and encased the aquamancer in a shell of black lightning, turning him to dust. When it was finished, the woman stepped through another invisible doorway, returned to the ship, and continued observing the massacre with crossed arms.

Will thought he might vomit. They couldn't fight that. He swallowed in rapid succession and took a step backwards. Caleb and Dalen were crouched behind a fountain, and Yasmina was helping Tamás and Marek pull the wounded to safety. Will looked around for someone in need of help, and saw a little boy trapped beneath an overturned wagon. Will raced towards him.

The boy was yelling in pain and clutching a pinned leg. Will set down his sword so he could tug on the wagon with both hands.

"Someone help me!" he screamed.

Caleb and Dalen dashed over to help. Before they arrived, a hulk of a man appeared next to Will, huge muscles popping out of the man's jerkin. The two of them were able to lift the cart. Not until the boy crawled to safety did Will realize the man who had helped him was Mala's boyfriend.

"Will! Look out!"

Caleb's voice. Will whirled in confusion, expecting to see a wizard casting more black lightning, or a ball of spinning fire. Instead he saw a coagulated shadow drifting towards him, reaching for him with outstretched arms. Streaks of silver light pulsated up and down the body of the shadow creature, yet it had clearly defined features, as if a human being had been molded into shadowy bas-relief.

The thing was inches away. Will had the sudden intuition that a touch would mean his death. He dove beneath the creature's arms, forced to drop his sword and scraping his chest and face on the cobblestones. The thing whirled and drifted towards him, its movements deceptively fast as Will scrabbled backwards, against the edge of the fountain. Golden flames roared atop the water, preventing his escape.

To his left was the overturned wagon. Will reached for his sword, but the shadow thing lunged forward on an angle, cutting off his escape routes and closing too fast for him to retrieve his weapon. Will knew it wasn't going to fall for another dive, and his options were to plunge through the liquid fire or fight the thing with his fists. Both seemed like certain death.

The shadow creature closed to within inches, and Will invented a third choice. He stepped backward onto the lip of the fountain and leapt as high as he could, just avoiding the outstretched fingertips of the shadow creature. In one smooth motion, Will rolled and landed by the wagon, picked up his sword, and turned to swipe the shadow creature full in the chest.

Instead of slicing through the ephemeral being, the sword stopped halfway, as if cutting through flesh. The shadow thing screeched, a terrible and prolonged human cry, and then it started flowing *into* the sword, first its torso and then limb-by-limb, until Will's sword had absorbed the entire essence of whatever the shadow thing had been.

"By the Queen," someone murmured behind him. He turned to find Mala staring at his sword with an awed expression.

Smoke filled the sky. A bolt of lightning struck the ground next to Dalen, shattering a section of mosaic tile. High above the square, a gypsy wizard was trapped inside a prison of white light, screaming for help as his magical cell carried him towards one of the flying ships. The golden fire inside the fountain next to Will coalesced into the form of a dragon, which leapt onto the square and swished its tail into the overturned wagon, sending it flying into a group of people. The monster turned towards Caleb. Without thinking, Will dashed forward and swung his sword through the elemental, causing the enchanted creature to turn to gaseous form and seep away.

"*Spiritscourge?*" Tamás said behind him, in a stunned voice. "Could it be?"

Ignoring the comment, Will looked skyward for the next threat. Instead he saw the airships heading back the way they had come, sails distended from the mage-summoned winds. Unused foot soldiers lined the rails of the warships, an afterthought next to the awesome power of the wizards.

The smell of smoke and death filled Will's nostrils, corpses littered the shattered courtyard, the screams of the injured pierced the sudden silence. His eyes moved first to his brother, standing safe a few yards away, and then to the rest of his companions scattered about the square. Their shocked gazes turned from the retreating ships and latched onto the sword in Will's clenched fist, thrust skyward in defiance as the city burned around him.

TO BE CONTINUED IN
THE LAST CLERIC

COMING MARCH 2018

Please visit www.laytongreen.com to stay up to date on The Blackwood Saga and Layton Green's other work.

Acknowledgments

An immense thanks to Michael Rowley, Rusty Dalferes, John Strout, and Mab Morris for helping shape this book. Sammy Yuen again applied his creative genius to the cover design. As always, my wife and family had my back during the writing process. While I will always dream of other realms, they have ensured this world is the only one I will ever need.

About the Author

LAYTON GREEN writes in multiple genres and is the author of The Blackwood Saga, the Dominic Grey series, and other works of fiction. His novels have been nominated for multiple awards (including a finalist for an International Thriller Writers award), optioned for film, and have reached #1 on numerous genre lists in the United States, the United Kingdom, and Germany.

Word of mouth is crucial to the success of any author. If you enjoyed the book, please consider leaving an honest review, even if it's only a line or two.

Finally, if you are new to the world of Layton Green, please visit him on Author Central, Goodreads, Facebook, and at www.laytongreen.com for additional information on the author, his works, and more.

18134619R00203

Printed in Great Britain
by Amazon